Her Giant Octopus Moment

KAY LANGDALE

Her Giant Octopus Moment

HODDER &
STOUGHTON

First published in Great Britain in 2012 by Hodder & Stoughton
An Hachette UK company

1

Copyright © Kay Langdale 2012

A CIP catalogue record for this title is available from the British Library.

Hardback ISBN 978 14447 3609 0
Trade Paperback ISBN 978 1 444 73610 6

Typeset in Plantin Light by Hewer Text UK Ltd, Edinburgh
Printed and bound by CPI Group (UK) Ltd, Croydon, CR0 4YY

Hodder & Stoughton policy is to use papers that are natural, renewable
and recyclable products and made from wood grown in sustainable
forests. The logging and manufacturing processes are expected to
conform to the environmental regulations of the country of origin.

Hodder & Stoughton Ltd
338 Euston Road
London NW1 3BH

www.hodder.co.uk

For my parents, Jean and Edwin, with much love

The publisher and author would like to thank:

David Higham for permission to reproduce 'Going Places' by Lemn Sissay, from *Rebel Without Applause* (Bloodaxe, 1992).

PFD (www.pfd.co.uk) for permission to reproduce 'Walking Away' from Collected Poems by C. Day Lewis © C. Day Lewis on behalf of the Estate of C. Day Lewis.

Faber and Faber for permission to quote from *The Waste Land* by T.S. Eliot © the Estate of T. S. Eliot.

Penguin Group UK for permission to quote from *Eyewitness Pond and River*, (Dorling Kindersley, 2003).

Warner Chappell Music Group for permission to quote from 'Tiptoe Thru' the Tulips With Me' (Burke, J./ Dubin, Al.)

Scout also reads from *Hatfield's Herbal: The Curious Stories of Britain's Wild Plants*. (Penguin, 2009).

I think I'll paint roads
on my front room walls
to convince myself
that I'm going places.

(from *Going Places*, Lemn Sissay)

I have had worse partings, but none that so
Gnaws at my mind still. Perhaps it is roughly
Saying what God alone could perfectly show –
How selfhood begins with a walking away,
And love is proved in the letting go.

(from *Walking Away*, C. Day Lewis)

I

It couldn't be her. Surely, it couldn't possibly be her?

Tess Hughes looked across the playground. She tilted her head to assess the woman. The body was the same: full-breasted, sturdy, strong, with neat shoulders, compact calves and a stance sure-footed to the earth. Same kind of clothing – that was indisputable. A will-of-the-wisp way with knotted and layered garments, seemingly masses of them – and her hair a wild tumble of fair curls skewered with a bronze pin. The face was lined, wearier, although she still had the expression of someone resolutely seeking something which eluded her.

Tess scrunched up her eyes, juxtaposing her memory of eleven years ago with the reality of the woman who stood on the other side of the playground, not engaging with anyone, her thumb worrying at a cigarette lighter. Strange, that amidst the hundreds of faces Tess had seen since, this woman had remained intact in her mind; clear, down through the years, like something steadfastly carved. She had been her first; Tess put it down to this. The first she had encountered, not long after training. She had felt a connection with her, being so newly in the same situation but with a little less intervention than the woman at whom she was now looking. At the time, the woman had perplexed her, intrigued her. She had not seemed the type to be predisposed to public service, to selfless giving. Empathy didn't look like this woman's strong suit. Tess had wondered if the woman might reveal herself as an evangelical Christian, or maybe a Buddhist. But, no, she had not. She had seemed unfathomable. An oddly vulnerable character, her nails bitten right down, whom Tess could not help feel was buying into the surrogacy process as a means of self-exoneration.

Tess's daughter Immie called to her across the playground, so that Tess was forced to stop staring. Immie was holding out something she had constructed in science – something to do with batteries, circuits. Immie was dangling her lunch-box in her other hand. Tess could see the fruit hadn't been eaten. That would have to be mentioned. She hated the fact that conscientious mothering was peppered with so many well-meaning admonishments. *Let them eat cake*; that would be so much easier. Immie was talking to a girl Tess had not seen before, although this was not surprising since her daughter had only been at the school for two weeks. Their move from London had felt timely. Tess had found rural life and a new hospital energising. Waking up to look out over her garden made her feel replete in a way she had not anticipated. The girl with Immie was slight, but purposeful in her walk. She held her circuit protectively under her arm. It was festooned with many more wires than Immie's. It had the air of some-thing far more ambitious attempted. A power station? A fairground? The child talked animatedly. Tess could see Immie nodding in agreement. The girl had an edge of benign neglect. Her tights had a hole at the knee; a button was missing from her coat. Her hair was in plaits that looked as if they had been tied some days previously. She parted quickly from Immie, as Immie reached Tess, and Tess caught a flash of green-blue eyes that were astonishing in their intensity.

'Bye, Scout,' said Immie, 'see you tomorrow.'

The child waved in farewell, and turned at a right angle to head for the woman across the playground. It had to be towards her – wouldn't that just take the biscuit? Life being what it was, with its remarkable ability to weave things together in ways that could never be anticipated, it would have to be towards *that* woman that the child headed, on this one day a week when Tess was able to meet her daughter from school. If that was the woman, wasn't the girl the child? Surely, she had to be the child? If she was the same age as Immie, it would be indisputable.

'Is Scout in your class?' she asked Immie brightly. (Always this tone, when what she was actually seeking was an answer in the negative.)

'Yes,' said Immie, 'she's next to me on the birthdays' list; we're almost the youngest in the class, but we are NOT the smallest.' (This said with a small out-puff of pride.) Immie went on to explain a science lesson, which had involved measuring each other's height, and plotting it across the months of each pupil's birth. 'It's genes and nutrition,' she said triumphantly, 'just as much as age.'

On a different day, this might have been the opportunity to mention the lunch-box fruit, but Tess thought better of it. Instead, she watched intently as the child approached the woman and held out her circuit like some kind of offering. The woman tweaked one of her plaits, and said something that made the child laugh. She reached up and kissed her mother and slipped her hand into hers, and they walked away.

At work the next day, Tess phoned her old colleague Mary Fitzpatrick, and asked her to look up the case on the database. The time-frame was so clear to her, entwined as it was with her own pregnancy and the nausea that had permeated the first twenty weeks.

'I think the child was born,' she said to Mary, 'contrary to everything we thought we knew at the time. I'd stake my life on it that the conceived child was born. She's the same age as Immie which matches all the original dates. The mother must have lied. There is no other explanation, unless you can think of one.'

Tess heard Mary pause. 'I don't know what to think,' she replied. 'These circumstances – I've never encountered them before. Would it constitute a crime? I imagine in the eyes of the father it would. Could there be litigation? Certainly all manner of accounting.'

'Well, we can't pretend I haven't seen her,' Tess said. 'That would make us accomplices, allies.'

'I know,' Mary said with resignation. 'I'll contact our legal department, and I'll get back to you when I have a better idea of the implications.'

Tess put down the phone. It occurred to her that some things, when set in motion, quickly achieved a momentum all of their own.

2

At parties, or any kind of social gathering, when Tess Hughes said she was an embryologist, there was always a palpable pause. Tess could count off on her fingers the spectrum of responses. There would be an anguished look between the couple who were contemplating, or had secretly embarked upon, IVF. There would be a complacent, self-aggrandising remark by a couple who would assert that they had had no need of intervention, as they had conceived their children *frankly, almost by looking at each other*. Someone else would ask her, tentatively, a little awkwardly, whether it felt like playing God – this assembling and disposing of life within the rational parameters of science. Someone else would ask where she stood on abortion, or on multiple implantations. There would always be a media-fresh story of a woman being attentively delivered of sextuplets in the American Deep South, or of a woman aged 58 being allowed to become a mother. *And what about embryo disposal?* the pro-lifers and Christians would always ask, not necessarily aggressively, but in a way which made her feel called to account. For Tess, explaining what she did was by far the noisiest element of her job; the interface with social strangers more crowded than anything in her daily life. If anyone had asked her not what she did, but what she loved about it, Tess would not have mentioned aspirations to playing God, or bestowing life with a sweep of a pipette, but rather the peacefulness, the calm, soft-lit order, the tone of quiet purposefulness which she felt to be missing from much of everyday life.

The atmosphere in the lab was utterly female. The paper was yet to be written on why embryologists were so overwhelmingly women. Perhaps it was to do with having small, deft hands. Perhaps it was the unrelenting, obsessive conscientiousness which made them check, check and check again the source and identity of each component they mixed. Perhaps it was their speedy light-footedness – cradling carefully a Petri dish or test-tube – moving between microscopes and incubators, keeping ova at optimum temperatures. So little was dropped; so little crashed to the floor. Even after many years of experience, this still impressed Tess. She and her colleagues moved at a purposeful, careful pace; stood over each other's shoulders while they confirmed the source of samples; looked supportively down each other's microscopes to decide whether they too felt that a particular egg was too grainy, too shrunken from its edges, to be viable. It was an atmosphere that never failed to move Tess with its gentle, neat, collaboration. They were invisible, she and her colleagues; absent from the photos of the doctors holding vernix-caked babies; absent from staff photographs on the walls of upmarket clinics. And yet they were there, right at the process's heart; stripped of identity in their blue hairnets, their latex-gloved fingers, peering down their microscopes, selecting and introducing, taking care of the embryos.

Tess felt so many hopes were compressed into their warm, softly lit lab. The lighting was kept dim to avoid activating the embryos. She loved this detail; she felt it a nod to their future humanity, like infants with a night-light to placate and calm them. The lab was sandwiched between two operating theatres. To the right of the lab, women lay, knees up, having eggs extracted. To the left of the lab, women lay, knees up, having fused eggs implanted. In each theatre, Tess felt that she stood like a silent, offering-bearing votive; a high priestess in the religion of fertility. She waited, unobtrusively, in the theatre on the right, to be given the eggs taken from a woman. A few days later she speed-walked to the one on the left, with the most viable embryo held in a tube in her hand.

In the interim, she felt the ambience around her to be akin to a group of taciturn, quilt-making women. Small, delicate, purposeful assays with a needle, and speech only when necessary. They did not listen to the radio; that would have been a distraction. Instead, the room was filled with the soft hum of the incubators, the low-level buzz of the back-up generator in case of a power cut. Winter or summer, the lab was kept at 37 degrees. Her work-space was blood warm, so that there was no thermostatic difference between where she stopped and it began.

In the corner of the room was a bin – no other word for it – where rejected embryos were discarded, along with glass dishes, used gloves, and other surgical matter. Tess always felt that part of the room was gloomier and darker than the cocoon of the rest of it. So much failed hope, spilling from a plastic rim. Viable embryos, in contrast, could now be kept for 55 years. Tess thought of them, frozen at life's very beginning, silently amassing alongside her as she aged and decayed.

Tess's main expertise was on the ICSI rig. This was a high-resolution microscope used for the highest level assistance. Instead of leaving a sperm and an egg to their own devices in a test-tube, the ICSI method injected the sperm right into the heart of the egg. As a process, it demanded the surest and speediest of hands. Tess would look down the rig, and choose the best sperm for injecting. She would then swiftly slap its tail with the needle, so that it could not damage the egg by swimming within it. She would inject it speedily, and return it to the incubator. Five days later, she would look at them again and decide which were the strongest. Survival of the fittest; natural selection; eugenics – of course this had all occurred to her as she looked down the microscope at the rapidly dividing, luminous blobs. Impossible to gauge who would be good, who would be clever, who would have grace. She never thought in that way. She assessed her embryos as she might fruit on a market stall. She was prosaic, matter of fact; sucking up the chosen contender with a deft flick of a pipette, and carrying it swiftly to the theatre to the left.

In the early days, she had looked beyond the women's knees in theatre. She had looked at their faces as they lay on the operating table, their partners usually holding their hands. Despair, wretchedness, hope, faith: she had seen them all etched there, along with the wincing that accompanied being prodded and poked. Tess felt that a scent emanated from the women, a baby-hunger as sweet and detectable as the smell of breast milk. Some cried while they were in theatre, particularly during implantation. Others moved their lips in private, fervent prayer.

After a while, she had stopped looking at their faces. It seemed to add extra responsibility, more burden; to make it more painful when all she saw down the rig were grainy, hazy eggs. She distanced herself from being able to picture the face at the end of the phone when she called to say how many eggs had fertilised (sometimes, none at all). And there was still the duration of the pregnancy to be viable. She had not enough depth, enough elasticity, to sustain all those multiple hopes.

When Joan Simpson came in, Tess was still allowing herself to be involved. 'She's a surrogate,' Mary Fitzpatrick told her. 'She's undertaking it for a couple where the wife was anorexic. Wrecked her system as a teenager, and nothing to be done about it now. Surrogate's eggs will probably be in good shape; my guess is they'll take nicely. Can you go in ahead of me? I need to go and check the incubators.'

When Tess walked into the treatment room, the grouping at

the head of the operating table struck her as a medieval trip-
tych. The woman who lay on the table had a mass of blonde,
tousled curls. The other, an Italian woman, stood to her left,
with her hand placed gently on the woman's forehead. On her
right stood a man who looked uncomfortable, embarrassed.
His body seemed arched from the table to avoid imposing
upon the prostrate woman. The surrogate looked self-
conscious, almost a little surprised to be there. Tess could have
believed it to be the portrait of the death of a persecuted saint.
An arrow protruding from her theatre gown would not have
gone amiss. Yet, 'Hello,' she said to Tess, in a tone which
approximated cheeriness. 'Are you going to make a start?'

'I'm afraid Doctor Fitzpatrick has just been called to attend
to something; I'm sure she won't be a moment.' The test-tube
in her hands suddenly seemed massive, conspicuous. The
woman's sheeted legs were already in the harness, ready for
the egg collection. Tess spotted a tattoo on her ankle in the
shape of a small, winged bird. The man noticed her glance,
and she saw that he saw it too. Tess sensed he tried to disguise
a wince of displeasure, and looked again at his feet.

'Hope your hit rate's impressive,' the surrogate said to her
brightly.

'I can't thank you enough for agreeing to do this,' the wife
said tremulously. 'We have no other hope. I've tried everything . . . everything.'

The surrogate patted her hand where it lay on her forehead.
'Don't worry,' she said, 'it'll do me good to do a good turn.'
(Tess would think, much later, of a quote she had once read:
'No good deed goes unpunished.' How could this be the
case?) However, the woman's awareness of her own benefit,
her own motive, made an impression upon her. She wondered
if anything could be construed as a truly selfless action.

Later, as she looked at eggs that were remarkable in their
robust smooth form, she wondered what had prompted the

woman to do it. There were rules on financial gain, even though they were a little dubious, a little open to abuse. There seemed no connection, no empathy between the woman and the couple beside her. Tess tried to imagine the circumstances that had led Joan Simpson to this point. She felt the absence of a palpable motive, but took solace in the knowledge that she was not required to judge. She skilfully flicked the tail of a particularly animate sperm.

When the woman came back for implantation, her hair was tied up in a scarlet wrap. Tess was struck by a resemblance, now, to a Renaissance portrait. She wore green eye-liner, and a turquoise bracelet protruded from a sleeve of her gown. Tess concluded that surrogacy lent itself to more relaxed time pre-appointment than for the usual patients, who were mostly on their knees on their bathroom floors, praying to their gods. The Italian woman sobbed quietly throughout the process. 'It'll be fine . . .' the surrogate said to her, shifting herself on the table. 'Just you be confident – I know this will stick.'

Two weeks later, Joan Simpson telephoned Mary Fitzpatrick to confirm she was pregnant. 'Nimbly done, Tess,' Mary said.

The couple whose baby it was to become came into the clinic to be told. Tess had been on her way to lunch when she saw them on the street afterwards. They were almost dancing a jig, she told Mary. She crossed her fingers for the couple – they looked like they would provide a child with a happy home, although she wondered if she should be espousing views on what constituted this, having found out two weeks earlier that she was pregnant by her lover who had left her after what had turned out to be a recriminatory, unreconciled, final fuck. If only her private life had been as smooth and ordered as her professional. However, she felt a connection with Joan Simpson who would be within days of the same due date as her. She thought of the next 38 weeks, both of them sailing serenely (she hoped) through pregnancy; one having a child whom she would bring up alone, and one having a child whom she would give up to others. How different it would be.

When Tess was ten weeks pregnant, having just vomited coming out of Baker Street tube station, she came into work and Mary told her that Joan Simpson's GP had phoned to say that she had lost the baby.

'She's done another pregnancy test, and it was clearly negative. She says she doesn't want to repeat. Too much of a disappointment, and she doesn't want to go through all the follicle stimulation again. I see no point in hauling her in, or having them meet face to face. The couple are coming in this morning for an update. God, I hate this part of the job.'

Later, Tess walked past the consulting room. The cries of the Italian woman could be heard through the wall. Her husband was holding her – she could see them through the glass panel in the door. The woman's black hair was streaming through his fingers. The desolation in her sobs made Tess place her hand on her stomach. She knew, as she had always known, that there was no possibility of shielding another from pain.

3

Joanie Simpson lay like a starfish beneath the duvet. She paddled her hand out across the pillow to tilt the clock towards her. She checked the time, stretched her arms, balled her fists, and yawned.

Waking up alone always seemed a small admission of failure. She poked her toes towards the corners of the mattress. Not that she'd ever met a man she'd like to spend the rest of her life waking up to. *Heaven forfend,* as her mother used to say. But she liked waking up next to men; actually, a merry, ongoing assortment of men, which Joanie construed as meaning that her appetite for life, for new experiences, for mostly enthusiastic sex, had not diminished now that she was almost forty.

It was a shame though. The sun was slicing through the window with a promise of early spring warmth, and Joanie felt toasty and content, and quite predisposed to the idea of a man, preferably with a hirsute chest and the tang of manual labour about him. It was preferable to the alternative, which was to continue the puzzle she had set herself. On the odd occasion when she felt inclined to melancholy or introspection – they were interlinked in her mind and she called them her mood indigo – she had dwelt on what might be said at her death. This was partly because of the itinerant life she had led, and the suspicion that there would not be many at her funeral. Nobody, certainly, who could track a thread through the years and say something definitively truthful and accurate. So,

Joanie had become preoccupied about the veracity of her obituary, about the ghastly prospect of nothing personal being said about her at all. Or, nobody listening, with the exception of Scout. With the resourcefulness by which she had always set great stock, she had decided to think up a little catch-all phrase about herself that would nail it properly; some jaunty, life-affirming observation that would make anybody who might be listening wish they had known her better, or for longer. Once conceived, she would write it down somewhere, and then there was always the possibility that it might be found and used to good effect. Scout could be relied upon for that.

The problem was the phrase itself. All that she had come up with so far – and it had borne examination over a number of days, but suffered from what might have been an overly religious overtone – was that *Joanie loved men*. Not like Jesus, obviously, not men in the *wider* sense (species rather than gender, with a predisposition for goodness and self-sacrifice) but men: the men she met, the men she intermittently fell in love with and invited into her bed. The men whose jaw lines, skin, spines, thighs, and buttocks – how she loved the line of a good masculine bum – brought her so much pleasure.

Women were a different matter. Joanie had never had much time for them. Her life was marked, she recognised it without distress, by an absence of long-sustained women friends. There was something about groups of women that set her teeth on edge. The thrum below their chatter was like a nail on a blackboard. She felt discomfited by – even intolerant of – their way of saying one thing and meaning another, of tucking insecurities beneath themselves like neat little kitten paws; the way they moaned and droned about things maternal, things familial and, so often, things menstrual. Bitchiness she had no time for. Or lipstick-smooth mouths saying something tart as acid. No, give Joanie a man any time, especially a man with freshly clean fingernails, and a resonant laugh which rumbled through his chest as she lay on it. One who might – in truth a little slowly and without any evident finesse – be able to say what he wanted, say what he felt, say what he meant, and with no *side* to him at all. No hidden agenda. No small, howling grievance padded liked wadding against the ribs. A small hymn to men – that was what she would have liked to have been capable of expressing. 'I am,' she said merrily to herself as she threw back the duvet, 'a living hymn to men.' God, how her mother, Alice, would be appalled.

Joanie sat on the edge of the bed and listened to the sounds of the house. Scout would have taken herself off to school. Thank God for a child who was resourceful, low-mainten-ance, and quick on the uptake. What a disaster the alternative would have been. How appalling the prospect of a whingeing little clinger with a honed line in emotional manipulation. No, Scout was a gift (she was aware quite how literally a gift). Alice had said *God knows how you ended up with one as sane as she is*, which Joanie thought a little unfair but probably justified.

Scout had been such an easy baby; gazing from the papoose with alertness and absorption. She had been quick to talk, quick to catch on. Joanie could remember her, aged six, frowning with concentration as she did up her own shoelaces. *I'll do it myself.* Joanie was grateful to Scout for many things, but mostly her independence of spirit and her ability to assess the lie of the land and act accordingly. Joanie was thankful that Scout had not left her feeling encumbered the way she conjec-tured some children might. She wasn't sure whether this was acceptable to admit, but she felt it anyway.

Joanie sat in front of the mirror and brushed her hair, stretching her lips wide to glance at her teeth, and running her finger along an eyebrow to see if it required plucking. Her hair had always been her best feature – she pulled at a curl and watched it spring back into place. If she'd ever been famous, she thought people would have gone into hairdressers and asked for a 'Joanie'. The fact that she hadn't been famous and, realistically, now, most likely wouldn't be, niggled at her. *Expectation unfulfilled* might be a better obituary. She traced the lines which were increasingly gathering around her upper lip, and pudged her finger at the crease that seemed to have taken up residence between her eyebrows. It was a source of some chagrin to her that she hadn't, felicitously, with light-footed serendipity, stumbled upon something that had catapulted her into the limelight – although she felt the word limelight itself evoked a queasy image of seasick green which wasn't entirely appealing.

When she was almost thirty, she had re-branded herself (this was how she saw it) from Joan to Joanie. *What's wrong with your proper name? I shan't call you any different*, Alice had said. But, for Joanie, the transition from Joan to Joanie was redolent of the women she wanted to evoke: Joni Mitchell (she kicked herself that she hadn't had the wit to change the spelling at the same time); Joan Baez (who someone told her went by Joanie to her inner circle). In trading Joan for Joanie she felt she had achieved a moniker that conjured up a woman on a beach, barefoot, wearing something white and floaty, perhaps accomplished on a musical instrument, or with a voice that sang clear and sweet. In truth, Joanie sang like a cat, and she recognised this was the point where her self-mythologising went too far. She'd told Scout – who, surprisingly, had a voice that could carry a tune – that the world was divided as regards to the behaviour of people who were tone deaf, those who sang gustily anyway, and those who had the wisdom to keep their trap shut.

She would like to have been creative. She'd had a few stabs at painting – a couple of ill-advised week-long courses. Hindsight had taught her not to sleep with the tutor on the second night: it was construed as an attempt to monopolise teaching time, and nobody put themselves down on the rota as your chore-sharing partner. She'd toyed with the possibility that somewhere within her there might be a poet. Haikus had, for a while, held appeal in that they were short and attractively random. (Nothing too redolent of discipline; she recognised that definitely didn't lie within her.)

A few years before Scout was born, Joanie had been a frequenter of hippy trails. She liked to think of herself as an aesthetically gifted traveller – bringing back rugs, wraps, pots, turquoise bracelets, from places beyond most people's ken. She dreamed of a shop somewhere exclusive like Tetbury, wafting in from her journeys, laden with shrewdly spotted objects of beauty. In reality, she'd sold a few manky rugs and some leather bags on a stall in Camden. People kept bringing them back and saying that it was impossible to get rid of the smell. Joanie had been fulsome in her suggestions (*Put half a cut onion in them, or some bicarb. Is there a windowsill it could sit out on?*) but had been mostly hassled into refunds. Her landlord finally evicted her, saying she'd made the flat stink. The problem with some people, Joanie felt, was that they couldn't overlook the downsides.

With aesthetics, she felt, it was all a question of tone. Her youthful travels had affirmed mostly what she knew before. Was that what was meant to happen? A journey in a VW van along the Silk Route with six young men had been what she liked to think of as a triumph of democratic giving in that she had slept with them all. This wasn't how her mother would have described it, but Joanie was not perturbed. Before Scout was born, Joanie, down on her luck and with a man and his child in tow, had come to seek refuge in her mother's back bedroom. Alice had stood in the kitchen one morning and said with exasperation that Joanie chose to construe as good-natured, *Why can't you get a steady job, a steady man, and a child that's halfway normal?* (Her last comment based on the fact that the man was a freegan and rummaged for discarded food in supermarket dustbins. Alice had come down that morning to find the boy foraging through her Addis flip-top for his breakfast.) At least when Scout was born, Joanie had fulfilled a third of her mother's plea.

The steady job was more of a challenge. Joanie liked to think that she might wake up one morning and discover her talents and deploy them henceforth. This hadn't happened yet, but that didn't mean it wouldn't. Her habit of what she described to Scout as *going on a break* – mostly when she'd been fired, was fed up to the back teeth of stacking shelves, or had enraged some supervisor by continually nipping out for a fag – allowed periods for what she hoped was reflection, when her true vocation might come shimmeringly to her. She would have acknowledged, if pushed, that her breaks mostly consisted of watching too much daytime TV, going for long walks in the afternoon, and looking lasciviously at married men in the hope that she might help them channel some conjugal boredom. She had moved house or flat almost as frequently as she changed jobs, with Scout always bundled uncomplainingly in tow.

When Alice died, Joanie had had a break to process that too, but concluded there was in fact not much to mull over. She decided she and Alice had a good, clear, mutual understanding, and beneath their differences, a recognition of each other's substance. Alice had left Joanie her house: a rural, two up two down that had been scrubbed, swept and polished within an inch of its foundations. Joanie became a homeowner, and from Alice's house conducted forays on to the job market. For the first time in her life, aged eight, Scout went to the same school for more than a term.

Joanie had initially focused on stripping the house of everything she felt to be emblematic of her mother's generation and outlook. The flock wallpaper, the swirly patterned carpet, the amber glass light shade, the dark wood headboards, the pink velour toilet mats. She'd chucked most of it away (only a fool, she thought, could call it vintage). She'd taken Scout to Ikea, and they'd piled three trolleys high with geometric rugs and glass shelving and white crockery and all manner of space-saving devices. She put a round ironwork table in the small backyard, and it was here she sat, on this morning, having a reflective fag and reading the paper, thinking about how much time her mother would have spent clearing the dead leaves that had compacted in the corner. She'd caught Scout dusting one Saturday morning – oh, there was Alice in her genes. Perhaps it emanated from the walls – all that good, decent, working-class respectability. Wherever it came from, it certainly wasn't channelling into Joanie.

Joanie made herself some porridge (she was currently experimenting with a slow-burn, low carb start to the day) topped with a little fruit and berry sprinkle. She was also plan-ning to extend this to a mid-morning snack of goji berries and almonds. The magazines she read reliably informed her that this was how supermodels snacked. She'd eaten two Twixes yesterday. Joanie suspected this wasn't quite the system cleansing that she should be aiming for.

Joanie's refurbishments hadn't included the doorbell. She'd left that untouched. Mostly because it hardly ever rang and also because it would have required electricians, re-plastering, re-painting. All that, Joanie felt, was too much faff, as well as unnecessary expense. When it rang, as it did on this March morning, with a chime that was the beginning of some old hymn, it irritated her because the doorbell was, in fact, a first impression. She made her way to the door – porridge bowl in hand – thinking it would not be the impression she would like to convey if it happened to be a replacement postman, or, a DHL man delivering a parcel, or someone enquiring about the electoral roll or the church register. Hell, this morning she would relish even a Jehovah's Witness or some nicely scrubbed-up, hesitant, besuited young Mormon. Some mornings, a little flirtatious conversation was all that was needed to get the day off to a swing.

Disappointingly, it was the same old postman. 'Recorded delivery, my dear,' he said. 'Can you sign?'

Joanie did her best loopy signature (always treat anything, she'd decided long ago, as if it were an autograph). She walked back through the house, kicked open the back door, and sat down at the ironwork table, her porridge bowl next to the post. Catalogues, catalogues, all manner of clothing catalogues. There was a bill for the electricity (there was always somebody wanting payment), and then the letter she had signed for.

Her first thought was that perhaps she might be due a hike in benefits. Scout's child allowance had recently gone up to £20 a week. Perhaps there was a tax credit for which she hadn't known she was eligible. The last year had had more breaks than usual. Perhaps she'd been paying too much National Insurance. Joanie loved it when the system kicked in with a refund. She opened the letter with optimism. But it wasn't about that. The letter wasn't that at all. It was from the legal department of the clinic where Scout had been conceived. It requested a meeting to discuss the possibility that the child she claimed she had miscarried had in fact been born. She noticed from the top right-hand corner that it had been copied to Scout's birth father and to Oxfordshire Social Services. The bright spring morning leap-frogged from her chest. She pushed her porridge aside. Up reared the past from the compacted leaves, shaking itself off and reeking of lies.

4

Mrs Pearson-Smith liked an orderly classroom. Scout couldn't have been happier in it. Regularly sharpened pencils in plastic tubs stood to attention like soldiers. Times tables and mathematical terms were written in clear, bold handwriting on a chart on the wall. At one end of the classroom was a poster that declared which author the class was studying this term, with a fan-shaped array of the said author's works. The children's exercise books were stored in filing cabinets, with different coloured separators indicating subject division. Scout was a book monitor, called upon to fetch and return the books at the beginning and end of a lesson. She would run her finger along the length of the file divides and wish that all things in life could be so clearly shown.

Mrs Pearson-Smith had a Good Work Book, which noted exemplary pieces of class work. It was made clear that entry to the GWB was not based on an absolute standard, but on what was good – or remarkable – for the individual concerned. Scout had come to appreciate the finer justice of this policy, even if at the beginning of the term she had to swallow a small sense of resentment when three pages of her own observations on the Fire of London were passed over for Billy Myer's scant paragraph.

Mrs Pearson-Smith had arrived new to the school that autumn term. She had come for interview in the previous term and, as Miss Pearson, had taught a sample lesson to the class. Scout thought she must have been a very pretty bride, and imagined she had brought to the wedding planning process the same organisation and thoroughness that she applied to the pencils and the filing cabinet. Scout was intrigued by Miss Pearson's metamorphosis into Mrs Pearson-Smith. Some of the children in the class had names which were both their parents' surnames, bolted together. The aspect that bothered her was what happened when Mrs Pearson-Smith's child married the offspring of someone else with two names. Scout envisaged a future when names could no longer fit into the boxes on forms which were supposed to contain them; a whirling accumulation of names that buzzed like a swarm of bees, and a time when a child would have to practise for years before they could spell their own name.

Scout gave thanks that she was just Scout Simpson, although she was intermittently preoccupied with what her birth father was called. Sometimes, she twinned her own name with the surnames of each of the children in the class and wondered if, by chance, she might have stumbled on the right combination. She couldn't ask her mum. It was definitely outside what could be asked. This was not the case for other areas, when Joanie, her knees hugged to her chest on the couch, would say 'Ask me anything, Scout, ask me anything you want to know.' This mostly involved what in Scout's view was a premature foray into the facts of life or a discussion of imminent changes in Scout's own body which definitely weren't happening; Scout was keeping a watchful eye. On the subject of Scout's father – their meeting, his character, his response to Scout's birth – Joanie was a closed book. A book closed so firmly Scout thought it would never be opened. So, whilst Scout felt free to ask her mother about all manner of things, her father wasn't one of them. Her maternal surname – Simpson – hung above her head in a way that made her think of it as a lopsided arch. Out there, somewhere, beyond her mother shut tight like a clam, was the other part of her name, just waiting to scooch up.

On the first day of term, Mrs Pearson-Smith had asked the class to write large name labels. She stopped by Scout's desk and said, *Oh my goodness – Scout – what a lovely name. Are you named after the girl in* To Kill a Mockingbird? *Atticus Finch is my favourite fictional father ever.* Scout thought that her response (*I'm not sure, Miss*) was probably the best option in a poor set of contenders. To say that she had never heard of the book would have made Mrs Pearson-Smith think she was ignorant or, worst of all, a child who did not care for reading. Scout's school library card – she could have shown her – was more crumpled and used than anyone else's. To say *Yes I am* – which would probably have created a favourable response – would have been a lie, and Scout was conscionable enough not to want to get the year off to a start based on falsehood. The truthful answer, Joanie had told her, was that she was named after the daughter of Demi Moore and Bruce Willis. Scout sensed this might not be the frame of reference that Mrs Pearson-Smith had been looking for (especially at the beginning of term when the composer to be played during registration was Mozart, and whom Mrs Pearson-Smith commended for his order, and his sense of musical propriety). Joanie, meanwhile, had elaborated on the supporting reasons for her choice: she'd loved the photograph of Demi pregnant on a magazine cover; she'd loved *Ghost*; she'd even liked *Die Hard*. This was enough justification for borrowing their daughter's name for her own. Scout was ambivalent as to the merits of her name, although now, she thought, perhaps she should try and read the mockingbird book. Recently, in a dentist's waiting-room, she had been flicking through a magazine and learned that Scout Willis's sister was called Rumer. Not Rumer spelt like rumour, but suggestive of it all the same. Scout gave thanks for small mercies in being named after the first child, not the second. Either way, she felt keenly that the route to her name had not been literary, but celebrity. While she was still a blank sheet for Mrs Pearson-Smith, she didn't want this to be the first thing attributed to her.

Scout was endeavouring to be a star in Mrs Pearson-Smith's class. The school had been trying to gain a Bronze Award for Eco Schools. This consisted of tackling waste, carrying out an audit, writing an action plan. Implementation involved collecting and measuring debris from lunch-boxes over a two-week period; writing a letter to parents about wasteful packaging: a new composting routine; and better litter collection throughout the school grounds. Scout had been the chief monitor in the measuring of waste in her classmates' lunch-boxes. She knew who came with wholemeal pitta bread, houmous and red pepper, wrapped in recyclable kitchen roll, as opposed to rocking up with Cheesestrings, Capri Sun, a Frube and a packet of crisps. She had been instrumental in composing the letter to parents; she had donned rubber gloves and poked around the corners of the playground looking for discarded wrappers and rubbish. Scout had made the Good Work Book for her contribution to the school's successful assay on the Bronze Award. Joanie hadn't seemed particularly impressed with the initiative, although Scout would have to confess, if pushed to spill beans, that it had been over a year since Joanie had packed a school lunch anyway.

Scout was not blind to the appeal of a life brimming with environmentally packaged healthy food. Mrs Pearson-Smith had toyed with the idea of a raised vegetable bed in the corner of the playground, so the children could grow fruit and vegetables, and eat them at lunch-time to contribute to their five a day. This sounded, to Scout, like heaven. When she and a small work party from the class had spent a lunch-time trying to dig a patch of ground, Archie Price had been caught peeing on it, resourcefully telling Mrs Pearson-Smith it was good for softening and enriching the soil. Most of the girls had recoiled in horror at the thought of eating anything grown there. (Scout had to give it to the boys; they had weighed up Archie's claim and decided it had merit.) Mrs Pearson-Smith had hastily abandoned the plan. There were other avenues to follow, she decided, to show she was pursuing the Outdoor Learning criteria stipulated in the Head's School Development Plan. The appeal of the possibility, however, remained in Scout's mind. Often, in Asda, as she looked at rows of ready meals, lined up in the freezer cabinet and labelled *Deliciously different!* or *Mouthwateringly tempting!*, she imagined a parallel life with a garden with a raised vegetable bed, peas bursting from pods and potatoes forked up from the soil. She had a weakness for cookery programmes, particularly the ones that involved some kind of crusade. She watched *Jamie's School Dinners* whilst waiting for the microwave to ping.

Scout had always loved school – even when the teachers had not matched up to Mrs Pearson-Smith's rigour and exactitude. In Reception class, at another school, when she was five, the teacher had mostly slammed in a video which instructed the bemused children as to the niceties of letter formation. Most of them would watch, mouths half open, or stifling a yawn, whilst Magic Pencil showed the sequence necessary to achieve a correctly formed letter. Scout would sit, legs crossed, and trace out the letters on the carpet, entranced by Magic Pencil's smooth, hands-free glide across a fake blackboard surface. Scout's own handwriting was now neat to the point of being mathematically precise. Times tables, spellings, Scout swooped upon them with relish. She would carry home the occasional homework worksheet, flat in her book bag, and protect it from any creases or splashes of rain. *It's not normal,* Joanie would tease her, *there's nothing wrong with a few creases or the odd smudgy finger-mark.* Scout, not wholly convinced of this (some of the boys turned their worksheets into torpedoes or planes within five minutes of getting them), continued to hand in homework sheets as if freshly flipped from a printer. In a world where most things could not be kept smudge- or crease-free, it was soothing to safeguard the areas that could.

When not at school, Scout's play was measured and neat. She would make intricate patterns with Hamas beads, and ask Joanie to iron them into hard, thin little mats. Scout had done a series of geometric patterns, some animal faces, and had worked up to what she called her DNA series, which had been inspired by a school trip to the Science Museum. *They're modelled on DNA molecules,* she said to Joanie. *It's really hard to make spirals with the beads.* When Joanie found them balanced precariously by the ironing board, she would call *Do you want me to iron these squiggle sets for you?* Scout wasn't sure whether this was entirely supportive or not. It certainly wasn't taking the respectful attitude to science encouraged at the Science Museum.

Scout had a dolls' house for which, she had a nagging suspicion, she was probably too old. The front of the house was painted sugar pink, and it opened by pushing up a small bronze hook. The dolls inside had wooden, sausage-shaped limbs. They didn't properly fit in the beds, and lay rigid with spoon-like red shoes sticking out from beyond the little gingham coverlets. Scout loved the tiny detail of the house. She ran her fingers around the painted circles of the electric hobs. She rearranged the living-room, and added some snapped matchsticks to make it look like there was a fire in the grate. She balled up red tissue paper to add a tiny glow of warmth. She made sure that the four people within the house were purposeful, engaged in domestic endeavour or recreation. Sometimes, she made the mother do what Joanie liked to do. She put her at the dressing-table, ready to paint on her lipstick mouth. She laid her on the couch watching Wimbledon on the television. (Scout had clocked, two years ago, that one of her mother's intermittent breaks from work always coincided with the Wimbledon fortnight.) She sat her at the kitchen table, with a tiny coffee mug by her hand. She put her in the bath, and made foam from washing up liquid so that the figure was swamped in white froth. She put her feet on a small footstool, and wished the doll's shoes were removable so that she could recreate Joanie, after a day stacking shelves, saying *God, my feet are killing me, Scout, I swear I'm going to end up with bunions or something.* Sometimes, Scout would sit by her mother and rub peppermint cream into her feet. Joanie would close her eyes and make small, purring noises like a cat. The room would gradually get darker, and the shadows fall long across the carpet, and Scout would think it was cosy and safe, her mother slack and easy on the couch, smelling of peppermint and cigarettes.

In school today, it was Rainforests. Rainforests, rainforests, how Mrs Pearson-Smith had managed to make them permeate all aspects of the curriculum. The children were looking at how areas of ground might support beef cattle, or sustainable logging or, alternatively, virgin rainforests for tourism and research. They had to choose an animal or insect and produce a poster explaining why it was suited to living in the rainforest. They were singing songs about rainforests, and tapping out rainforest rhythms on instruments from the school percussion box. They were writing compositions. Scout had been particularly proud of hers, written from the perspective of a kapok tree at the moment it was felled and came crashing through the canopy. They were learning about the ozone layer, about all the environmental disasters stored up and ready to come tumbling about their adult heads. Mrs Pearson-Smith had pinned up a map of Brazil, and Scout had coloured in the vast trajectory of the Amazon. It all seemed so big, and so far away, yet she understood from a television programme it was something she had somehow to safeguard. She wondered what it would be like to be someone in power, someone who got to decide what happened when. It would be encouraging to know that one day you might have a say. Otherwise, learning it all was just a way to feel helpless, to know everything was going horribly wrong, unable to do anything about it at all. She had voiced this opinion to Mrs Pearson-Smith, on her way out of the classroom one day, her brow furrowed with anxiety. Mrs Pearson-Smith had been brisk and positive, and said the Bronze Eco Award was carried to them by the tide of the Amazon. Scout wasn't sure whether this was an entirely accurate image, but she'd turned the central heating thermostat down to sixteen degrees, hoping Joanie wouldn't notice, and had started taking her daily shower in water only just lukewarm. She wasn't exactly sure of the connection between this and safeguarding the rainforest, which, she thought, however destroyed and exploited, still seemed a very beautiful place to be. Perhaps one day she would go there, although this seemed as likely as living on the moon. On the news, she had watched the leader of the United Nations, the President of the EU, and the President of America. They all had power to make decisions for the good, and whilst she suspected they weren't showering in lukewarm water, or turning down their heating, she liked it that Mrs Obama had planted a vegetable patch. She suspected that no one was peeing in hers to soften and nourish the soil.

Scout thought it a little unfair – this gifting to her generation the problems which greedy, careless, consumption had caused. She wondered if her generation would grow up the least carefree of any. No wonder she felt anxious asking Mrs Pearson-Smith if it was fixable. No point tapping out rainforest rhythms on percussion instruments, she wanted to tell her, when the whole lot's going to come crashing around our ears.

Scout finished carefully drawing her tree frog. The edges were perfect, no over-spilling of colour at all. She had ruled neat lines to show the adapted features, the sticky pads on its feet which helped it to jump from tree to tree, and its long curly tongue. The school bell rang, and Mrs Pearson-Smith told them they could pack away their books. She came past Scout's desk and said, 'That's lovely, Scout, that will go on the wall.'

Scout put her things away and collected her jacket from her peg. She went out into the playground and scanned it quickly to see if Joanie was there. They had no fixed arrangement; she was either there or she wasn't. Sometimes shifts changed, and she was back in time to come and collect Scout from school. Sometimes, particularly when she was working in pubs or wine bars, she took a nap around this time (*No one likes a barmaid,* she told Scout, *who looks as if she is just desperate to get into the flop*). She wasn't here. She definitely wasn't here. Scout's eye was well trained enough to look away from the gaggles of mothers to the periphery of the playground where Joanie might be standing. Her mother, she felt, with a small twinge of unease, did not have the interest in friendship that some of the other mothers had. Joanie usually stood alone, gazing at her boot toes, or examining her fingernails. She always looked up and laughed when she saw Scout coming. Scout couldn't fathom why, but she thought it was probably a good thing.

5

When Scout got home, Joanie wasn't doing any of the things she might have expected her to be doing: having a cigarette out at the table in the garden; setting the Sky box for something she wanted to record; or ironing one of her tops, her mouth pursed in concentration. Instead, she was moving around the house like a whirlwind. All of their clothes seemed to have been piled in heaps on their respective beds, and she was rifling through them, snatching pullovers, tops, shorts, jeans.

'Scout,' she said purposefully, 'come here and let me measure if this still fits you.' She held up a summer dress against Scout's frame. 'That'll do,' she said, and stuffed it into a black bin bag at her feet.

'What are you doing?' Scout asked. Maybe it was one of her periodic clear-outs, perhaps she was taking a bumper load to the local charity shop. Scout was mindful of previous periods in their lives, when Joanie had asserted that *Too many belongings are like ballast, they just drag you down*. Once, she had suggested to Scout they should only keep as personal belongings those which fitted into a single rucksack. *Like snails*, she'd said. *Everything else is clutter.*

'We're going,' Joanie said abruptly, her cigarette clamped decisively in the corner of her mouth.

'Going where? Going when? For how long?'

'Somewhere. Anywhere. Now. I don't know.' (Joanie had always prided herself on her ability to be succinct.) 'And don't give me any of your fretful stuff. There's a Sainsbury's Bag for Life with an elephant on it downstairs by the radiator. You can put some of your own things in there, you know, things you'd like to have.'

Joanie left Scout's bedroom and returned to her own, and began the same bin bag stuffing frenzy. She swooped all the cosmetics and skincare from her dressing-table into a small tote bag. She opened a shoe box from underneath her bed, and shook some paperwork into another.

Scout sat on the edge of her bed. She bit her lip, looking at the mess her room was in. She made a half-hearted attempt to put some of the rejected clothes back into her wardrobe, and smoothed out a patch of crumpled duvet with the palm of her hand. She walked downstairs and picked up the Bag for Life. The bag's cheery title seemed painful now, named in anticipation of a life spent repeatedly going to the local Sainsbury's. Now, it was a bag for *her* life. A new snail phase. Whether she liked it or not.

Her pencil case went in first, with her crayons and her ruler. Then her hair bobbles. Then her Scrabble set. The book by her bedside was from the school library. She stroked the cover with her fingertips. Now she wouldn't find out how it ended. That seemed reason in itself to cry. Stealing a school library book – she could imagine the disappointment on Mrs Pearson-Smith's face. She left it on the table. She opened the dolls' house and looked wistfully inside. She thought of taking the small china kitten, curled up in its own little wicker basket. It would probably break, so best left too.

She picked up the bracelet-making set she had been given by Joanie for her last birthday. That would be a good thing to take. She could make bracelets while Joanie was doing whatever it was that she needed to do. Scout sat down on her bed again, and swallowed the inclination to cry. *Somewhere.*

Anywhere. Now. Perhaps this was because of what Joanie always used to tell her. *Your mama's a free spirit, your nan is a rooted plant*. Scout wondered if she was also the rooting kind. She liked opening and closing the same bedroom curtains each day.

'Scout, come on, hurry up,' Joanie shouted from the bottom of the stairs. 'Christ, you've only got one bag to pack, do you have to take all day?'

Scout picked up the bag and looked steadily around her bedroom. She clutched the bag to her chest, and made her way downstairs. She walked out on to the street, where Joanie was shoving bags into the boot of the car. One of the neighbours stopped, as if about to pass comment, and Joanie said, brightly, cheerily, 'Sorry, can't stop, too busy to talk.' Scout had to admire her mother's ability to make people bounce off her, when required.

Scout watched as Joanie locked the front door and came briskly down the path. She got into the driver's seat, checked her appearance in the car mirror, twisted a couple of her curls with her index finger and thumb, and then patted Scout on the thigh, saying, 'Come on, sweetie, think of it as a road trip.'

Joanie started the engine, and Scout knew it would be a mistake to turn round and look back. She focused on the cat's eyes in the middle of the road. Really they didn't look like cat's eyes at all.

'We're like Thelma and Louise, or Bonnie and Clyde,' Joanie said with an enthusiasm that Scout thought was not entirely genuine. Anyway, weren't they criminals – or in Thelma's and Louise's case (one of Joanie's favourite films) didn't they become criminals? Were she and Joanie criminals, and in which case what had they done? Try as she might, Scout couldn't think of anything that justified this sudden dash for *somewhere, anywhere*.

'This is our getaway vehicle,' Joanie said, laughing, and turning on the radio. Scout questioned whether 'getaway vehicle' was what the Vauxhall Corsa's designers had had in mind. Finally, she plucked up courage to ask, 'But what about school, what will Mrs Pearson-Smith say?'

'That's all sorted,' said Joanie, breezily. 'I've e-mailed school and told them we're leaving the area. I've told them from now on you're to be home educated. I'll be in charge of your learning, so they won't need to send a reference to another school.'

Scout looked at her hands clasped in her lap. No more Mrs Pearson-Smith. The sharpened pencils. The filing cabinets. The Amazon snaking its blue, wide way across the classroom wall. Her tree-frog poster probably wouldn't go on display now. She was due to be in the Good Work Book on Friday. Would they mention her in her absence? She felt as if she had a small, black hole in the middle of her chest. She looked sideways at Joanie as they waited at a traffic light.

'But you're not a teacher. You don't really like the stuff I do at school. How can you teach me? Who will teach me?'

'Home learning's all the rage. I've read about it in the paper. The first few weeks feel a bit directionless, but then you get into a routine. I read about someone who went to Oxford and they'd never been to school in their life. I'll buy you a few books, we can supplement things with trips to museums and exhibitions. How hard can it be? Let's face it, you're hardly doing A levels.'

Scout didn't answer. She considered the prospect of own-learning. She tried to picture Joanie taking her to a museum or exhibition. It was hard to get past the image of the café, or her mother having a smoke on the steps outside.

They were on the M40, rattling towards Birmingham now. *Nice big city,* Joanie had said. *It should be okay for me to pick up some work.*

'Are you hungry?' she asked Scout. She was. 'There's an M&S at the next junction. Special treat. You can have whatever you want.'

Scout admired hunger. Whatever you were thinking or feeling, it always came out top. She liked M&S. She liked it being advertised as *your M&S*. Sometimes she imagined herself in one of the supermarket trolley sweeps she saw on daytime TV, piling her trolley high with all the things she liked from *her* M&S. At the checkout at the service station, she clutched her wire basket which contained mini scotch eggs, orange chocolate-covered biscuits, popcorn with added nuts and lime juice cooler. 'Thanks Mum,' she said to Joanie, as the assistant rang the items through. Perhaps there would be compensations for being on the road and own-learning. The assistant smiled at her, and said to Joanie, 'What a nice polite daughter.'

In the car, Joanie said, 'Do you know, Scout, at the checkout I suddenly felt really old when you called me Mum. We're more of a team, you and me. I'd like you to call me Joanie, not Mum. That would make me happier. Is that okay for you?'

Scout bit into the thick chocolate of her biscuit. She looked out on to the motorway lanes, at the lorries thundering next to them on her left. So, calling Joanie Mum made her feel old. Scout wondered if Joanie had considered that not calling anyone Mum might make Scout feel she didn't have one. Like not calling anyone Dad, either.

'Yes, fine,' she said quietly. The biscuits were making her feel a bit sick.

6

You had to credit Joanie, Scout thought. When she wanted to she could certainly crack a pace. It was only three days later, and after two nights spent in a cheap B&B, Joanie had found them a tiny flat in a tower block, and had got herself a job at the Sleepeasy Hotel near to Spaghetti Junction. 'I am a chamber maid,' she said to Scout in a mock French accent. Her mother's enthusiasm for things was always comforting. When they had come up in the lift (which smelled of pee and had graffiti sprayed all over it) to the flat, Joanie had carried their bin bags inside, pronounced it *Grotsville and Grubsville!* and told Scout they would scrub it clean.

The scrubbing-it-clean part hadn't actually happened. Joanie had popped down to the corner shop for some fags and some cleaning products, then poked away at the mould at the window-sill corners for a bit before saying to Scout, 'That's me done,' and putting her feet up on the couch. Scout thought the couch had all manner of dodgy stains but, again, had to admire Joanie's foresight when she pulled from a bin bag an Indian throw taken from its place by the stairs at home. 'Ta- daah!!' said Joanie, as she thrust it out like a magician uncovering his table of tricks. The wall hanging floated down on to the couch and cloaked it entirely. 'See,' Joanie said, 'take it from me, Scout. When it comes to housework, you can either work hard or work smart. Scrub at stains on a couch or magically cover them away.' She patted the space on the couch next to her. 'Come and sit with me. Shall we get fish and chips for tea?'

Scout put down the washing-up brush with which she had been poking the sink plughole. It was brown with the staining – she presumed – of other people's tea. She wondered what succession of faces had sloshed tea remnants down this sink, looking out through the plastic window frame on to a largely vandalised small playground and one straggly tree. The tree was beginning to leaf – Scout was comforted by this. She swooshed a little bleach into the sink and wiggled the washing-up brush until the stainless steel started to reveal itself.

Joanie hadn't bought any books yet. Scout had no clue as to the nearest museum or exhibition. Perhaps this period was the weeks where everything was a bit directionless. She wondered if she should write out a few mathematical times tables, just in case she should slide towards forgetting. It was painful to think of the classroom at school, and what work they might be doing. What would Mrs Pearson-Smith have done with all her exercise books? Had they been taken from the cabinets and neatly put aside? Or, if Joanie had made it so clear that they were not coming back, would they have been tossed in the bin? All that neatness, Scout thought, all that thinking and careful, precise effort. (*Think like mad!* she always told herself when Mrs Pearson-Smith gave her a piece of extension work.) Surely Mrs Pearson-Smith wouldn't bin it all? She thought she could trust her not to. Although, as she looked at her mother, now blowing perfect smoke rings from the couch (this used to make Scout laugh when she was younger, and Joanie had followed each ring with a Native American-Indian whoop), Scout wondered whether trusting, or thinking you could guess correctly what an adult might do, would be an unrealistic expectation.

'Sausage and chips, cod and chips, haddock and chips,' Joanie was saying. 'I'll nip down and you can get into your pyjamas and we can watch some TV. I'm off early in the morning for the breakfast shift.'

Scout went into the bathroom as the front door closed behind her mother. The grouting between the tiles of the shower was rimed thick with black. She ran some warm water in the sink, stripped off, and rubbed her flannel with some soap. *This is called a sponge wash*, her nan, Alice, had told her long ago, when they had lived with her for a while. She changed into her pyjamas which smelt of home. Scout was struck by the ability of unexpected things to surprise you to tears.

Joanie came back and Scout sat, her body curled into her mother's, eating chips and watching TV. Joanie had bought a bottle of chardonnay and chilled it by using the kettle as an ice bucket. Later, as Scout lay in her bed, she could see Joanie lying in her bed on the other side of the thin strip of landing. The flat was on the third floor, and the sodium street lamps threw up enough light to reveal her mother's face. Joanie was sleeping soundly. Scout could hear the soft, neatly spaced snores she made when deeply asleep. Outside, someone was shouting. *Fuck off, you wanker.* She heard the crunch of an empty can being crushed to the ground. The swoosh of cars going past on the main road made an oddly soothing sound. Rain had fallen, and the puddles in the gutters splashed up on to the kerb as each car passed.

'This is my new home,' Scout said to herself, counting the cars as they passed. Someone hammered on the lift door. A loud laugh carried out into the night. Her mattress smelt a bit weird. Probably best not to think about why. She wondered what home actually meant. As long as Joanie was with her, did that make anywhere count? Perhaps home was portable, transplantable, truly like a snail's. Since Alice had died, she had only Joanie to love. Sometimes, Scout thought, this might count as having all your eggs in one basket.

7

Ned Beecham read the letter for the third time, folded it and placed it back inside its envelope, then took it out and read it again. Repetition, he decided, or repeated exposure to the neat, uniform words that trotted across the page, did not make it any less bewildering. A child. A child whom he thought had not made it to its first trimester was seemingly alive, alive, almost eleven, and now hot footing it across the country with a mother who had been notified by the clinic's legal department that they, and Social Services, wanted to discuss the matter. What did that mean for him?

Ned's hand passed over his brow, and settled on his lips. What form of words to tell Elisabetta, he wondered. What form of words, before that, to make it something he could assimilate for himself?

Ned unpicked the years, back to his recollection of that time, at the clinic, in what seemed another age entirely. He shrank from the memory of the inroads it had made upon his own dignity, his own privacy. Sperm counts, sperm samples. Sample pots given to him, and returned excruciating minutes later with glistening contents. Elisabetta's face, through that period of their lives together, with an agonised quality. If he had been able to, he would have painted her; the planes of her face contorting and dissolving upon themselves, so that she would have been a woman disintegrating. Instead, she told him, clearly, fire-eyed, she was a woman consumed for a second time, but this time by her own self-blame. When the gynaecologist explained to them that her anorexia as a teenager had irreparably damaged her ovaries, the image flashed into his mind of the Space Invaders game he used to play in pubs as a teenager, where round, determined icons moved purposefully forward, chomping everything in their path. Elisabetta's body, aged fifteen, had begun to consume itself from within. When he saw photos of her from that time, he could hardly recognise her; the visible jab of her elbows, her knees; her femur, her jaw bone, cheekbones, protruding from her skin. It had been an isolated episode, sparked by some predictable teenage angst. Good God, he had seen it often enough at the schools where he had taught; girls of fifteen, sixteen, suddenly shrinking, yellowing, elongating, their legs assuming the fragility of young giraffes. Elisabetta had recovered her equanimity and cherished again the food that was the hallmark of her Italian family life. But in her case, there were consequences, consequences that had rolled quietly, furtively, invisibly, fourteen years into the future. When Ned met and married her she was a beautiful woman, her bones smoothed in soft, olive flesh, her eyes bright, her hair gleaming. Ned had been a man bowled over by his own good fortune. He had stood at the altar of a church in Lucca and beamed.

It was only when they began trying for a child that the damage was revealed. Inside her body, her fallopian tubes and ovaries, were gnawed at, diminished. An ultrasound showed frayed edges, tatters of flesh awash in the scoop of her abdomen.

The surrogacy option had been something to which Ned had been slow to concede. It had a curious anonymity and intimacy which he found hard to reconcile. They had met Joan Simpson on a couple of occasions and she had seemed straightforward, what his own mother would have called *of good cheer*. He might have steered more towards *blowsy*. The thing Ned felt most uncomfortable about, and which he had never told anyone, was how completely unattractive he found her, although he recognised that this was a subjective not an objective response. Compared to Elisabetta who was so dark, lean, and supple, this woman reminded him of a plump china doll, with little-girl tousled blonde hair and a mouth that smiled too readily, without the smile gaining purchase on her eyes. She was large breasted – again, why should he have baulked at that? She seemed bovine somehow, made of too much creamy, buttery flesh. At the ovum collection, Ned had stood at her head and winced as he noticed two things. She had a tattoo of a swallow on her ankle (appropriate now that she had shown this predisposition for flight), and her nails were bitten, chewed right down to the quick. Ned could never have kissed a hand with nails gnawed like that. It seemed a ridiculous thing to focus on, but it bothered him as he stood there. He would have chosen distance from her. He wanted to turn his head away from her raised, sheeted knees. Instead, the contents of his body had been fused with hers, and were now to seek refuge in her blood-warm womb. In the natural way of things, this woman's egg and his sperm would not have meet in consensual passion. They wouldn't have exchanged six sentences, let alone a look of desire. He did not kid himself that she was looking at him with anything other than cheery goodwill. If he had mentioned his reservations to Elisabetta, he knew he would have made her cry. Her need to become a mother seemed as physical as heartburn. It had been hard enough to find anyone prepared to do this for them. *Like hen's teeth, these women,* she had told him. He was always impressed by her grasp of idiomatic English.

When the doctor told them that the woman had miscarried, Ned had felt guiltily relieved. Not predominantly so, as he held Elisabetta sobbing in his arms, but quietly, secretly so, and he was uncomfortable accepting their families' commiserations. His mother's especially. He would like to have told her that it was an odd relief. He compressed and tucked away what he could only describe as a stubborn feeling of gladness. He wondered if its ascendancy was actually morally appalling. It would probably have been different, he reassured himself, if the surrogacy was just a question of a borrowed womb. If it had been his and Elisabetta's embryo implanted in the woman it would have seemed entirely different. The years had rolled on and Ned was utterly comfortable with the episode as consigned to the past, and now there was this letter, this daughter, this direct challenge as to how much of a birth father he could or should feel himself to be.

The issue of children, anyway, had been reshaped with time. Three years ago, he and Elisabetta had travelled to China and adopted a baby girl they had named Maia. They were a family. Elisabetta was happy. She taught Italian part-time at a local independent girls' school. Maia was in the Nursery class. She was a bright, quick, elfin child. Ned was Head of the Classics department in an independent boys' school. He was also a Head of House. Elisabetta's parents' wedding gift to them had been a tiny villa outside Lucca. They spent two months of the summer there, awash in sunlight, good food and wine, and visited by a steady stream of family and friends. Last summer they had dug out a small pool. Maia had played in it all day, like a duckling. Ned felt proud of the jumble of threads which had knitted them together: England, Italy, China, the languages of English, Italian, and his own days spent teaching Latin and Greek. Initially they had agonised about finding Asian dolls for Maia to play with, to affirm her cultural identity. They had peopled her dolls' house with small Chinese figures. Now, it all seemed unimportant, everything was a glorious mish-mash. At the senior school she would go on to, Mandarin was taught from Year Seven. His daughter would know English, Italian, Mandarin, Latin, French. She would be taught by Elisabetta to cook osso buco. His own mother would teach her to make Yorkshire pudding and cup cakes. She would play lacrosse, hockey, netball, tennis. Facebook would hand her a world of connections. She would be English, European, Chinese. He was not worried about Maia. Once he had successfully banished the memory of the stark, bare orphanage in which she had begun her life, he saw the life they had given her, and what she had given them, as entirely felicitous.

And now this. This other girl. This child he had conceived with that woman. The woman he had found repellent. He could still remember the sight of the swallow tattoo on her rounded ankle and the small negative charge it gave him. She had named the girl Scout. He wondered if that came from *To Kill a Mockingbird*. That would be unexpected, surprising. What was she like? What kind of life had she been living? *Itinerant, until the last three years*, the letter said, and now, at the first hint of discovery, what appeared to be a random burst for elsewhere. Would there have to be DNA tests before he even began to get his head round what he wanted to do? The clinic seemed absolutely clear about the date of implantation and of her birth. The letter from their legal department suggested he consult a lawyer. It would be likely he had a case, if not for custody, for contact. Apparently, it was in the best interests of a child to know both genetic parents, if possible. How odd that the embryologist – he couldn't even remember where she had stood in the room – should have such a distinct memory for faces, and had been able to place Joan Simpson so many years later. You couldn't have scripted it, or fail to be impressed by a secret's tenacity in wriggling itself out into the open. Ned stood in the kitchen and heard Elisabetta singing to Maia upstairs. He would simply show her the letter. That way, he would not agonise about how he presented the facts.

The facts were that Joan Simpson had deceived them. Had deceived him in particular. Had lied to them about a child which was biologically half his. A child who had seemingly grown up fatherless with God knows what account of his own involvement or attitude. Did the girl know the circumstances of her conception? Did she know he had no idea of her existence? It was almost twelve years ago. So much time had gone by.

A biological daughter. A daughter already shaped and sculpted and nurtured by a woman with whom he felt so little in common. It was unpredictable. Dealing with unpredictability was not his strong suit. Ned loved Latin. He loved its order, its internal logic. He loved showing his pupils how to take a fine crow-bar to a sentence, how to dissect its grammatical parts, how to attach to it appropriate cases. He still gained pleasure from the tables of different groups of verbs, in words declined, chanted, recloaked in different grammatical shapes. In Latin, there was form, substance, solidity. He liked to see its shadow cast long in English and Italian words. His mind-set was one which liked to pursue things to a conclusion. Ned was methodical, meticulous. How these qualities were applicable to this situation was not apparent. And yet, he was not a man to shirk his responsibility. Was Scout his responsibility? Even after all this time?

Scout. His daughter. His now two daughters (both by circuitous routes – what should he deduce from this?). A lawyer. Where to begin to find a lawyer who would know something of this? There were three more days of term before school broke up for the Easter holidays. They were due to go to Cornwall to spend some time with his parents and his brothers. He would talk to Elisabetta then. He would show her the letter when they walked along the beach. There was something about space, light and water which made bomb-shells more palatable, more easily assimilated. It was not like reading the letter, as he was doing, in their small lime-white kitchen, which did not seem to have space enough to contain its unruly reverberations.

8

Scout wondered, as she poured herself a bowl of Frosties, whether she was winning at shaping her day into some sort of routine. Joanie hadn't eaten breakfast; she said she'd get it at work. Scout had washed up her mother's coffee mug, and rinsed out her ash-tray. She sat down at the table and wondered how she would fill the day with some learning. No books, yet, had been forthcoming from Joanie. On Saturday she had worked, and on Sunday she'd said she was 'far too knackered to be thinking about doing anything'.

Scout had a picture of how Joanie spent her day. She had made Scout laugh with her account of the rules and guidelines for cleaning a room. 'Sheets turned down to the left, visible as the door opens. Hygiene seal on the loo; new plastic bag over the water glass. Shower curtain concertinaed neatly to the right. Shower head always facing the hot tap. Mini bar tray to be stocked with equal sachets of coffee and tea, double the quantity of UHT milk. Headboard always to be hoovered behind in case of forgotten items.' ('That's pants,' she told Scout, 'pants and discarded condoms, although I haven't found any yet.') She told Scout of the trolley which she pushed from room to room, with little hooks on which to hang bottles of cleaning products, and a pull-out section for new, pressed sheets. 'I'm quite the bee's knees of order,' she said, 'although I use one of the drawers for my Silk Cut and some chocolate.'

Joanie hadn't asked her what she was doing that day. Maybe Joanie had such confidence in Scout's ability to own-learn that she didn't think it necessary. From the window last week Scout had spotted a van called Mobile Library. That was Wednesday, which it would be again tomorrow, and she thought she would go out past the playground and see if she could join. The estate in the day was not as empty as she had anticipated. There were young mothers with babies in push-chairs, sitting on the bench by the swings. They texted speedily, and held up their phones to show each other photos. Their babies sucked bottles and pulled at their mothers' earrings and hair. There were women in burkhas who moved swiftly between one flat and another, or quickly down to the shop. There were a few old guys who sat outside the pub across the road. There were gangs of boys, truanting from school. They stood, hunched over, hands in pockets, hoods up. Scout didn't like walking past them. She quickened her pace and felt as if her knees might bash against each other. Altogether though, the place wasn't without an odd, grim, grubby cheer.

Scout sat at her third-floor window, behind a tobacco-stained net curtain, and thought the estate was a kind of rainforest, with layers and layers of inter-connected life. An ice-cream van came sometimes, its tune plaintively ringing. The dustbin men ran along the long low wall which separated the bins, chucking bags to each other, as agile as monkeys in a way that Scout found unexpected. A pair of policemen walked around and around the small, bald communal garden. There was a sign which said No Drug Dealing, but someone had scored out the No. The beech tree's leaves were unfurling more each day. Someone had thrown up a pair of knickers, and they were caught in a branch. No one seemed to be crying though; no one was throwing themselves off the parapet that ran around the top of the blocks. Scout wondered if this was evidence enough of being happy, or if people held sadness curled tight inside them so that you didn't get to see it.

'When you go down to the shops today, add up what you buy in your head. That'll be Maths,' Joanie had shouted as she pulled the door to with her foot. Scout wondered whether Mrs Pearson-Smith would count this as Maths. She made her bed, washed her face, brushed her teeth and took some money from the jar by the sink. She put the key in her pocket and closed the door carefully behind her. She made her way down to the 7–11 shop which took up part of the ground floor.

'Why you not at school?' the owner had asked. 'Truanting is not way to success.' Scout had explained that she was responsible for teaching herself. 'School is better,' he said, and Scout wished Joanie had been there to overhear.

He was called Aatif Mohammed. Scout had deduced this from the sign above the shop door, which said he was permitted to sell intoxicating liquor. He had four older children who helped out after school and at weekends. His wife ran the Post Office counter, which had envelopes in a rack arranged in increasing sizes. They had another daughter, Lavanya, who looked about two years old and sat on a small stool by the till. Mr Mohammed said she was named after her grandmother. When Scout waited in the queue, she would squat down and take the little girl's hands between her own fingers and thumb. She would waggle her wrists and make her tiny bangles jangle. They called the child Nona for short, which Mr Mohammed told her meant butter. Scout preferred coming to Mr Mohammed's rather than walking down the main road to Tesco. She thought it might be a little bit more expensive, but it felt friendlier, more personal. Mr Mohammed told her that he was having one of the new mosquito devices fitted; it was meant to ring out at a high frequency and would stop gangs loitering outside his shop at night. Yesterday he had been testing it, plugging it in at a point behind the till. 'Can you hear it?' he asked her. 'It's meant to whine like a mosquito. Adults are not meant to hear it, the frequency is too high. Only children and teenagers.' Scout had tried with all her might to hear the whine of a mosquito. Perhaps it was blocked by the background drone of the road. Perhaps it was the noise of the other people in the shop. She had shaken her head. 'Never mind,' Mr Mohammed had said, 'perhaps you have astonishing mature ears.' Scout wondered if Nona could hear it, and whether she would be kept awake by the gangs beneath her window or by the device to deter them.

The shop was always well stocked. There were cigarettes, newspapers, pies and pasties, sweets, chocolate, biscuits, and tins of sausages, tuna, beans. There was a freezer with ice creams and frozen pizzas and chips and, at the back, a shelf of Indian food – basmati rice, lentils, spices, and flour for chapatis. Scout saw there was also a section of Polish food. 'Sign of the times,' Joanie had said when Scout had come home with some Polish ketchup.

Today, Scout put in her basket a Double Decker, a loaf of bread, some ham, two pizzas and a carton of milk. As Mr Mohammed started to ring the prices into the till, Scout placed her hand over its window with its emerald-green digits. 'I'm trying to add it up in my head,' she said, 'before the till tells me. It'll be good for my Maths.'

'Very good for your Maths,' he said. 'How much I am charging?'

'Six pounds and seventy-eight pence,' said Scout.

'Very good indeed,' said Mr Mohammed. 'Now tell me how much money if you have bought two Twixes, two Mars bars, and big Galaxy.'

'Two pounds and forty-eight pence,' said Scout. 'But I'm feeling quite sick if I eat all of that.'

'See, Nona,' Mr Mohammed said, gesticulating towards Scout, 'each day we will do Maths and you will listen up and be Maths genius even before going to school.'

The child rocked back on her small red stool. 'Two pizzas,' he said to Scout, 'multiplied by a carton of milk,' and then, 'thirteen times table, no pauses please.'

'She will soon be faster than till,' he called across to his wife.

'He will make more than grocer of you,' she said to Scout. 'This is always his wish.'

When Scout went back up in the lift, her shopping in a candy-striped bag (probably too thin to recycle and use again, but she wouldn't think about that now) she felt buoyant. That was Maths. That was definitely Maths. Even Mrs Pearson-Smith would count that as Maths. Now, if she played Scrabble with herself that would be Spelling and Word Skills. If she could find a nature programme on TV this would be her best own-learning day yet. Perhaps there would be a wildlife programme that focused on South America. Perhaps there would be another animal whose adaptations she could add to her knowledge of the tree frog. Perhaps she might glimpse the Amazon. She thought again of the map on the wall at school. Nicola Tate, who used to sit next to her, would whisper *Boring, boring, I'm going to die of boring* when Mrs Pearson-Smith scanned pages of the atlas on to the screen of the white board. She'd love my life now, Scout thought; she'd probably eat crisps and watch TV all day and Joanie would be okay with that. Joanie always said that classrooms couldn't teach you, only life could. Sometimes, Scout secretly worried whether she was the kind of daughter her mother would choose.

Later in the afternoon, she went back down to the shop to buy herself an ice lolly. Mr Mohammed had placed a stool next to the one for Nona. 'Here, for you to sit,' he said proudly, passing her a piece of paper. On it, he had drawn the floor space of the shop, marking the length and the breadth with their respective number of metres.

'Area of rectangle,' he said. 'Length times breadth. What is the area of my shop, in square metres please?'

Scout calculated the answer, and Mr Mohammed used his biro to add a swooping, jubilant tick.

'Now triangle,' he said. 'Area of triangle is half base times vertical height. Always remember, area in square metres please.' He wrote a small neat m, and put a little ^{2} above it. 'This is how you tell it,' he said, 'this is how you show it is not just one set.'

He drew her a triangle, and Scout calculated its area. Her one regret, leaning on her knees to write, was that her numbers were not as neat as they could have been.

Scout went back to the flat and sat at the kitchen table. With her ruler she measured out ten rectangles, ten triangles. She wrote the formulae at the top, and underlined them with a red biro Joanie had brought home from work. She ruled a neat line beneath each answer she calculated. She would ask Joanie if she would buy her a clear folder when she was next in town. It would be her Maths folder, she thought, and she would place in it all the things Mr Mohammed taught her. She put the work neatly on top of the kitchen cupboard, wiping it first with kitchen roll to make sure it was not greasy or dusty.

Scout sat at the table feeling unexpectedly happy. She wondered when her mother would be home. This would be the first day she had news to tell. Scout always looked forward to Joanie's return. She wondered if her mother ever considered how long each day felt inside this small, dingy space. The walls, she had decided, leaked sad feelings; feelings of not being able to turn anything to the good. She sat upright at the table, bolstered by her Maths formulations. She would bounce them back at the walls, make them absorb her productive day.

Scout stood up, and decided to lay the table. She put out knives, forks, plates, two water glasses and a wine glass for Joanie. She put the pizzas on a baking tray, covering it with foil first because the tray was thick with the burned-on remnants of other people's food, and turned the oven to the correct temperature so the pizzas could be put in as soon as Joanie got home. She tore off two pieces of kitchen roll and folded them into triangular napkin shapes. For good measure, she took out her ruler, measured the base and the height, and calculated their area, remembering to double the number because the napkin was folded.

When Joanie came through the door, she was already pulling at the poppers of her uniform and kicking off her shoes. 'I've got a date,' she said jubilantly, 'I'm going out on the razz. Mick from the storeroom has asked me. I thought there was something brewing!' Scout sat at the table and watched as her mother went from her bedroom to the bathroom and back again, naked except for a spotted shower cap. She was singing noisily, and wiggling her bottom. She wiggled it at Scout, who managed a smile.

Her mother pulled on a blue dress from her wardrobe, and a long dangly necklace with crystal clear hearts. She touched up her nail varnish, spritzed on some perfume, and applied mascara. She teased the curls by her cheekbones into more defined ringlets. She lipsticked her mouth, and came into the kitchen to plant a perfect motif on Scout's forehead.

'Oh, you've laid the table for tea,' she said, 'I'm sorry, I haven't got time to eat. Enjoy yours, and don't worry, I won't be back late.'

She slammed the door behind her. Scout could hear her still singing as she waited for the lift. The flat seemed to wobble like water, to carry the memory of Joanie's brief disturbance of its stillness. Scout felt it washing over her in small, short waves. Seventeen minutes, Scout thought, looking at her watch. Even by her mother's standards that was fast.

She took her pizza from the oven. The edges were slightly blackened, but she ate it anyway. Afterwards she washed her plate carefully on the rack, and put Joanie's unused crockery away. The plate looked back at her, like some misplaced, fallen, white moon. The area of a circle, she thought resolutely. There must be a formula for that, too.

9

Elisabetta Beecham walked with her husband on a Cornish beach on a morning early in April. Above them, the sky was scrubbed clean of clouds. A confident wind whipped from the water, bringing salt to her cheeks.

Ned was holding her hand. He always did this a little awkwardly, his fingers interlaced with hers so that the resulting clasp felt like a tangle of nubbly, knuckley ginger. It was both gentle and committed, and thereby typical of him. It was one of the things that had initially drawn her to him: his slightly formal, English reserve. Her own upbringing had been characterised by volatility, loud voices, huge warm scoops of gesture. There had been a quiet sense of homecoming in Ned's early, tentative affection. She looked at him now as he walked beside her. Strawberry blond. Only the English could come up with that as a colour for hair. If Ned grew a beard, it came through auburn, almost red. His skin became no more than honeyed with sunshine. He was drawn from a palette entirely different from hers. It was one of the things she had lamented, in the years when she had wept over not being able to bear his child: the prospect of mixing those colours, of perhaps having a brown-eyed, strawberry blond child. Maia had changed all that. It had been such a relief to celebrate her difference; to easily, instinctively, love their new daughter and to put aside what had become a fury with herself, and with her past.

Elisabetta sometimes wondered if she had fallen in love not just with Ned, but also with his entire family's perfectly pitched understatement. In the dark days, when she felt she had wept her windpipe raw, there had been sustaining consolation in the touch of his mother's hand, pressed lightly, wordlessly, to her shoulder-blade when she entered a room where Elisabetta had been crying. Even now, Elisabetta was always heart-warmed, watching Edward, her father-in-law, place his hand in the small of Prue's back as she walked before him. There was a tenderness she could see in their dealings with one another. It did not involve loud declarations of love, or hot blasts of recrimination. Her parents-in-law's home felt like a staunchly resolute refuge, bolstered by compassion and good sense, and washed through with blue Cornish light.

Elisabetta had learned to love English light. She had forsaken the ochres, the umbers, the russets, of her native Tuscany, and had learned to cherish the blue-green light of an English spring morning, the smoky, smudgy grey of an autumn twilight. She had even learned to love the intermittent slate of the sea, in such contrast to the aquamarine, the turquoise, of the sea of her childhood. Now, today, in Cornwall, its blue-greyness was tipped with a flinty edge, a seagull wheeled and called high above her, the waves sucked and smacked against the hollow of a nearby rock and threw out spumes of foam which scurried away between pebbles.

Her mother complained she needed glasses to read in English light. *At home I can see everything, read everything*, she said, palms upturned in familiar exasperation. *The English,* she said, *they look through soup. Cold hands, cold hearts*, she had told her, walking through London one long-ago raw February morning. Elisabetta was confident her mother had exempted Ned from this judgement. At the loud, noisy table in her parents' home, he was held in affectionate, bemused esteem, as her family argued, disagreed, slammed their hands on to the table and made the serving bowls jump.

Now, as she looked back along the beach, she could see Prue holding Maia's hand. They were leaning over a rock pool. Prue could be counted upon to know the name of each determined thing within it. On the way down to the beach through the woods, she had been showing Maia flowers, crushing wild garlic between her fingers to release its smell. And then, 'English bluebells,' she told Maia, 'these are English bluebells. The Spanish ones don't smell as good.' Her own father took Maia hunting for fungi and truffles, his broad, brown fingers pushing back leaf mould and soil, his finds held up in triumph like trophies. It made Elisabetta smile, the sight of her small Chinese daughter, schooled by her grandparents in English and Italian pastoral ways.

Ned suddenly stopped walking. 'There's this,' he said, passing her a letter which he had folded so carefully within his jacket breast pocket there was no clue it was contained there. Elisabetta stopped, her boots sinking a little with the suck of the sand.

A letter. For a moment she was baffled. Who would send them a letter that Ned would hand to her so gravely? Her stomach flipped. She looked to his face for guidance and then back to the letter, still proffered in his hand. No clue. She looked back along the beach to Maia. Surely it couldn't be anything to do with her adoption, not after all this time?

'You are frightening me,' she said. 'Say something. Who is it from?'

'Read it first,' he said insistently.

She opened it. The typeface danced before her eyes. There was a child. There had been a baby. The blood roared and thumped somewhere deep inside her ears. It seemed Joan Simpson had lied. She read it, and re-read it. There had been a baby, after all, and this letter quietly, baldly, calmly, affirmed it, when surely someone should have been screaming it from the cliff top? From the wide bowl of the sky, things came raining down; raining down on to her skin as painfully as knives, forks, spoons, pots, pans. That time, that dreadful time, those years of trying to conceive, her tattered innards, the antiseptic smell of hospitals, clinics, the desperate knot of hope and despair in those places. And then Joan Simpson. Her hair on the pillow. Her own hand on Joan's forehead. Joan's eyes which had been clear, without emotion, at the point of implantation. The grief, on hearing of her miscarriage. An afternoon spent quietly, utterly still at home, her hands in her lap, her face drawn, her lips grey, accepting that all routes had been attempted, pursued, and that it was time to give up. All hope lost. Yet the baby's heart had beaten on.

She looked up from the letter, and out to the horizon where the water met the sky. Impossible, so often, to detect, where one became the other. She could feel Ned looking at her face, trying to read signs, indications of response. Such a myriad of emotions, jostling and elbowing to the surface. Wounds long since assuaged and made smooth to the touch, by time and by Maia's arrival. Old, forgotten shards of pain, resurfacing and flexing familiar, keen edges.

'Am I angry?' she said softly. She bit deep into her lip, and tasted the sweet iron of blood. It felt right that this letter had drawn it. 'I think so. She lied to us. How could she? It was supposed to be our baby. She could have said she had changed her mind. Then we wouldn't have thought that we had lost that one too.'

She looked down at her boots. 'How long have you known this?'

'Only three days.'

Three days, she thought, thinking of his silence beside her in bed last night. If she had tried to keep this knowledge from him for three days she would have burst like a dam. Why had he not needed to tell her? Was he not angry? The child had been stolen from them both, but more physically from Ned.

'I wrote her a letter of consolation, of condolence. I thanked her for trying. I said I was sorry for all she had gone through on our behalf.'

'What's more pressing,' he said softly, 'is what we do now. Apparently there are choices to be made. Do we talk to lawyers, try to find her, and meet her? We need to understand if we think of her as our daughter.'

His words tumbled to the sand. He was logical and precise. He had had three days to digest it. Three days to consider options. The information was still stunning its way into her, cell by cell. She fished for a response.

'I don't know. I don't know. I am so shocked. They must be certain, mustn't they? It couldn't be a mistake?'

'They seem very confident of the dates – the implantation and birth date. If they find her, they will want to confirm it with a DNA test. But it's how we find her that bothers me. I don't want her to feel hunted down, but I expect that's the outcome.'

'We should take advice. Someone must know about these things.'

He reached to take her hand; she misinterpreted the gesture and gave him back the letter. She resisted the temptation to throw it wide to the sea. He refolded it and put it back in his pocket. Prue and Maia were approaching. At some point, in the next few days, Elisabetta knew he would discuss it with his mother, as a tablecloth was folded, a knife sharpened, a dog's paws rubbed dry. Consensus would be reached, calmly and reasonably, in a place far beyond the wild injustice that winnowed at her collar-bone now. She shook back her hair in the face of the wind.

Maia ran and clutched at her knees. She scooped up her daughter, kissed her gleaming black hair. She smelt of sea grass, of salt-water, of the fragment of crab shell held stead-fastly in a small, furled palm. Maia's adoption had confirmed what Elisabetta had always felt to be true: the ability of love to refashion the heart. And now there was another child, haphazardly, inextricably, connected to them too. A child who needed to be tracked down, but what might that make them?

10

Joanie breezed into Scout's bedroom, saying, 'Doughnuts, hot chocolate, breakfast in bed!' She put a six-box of warm dough-nuts on the floor, and two lidded paper cups. She opened Scout's curtains and let in the light. 'While you wake up, I'll have a quick shower,' she said.

Scout wondered whether it was a peace offering. Was it the blue dress or her nightie beneath her dressing-gown? Best not to look. What did Alice say? *Ignorance is bliss.* Possibly. Certainly smoother. She closed her eyes again, and stretched her limbs beneath the duvet. Joanie quickstepped into the bathroom, and Scout heard the shower begin to run. Last night, she had lain awake waiting for the sound of Joanie's key in the lock. She'd listened to the swoosh of passing cars, waiting for the empty space of the flat to be filled. She'd listened for Joanie's heels tip-tapping along the corridor outside, or for the sound of her laughing with Mick from the storeroom. The pizza had given her a tummy-ache. She'd wondered if Mr Mohammed's family were all having their supper around a big rectangular table. She'd fallen asleep calculating its possible area.

Joanie emerged from the bathroom wrapped in a towel, her hair wet. 'Budge up,' she said to Scout, balancing the doughnut box on the bed, and climbing in next to her. Water dripped from her hair and down the channel of her cleavage. She passed Scout a hot chocolate, and Scout sucked hesitantly at the hole in the lid. She decided to be careful not to give the impression

she was in a sulk. Joanie never had time for that. The hot chocolate caught the softness of her inner lip with its heat. Joanie put
her arm round her, and gave Scout a big kiss on the top of her
head. 'How's my darling this morning?' she asked. Joanie
smelled clean, like mown grass. Scout wondered if she should
say there was no need to feel sorry. Joanie didn't usually require
forgiveness. Usually, neither of them said anything. It was better
to say nothing; but not in a way that might seem she was sulking.
Maybe the doughnuts and hot chocolate weren't saying sorry
anyway. It was sometimes hard to tell.

'Fine. I'm fine. Did you have a nice time?' Scout hoped
Joanie might describe it. There were not enough words in this
flat. There were too many vast, dinosaur ribs of silence. She
wanted Joanie to throw back her head and laugh, and fill the
room with some warm, sloshing sound.

'Fantabulous,' Joanie said, tucking the duvet around them.
'There was an ice sculpture on the bar shaped roughly, very
roughly, into what I think was a dolphin.'

When Scout got up, the solitary plate was still in the draining
rack like a small, solid reproach. She put it away quickly. She
would think of it only in terms of Maths as yet unknown.
Joanie went into work late, saying 'Who cares? I've been brilliant, I should have some credit in the bank.' Scout went down
to the shop to buy lunch. Mr Mohammed was waiting with a
narrow-lined A4 pad.

'Prime numbers, today,' he said. 'Definition of a prime
number is a number that can only be divided by one or by
itself. Another way to say this: its factors are only one or itself.'
He handed Scout a sheet of paper. 'Copy definition down,' he
said, 'and then tell me if the numbers on this list are prime or
not.'

Scout tried to put out of her head the thought that if Joanie
were a number, she would probably be prime. Probably definitely be prime. Was it a choice you made, to be divisible only

by yourself? Or, if you were a mother, did it mean by definition you had divided? Scout wondered if there was a special
name for a number which was not a prime. She would ask
him later. She sat down next to Nona, and gave thanks for Mr
Mohammed.

Later in the day, from her window, she saw the mobile
library arrive. She pulled on her jacket and went down to
where it was parked. The woman inside seemed surprised
when Scout entered. 'Goodness,' she said, 'a new reader. I
usually only get one at this stop.' She had a pink face, and eyes
that were round and blue like a doll's. The wedding ring on
her finger had puffs of swollen flesh either side of it. She wore
a matching striped top and cardigan, and some beads at her
neck. Scout decided she seemed all powdered wobble and
softness. She didn't look the kind to be driving what was basically a truck full of books. Scout read the badge pinned to her
chest. *Mary Crawshaw.Volunteer.* She took a bold step forward,
running her finger along a shelf of books. The van smelled
musty. She wondered if she was ever going to be anywhere
that smelled nice again. 'Shouldn't you be at school?' the
librarian asked. Scout thought about taking up wearing an
own-learning badge.

Despite its obvious defects, the mobile library looked like a
small treasure trove, even though Scout could see most of the
books were dog-eared, yellowing, with pictures of women in
vast ball gowns looking up at men with moustaches (this in
the section labelled Romantic Fiction in Mary Crawshaw's
neat hand).

'I'd like some books to help with my learning, please,' she
said. Mary put her thumb to the dimple of her chin and looked
purposefully at the Non-Fiction/Reference section. 'How
about *Kings and Queens of England*?' she said. 'That can't go
out of date. And I've got a nice one here on things that live in
ponds. This is new,' she said, picking up a small paperback

called *Hatfield's Herbal*. 'There's not much of a budget for new books. Mobile Library is always last in the line, and I have to say sometimes I'm a bit perplexed by what they choose. At a push, would that count as Science?' Scout read the first page intently. She wasn't sure, but it looked interesting.

'It's nice to have a new reader,' Mary Crawshaw said. 'I'll have a poke around in some of the other vans. Most of what is borrowed is either stories of women wanting to find husbands, or of tragic childhoods. I don't think anyone's going to be fighting with you over *Pond and River*. Don't you have a computer? That's the way everybody mostly learns now.'

Scout shook her head.

'They say all books will be read electronically soon. Then this old van will be for the dump, and probably me too.' Scout thought that would be a loss; both the books and Mary Crawshaw, with her powder-blue eye-shadow and her scent of talc. 'I'd like to live in this van,' Mary told her encouragingly which, although only half-meant, she could see had a positive effect.

'Let's do you a ticket,' Mary said. 'I don't suppose you have a photo? Never mind, I'll just write a description in the box. You're hardly being stampeded by a queue, are you, and it's only me who'll be checking.' Mary wrote in the box *Looks about ten, straight hair in plaits. Sweet face*. Scout would be eleven soon. Her hair curled sometimes, in the right sort of rain. Normally people noticed that her eyes seemed both blue and green. Why quibble? she thought. She scooped the books under her arm.

'Hello, Mr Groves,' Mary said into the space behind her, as Scout became aware of someone coming very slowly up the steps. 'This is my other reader,' Mary said warmly, 'you two must be neighbours. How are you this week?' she asked, stepping forward to help an elderly man into the van. 'This is

Scout,' she said, gesturing to where Scout stood with her books next to the flip-down counter. The old man nodded his head deferentially and offered his hand to Scout. The veins stood out on it like blue-green tributaries of the Amazon. 'Hello, Miss Scout,' he said, and Scout thought she had never met anyone so old, or so formal.

Later, as she inched back with him towards the lift that would take them both to the third floor, she wondered how old he was, and decided it would be impolite to ask. She carried the one thin book he had borrowed from the library. ('Anything too long and he forgets the beginning by the time he gets to the end,' Mary Crawshaw had confided.)

As they stopped by the lift, one of the boys from the block gang ambled over towards them. 'Hey, sir,' he said, 'any chance of lending me a couple of quid?' Scout instinctively put her hand to Mr Groves' elbow, and was surprised to see him burrowing into his jacket and removing a brown leather wallet. He took out three coins and gave them to the boy. 'Pay you back tomorrow,' the boy said. 'Honest, I'll pay you back tomorrow.' He pocketed the coins and laughed as he walked back to his friends.

Scout watched him retreating, and Mr Groves slowly, carefully, putting the wallet back inside his breast pocket. 'Do they ask you for money often?' she asked, pressing the button for the lift. Mr Groves didn't answer.

Outside his flat, four doors along from Scout's, he retrieved a key from his trouser pocket. 'Would you like to come in for tea, Miss Scout?' he asked. 'It would be nice to have a guest.'

Scout wondered what Joanie would say. She ran through her head all the stranger-danger lectures she'd been given at school. This man looked so frail the wind would blow through him, not round him. Before a strong light bulb, she thought, he would probably be see-through. If she huffed and she puffed she could probably blow him right down. She said,

'Yes please, I'd like that,' and gave him a little bow with her head.

'Delightful,' he said, pushing the door open into his tiny hallway.

Scout expected the flat to be grimy, or smell of old person's pee. One Christmas at school, they had sung at an old people's home and, despite the evidence of at least three trolleys wheeled about by cleaners, the rooms had a smell that made the inside of Scout's nostrils burn. Mr Groves' flat, in contrast, smelled super-clean. It was chock-full of things which were spotless and polished. Brasses on a leather strap hung by the fireplace. Crystal vases on a sideboard caught the light and scattered it. The door handles were gleaming, the taps shone like small beacons. It smelled of polish, of endeavour, of domestic precision. Scout had a vision of Mr Groves moving slowly and painstakingly around the small space, polishing and wiping like a determined beetle.

'Tea?' he asked, reaching towards a tray on the sideboard. His voice was so thin, so reedy, Scout imagined his vocal cords hardly vibrated. She watched as he tremblingly carried the tray towards the kitchen table. He boiled water in the kettle, swooshed it round the pot, and then emptied it out into the sink. He measured out two teaspoons of loose leaf tea, put it into the warmed pot, and filled it with water. He filled a small jug with milk, his hands precise and careful. He arranged two cups and saucers on the table, and produced a bowl of sugar with a spoon that fanned into segments like a seashell. He poured tea for Scout, and she sipped from bone china that felt thinner than her eyelids. 'This is how tea should be prepared properly,' Mr Groves said. 'It is one of the few things I know.'

'How do you know?' asked Scout, who did not usually drink tea but was drinking this because nothing had ever been prepared for her with such soothing, meticulous, ritualised care.

Mr Groves reached into a drawer, and took out a pair of white gloves. He passed them to Scout. They were old, yellowed, and a little frayed, but Scout could see each individual finger was beautifully stitched.

'I was a butler,' he said, 'all my working life. In a grand house, Houghton Hall, for the Broughton-Fowler family. Things were done properly. Manners. Etiquette. The correct laying of a table. It's a lost art. People have no time any more.'

'I've got time,' Scout said. 'I've got plenty of time. You could tell me about it.'

Her voice seemed quick and loud in the room. There was something about him she liked and trusted. She felt perfectly safe. What he had to say might be interesting to hear. It would all be learning, all own-learning, and anyway, there was only herself to decide what qualified as such. Joanie probably wouldn't mind at all.

11

Scout pushed the window open a tad to let in the brisk April morning. On the kitchen table she had put out some paper, her crayons, and *Pond and River*. *After the dull, cold days of winter*, she read, *spring is here at last*. She cast her eye over the pictures of plants. *The caterpillar of the puss-moth feeds on sallow and poplar, both found in damp or moist soils, so puss-moths are often seen near pond and river*. Scout inspected the illustration. A puss-moth sounded more interesting than it looked, but this probably shouldn't be held against it. She looked at a photograph of two Petri dishes containing tadpoles from a small pond and tadpoles from a large one. The small pond heated up more quickly, so the tadpoles grew bigger, more quickly. Perhaps it was the same for humans, she thought, and a question of luck as to the space in which you were born. She was drawn to the names of the plants – ragged robin, cottongrass, marsh horsetail, loosestrife, meadowsweet. They sounded as if they could be munched. She copied them out in her neatest handwriting, and decided she'd start a new folder called Nature. She would not draw diagrams of a tadpole changing into a frog. She'd done that in Year Two. She thought of the tree frog poster she'd been working on at school. Perhaps she should find another frog – an English one – and write about that. She flicked through to the back of the book, and became absorbed by the *AMAZING FACTS! Cane toads lay 35,000 eggs a year. Fishing bats' echo-location can detect a minnow fish's fin as fine as a human hair. Frogs have top teeth*

*but not bottom, so they can grip but not chew. Newts find their way
back to the pond they were born in, using sight and smell.*

Joanie seemed to have had difficulty finding her way to bed
last night. She'd come in late, and crashed towards it, swearing
to herself as she pulled off her boots. Scout guessed it had
been a vodka night, not a white wine one, not that she would
have asked. This morning, Joanie had lain in bed, her palms
pressed to her eyelids, and asked Scout to bring her an aspirin
and a black coffee and not to open the curtains. She'd got
dressed, swearing softly again, her cigarette clamped at the
side of her mouth as she zipped up her boots. 'Bugger bugger
bugger,' she said, as she reached for her handbag on the
bedside table.

'What would you like for tea tonight?' Scout had asked
tentatively, mentally casting her eye along Mr Mohammed's
shelves. 'Oh God, don't even ask me about food. I can't even
think about food.' Scout had sat quietly while Joanie gathered
her keys, her lighter. She thought about telling her that Mr
Groves was going to explain procedures at a pheasant shoot
today, but decided not. Chattering was probably best avoided.
She sat on the couch, with her hands in her lap. She fixed her
eyes on a blotch on the wall. She remained sitting for a little
while after her mother had gone. Then she smoothed the
creases on the knees of her jeans, and picked up her library
books.

Scout copied out a small piece on why a frog's call,
despite being so loud in proportion to its body, doesn't
blow its own eardrums. The secret was that its ears are
connected to its lungs, so the vibrations disperse through
all of its body, not just into its ears. How clever, she thought,
how unbelievably, intricately clever, but she worried a little
that this was just copying, just lazy learning, not *thinking
like mad* as she had done for Mrs Pearson-Smith. She put
the book aside, and wondered if there was a pond tucked in

the scrubby land between the tower blocks and the next main road. She tried to imagine listening at night and hearing a frog croak above the other sounds that had become rapidly familiar. Unlikely. There was perhaps only so far she could go with this. She picked up *Kings and Queens of England*. Each day, she was jotting down key facts on one chosen monarch. So far, she was impressed by Edward III making members of parliament sit on woolsacks to remind them how important wool was for English trade and prosperity. If she progressed through the book, she'd have a folder that went from William the Conqueror to the present day. In Year Five, when they had studied Victorians, she'd done a time-line on Queen Victoria. She'd liked it that Victoria became Empress of India when her time-line was almost done, and that her Empress crown contained the biggest diamond ever found. That seemed a good way to top off her reign. None of the other kings and queens she had looked at in the book had so far matched that. Today, she chose Henry V, and gave him a small colourful banner beneath his name. She wrote *Good at fighting the French* in curly bubble letters she thought suited banners and crests. Then, she picked up *Hatfield's Herbal*, and read about ash trees. *Shepherds' crooks used to be made of ash as it was said it could never hurt sheep ... A wagon with an ash axle was believed to go faster than any other.*

Scout wondered how people decided what they believed. Did they believe what they actually saw with their own eyes, or what they felt was true? The second option would apply to God. Yesterday, she'd decided she was having some trouble imagining Him here in this flat. The village rector, who came weekly to school, had told them God was present everywhere. E-V-E-R-Y-W-H-E-R-E. This meant He ought to be here. There had been a picture-book version of *Alice in Wonderland* in the school library. One drawing – across a double page

– showed an enormous Alice squashed into a very tiny room, her elbows jammed up against window frames, her shoulder pushed to the ceiling. That was how it would be for God, Scout thought, if He *were* actually in this room. It was hard to think of Him here. Apart from her own silence, and her small, quick movements, this flat contained only an absence or presence of Joanie. There didn't seem space for much more. Perhaps it was better to try and imagine Him Christmas-style, tucked up in the flat as a newborn baby. She tried to summon Him up, swaddled. This didn't seem to work either. A baby brought with it all the accessories the teenage mums had on the bench near the communal garden: bottles, dummies, mobile phones, buggies, Diet Cokes. No, Scout thought; not that sort of baby.

Up to now, she'd never had any problems picturing God, admittedly only massive behind the altar when they went to St James for Harvest Festival or Christingle, but she could not see Him here. Not even in the way that sometimes got written about in the papers, when a damp stain on the wall looked like Him on the cross, or the Virgin Mary's face, and then pilgrims came flocking. (*Jesus on a piece of toast* – she'd read about that in a newspaper.) She looked up at the damp stain that rippled from the corner of the kitchen ceiling to the pendant light. That just looked like nothing or, at a push, maybe reeds from a river, sucked along by the current. There was no escaping the fact that some things were just plain unremarkable whatever you might hope for. She tentatively hummed a song they sang when Year Sixes were leaving: *And it's from the old I travel to the new, Keep me travelling along with you.* Her humming petered out, somewhat lacking in conviction. God, she hoped, would understand why. It wasn't her fault if the flat felt beyond His attention.

She got up from the table and walked three times between the window and the bathroom door. She ate two Jammie

Dodgers and drank a glass of milk. According to her watch, it would be break-time soon. If she had a skipping rope, she could go down to the communal garden and skip. It had occurred to her, with some anxiety, that she wasn't doing any P.E. This would be bad for her heart, her muscles. They'd done a whole project in Year Four on why exercise was crucial. She resolved to run up and down the stairs to the ground floor three times – that should make her out of breath. She'd do that before going down to buy lunch. She could then do whatever Mr Mohammed was setting for Maths today, and sit there with the confidence that her heart, lungs, and leg muscles had done their work too.

Later, she sat on the second stool by the till while Mr Mohammed embarked upon fractions. As a learning tool, he was using a pizza that had been squashed by the chest freezer lid, and so was not fit for sale. 'Better,' he said, 'that its use is to a different end. A pizza for education, not a pizza for nutrition.' With a small penknife he cut it into respective parts. He taught Scout to add fractions, to subtract them, always to give them the same denominator before trying to do anything else. Nona sat beside her while she wrote out her answers. Her bracelets jangled as she pulled on the fringe of Scout's cardigan.

'And now also,' said Mr Mohammed proudly, 'a dictionary. I have located a dictionary. After Maths it is your job to find some English words to teach me. The only condition is that they must not be known to you either. You must skim down the page and find a word that you do not know. Ask me if I know it, and then if I can't tell you, you read me out the answer. This way we will both be better at English vocabulary. We are both improvers.'

Scout opened the dictionary randomly, at a page of words starting with the letter D. Her brow furrowed with the effort of discrimination.

'Deracinated,' she said, 'de-rac-in-ated,' stressing the syllables.

'No idea,' said Mr Mohammed. 'You have me from the off. First one unknown to me. So what is deracinated?'

'To be uprooted, to pull out by the roots. It's not just for a plant. It can be people too.'

'I can see that, like for my parents who came here and thought they had arrived into permanent monsoon.'

'Jaunty,' said Scout. He shook his head. 'Easy and sprightly in manner. Perky.'

'A jaunty walk would be a good thing if possible. This I am guessing.'

Scout warmed to the task. 'Susurrate,' she said, moving her finger through the pages.

'Again, you have me,' he said. 'I think you are better at Maths than I am at dictionary.'

'To make a whispering sound,' said Scout, 'like the wind makes through the leaves of a tree.'

'I see that. Very nice. Very fitting. The word sounds like it is.'

'Onomatopoeia,' said Scout. 'My teacher taught me that. It's when a word sounds like what it means.'

'Then we have one,' said Mr Mohammed, 'we have one of your onomatopoeia. Sus-urrate,' he said to Nona, blowing the word through his lips. Nona laughed and sucked her teeth at him.

When Mr Groves answered the door, he tipped his head in his customary fashion. 'Good afternoon, Miss Scout,' he said, 'I hope you have had a productive morning.' He helped her remove her cardigan, and hung it carefully on the hook at the back of the door. 'Tea will be ready at three, Miss,' he said. 'Today, I made the presumption that you might enjoy some crumpets and jam. That was Miss Maudie's particular favourite when she came in from riding.'

Scout sat in Mr Groves' tiny sitting-room, and felt it to be a parallel world, one in which her horse might be being taken to the stable by a groom, whilst a maid pressed her dress for dinner. She envisaged bells rung in bedrooms, and servant feet quickly anticipating the need. 'The problem is, Mr Groves,' she said, 'I wouldn't be in the bedroom, putting on a dress made of silk and shoes of the finest leather: I'd be the one polishing them, or running up the stairs when the bell's rung by Miss Maudie.'

'Not in this version, you're not,' Mr Groves said. 'In this version, you are the young lady of the house. You are ringing the bell.'

'Hello darling,' Joanie said, as she came through the door. She planted a big kiss on Scout's lips and wrapped her tight in her arms. Her mother smelled, gloriously, of perfume, of polish, of cigarette smoke, of the boiled wool of her coat. Scout breathed her in.

'Sorry I was such a grouch this morning. God, I can't remember the last time I felt so dreadful. I had a full English at eleven, that set me right. What did you buy for tea?'

'Pie. Steak and kidney pie,' said Scout. 'And some frozen peas, but they were a bit hard to jam in the ice box.'

'Delicious,' said Joanie. 'I'm starving. You are a star.'

Her mother sat down on the couch, flipped off her shoes, and put her feet on the footstool. She stretched back luxuriantly, and lifted her hair so that it streamed out behind her. It reminded Scout of the twirly ribbons they held when they danced around the maypole at school.

'What did you do today?' Joanie asked. 'Did you have a nice day? You should get out a bit more. You're looking a bit pale. Come the weekend, we'll go somewhere and I'll make a nice spaghetti bol for after.'

Scout opened her mouth, ready to tell her mother of crumpets, pheasant shoots, common denominators, frogs' teeth, and puss-moths, and that just twice up and down the stairs had given her an unbelievable stitch. She also toyed with asking her if the damp patch in the bathroom might look like anything to her. Sitting on the loo, just before Joanie came home, with her head tipped to one side so that her ear was almost touching her shoulder, Scout had wondered whether it might not resemble Moses tucked cosily in his basket. She would ask her to look, and see if she thought so too. She was sure there was no danger of an inrush of pilgrims. She took a deep breath, ready for it all to come spilling out. Then, she saw that as one of her mother's hands reached into her bag for her cigarettes, her other, absent-mindedly but purposefully, slid along the couch, deftly locating the TV remote control.

'Just this and that. Just this and that,' Scout said, hardly missing a beat, as the television loudly, brightly, flickered into life.

12

Joanie sat on the couch, shifting restlessly. She had humoured Scout by sitting on the loo for ten minutes, her right ear pressed to her right knee, trying to see Moses asleep in his basket in the top left corner of the ceiling. She'd given it her best shot, but there was nothing doing. She went to light a cigarette, and resisted. She thought, perhaps a glass of wine, or a Scotch, and thought not. Horlicks? Cocoa? Probably none in the cupboard. Who was she kidding? Definitely none in the cupboard; grotty, crappy, MDF, peeling cupboard that it was. Her good mood was evaporating. This hand-to-mouth living sucked. Her job sucked. Picking up after other people. Cleaning up after other people. Stupid trolley which had a dodgy wheel so that she caught her ankle trying to steer it through doorways. Other people's stinking, stained bed sheets. Other women's sanitary towels and tampons just tossed into the bin. Gashes of bright red blood. No inhibition, modesty or prudishness. They could do with a little more of that at the Sleepeasy Hotel.

The vast majority of her co-workers couldn't even speak English properly, but probably had degrees in genetics or archaeology. The ones who could speak English mostly didn't give a shit. *Morning*, they said brightly to a guest as they met in the corridor. *Tosser*, they said when they'd passed. And to come home to this, Joanie thought, casting her eyes over the dingy paintwork, the stained furniture, the crappy carpet, and Scout with her eyes like saucers, fastening on to her the minute she walked through the door, wanting God knows what, but needy, now, in a way that made Joanie's chest feel tight, and made her feel as if the oxygen was being sucked out of the room. Did other mothers feel like that? Typical if it was her only claim to uniqueness. She relented on the cigarette and lit it with a crisp flick of her lighter.

She'd watched a wildlife programme with Scout once, narrated by David Attenborough; she'd always liked his voice. It had filmed the Giant Pacific Octopus. When pregnant, the female would find a small crevice in a rock, scuttle inside, lay her eggs, and lie there obsessively cleaning and aerating them, protecting them from sea-stars and crabs for seven months, until they were ready to hatch. Then, tenderly, she would help ease them out of their jelly casing, and waft them carefully outwards and upwards to begin their life. Then, weakened, not having eaten for the entire period since entering the crevice, she would die – just peel and disintegrate away – a testament to devoted and self-sacrificing maternal instinct. The very thought made Joanie shudder, let alone the memorable image of the shrinking, failing, octopus dying in its birthing bed. If that was what motherhood required, Joanie thought, they could count her out. Love shouldn't mean self-sacrifice. She'd decided that early on.

It was raining, a soft mournful rain, which wouldn't help her mood. It seemed to patter on the plates of her skull. Across the hallway she could see Scout, turning over in her sleep. She murmured more in her sleep these days; muttered conversations to herself about goodness knows what. Joanie didn't want to think about how she was filling her days. Best left unexamined. She'd talked about the old guy, a butler; the shop guy teaching her Maths – what was that about? The mobile library. It probably wouldn't stand up to much scrutiny. Perhaps she should ask her more questions.

Yesterday, an old crow woman on the ground floor, waiting, probably deliberately, for Joanie to go past, seemingly doing a bit of half-hearted wiping of her door frame. 'Excuse me, (voice a bit quavery but steely in intent) is it your daughter I see coming up and down from the third floor? She should be at school.' Joanie clocked her gist. Interfering old bat, just the kind likely to pick up the phone and call someone. A whiny and concerned tone wheeled into place; shiny, polite words for public consumption hauled on to her tongue. 'I don't like to presume, and you may be aware already, but I just feel, as a member of the community . . .' Well, she'd bat that one right back if and when it came. The Sleepeasy Hotel had her National Insurance details, all her bank stuff. Realistically, anyone looking for her with purpose would find her, but she'd be up and off. Years of practice, pre- and post-Scout. She'd done nothing wrong. Not strictly wrong. Nothing there was a law against. Probably not even a law about. She'd just chosen not to turn up to a meeting she'd been invited to. There was no way they could force her. Social Services would be unlikely to chance their arm. She stubbed out her cigarette. She looked across into Scout's room.

Scout looked smaller, younger, when she was asleep. She couldn't understand mothers who chose to sit at the bedside of their sleeping child, listening to their in-breath, their out-breath, and feeling it as bellows to their own lungs. When she did look at Scout asleep, she felt as if responsibility had her by the ribcage. It pulled her up short so was best avoided. Scout still looked small enough for someone to scoop her up and carry her away. Going out for a night and leaving her to put herself to bed seemed a bit neglectful. Yet, it was never her intention to go out for more than a couple of hours. When she said yes to Mick the storeman, she'd said to herself she'd be back by 9.30, she'd just have a quick drink and leave. Scout would be brushing her teeth as she walked through the door.

It never turned out that way. She was always so caught up in the moment, absorbed by a man's body, feeling her own body flicker into light and warmth, all glowed-up, and a million miles away from her stupid job. Scout became less substantial in the context of a bar, a nightclub, a noisy restaurant. She seemed to evaporate, no matter how hard Joanie tried to picture her in her pyjamas, kneeling on her bed, patiently tugging her bedroom curtains closed.

In the mornings, Joanie felt the hammer blow of alcohol to her head, and in her bones, wiggling and turning like a persistent worm, a small voice, saying *You've done it again; you're a crap mother. Crap crap crap.* Later in the day, feeling kinder to herself, she'd reconsider. Scout was warm, fed, clothed, loved. That was more than most. She wasn't overly ministered to, that had to be acknowledged, but Joanie felt she could justify that as a better preparation for what was to come. Life wasn't generally in the habit of bending over backwards for anyone. More likely to poke you in the eye with a stick. Perhaps if you learned that, early on, from your mother, you were better prepared. No possibility of subsequent disillusionment. As an additional benefit, Scout's perceptions of romantic, sustainable, monogamous relationships with men weren't likely to be overly rosy either. That had to be helpful. What did Alice say? *One thing you're never short of is finding justifications to do what suits you.* Thank you, Alice. Not that self-improvement or self-questioning had ever been Alice's brief. Her version of mothering was mostly a compilation of tedious, infinitely repeatable, domestic duties, with no vision of what else she might be. Scout couldn't accuse Joanie of that. Not that Joanie had exactly nailed what else she herself might be, or garlanded herself in achievement or accomplishments. That could be posted under 'work in progress'.

'Don't beat yourself up over it,' she said out loud to herself. How odd her voice sounded, speaking to no one in this grubby little space. Did Scout ever talk out loud, and fill its poky little corners with conversations with herself? Perhaps she should ask her. She should try to be more interested in the detail.

Scout's resilience was awesome. It was gobsmacking, her daughter's ability to not complain. Joanie wondered if she'd come home one evening and find Scout in bed, sobbing, the covers pulled up over her head, or standing, defiant, arms folded, and asking either for an explanation or her old life back. But nothing. Nothing at all. What if Scout was storing it up, fit to burst with a torrent of blame, someday soon? She should be on her guard for that. Alternatively, perhaps children loved with total, passive acceptance. How brilliant would that be? Although, maybe in Scout's case it could be more indicative of not being swamped with other alternatives. Perhaps there was an unfailing comfort in being wherever your parent was. Pretty impressive, whatever. Scout didn't seem physically big enough to contain all her strength of purpose. Her frame was so thin, so unlike Joanie's own (here, she squeezed the plump round flesh of her upper arm and was tempted to plant upon it a big fat kiss), it was hard to imagine that she mastered such sturdy resolve. Put up or shut up. Perhaps Scout had plumped for both.

Was her frame like her dad's? Joanie couldn't remember how he was built. She disliked picking over that whole episode and revisited it as little as possible. She could remember his wife, Elisabetta, crying. Thinking about it, now, made her feel uncomfortable. It jostled and pushed under her skin, all jabbing elbows and fingers. Her preferred option had been to parcel it firmly away. That had worked for years, and now, on this night, in this bloody shitty place, it was all coming back, knocking on her skull, trailing images she'd wanted to forget.

If asked to explain, if asked to explain honestly, Joanie would have to acknowledge that often when she made decisions, a week later, a month later, six months later, she would be truly amazed the course of action had come from her. Unbelievable. So many of the decisions in her life felt like they had been made by a different person. *Unaccountable*, Alice said. *You change with the wind*.

Surrogacy. How mad was that? If Alice had known, she'd have gone to town on what it revealed, but Joanie thought it was mostly a come-uppance for watching too much daytime TV. That was where it all started; lying on the couch mid-morning and watching a woman give an interview about how she'd gifted five couples with the baby of their dreams. How the audience had loved her, how they applauded her. *Wow*, said the woman interviewing her, *you're amazing*, and the surrogate sat there looking like a glowing goddess, awash on a sea of tearful gratitude and respect. Big-up for her. She'd got to Joanie, tapped right in to where she was hard-wired. She wouldn't mind a slice of all that awe. After she'd turned off the television, she'd lain on the couch, eyes shut, and imagined herself with some of that power. It would be like being a fairy godmother, bringing mothers, fathers, grand-parents to life. *And so you* shall *be a parent*, she imagined herself beneficently saying. How fertile she'd feel, how effort-lessly able to create life. How deeply appreciated. That would make a nice change.

That programme had been the trigger. She'd hotfooted it to a clinic and after what seemed a very brief discussion, been given a list of prospective parents from which to choose.

Ned and Elisabetta Beecham jumped right out. She'd always liked Italy. Teachers were mostly reliable. He came from Cornwall. Perhaps the child would go to the beach a lot. When she'd met them, it had been everything she'd hoped for. Elisabetta wept and held on to her hand. *I can't believe you would do this for us,* she said. *Surrogates are very special people,* chipped in Paul, the advisor. Joanie had just smiled and felt like a painting of the Madonna.

A few weeks later, she'd hadn't felt quite so buoyed up by what a special person she was. Instead, she was becoming quite enamoured of the images in the pregnancy guidebooks she had been given by Elisabetta. How gorgeous they all looked, these women, with their glossy hair, glowing skin, and jam-packed bellies. She started to dwell on the pictures of breast-feeding, of cradled newborn infants, of tousle-haired toddlers. That looked pretty powerful too. The golden image of herself as a mother, rather than as a surrogate mother, seemed to be growing as vigorously as the baby inside her. The notion of gratitude, of the power to bestow happiness upon others, began to seem small in comparison. What were the Beechams to her? Perhaps becoming a mother would make her feel complete in ways she had never considered. Complete and very photogenic, which was always a bonus.

At nine weeks pregnant she lay on her bed one evening, listening to the radio – Mama Cass singing *Dream a little dream of me* – and envisioned herself on a beach with a blonde beautiful baby on her lap, with a vibe that amounted to so much more than she was on her own. And that was it – Mama Cass, and the radio; the evening light across her stomach, and an absolute falling in love with herself as a glowing, golden mother. How small and stick-like the Beechams seemed in comparison. How they scritch-scratched out of her mind, along with her desire to bestow life-changing happiness.

Joanie always thought of that moment as her biggest crush; not on some bloke but on an image of herself. She'd always felt something was going to come along to transport her into what she wanted to become. The shrimp-sized baby would do it. She was sure of that.

The next step was easy to rationalise. The baby was in her body. She was nourishing it, breathing in and out for its benefit. It was hers more than anyone's. Just let some lady try and say different. The main obstacle became how to extricate herself. Ms Fertility Goddess doing an about-turn and making a dash with the baby.

Yet the lie had been easy. It was perhaps reprehensible to admit it, but the lie had been easy. She'd sobbed to a potato-faced midwife who squeezed her hand sympathetically, and patted her knee. She reported great clots of blood, bright bright redness, and then as if a period gently finishing. A few days later, she'd gone to the doctor's and taken a pregnancy stick into the loo, and tipped some water on it, and a little Fanta from a bottle in her bag. She had come out and shown the doctor the clearly *Not pregnant* window. She'd bitten her lip, as if holding back tears. He had been sympathetic, a little awkward, and asked her if she wanted a D&C to ensure against infection. She'd said she was physically fine, no temperature at all. He asked her if she wanted to try the procedure again. She said no, it had all been too traumatic, and was it possible for him to phone the clinic and tell them she'd had a miscar-riage. She didn't want to do it herself or to face the couple – it would be too stressful, too awful, after their hopes had been built up. She had stayed at the same address for a week longer (just long enough to get a wretched commiseration card from Elisabetta which was the only time during the pregnancy she felt anything less than robustly well). Then she had upped and offed – moved down to the coast for the rest of the pregnancy. When she presented at a doctor's, she said she had been in France for the last six months, had just discovered she was pregnant – probably about fifteen weeks she thought – her cycle had always been irregular. It was her name change that facilitated the final smooth, easy passage of the lie. Her old NHS records had been in the name of Joan. She said she had lost her card, her number, and was issued with a new one, this time as Joanie. A whole new start.

She recognised, now, as she sat on the couch, that some might point a finger. It could be construed as a little cold-hearted that she hadn't thought of the Beechams again during the pregnancy, not even when she first held Scout. Scout was hers, hers alone. She'd had no trouble assimilating that. *Some people make their own truth*; that was what Alice would have said.

The first year of motherhood had suited her down to the ground. She went to festivals, to beach camps, to protests, with Scout tucked pertly in a rainbow-coloured papoose. She felt tinged with Mother Earth fecundity, with bohemian sass. There had been a tricky patch later, when Scout had become less portable, more mobile and wakeful, and needed something resembling structure and pattern. Joanie had made a bolt for Alice's, for her mother's soul-destroying, predictable routine, and practically handed her over. There had been a minor brush with a well-intentioned, earnest-faced social worker, some bleating about not having to be a good mother, just a good-enough mother. Joanie had smoked a large joint afterwards – she liked to think in a spirit of good-enoughness – and then it had settled into plainish sailing. Inheriting Alice's house marked the first time Scout had lived longer than six months in any one place.

The problem – and now Joanie had got into her bed, and was looking up at the car headlights as they swooped across the ceiling – was that, however much she loved Scout, more recently Joanie couldn't shed a small, stubborn feeling that she wasn't living the life that she wanted to live. Eleven years on and Joanie was not the person she wanted to be. Completeness hadn't actually materialised, although in truth it wasn't Scout's fault. Perhaps it was an illusion to think someone else could make you complete. Even worse, maybe motherhood wasn't all it was cracked up to be. And now that she reconsidered it (perhaps distance had lent perspective), it looked as if she'd walked into it thanks to Mama Cass singing on a warm summer night. Dream a little dream indeed.

At some point she might be forced to tell Scout everything, although she shrank from the thought of Scout's candid, blue-green gaze. She hoped she would not be rumbled into having to tell. Maybe if you buried something deep enough it need never come out. She'd always made it clear to Scout any questions about her dad were strictly off limits. How long she could count on her adherence to this was difficult to tell. It might be another thing which went AWOL in puberty.

Joanie chewed at her fingernails and turned to the wall. It was killing. If she had believed in God, she'd have shaken her fist at Him. Screw Him for giving her the ability to imagine herself as more and better without the capacity or tenacity to achieve it. Maybe she should abandon what little was left of Him from Alice's indoctrination and perhaps give Buddhism or Hindusim a shot; pin her hopes on reincarnation and hope to come back better. Some things were evidently worth waiting a lifetime for. Go through it all again and next time be effortlessly accomplished and feted. Like Trudie Styler with her new yoga video where her headband matched the lavender border in the garden of her Italian palazzo. Or Nigella Lawson dressed as the spirit of Christmas on the cover of a Sunday magazine with a raft of new recipes. She reminded herself as she fell asleep that reincarnation might also involve coming back as a cricket or a long-eared bat. Or someone properly good, like Mother Teresa. That would be truly killing.

13

Elisabetta and Ned sat in the waiting-room of a solicitor's office. Elisabetta noted the potted yucca plant in the corner. Someone had dusted it. Its leaves positively gleamed. This must be an indication of attention to detail. On the receptionist's desk was a white orchid. This was in similarly robust health. Someone was fastidious. The receptionist was pretty. She had glanced at them once or twice as they waited for their appointment. Understandable, Elisabetta thought, to be a little curious. She reached over and took Ned's hand and held it between her own. What would be the most common reason for a couple in their forties to be visiting a solicitor? Divorce probably. Maybe the receptionist tried to gauge the depth of mutinous siege between couples; which one had had the affair, or which one simply could no longer bear the touch of the other. Elisabetta looked across at the receptionist. She was studiously avoiding eye contact now. The English were always so adroit at lifting the edges of things, peering briefly, conclusively, beneath, and then looking fixedly the other way.

Prue had been taken aback. It was the first time she had seen Prue like that. Perhaps it was the notion of a grandchild genetically hers. Perhaps it was the complete incomprehensibility of a lie so brazenly told. She had sat with her hands in her lap, her lips slightly parted as if physically trying to swallow Ned's words. Edward had said, 'It could be something of a Pandora's box', which Elisabetta had puzzled over. Was Scout supposed to be Pandora, unleashing awful things upon them, or was Scout herself coming out of a box which would have been better kept closed? Ned didn't want to talk about it. The nuts and bolts – calling a solicitor, arranging an appointment, yes, he had talked about that, but not its breath-stopping magnitude. A child of his who had been alive these past eleven years, breathing in and out, perhaps walked by in a queue, or passed outside a cinema, or in an airport. Connected but unknown; carrying the imprint of his paternity, invisible to the eye. When they had gone through all the adoption procedures for Maia, she thought of the forms filled in: *Childless* – ticked; *Number of siblings* – None. And yet Scout had been there, breathing in, breathing out; limbs growing, lengthening, acquiring words, habits, preferences. Everything had been so monumentally incorrect.

Ned would not engage in speculation as to what she might be like. In contrast, Elisabetta found she woke each morning, composing a girl's face, not Maia's much-loved one but a smaller, feminised version of Ned's. She hadn't been able to come up with an alternative to Joan Simpson's curls. They would have made their mark. She couldn't imagine how they would not have assumed dominance over Ned's straight, compliant hair.

She didn't want to think about Joan Simpson. She felt anger in her throat, stuck like a hard-boiled sweet. What expression had Ned's brother Robert taught her long ago? To pull a fast one, to hoodwink? She'd certainly done that. This woman with her round, fat, successful ovaries and her cosy, cocooning womb, who had stolen Ned's sperm, and ridiculed her own half-consumed innards.

Let it go, she said to herself, *let it go*. She focused her gaze on the orchid on the desk. The receptionist checked her computer and looked up.

'Would you like to go through?' she said. 'Miss Philips can see you now.'

Susan Philips was younger than them. That was the first thing that struck Ned. She looked like a slip of a girl, like one of the teaching students on their probationary year. She didn't look like someone capable of carrying what he was sure were the bulky and awkward dimensions of family law. She had a smattering of freckles across the bridge of her nose. She repeatedly tucked a strand of hair behind her right ear. Her fingers were devoid of rings. Her nails were filed shortish and square. Ned focused on her hands whilst he summoned the vim and vigour to look her straight in the eye. It occurred to him that halfway through this meeting it might feel as if the ceiling were about to cave in, as if, with a great roar and tumble of cornices and plaster, the implications of what he was doing here might be emphasised.

Susan Philips began by explaining the procedure. 'You can apply for contact based on the principle that it is in Scout's interest to know her genetic parent,' she said, 'but it's problematic because we don't know where she is. We have no information on Ms Simpson since she left her home in Oxfordshire. If we can locate her, we can serve her with an application and she will have to come to a hearing. A social worker or guardian would be appointed to represent Scout's views. He or she will have to ascertain what the child knows, and whether she knows the truth of her birth circumstances or not. You may have to undergo a paternity test. Scout would have to be consulted in any contact decision because of her age.'

Ned decided Susan Philips' voice was without any emotion. Perhaps the whole thing amounted to a dispassionate process. A dispassionate conception; a dispassionate lawyer. Elisabetta seemed to be the only one who had alighted on some kind of instinctive emotion, some kind of innate connection albeit mostly on his behalf rather than her own. He was still struggling to get past the fact that he had been secretly assuaged when he thought the pregnancy hadn't worked. If he could get past that guilt, perhaps he could open his mind to the child.

Susan continued. 'You need to decide how far you want to pursue this, and what exactly it is that you hope to achieve. You also need to be aware that you will not qualify for any form of legal aid. It could be expensive. The child's mother may be deliberately obstructive and may draw out proceedings. It may be lengthy but the process usually, eventually, works. It's sensible to be clear about what you hope to gain from it from the outset.'

Although Susan Philips was young, her voice was old. Its modulations, its warmth and softness, had been chipped away by the reciting of procedures, legalities, caveats. It was not world-weary in tone; it was, more accurately, people-weary. He guessed that she probably didn't see them at their best. She was tough – he saw that now. Her expectations as to behaviour were most likely to be jaded or cynical. The hair tucking, the girlish nails, were easily misread. She probably didn't particularly care what either of them was feeling. What she wanted was clarity. Clarity of intent, of purpose. Clarity of procedure. Everything shipshape. Her faith in the law, not humanity, intact.

After the meeting, Ned and Elisabetta went for a coffee. Elisabetta sat blowing on her cappuccino.

'She seems to know what she's doing,' she said.

'She looks as if she wouldn't recognise doubt if it came up and bit her.'

'That's probably unfair.'

'I'm just having trouble seeing Susan Philips as the beginning of a trail that leads us to Scout. No one actually starts looking. It's not like hiring a private detective.' Ned tried to distance himself from the image of snuffling bloodhounds that came to him unbidden. 'Perhaps what she's actually achieving is making us understand what we want to gain.'

'This we already know. One: we are righting a wrong. Two: we would like to have a relationship with your daughter. Three: if she chooses to, Scout may like being part of our family.'

Elisabetta tapped the fingers of her left hand with her right thumb as she counted. Since that day on the beach in Cornwall, Ned thought, her eyes raw with shock, there had been a hardening of her resolve, an emerging determination to find Scout.

'But you can't assume any of that when we have no idea what she is like. No idea of the formative life she has lived.'

'The same then as Maia.'

'No, not the same. Not the same at all. Maia was too young, too uninfluenced, too unformed, to have become anything. Scout's almost eleven. She might have been told a completely different version of her conception. And, after this, she might hate us, especially if she thinks we have hunted her down, which in truth we would have done, however unlikely that outcome seems now. Children are loyal. We both know that. She could be perfectly happy with her mother. I could be nothing like the father she would like or thinks she might have.'

'Alternatively, she might not be completely happy. She might feel the absence of her father. You might be, how do you say, just the ticket.'

Elisabetta put down her cup, reached across the table and placed her hands on his face. He was reminded, despite himself, how he had always loved the shape of her top lip. 'She's half of you,' she said simply. 'How could she be anything but lovely? And how could she not be heart-warmed in that in all of this you just tried to be her father?'

Ned looked across at her. How could she be so certain?

Later, at home, with Maia tucked into bed, Elisabetta poured herself a glass of wine in the kitchen and began to make some sauce for pasta. The knife flashed confidently as she chopped onion, garlic, butternut, sage. She thought about what Susan Philips had said. It was straightforward applying her advice to Ned, but what about to herself, what was *she* trying to gain? Ned would be Scout's father. Joan Simpson was Scout's mother. What did that make her? Probably completely peripheral. She would become a stepmother, with all that potentially negative baggage. And yet, despite that, she couldn't suppress a small, instinctive certainty that this child was worth trying to gain. She shook her head. It was probably an over-emotional, irrational perception that somehow they could save her. Scout most likely didn't need saving at all, and why should she presume that she might? Elisabetta suspected it revealed more about her own self; always this desire to fix and to mend. To gather to her that which probably didn't need mending or saving at all.

She leaned against the oven, and poked the butternut around the pan with a wooden spoon. Where was Scout? What was she doing? A pin in a haystack. Was that how it was said? She looked at the space between her body and the work surface, between the work surface and the front door, the door and the road outside, between the road and the outskirts of London, between London and the motorway. It thrummed with distance, with separateness. Where was Scout? Who was she? How even to begin?

14

Scout sat at the kitchen table, a knife, fork, and spoon arranged very carefully in front of her. Evidently, she wasn't going to use the knife and fork to eat her Frosties, but she'd put them out anyway. A place setting. A proper place setting. Well, almost proper; she now knew the principal pieces in a place setting actually numbered seven.

Yesterday, Mr Groves had taught her about cutlery. Anyone who thought they knew anything about cutlery before listening to him would find themselves feeling very foolish. He had sat her down at his walnut table, and set before her a wooden canteen with green felt lining. He had opened it briefly, its contents gleaming within, and then closed it, saying, with a small tip of his head, that they would begin with definitions. A cutler, he said, makes cutlery. Cutlery is primarily knives, including carving knives, forks and steels. Knives were also made for cheese, butter, fruit and cake. A fish knife had a silver blade, tapered to separate the flesh from the bones. A *tang* is the part of a knife that slots into the handle. A knife is *whetted* to a very fine edge. Spoons and forks are called flatware, because they begin their life flat, and then are beaten or pressed into shape. There are spoons for soup, which have a more rounded bowl, and spoons for grapefruit, and for eggs. The number of traditional English designs ran to very many. They included Onslow, Kings, Dubarry, Fiddle, Old English Thread, Queen, Bead, William and Mary. Each one he'd described to her, drawing its shape on a small, yellowed pad of plain paper.

This is Kings, he said, drawing ends tipped as if with scallop shells. *This is Fiddle*, he said, drawing a shape like a violin. Then, he opened the case. *Rattail*, he said, with a prolonged out-breath of pleasure. *Given to me by the Mistress, for service of thirty years*. Actually, he confided, taken from the third best set, but good enough for me; plenty good enough for me.

He took out a spoon and handed it to Scout. She turned it over and saw a smooth raised ridge running up the back of the spoon bowl. 'Rattail doesn't make it sound very nice,' she said, 'but it's lovely to touch.' She traced the length of the knife and the fork with her index finger, and picked up a small teaspoon which Mr Groves said could be used to eat coddled eggs for breakfast. *Coddled eggs*. Now, as she sat with a Frosties box in front of her, plus her knife, fork and spoon, the 280 bus visible through the kitchen window, it seemed a galaxy away – a place where a coddled egg might be eaten with a small silver spoon from a porcelain dish, in a room especially called the Breakfast Room. Scout wondered if coddled eggs had given their name to the word mollycoddled. This was the flaw in own-learning. It was pretty much impossible to answer your own questions. Not the questions you asked yourself whilst secretly, gleefully, actually knowing the answer, but the questions to which you had no clue, no idea at all. She wouldn't ask Joanie. She didn't like being put on the spot.

Scout didn't feel like eating Frosties any more. They seemed something of a disappointment. Instead, she ate a banana, and three iced ring biscuits, and drank a glass of orange juice. She put the cutlery and flatware back in the drawer. She didn't think they could make any claim to a particular shape or design. It certainly didn't resemble anything Mr Groves had drawn. Her faint hope that it might be Bead was crushed when she thought what might be a raised edge turned out to be food she could scratch off with her thumbnail. They certainly weren't silver. Nor silver plate. Probably not even stainless steel. Just any old metal that was perfectly, easily, stainable.

Scout thought it must be nice to be Mr Groves, eating his supper from knives and forks taken carefully from the canteen. It must make each meal into some kind of ceremony, some sort of contained, proper moment, which bore no resemblance to how she cut and forked food into her own mouth.

He had given her a soup spoon, and a bowl of water standing in as soup. 'Very good not to slurp,' he said. 'The finest consommé can be very taxing.' Scout had puckered her lips round the edge of the spoon and practised until the water entered her mouth as silently as the air breathed in through her nose. 'Very good, Miss Scout,' said Mr Groves, 'very good indeed. You are an excellent soup drinker. No butler would be looking, secretly appalled, at you.'

This was good to know, Scout thought now, as she pushed the cutlery drawer closed. *Heaven forfend*, as Joanie would have said, that a butler might look at her, secretly appalled. Perhaps that would be her ambition in life. To one day sit at a table and eat soup from a silver, round-bowled soup spoon and no one to guess that she'd been taught by Mr Groves, practising with water, her Maths sheets brought up from her session in the shop and tucked carefully beside her out of splashing's way.

Scout sat down at the table and looked at her watch. Too early to go to Mr Mohammed's; there were always too many customers mid-morning, too much passing trade. Yesterday, she had triumphed again in the dictionary game. *Eponymous*, she had asked. *Esoteric*. She pushed herself back from the table. She pressed her fingertips firmly to her closed eyes, and tried to determine, when the blackness cleared, what colour she would see. *Not much*, she was deciding, faintly disappointed. The last time she had done this – perhaps it had been in the full glare of sunlight? – she remembered a kaleidoscope of colour.

Then the doorbell rang, which actually made her jump. The doorbell had never rung in this place. No one had ever come to the door. She sat at the table, waited while it rang a second time more shrilly, more insistently, and then walked softly to the door, her hand tentative upon the lock.

When she pulled it open – just a centimetre, just a fraction (she was confident she could close it quickly if it was anyone bad), there was a woman standing there. A woman with hair so red it looked on fire, and with a clipboard in her hand.

Scout wasn't sure if clipboards were ever a very good thing. They'd used them once on a school trip where they were supposed to be drawing types of buildings in Thame High Street. Billy Myer had whacked Oliver Benson over the head with his, and Mrs Pearson-Smith had threatened to confiscate the lot if anybody followed suit. *And then you'll just have to lean your paper on your knees or the wall.* Scout had heard the teaching assistant, Miss Morris, say, under her breath, 'In his hands, it's not a clipboard, it's a bloody lethal weapon.' Scout wondered if, in a grown-up's hands, especially one with hair so red it was flaming down her shoulders, it could also be counted as such. She suspected it might.

'Hello. My name is Sylvie Austen, I'm from Birmingham Social Services Family Department. Is there an adult at home? Is there an adult I can speak to?'

'Umm . . . My mum's just popped out. Just popped out. She'll be back shortly.'

'That's good. About how long is shortly do you think?'

'Perhaps half an hour. Half an hour. Something like that.' Scout waved her hand randomly, as if wafting something away, aware she was mumbling, sheepish. She lifted her chin to try to meet the woman's eyes with her own.

'Well, thank you,' the woman said. 'Thank you. I'll call back.'

Her tone had a forced brightness to it which made Scout's teeth hurt. She closed the door, and stood with her palm to it, breathing more noisily than she thought she usually did. Her heart went thumpitty-thump in her chest. She breathed in purposefully, and dropped to her hands and knees. Carefully, quietly, she crawled into the sitting-room, and sat with her knees tucked to her chest, under the window which looked out to the front door on the left. The woman was still there. She was leaning against the rail which ran along the landing. She was texting. Scout lifted a corner of the net curtain. It twitched slightly. The woman seemed to catch it in her peripheral vision and glanced over. Scout dropped to the floor. The carpet smelled horrible. She hadn't lain on it before. She used her thumbnail to track between the blue weft and weave of the tufts. It was dusty too. She worried that she might sneeze. The distance between her and the woman was probably not much greater than the length of her leg. She heard the woman move – her heels made a noise on the concrete as she shifted position. The woman cleared her throat. Scout inched away from beneath the window-sill (surely the woman could hear her breathing?) and, in the absence of a better plan, crawled across the hall and under her bed, where Joanie had stashed their bags. There was a crackle and rustle of polythene as Scout dragged herself forward by her elbows. She lay under the bed, finding the small, tight space oddly soothing. She closed her eyes. Perhaps she should think of it as a flotation tank. Joanie had once had a craze on flotation tanks. 'I float all my cares away,' she had told Scout, 'I imagine I'm back on the kibbutz, by the Dead Sea.' Scout shifted position. The polythene was quite scratchy.

Was Sylvie Austen still standing outside? What did she want? Perhaps she should have mentioned her own-learning. Perhaps it was just a simple check on that. She should have gone to the door with her Maths sheets, and given her an example of geometric reasoning. That might have sorted it. She looked at the luminous hands of her watch. Joanie had asked her, when she chose it for a birthday gift, *Why on earth would you want a watch you can see in the dark, when the other one's much prettier?* Point proved, Scout thought, noting that it was twenty minutes since the doorbell first rang.

Sylvie Austen was obviously a woman who paid attention to detail. Scout should have deduced that from the clipboard. Sylvie Austen wasn't a woman who was going to lean on the wall, or her knees, to write. No sirree. Everything would be neat and correct. The doorbell rang again at precisely 11.30. Scout crawled out from under the bed and brushed the dust from her jeans. She had pins and needles in her arms. She went into the kitchen and reached to the top of the cupboard to get down some of her Maths sheets. She put them against her chest like a battle shield and went to the door. She toyed with the idea of an attempt at whistling, and decided now probably wasn't a good time to give it a go. She opened the door and there was Sylvie Austen, her arms folded round the clipboard, leaning slightly forwards, creased over at the waist. Scout thought afterwards that if her body had been a line in one of her geometric reasoning diagrams, joined to the perpendicular of the door frame, and then the concrete line of the floor, it would have made a kind of Social Services triangle.

'Not back yet?' Sylvie said encouragingly, with the kind of smile that Scout thought adults made when they wanted you to be very aware they were S-M-I-L-I-N-G.

'No, not back yet. This is the only door.'

'Has she perhaps phoned to tell you she's running a little late?'

'Umm, I didn't hear the mobile, but I was concentrating on my Maths.' Here, Scout brandished her sheaf of papers with what she hoped was confidence. 'I'm own- learning. I'm doing my Maths. Sometimes I forget to pick up the phone.' Scout crossed her fingers behind her back. How bad a lie was claiming to have a mobile when you didn't?

Sylvie Austen didn't seem to be bowled over by her Maths productivity.

'Can I just check your name?' Sylvie Austen was tracking her finger down a list. Scout wondered how many options there could be.

When the woman had gone, Scout worried she'd made a blunder. She hadn't waited for the woman to offer her a name, to show that she actually had some inkling of who she was. Instead she had blurted out *Scout, Scout Simpson*, and the woman had written it down. She'd left, and this time when she closed the door, Scout leaned her back against it and slid down it like a folding concertina, until she had her arms wrapped round her legs and her eyes pressed to her kneecaps. She sat there for some time. She didn't think Joanie would be at all pleased about this. She didn't know quite why, but she thought Joanie would definitely not like the sound of this.

She sat for a while longer. Mr Mohammed would be having his lunch. She'd go to Mr Groves instead, and offer to go with him for a walk around the communal garden. She checked her watch again – it was 12.20, he would be up and spry. He'd told her he did not like visits in the morning. *It takes me a little while, Miss Scout*, he said, *to get things as they should be, myself as I should be*. She'd had a vision of Mr Groves in his pyjamas, perhaps shuffling barefoot to the loo, his white, fine, hair unkempt from the pillow. It would be appalling, she felt, an invasion, an intrusion, to see him like that. She imagined the vast number of small, intricate, slow and painstaking movements which got him washed, brushed, clothed, his shoelaces evenly tied. To see Mr Groves how he didn't want to be seen would not be friendship at all.

When they left his flat, Scout had looped her arm through his. She wasn't supporting him, like she would someone who

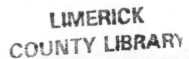

couldn't walk properly, they had agreed on this. It was, instead, what Mr Groves called a *gesture of solidarity.* They stood by the lift and, as Scout pressed the button, one of the hoodie boys came and asked to borrow some money. This time Mr Groves gave him £5, smooth and crease-free from his wallet. 'I think you forget to get it back from them,' Scout said. 'I think they ask you because you give it to them and then you never ask for it back.'

'Do you think so?' he said mildly. 'I think it probably does slip my mind.'

Scout wondered how he could remember so much detail from the past, and then things like a boy asking him for money by the lift made no mark, like water passing over water.

Scout and Mr Groves inched purposefully round the garden. There was a bench they sat on together after three careful loops. Scout looked at the toes of his polished brogues. Could steps get any smaller, any frailer?

'Four wing tip Oxford brogues,' he'd told her. 'That is what these shoes are. Polished with burgundy cream. They'll see me out.'

Even shoes in Mr Groves' world had a name, Scout thought. Even shoes had something which confirmed their identity and made them distinct and real.

The wind ruffled his hair as they walked in the bare, bald garden. It was like a dandelion clock. At any moment it might lift away from his scalp and float off in the breeze. Scout took advantage of the sunlight to scrutinise his skin. It was almost translucent. There were brown spots, and great snakes of veins. The bridge of his nose was as prominent as the ridge on a rattail spoon. He wore some sort of cologne; he smelled of limes, of mandarin oranges. He was so clean, so *dapper.* She'd try that word in the dictionary game, she resolved, although it was cheating because she knew it already. She held Mr Groves' arm tighter. The paving was uneven in places. His breath seemed to whistle out of his chest. His ear lobes were the biggest she had ever seen. She'd read somewhere that ear lobes were the only part of the body which carried on growing for all of your life. Beyond the garden, she could see Mr Mohammed holding up Nona to wave at them over the venetian blind which covered half of the shop window. Scout waved back, a long-armed, sunny wave. Nona shook her bracelets. Mr Groves creased up his milky eyes with the effort of trying to see too.

'It's a shame there are no flowers,' he said. 'I'd like you to see a good herbaceous border. The gardeners at Houghton, what they coaxed from that soil. The colours, from March through until October, it was a sight to behold.'

He told her about a party, a summer ball, in 1948, the year Miss Charlotte had come out and had been presented to the King. How Houghton had been scrubbed, he said, footmen on ladders, the great staircase waxed. On the lawn, vast trestle tables with jugs of Pimm's, and strawberries from the kitchen garden. Asparagus steamed in bundles and served with light, foamy, hollandaise sauce. The tablecloths, he said, had been whitened and starched so they could practically stand up by themselves, and crystal glasses so perfectly dried and polished they caught the flashes of evening sunlight and threw it right back. In the kitchen, a veritable army chopping, and slicing, and cooking. A meringue, a pavlova, he said, almost as big as this bench, baked in sections and then put together, gleaming with summer fruit. And the roses, roses from the garden, petals thick and creamy as wax, and he was in charge, in charge of it all, running like clockwork. The guests danced in the Great Hall until morning, he said. Breakfast was served promptly at eight. Eggs Benedict. Kedgeree.

'If there had been a Good Work Book at Houghton,' Scout said, 'you'd have been in it. No question of that. You'd have definitely been in it.'

15

James Baxter sat in his study on a Sunday afternoon, the repleteness of a good Sunday lunch making itself felt. In the kitchen he could hear Molly, his wife, putting away the last pots and pans. She would be wiping around the base of the taps at the sink; she preferred the granite perfectly dry, its blackness matt and uniform. James wondered if this was what bolstered an enduring marriage: the accrued detail of everyday preference and habit. Molly was fastidious. This was something he had always admired in her. Their house ran smoothly; it was ordered, clean, exact. She was not without assistance; James Baxter was not a man who expected his wife to clean the bath, but he was attentive enough to realise how in the last decade the nature of that help had changed. No more fifty-something women from the village, sourly wringing a mop in a bucket, and lethargically flicking a duster so that ornaments sat in their own puddle of dust. No, now there was a succession of young, quick-eyed girls. Poles, Brazilians, Portuguese. On their way from somewhere, on their way to somewhere else. Sending money home. Gathering up a new language like coins. They called him Boss. *Yes Boss*, they said if he asked them to press his suit. *Make sure you've seen work permits, visas, passports*, he said to Molly. *Everything above board. You know how it must be.*

Molly was entirely trustworthy, could be relied upon to be thorough. Sometimes, he felt his watch could be set, his life arranged into chapters, by Molly and her ways; talking to him this morning as she prepared potatoes, leeks, carrots, her coat for church on the back of the chair, her hands quick and economical in their movement. Molly went to church alone; it was not a cause of marital dispute. Her God seemed to fit smoothly into her life like a pebble into her palm. She had shown no evident disappointment at James's inability to feel similarly. On Sunday mornings, she went to church while he walked the dog. For a while he had seen this as a pastoral alternative, a small hymn of thanks to Creation as he walked along the bridleway by their home. More recently he'd acknowledged it as more Darwinian, more Humanist than that. James Baxter was determined not to become a deluded, self-satisfied old fool. With regard to God, James's years in crime and family law and, even more so, the years since he had been appointed to the Bench, had convinced him that it was difficult to see evidence of any form of benign, godly intervention. No still, small voice of calm whispering cessation into the ear of a man bashing his wife's brains out with a skillet. So, James walked the dog and Molly went to church, and when they returned she would tell him the congregational gossip (who was being prayed for, or that the congregation numbered only twelve today), and he would tell her that the winter wheat was through already, or that the banker who owned Manor House had put down black pheasant for the shoot. Molly probably knew this already, seeing as she walked the dog every other day of the week, but James suspected she indulged him by allowing him to tell it to her as news. She had done this with the children when they were small; bestowing upon them a small feeling of triumph because they felt they had brought her something new.

The children had been there today for lunch. He could hear them talking in the drawing-room. Children. Ridiculous, really, that he thought of them as such, when the youngest of the three had almost finished university. They were different from him and Molly, from how they had begun. How much this was a product of the times or of background James couldn't decide. He was a working-class boy made good. A grammar school boy, chosen by Oxford, called to the Bar. The years in between had smoothed out his accent, and honed his mannerisms into something sleek, urbane. His generation of lawyers had made their assays to the Bench, to Heads of Chambers, to the High Court. They had become fattened and smoothed like geese for Christmas, their pinstripe suits increasingly broader, of better cloth; their shoes made to their own lasts. What had someone once told him? If you stand by the table long enough, a seat becomes vacant. He and his colleagues, he saw, had been fingered by the Establishment. Now, they were embossed with its patina, burnished by its laurels. The hunger which had won him those prizes had been cloaked, satiated. In his children he saw, with something akin to mild disappointment, there was no evidence of it at all.

Affluenza. Was that how it had been described, this stifling of appetite by the plenty of an affluent upbringing? Was it unkind to think that his children lacked any depth of application? Nowadays, immediate gratification was all, everything so instantly, speedily Googled. Maybe it was just that the upsides of sustained endeavour were no longer convincing. In a world which offered no certainties, perhaps it was difficult to put your shoulder to the wheel. What was it he had read – when people stop believing in God they either believe in everything or nothing? James wondered if what people mostly believed in now was not God, or Good, but Goods – things that could be bought by shopping and which required ongoing upgrading.

This was not a line of thought that was productive to pursue. Since his recent speech to his colleagues, at a dinner, James was aware that everything he now said might be considered an extrapolation of his statement upon society at large.

He had not intended his speech to gain the coverage it had –
plastered across the front page of two newspapers with a
(frankly) stiff-starch photograph of him and Molly from
when he had been made a High Court Judge. His observations had been meant for his colleagues, some of whom were
complacent in the face of societal change. Too many, he
believed, were too snug in their clubs (golf and gentlemen's),
too immersed in the social apartheid of their daily round, to
see that beneath them, around them, the fabric of the temple
was tearing. His speech had been trumpeted as the judiciary's
recognition of the disintegration of family life, and of society
itself. Now, in the media it was referred to familiarly, chum-
mily, its particular observations and recommendations
reduced to infinitely chantable plainsong. (Single mothers,
absent fathers, no employed adult, absence of any place for,
or significance of, education or work.) Lucky, seeing as the
media was now inclined to regard him as a paragon of virtuous
family life, that there was no mistress tucked in a flat in
Kensington, no episodes of S&M in a bordello in Chelsea. He
was sure some journalists would have poked around a little.
How the media loved that – a judge caught with his trousers
around his ankles. James gave thanks for his own squeaky-
clean marital record, which was largely a reflection of both his
love for Molly and a certain predisposition to concentrate on
one thing at a time. He could only wonder at colleagues who
were serial philanderers. The complexity of spinning labyrin-
thine lies was a prospect he found exhausting. Molly just
dismissed them as randy old goats.

He understood the speech would be his three minutes of
fame, although it had created some political waves, and an
invitation to join a Tory think-tank. (The answer to that was
No. James felt the judiciary should be resolutely apolitical.)

What a plethora of inadequate, tainted lives he saw in his
court. Mouths half open in gobby disbelief. Malnourished faces

with the absence of education marked upon them as clearly as tattoos and piercings. The number of children his judgments swept from parental care into the aegis of the social services – the range of options and forward plans was boundless. Did they thrive better, he wondered, did they escape the doomed option thrown at them at birth? The jury would probably always be out. James was sufficiently open-minded to acknowledge this. So much effort, he sometimes thought wearily, so much effort in trying to right what was wrong, heal what was damaged. Barristers in his court legitimately trying to get to the bottom of parental accounts that twisted and turned in their complexity. He often thought of Solomon, who'd suggested a baby be cut in half to gauge which of two women was the child's real mother. If Solomon pulled that stunt now, James suspected, it might not be that clear-cut. He'd probably be sued for post-traumatic stress disorder, for horrifying the women. *Who should decide?* James had mulled on that for years. Some of his colleagues had slipped into their ermine and wigs as easily as they had their prep school blazers. The residue of his faith, and a small, persistent, stubborn anxiety that social issues could not be chloroformed and pinned down like moths, made James inter- mittently uneasy in his judgmental shoes.

On James's desk were the court papers for this week. He cast his eye over the first case. This was a new twist. A surro- gate mother who had concealed a successful pregnancy and now, upon discovery, had absconded with the child. How had it come to light? No doubt some social worker or solicitor would be quick to let him know. He wondered if the child knew. The father now did. That would be complex; *I think you are my daughter* – which Shakespeare was that? A child conceived by strangers. What a tangle this new biology could create.

The clock ticked sonorously on the mantelpiece. Steadily, the bundle of papers slid from his hand across the expanse of his belly. When Molly came in, James was snoozing. She removed the papers from his abdomen and replaced them on the desk. She looked out of the window, hearing laughter from the garden. Philip was teasing Minty; it had always been so.

Beyond James's breathing, the house was quiet. There was always this lull on Sunday afternoons, it was something she treasured. It spoke of some kind of connection; a quality beneath all their differences which expressed something shared.

She stood very, very still, her fingertips resting on the solidity and clutter of James's desk. She had a vision of herself as a Carmelite nun in a bald, tidy room. Ridiculous really; she didn't even know what Carmelite meant. She just liked the notion of calm the word carried.

She straightened her spine. She shook herself like someone scattering raindrops.

Tomorrow would be busy. The fridge was empty. There was her father to be visited. A dentist's appointment. The boiler needed servicing.

She thought of James and her children. There was great love. Great love. She knew that. It was just that it was festooned with so much detritus. So much clutter. The trick, she thought, was not to let the eye be distracted. That was the thing.

16

Sunday nights meant a bucket of Kentucky Fried Chicken, eaten in pyjamas, mostly with a DVD or the television on. Sometimes they played Scrabble, but Joanie would end up using words that weren't in the dictionary. Tonight she'd tried *vajazzle*, which she said meant to sparkle up. She predictably, unfailingly, good-humouredly, lost every time. It was not deliberate. Scout had watched carefully and was confident of that. Even if it had been, Scout still loved winning. The click and shuffle of the Scrabble pieces on the board. The whoop when, with a flourish, she would lay down a word like *delirious*. Her mother always laughed when she lost. She would stretch back and say *I am so RUBBISH at this*. Scout thought Joanie truly didn't mind losing, whereas Scout constantly re-counted her points to check she'd missed none out. *A bit over-competitive*, a teacher had said to her once. And, *Learn to be a little bit more patient when others don't grasp things as quickly as you.*

Sometimes, she wondered if the enthusiasm she and her mother expressed over the Kentucky Fried Chicken wasn't slightly hollow. *Yum!* Joanie would say, her lips grease-slicked from the crumb coating. *Yum! Yum!* Scout would reply, rubbing her hands or her tummy. Scout thought that really they'd stopped liking Kentucky Fried Chicken some time ago. They used to have it in their real house too. Joanie started buying it because she said it demonstrated she'd escaped from Alice's rigid, inescapable, Sunday-dominating roast. (*Cooked to death*, she said to Scout. *If it went in the size of a turkey it came out like a pigeon.)* Joanie said the Kentucky Fried Chicken bucket was a triumphant snook to her dull childhood Sundays. Scout thought Alice would be sorry that her commitment to cooking dinner had resulted in KFC.

Scout nibbled on a piece of corn on the cob. It felt slimy to her teeth. Hard to imagine it growing in a field somewhere. Perhaps it didn't. Perhaps it had never even seen the light of a sunshiny day. Perhaps there were battery chickens, and battery corn, grown inside glass somewhere, all ready to be Kentucky Fried. Scout wasn't sure whether the chicken had given her indigestion, or whether it was just the sensation she sometimes got when she wanted to say something, but was not sure of the response it would get. Mostly it was when she was certain it wouldn't be enthusiastic.

Joanie looked so happy tonight, so soft in her face. She was swigging beer from a bottle. She'd got her hair tied up in a scrunchie and was wearing a pair of old tracksuit bottoms. Scout knew nobody who could sit cross-legged as perfectly as Joanie. The outsides of her thighs opened flat to the floor, like two perfect triangles, her feet tucked up into her groin. She could deal cards, play board games, her upper body moving forward and backward, her legs folded beneath her like a perfectly balanced statue. Joanie had propped the window open. Today had been warmer – 'Summer's on its way,' she'd said, 'let's go for a walk.' They'd gone for a walk, and Joanie had held her hand, and bought her a white chocolate Magnum. Scout wondered if the Magnum was why she was feeling queasy – the Magnum and the Kentucky Fried. There was no five a day in that. She thought of the healthy lunch-boxes at school. Maybe she could talk to Mr Mohammed. Perhaps he would buy some houmous at the Cash and Carry and sell it in the chiller cabinet. Did Polish people eat houmous? It might be one of their favourite things. Maybe he would think it was worth a try. He wouldn't mind her asking.

Sylvie Austen hadn't come back. Or at least hadn't come back yet.

'You've got that face on,' Joanie said suddenly. 'That face when you're busy thinking about something which is nothing to do with this.'

Scout took a sharp intake of breath. Joanie was good, Scout had to acknowledge, her mother was good. There she was, seeming all relaxed and inattentive on the couch, and then quick, like a lizard's tongue darting out, fastening on to her uneasiness. She swallowed hard.

At school, one Mother's Day, they'd had to design a poster called *What my mum does for me.* The class had written things like *Makes my birthday cake,* with a big glossy drawing of a cake, or *Puts a hot water bottle in my bed when it's cold,* with a picture of themselves asleep. Scout had puzzled over what to put. Joanie wasn't so hot on the things her classmates were coming up with. In the end, she drew a self-portrait, and wrote underneath it *My mum can read my face* and added a choice of flashcards with words like *Happy, Sad, Worried, Joking* which could be stuck to her forehead.

Joanie didn't look like she was going to abandon tack. She was watching her intently.

'What did you do with Mr Groves today? What did he come up with?'

'He taught me to walk round the garden with a book on my head. Posture. He said you can't put a price on good posture. I decided afterwards it was a kind of P.E. lesson.'

'That sounds like a good investment. If we had a sports car, he could probably teach you to get out of that. Perhaps even with the book still on your head. And what about Mr Mohammed?'

'Perimeters. We did perimeters.'

'Excellent again. So are you going to tell me what's bothering you, or shall we go on to what you had for lunch?'

'A cheese sandwich and a bag of salt and vinegar crisps and a finger of fudge.'

'Sounds very nice. Now to the thing that's bothering you.'

Scout felt rumbled.

'Someone came; someone came from Social Services. She rang on the doorbell and I answered it without thinking. I told her you'd be back in half an hour and I thought she'd go away. But she didn't, she stood there, and then she rang the bell again later. I told her I was own-learning – I showed her my Maths, and she asked my name and I told her, and then she went away. Will something bad happen now and is it my fault? Why did she come? Do you think she'll come back?'

Joanie pulled her knees up to her chest and retied her hair in its scrunchie. She waved her hand as if wafting away a fly, and made a sound like *tsk* through her teeth. Elementary, she thought. Why hadn't she told Scout never to answer the door?

'Who knows?' (Now with a double waft of her hands.) 'It's probably because of that busybody downstairs. Old bat. Some people just can't keep their noses out. She asked about you last week. I thought I'd put her off. Interfering old cow. It's not your fault anyway. It's not your fault at all. Don't give it another thought.'

Joanie went very quiet. She didn't look cross, but she looked as if she was giving it several other thoughts herself. Scout wondered if she was worse than cross. Joanie got up, collected the Kentucky Fried packaging and started stuffing it into the kitchen bin. She poured the left-over Coke into the sink. She straightened the cover on the couch and banged the cushions with her hand to plump them back to shape.

'It's late, Scout,' she said, 'you should get ready for bed. Pack away the Scrabble. Even though you haven't got to get up for school in the morning, you should still go to bed at a reasonable time.'

She was brisk, efficient. Scout wondered if she was like this at work, wheeling her trolley along the corridor, taking no nonsense, getting on with what had to be done.

Scout trickled the Scrabble pieces through her fingers and into the little drawstring bag. She kept her eyes downcast as Joanie emptied the kitchen bin, knotted the plastic bag and put it by the door, ready to take down in the morning. 'I feel like strewing it right outside her front door,' she said. Scout reassured herself that she was just saying that, it wouldn't actually be something she would do.

Scout went to the bathroom and washed her face. She opened her lips and peered at her gums, her teeth. They looked clean enough, but you couldn't really tell. You could buy plaque disclosing tablets; after you chewed them, they showed all the unclean parts of your teeth in bright, grainy pink. It was like in life, Scout thought. Sometimes things looked all right but you weren't looking at them correctly. Her teeth could be going rotten. That was another thing to worry about. She couldn't see how a trip to the dentist would figure in their current living arrangements. And what, thinking back on the afternoon, was the point of good posture if you had a mouthful of rotting stumps? Debutantes probably had the pearliest white teeth. Their teeth would exactly match the white of the coddled eggs they ate for breakfast in the Breakfast Room. If, in an unfortunate mishap, they touched a tooth with the teaspoon as they ate, it would ring with the perfect ting of silver caught on flawless, plaque-free enamel. She put some paste on her brush.

'What would happen if I got toothache and needed to go to the dentist?' she called across the hallway.

'I'd find one and make you an appointment.'

'How would you know where to go?'

'I'd look it up.'

'How would you know if he or she was a good one?'

'Dentists are mostly good, especially for children's teeth.'

'But what if the one you found wasn't?'

'Why wouldn't they be, and Scout, you haven't even got toothache.'

'Sometimes something can be wrong with your teeth without you having toothache. I was just wondering, if I did have it, what you would do, and what would happen.'

'Well, stop wondering. I'd fix it. Think about something else. Think nice thoughts.'

Scout got into bed. The dark seemed thicker, murkier. Odd, when she had been alone here at night, it had never seemed as spiky and edgy as it appeared tonight. 'Mum,' (she wondered if she could risk throwing this in occasionally when not in public) 'Mum, were you ever scared of the dark when you were a child?'

Joanie appeared in the doorway. She came and hovered at the edge of the bed.

'No, not at all. Mainly because Alice always insisted on the landing light being on. She was always obsessed with being able to see the way clearly to the bathroom if you got up in the night. Don't you remember? When I left home, it was a revelation, the thickness of a completely dark night. If the darkness is bothering you, remember it's just what's left when the light has gone, and unless something happens to the sun, the light always comes back. Come on, go to sleep. Stop fret fret fretting.'

She kissed her, and left the room.

Scout drifted into sleep, reassuring herself that if the sun not rising had been a possible outcome of climate change Mrs Pearson-Smith would have told her. She'd have put them on their guard.

Joanie sat down on the couch, sucked hard on her cigarette, and bit at her thumbnail. The situation was a mess, or at least it was becoming a mess. Would they come calling again? They had a reputation for persistence. How much communication would there be between counties? You never knew with computers. If it came down to people's efficiency, probably very little. She reassured herself she was probably a very small fish to fry. Perhaps, also, it depended on how Ned Beecham had reacted to the news. Would he have to be the one to set things in motion? Maybe he'd moved on and had a whole new family and didn't care at all. That would be handy. She didn't want to think of the alternative. Had he and his wife looked capable of dishing out some retribution? Joanie suspected her course of action might look worse from the outside than from her own perspective. Alternatively, somebody in authority might be intrigued, and fasten little piranha teeth into the skimpiest of detail. A lawyer with the thrill of the chase. Perhaps it was inevitable that the social worker would come again. If she did come, maybe she'd find Scout in a syringe-sprinkled garden, practising good posture with a book on her head. That would be novel, for whomever came sniffing for neglect. How to file that observation would give them some food for thought.

Joanie kneaded the muscles of her shoulders with her fingertips and glanced across at her empty bed. She felt rattled. Oh, for a bed filled with a broad-armed, warm-skinned man. That was what she could do with. Not Social Services with all their crap.

17

Sylvie Austen sat in the meeting room, waiting for her manager and her colleagues to arrive. She sipped from a mug of green tea with peppermint. The nutritionist who wrote a column in the newspaper she read said that green tea was very good for the prevention of varicose veins. She rubbed her hand down the length of her calf meditatively. She was only thirty, she hadn't even had children yet, but her mother's legs and her grandmother's had varicose veins snaking down them. It was a logical anxiety. She peered to see if there was anything visible. A few thread veins, a couple of slightly raised areas. She blew on her tea and took a large gulp. Sylvie was a great believer in prevention being better than cure.

She felt quite the detective this morning. Extraordinary, how sometimes you were looking for one thing and you found something completely different. A kind of unforeseeable serendipity, which was all the more remarkable considering the squalor, poverty, moral chaos and generally loveless ethos in which most of her work was steeped.

Sylvie still sometimes wondered what it was that had prompted her to go into social work. She was familiar with all the guff about wanting to mend society, to bring care and compassion into areas where there was none, to shine light into murky corners. Yes, yes, all that rhetoric still held, and she was sure she could actually remember believing it. It was more apparent in the faces of her younger colleagues, who still felt there was everything to play for, than in the more weary,

resigned faces of her elders or betters, who occasionally –
politically incorrectly – wished for a colony to which they
could ship all their problem individuals, or a mass sterilisation
programme, starting with their own particular case-load.
Working for the Early Years and Family Support team had
attained a mildly ironic ring, in that there was very little resembling a family that came into Sylvie Austen's view on an
annual basis.

Love. It wasn't that she didn't witness it: it was love morphed
into alternative shapes and contexts, but visible, desperate, all
the same. Drug-addicted mothers who clung to their babies
while out scoring heroin at two o'clock in the morning. You
certainly stood no chance of taking their children into care on
an abandonment claim. They had to be physically wrenched
from their mothers' syringe-marked arms. Sylvie Austen sometimes felt that love, in its grimy, seedy form, could tug at the
heart-strings more effectively than any saccharine Valentine
card or movie. She had concluded that love was at its most startling when displayed in the context of a shipwrecked life, or
when death, or any number of darknesses, threw it into relief.

The children who had been through her hands! Some
adopted, taken away at the local authority's behest. Children
with teeth rotted from drinking juice out of bottles: limbs
fractured in God knows what sequence of events (*She fell out
of her high chair, She fell down the stairs, She tripped by the
swing*). The real version usually made an appearance eventually. The women she dealt with who shacked up with all
manner of hopeless, predictably shitty blokes, who drank, and
took out their temper on children they had not sired.

Sylvie had lost count of the times she had come home from
work, thrown her clothes into the washing machine, and stood
under the shower, scrubbing at her skin and her hair, trying to
wash off the taint of a flat or house reeking of fags, booze, dog
shit (usually from some kind of weapon dog – a pit bull or a

Rottweiler) and filled with pale-faced, nit-ridden children with any number of leagues between themselves and a freshly cooked square meal. A feeling, soul-sapping, as she sat afterwards wrapped in her bathrobe, that some things were beyond fixing, or at least beyond her capacity to so do. One of the receptionists had said to her helpfully, after some media coverage on another authority which should have taken a child away from its mother and her boyfriend before it was beaten to death, *You can't do right for wrong.* Yes, indeed.

Sylvie wondered at what stage in her life it had seemed a good idea to work in an environment where notices informed clients that it was *an offence to physically assault our staff.* Sylvie had been jostled a couple of times, slapped once, had the door pushed or slammed in her face many, many times. She'd lost count of the times she'd been told to *Fuck off, it's none of your business.* Sometimes, she wondered if they had a point.

The money that was spent, the thousands and millions of pounds that went on trying to repair, to make good, to equalise, to create opportunities, offer chances. Sylvie saw her work arena as the septic underbelly of society, festering beneath all those who lived upright, morally complacent lives. Sometimes, faced with a woman, three of her children already taken into care, pregnant with a fourth, assuring her that this time she'd do better, she'd do differently, Sylvie would see it all unfold before her: the Emergency Protection Order, the appointment of a guardian for the child, the hearing, the barristers, the spell at a mother and baby unit, the character assessment, the forward plan discussing options for support. A little later, predictably, the fourth child would be taken into care, and Sylvie would put money on going through the same process with a fifth. Sometimes, she wondered if she actually changed anything at all.

Scout Simpson had been a surprise. Highlight of the week, in fact. Waving the little bundle of papers she said was her

Maths. Something earnest about her. A little sheepish in her first conversation, and then patently giving it her best shot. A woman had rung from the flats. Hers was a familiar voice. She shopped the truants and the drug-dealers; got particularly animated when she thought she'd spied a flat crammed with illegal Chinese immigrants.

'It could be like those cockle-pickers,' she'd said to Sylvie, 'exploited just like those cockle-pickers.'

'I don't think they'll be travelling to the coast from here,' Sylvie had said, wanting to parry the woman's salacious enthusiasm. Nothing like disarray in others' lives to confirm to someone their own hearth was of model neatness.

'There's a child,' she'd said, 'a child of school age. Not been there long. The mother goes to work – not night work, looks respectable, relatively. Although does go out at night. Kid's on her own all day. I see her down in the shop most afternoons. You want to look into it. She should be at school.'

Sylvie had been expecting Scout Simpson to be someone else. There'd been a child across the city – one of her colleague's cases – who'd moved unexpectedly, just as they were about to consider foster care. It was her name Sylvie had been thumbing through for, when Scout had piped up and told her who she was. Sylvie had written it down with the weariness that came from knowing that there wouldn't be time, resources, staff – or even motivation – to pursue this one further. The child was plausibly claiming to be home educated; she looked clean and well nourished. The police had not been called to the flat for any public disturbance. The mother was perhaps doing a small part-time job. Sylvie had written down her name assuming she would put it aside and get on with more pressing cases. Then, on an inter-county e-mail from Oxfordshire, the name popped up on her screen: *Scout Simpson – Location Order*. The mother had absconded. Upped and offed. A Location Order had been filed by the father. All too familiar.

Sylvie's colleagues came into the room and sat down. Scout Simpson was number three on the agenda. Sylvie, it was decided, would go back to the flat and try to talk to the mother, this time armed with notification of the Location Order. Then, if she absconded again, the mother could not plead ignorance. They would try to achieve cooperation; this was always at the vanguard of good practice.

Against *Optimum outcome*, Sylvie wrote Mother returns to Oxford team and agrees to meet with birth father to discuss options. She thought of the child, trying to hide from sight underneath the window sill. There was always a child in the middle, trying to please everyone.

18

Elisabetta was finding it hard to concentrate on the simplest of things. In the supermarket, hand poised to remove something from a shelf, or putting carrots into a bag, she would find her gaze snagging on children, always girls, always aged around eleven. As she drove down the street, they caught her eye as they walked along the pavement. At school, when she hurried across the playground she looked at the children in Year Seven, the ones she did not teach because Italian was not offered until Year Nine. On the tube, she found herself scanning and re-scanning the platform, the other passengers, the stairs or escalators leading up and out into the air. She wasn't actually looking for Scout. She wasn't actually expecting to see her. She was clear on this. Instead, it was some kind of absorption process, some kind of inhalation of all the patterns and permutations and possibilities a girl of this age might possess. Elisabetta was learning them; their body language, their posture, their movements, the tone of their voices.

At night, Scout came into her dreams. Sometimes she was walking towards her, sometimes running away. Once, she was holding a box containing a pale blue robin's egg. Her hair was red, her skin cream, her eyes green. She ran along a beach, her bare feet leaving no trace in the sand. Sometimes she looked like Prue, sometimes like Ned, sometimes her hair was blonde and tousled, festooned with awful, gaudy, wide ribbons. Sometimes she looked over her shoulder with an expression of something like reproach. Elisabetta's own body dolphined in and out of the dreams. She had breasts that withered and fell away, teeth that dropped out at a touch, innards that looped around her like a theme park ride. Her hands were either empty, or clasping Maia's. When she reached out it was into bald, white, empty rooms. *You don't understand,* she was telling a police officer, who was refusing to believe that her child was lost. *She was meant to be my child. That was the agreement. She was meant to be my child.* She searched for her on Oxford Street, on the new junction with Regent Street where pedestrians could cross every which way. She walked each one of the permutations, crossing and crossing again, and the child was ahead of her, barefoot, glimpsed, and then lost in the crowd.

When she woke, she was laced with sweat. She could feel it on the edges of her collar-bones, between her breasts, in the hollow of her navel. Ned would be sitting up beside her. Did she cry out, she wondered? He did not ask her to tell, he simply held her in his arms. The soft old T-shirt he slept in dried her skin, the comforting feel of it helped slow the speed of her heart.

In the morning, over breakfast, she felt an embarrassed awkwardness. They would talk overly of Maia, noting everything she did, stating the obvious, repeating the choices she had made for breakfast. ('Strawberries? You definitely want strawberries this morning? You're sure you wouldn't prefer a boiled egg?') Ned would talk of a particular pupil, or of a parents' evening that night. Elisabetta found herself talking of the weather, conjecturing whether it was warm enough to go without a cardigan, or whether Maia would need sunscreen in her school bag. All these words, Elisabetta felt, rushed into the vacuum of their silence, all the things that suddenly seemed unable to be said. *Do you think of her? What do you think of her? Do you think they will find her?* These words had an unsayability that had nestled into the spaces between them. Was he thinking it too? She knew when she reached down to kiss him as he sat at the breakfast table, that he knew and she knew and this silent knowledge was one of the things that would make their marriage endure. Ned's skin, the feel of him, the smell of him, the secret places of his body, all this was imprinted on her, inhaled by her, absorbed into her bones. The words would be later. Surely the words would be later? Until then she would dream of a barefoot child, and stand in supermarkets, mouth half open, caught by the delicacy of a fine-boned neck, a pony-tail moving in fluid synchronisation with a head lightly turned.

19

Today was going to be hot. It was a beautiful May morning. Scout pushed back her duvet and squinted up at the sky. Perfectly blue. Probably the kind of day when the family at Houghton woke up and said *Let's play croquet* or *Let's put on our bathing suits and swim in the lake.* Mr Groves told her he used to carry down towels, a pile of towels, taken from the linen press. He'd put them on a bench by the lake and the young masters and mistresses would come tumbling out of the water, shrieking and shivering, he said, for it seemed always to be cold, and sometimes with emerald streaks of weed clinging to their limbs, their hair. Master George had tied a rope to an oak tree and would swing out across the water and drop like a stone, plumb centre into the lake. After swimming they asked Cook for lemonade, which was made in huge glass jugs from fresh lemons and sugar and water. Mr Groves would take it out on a tray and serve it at a stone table on the terrace. Sometimes, Cook made them thick hot chocolate. Miss Louisa scooped the cream from the top with her fingertip and fed it to Peaches, her mother's pug. The Mistress always called to them from the Morning Room as they ran out through the french doors, *Wear your hats, girls. This sun is merciless. If you don't, your skin will look like Cook's.* Last thing at night, Mr Groves said, he would walk across the lawns, and retrieve hats from by the swing, the tree house, the croquet lawn, the lake. He would hang them on hooks in the Boot Room, each thing in its rightful place, ready for the morning when they would be scattered again. Scout had told him she thought it must take patience and an even temper not to be cross when the hats were left everywhere. He replied it was one of his favourite parts of the day, to walk through the gardens in the gentle dusk, the swallows swooping near the eaves of the house, and the fragrance from the borders; the roses, the day lilies, the jasmine, the nicotiana.

Scout looked round her tiny room. Each thing in its rightful place wasn't really an option. She wondered if she should perhaps try for some kind of system, get some hooks and some stickers to label them. It was hard, though, to make this feel like her real home. When her clothes emerged from the washer dryer machine, they were crumpled as if they'd been left on the bedroom floor. She tried to fold them, to smooth out the creases with the flat of her hand but it didn't make much difference. They did not give the impression of clothes freshly laundered. They didn't look like things which might emerge from a wardrobe or a linen press at Houghton, of that she was sure.

Joanie had been quiet. Not grumpy, just quiet. She left in the morning – today with some peanut butter on toast in her hand as she went out of the door. When it closed behind her, Scout found it hard to shake off the feeling that there were more hours in the day than she could fill. More Maths and dictionary with Mr Mohammed – that would be a highlight. He was going to teach her to draw triangles accurately with a pair of compasses. He had bought her some from WH Smith in town. She had asked to repay him but he had refused. 'For my star pupil,' he said, 'for a mathematician of rare distinction, it would be my pleasure to buy a compass.'

The dictionary competition was, on balance, she thought, about even-stevens. Yesterday, he had given the correct definition for *gregarious*. Scout and Nona had clapped (Nona was good at joining in). Today, Scout would find something harder.

Perhaps, also, she could continue with *Pond and River*. She'd had it out on loan for three weeks now, but Mary Crawshaw said there was hardly pressing demand.

She got out of bed, and picked up the book from where it lay on the top of the drawers beside the window. She could do Summer Underwater Weeds. That would be cool and silky. She read *Tape grass, Bulbous rush, Flushed rush, Water violet*. She imagined them stuck to the limbs of the Houghton children. She saw Master George fly through the sky on the end of a rope, crashing down into the water, dispersing blanket weed, sinking down through the duck-weed, the water green and smooth. Master George was probably an old man now, but she didn't want to think about that. When she thought of stories she loved – Thumbelina cradled on a leaf, floating downstream, and the prince who scaled an ice mountain to rescue a princess by cleverly taping eagle claws to his hands – the Houghton children were as vivid, as fixed in her imagination, their lives full only of beautiful things.

Scout wondered if your eyes felt different if they only looked at things that were lovely, well-made, perfectly done. Maybe your eyeballs always felt at ease. Now, if she closed her eyes, she could imagine Miss Maudie's pony, saddled up by a groom, waiting in the courtyard for Miss Maudie to come out of the house, and Maudie appearing, adjusting her gloves, her jacket, her riding boots gleaming with polish, a stock tied neatly at her neck. Scout had never actually been on a horse, but this did not prevent her sharing Miss Maudie's anticipation of a gallop along the Great Mead, the pony's tail and mane streaming, Miss Maudie's posture just so.

When Scout went down to the shop, Mr Mohammed was finishing setting up a new fixture. It would be Father's Day soon, and he had succumbed to a range of pop-up cards, displayed in their own Perspex, cuboid shelving. At the top of the shelf, 3-D silver letters announced *A miracle in paper engineering!* 'Too expensive,' Mrs Mohammed said from behind the Post Office counter. 'He is thinking our customers have more money than they do. He would send this card to his father if he were still alive. This is what attracts him.'

'Smitta is never as optimistic as me,' Mr Mohammed said, tightening the shelving with a small screwdriver. 'People will spend money on their dear dads. Of this I am confident.' He took out a duster and polished his finger-marks from the Perspex.

Scout stepped back and looked at the fixture. *SUPER DAD!* said one card, picturing a football, a rugby ball and a golf club spilling out of a box. *BEST DAD IN THE WORLD!* said another, the letters joined by some complex origami and pouring out of a champagne bottle. Another, with a picture of a movie star from long ago whom she couldn't name, said *Of all the dads in all the world, I'm so glad you're mine.*

Scout felt a small pit-pat in her chest. Perhaps she should ask Joanie what he looked like, or what he did. Then she could at least imagine to whom she might send a card which said triumphantly, bursting from a crown like those contained in crackers, *YOU'RE A KING OF A DAD!*

He would probably have been burly. All the men that Scout glimpsed with Joanie, all the ones who rocked up and knocked on the door of their real house had been burly. They had big hands like butchers, and forearms which were wider than Scout's legs. They often had quite a lot of hair; dark hair on their heads, chest hair, wiry hair on their wrists. If they sat on the couch, they would give Joanie's bum a light little slap as she walked past, and Scout would think everything was fleshy, everything came down to skin on skin. In their old house, she had often woken at night, hearing a deep, chesty laugh. Men made her mum sing. She'd clocked that too. Often, in the mornings after Joanie had been out with a man, or a man had

come back to the house, Joanie would sing as she put stuff in
the washing machine, or hum as she brushed her hair.
Sometimes the men tiptoed out early – Scout had gone to the
loo once and seen one going down the stairs, his trousers and
shoes bunched in his hand. She wondered where he was going
at this time of night. Perhaps he had another house to go back
to? Men's underpants, baggy and saggy at the back, were not
a good sight. Or, the very white skin of an actual bum, glimpsed
by Alice's landing light.

Lord and Lady Broughton-Fowler had a bedroom with
their own dressing-rooms and bathrooms either side, Mr
Groves had told her. Scout had decided it was probably unac-
ceptable to ask if that meant they had never had a conversation
with one of them sitting on the loo. She and Joanie often did.
It had a cosiness all of its own. At Houghton Hall, Mr Groves
would attend to Lord Broughton-Fowler in his suite to the left
of the bedroom. Lady Broughton-Fowler's maid attended to
her in her suite on the right of the bedroom. She had a
dressing-table with glass bottles containing her perfume, and
hairbrushes made of silver with her initials engraved on the
back. Perhaps they only saw each other clean and lovely and
after the loo, either ready to go down for breakfast or to dinner
or riding, or in a nightgown ready for bed. Scout wasn't fooled
into thinking that this meant things were always happy. Mr
Groves told her that in the Great War, the previous Lady
Broughton-Fowler had lost three of her boys who had been in
the Cavalry. She had retired to her bedroom and wouldn't get
out of bed. She ate only milk soup and became as thin as a
rail. All the engraved hairbrushes in the world couldn't change
that. Lord Broughton-Fowler had to open the fête by himself.
The Hunt stopped assembling in the courtyard, and had to go
to the Manor instead. It was the sound of the horses, she said,
she was unable to bear it. When she died, Mr Groves said, her
coffin was as light as a feather. It could have been carried by

the one son who remained. Scout imagined that the next Lord Broughton-Fowler wouldn't have been burly, either.

She turned her attention from the cards.

After Maths and dictionary (she got him with *uxorial*), Scout bought some Sellotape and went to see Mr Groves. 'It's for your wallet,' she said, 'I wrote this out for you to stick in your wallet.'

Mr Groves took the small piece of card she gave him. In neat, careful, block capital letters, she had written: THEY ASK FOR YOUR MONEY BECAUSE THEY KNOW YOU FORGET YOU HAVE GIVEN IT TO THEM. THIS IS TO REMIND YOU. He showed her it didn't need to be stuck in. There was a small window for a photo opposite the section that held coins. 'You should put a picture there as well,' Scout said cheerfully.

'There's no one I have a picture of,' he said. 'I think I was married to Houghton Hall.'

Scout thought that perhaps for an Art lesson (which reminded her, she hadn't had one of those since she'd been in the flat), she'd draw him a picture, one that could be folded out. She would draw him, but a younger version of him, walking with stronger, bigger steps, in a garden at twilight. She would colour in many different types of flowers. In his hands she would put all the sun hats he had carefully gathered.

20

When the doorbell rang, Scout knew it would be her. She sat at the kitchen table for a moment, then put her pen and pencil carefully back in her pencil case and zipped it quietly shut. The crayons she could do nothing about. Her pencil case had a design of pink and white marshmallows. Scout looked at them for a while. They looked soft and pillowy. Under her breath she was counting, waiting for the doorbell to ring again. Joanie had told her not to open the door. She would sit here quietly, her hands neatly folded in her lap, and not move an inch. The woman would tire of waiting. Eventually.

Scout decided it was best not to think about the importance of making no noise. It would cause the back of her throat to feel dry, make her want to clear it, or perhaps even to cough. She swooshed as much spit as possible and swallowed with purpose. That would probably fix it. Turning her head slightly, she peered down the hall to the door. She was suddenly aware of wanting to wee so crossed her legs. She should think of anything but her throat or her bladder. Her legs felt a bit shaky. It was easy for the image of the Social Services woman to morph into something else; to change into something bad, like in a scary film, waiting to come and get her. *It's only a woman with a clipboard standing out on the landing.* She would have whispered this to herself, but she thought it might set off her throat. Instead she traced the sentence with her fingertip, along the lip of the table. She switched from her left hand to her right when she crossed the mid point of her body. She leaned slightly forward. She couldn't hear anyone beyond the door. Then, a voice. A voice murmuring to someone. A woman's or a man's? Perhaps she had come back accompanied. Could it be someone down by the lift?

She leaned forward a little more. Slowly, heart-stoppingly, she watched as four pale fingers pushed their way through the letter-box. The nails were varnished pink. The fingers held the letter-box open. Scout sucked in her ribs and made herself thin to the back of the chair. A voice came next. It was her voice, the same woman's. If Scout had not been so busy trying to be absorbed into the chair, she was confident she would have seen a flash of red hair. Perhaps that would come spilling through the letter-box too. 'Scout Simpson,' the voice said, 'Scout Simpson. Are you there? Can you answer the door if you are there?' Scout calculated there would be a number of seconds, perhaps only five or so, before the mouth was replaced by two peering eyes. She put her hands beneath the seat of the chair and lifted it at the same time as taking two steps backwards. Now, she was sitting pressed up against the front of the cooker. The switches for the front rings were jamming into her shoulder-blades. Good job it wasn't a gas cooker or she could gas herself. Or blow up the whole block of flats. Scout could no longer see the letter-box. She could hear the fingers rustling. The voice came back, less fuzzily this time. 'Scout, we are trying to help you. We need to speak to your mum. She knows what it is about. She will know why we are here.'

Scout realised she had forgotten to breathe. She felt her fingertips tingle, and took in a great suck of air. It sounded so noisy going into her chest, she wondered if it had made a great gusting sound, as if she'd drawn in all available oxygen from along the hallway. There was silence from the letter-box. The doorbell rang again. Scout's scalp began to itch like mad. She unclasped her hands and allowed herself the luxury of scratching. *Scritch scratch* went her nails on her head. It sounded impossibly loud.

'We're going now,' said the voice. 'I'm pushing a letter through the door. We'll be back in the morning. I hope we can talk with you then.'

Scout heard the sound of something dropping on to the doormat. She heard the footsteps walk slowly away. She was sure there was more than one set. She walked quietly into the bathroom and sat down for a wee. A few minutes longer and she'd have definitely wet herself.

Waiting for the lift, Sylvie Austen turned to her colleague, Sam. 'Poor little thing,' she said. 'She's not lacking in initiative. She lifted the chair and moved it backwards. That must have taken some doing. She looked like she'd been colouring at the table. Mum can't be getting it all wrong.'

Scout watched television until Joanie came back. There was no point trying to do any school-work. She could only keep looking at the sealed envelope she held in her hand. When Joanie came through the door she was brandishing a bag. 'Ta-daah!' she said. 'I was walking past the Oxfam bookshop, and I saw them in the window. Someone's obviously given up travelling.'

Scout looked in the bag. It contained about half a dozen *Rough Guides* to European cities.

'Is that Geography? Or History? Or possibly Foreign Languages? Probably all three!' Joanie said. 'You see, I told you we'd get into the swing of this home schooling thing.'

Scout put the bag on the floor and gave her mother the letter. Joanie opened it, turned towards the window and speed-read it. Damn it, she thought, he *had* slapped some-thing on her. A Location Order. What the hell was that? She read on a little further. It related only to Scout. Where she herself was didn't matter. She was advised to take Scout to a police station, or risk committing a criminal offence. Criminal offence. That certainly took it to another level. Damn him, and Social Services, for their surprising efficiency.

She chewed at a nail and toyed for a split second with the cooperative option. Should she meet them? No way. Once they'd got you, you were pinned and wriggling. Since when had making a dash for it ever failed her? To bolt it was. Joanie had never been convinced that people who took time over their decisions actually made better ones. She felt a rush of adrenalin.

She went into the kitchen and put on the kettle, absentmindedly moving the chair back to the table from where it still stood pressed to the cooker. She reached into her bag, took out her purse, gave Scout a £10 note and said 'Run down to Mr Mohammed and buy a couple of rolls of dustbin bags. Say goodbye to him. We're leaving tonight. Don't gawp at me! Leg it down there. We need to dash.'

Scout said to Mr Mohammed, 'I'm leaving. I don't really know why but we have to go. Thank you for the Maths. Thank you for my compass.' She picked up Nona and kissed her, and squidged her buttery softness. She tried not to cry. Mr Mohammed had not known what to say. He wouldn't take the money for the bin bags. While she waited in the queue she'd noticed he had not sold many of the Father's Day cards. Perhaps Mrs Mohammed was right. Perhaps people didn't have the money, the inclination, or the fathers. 'I hope you sell all of your cards,' she said, as she stood on the threshold of the shop holding the bin bag rolls. Mr Mohammed put his palms together and gave her a little bow. Scout noticed that from his palms to his elbows to the top of his head made an almost perfect equilateral triangle.

When Scout came back into the flat, Joanie was like a

whirling dervish. It was the same as when Scout had come back from school in March, only this time the space was smaller, and the decisions easier. She was leaving nothing behind. 'Put this somewhere if you want it,' she said, taking all the Maths down from the top of the cupboard.

When they had finished packing, Joanie got one of the trashed supermarket trolleys from down by the garden and brought it up in the lift. She put the holdalls and filled dustbin bags into it and started taking them down. Scout stood in the sitting-room, looking at the bare couch. The place had never felt like home until now. 'Come on, Scout,' said Joanie, 'I'm going to lock the door and push the keys through. It's late, and time we were making a move.'

'I just want to post something,' Scout said. 'I'll see you down by the car.' Joanie took down the last trolley load. Scout could hear her heels click-clacking along the hallway. She took out her drawing, and went along to Mr Groves' door. It was 9.30pm. He might be afraid if she rang the doorbell now. He might think it was the hoodies, perhaps the worse for drink or drugs. She'd never seen so many bolts and locks as on the inside of his door. Even if he wasn't afraid he would perhaps be in bed, or almost. He would be wearing pyjamas, slippers. He wouldn't want her to see him like that. *Waistcoat on*, he would say when she came to the door after noon. She'd wondered how long it took his swollen old knuckles to do up the long smooth row of buttons.

On the back of the drawing she wrote *Thank you, I'll miss you, love Scout*. She put three kisses underneath, and wondered about adding something about not slurping soup or always walking with her best possible posture. The paper was becoming blurry and she realised she was crying. She pushed the paper through the letter-box and ran down to where she knew Joanie's car was parked.

A drawing of Mr Groves fluttered softly down and landed

square on the mat. It showed him in a long-ago flower-filled garden, holding a hat that resembled a beanie owned by Scout. He paused on his way from the bathroom, and stooped slowly to pick it up.

21

'Bye-bye Brum,' Joanie sing-songed as she swung on to the M40. 'Bye-bye Sleepeasy Hotel. Bye-bye Social Services, bye-bye anyone else who might be interested in us. We're off to the seaside!'

Scout had to admire her mother's ability to adapt. She'd gone a bit pale when she first read the letter, and sworn under her breath when she'd read it again, but then she'd posted it into the toaster and watched it shrivel and burn. Scout had opened the kitchen window in case the smoke alarm went off. Joanie had chewed her thumbnail furiously while the letter smouldered. Now, she seemed fine, if anything a speeded-up version of herself. Her voice was a little louder than usual. She was laughing with her mouth open really wide. 'Never waste a crisis,' she was saying. Was she just throwing out sayings? Were they supposed to be comforting? 'The person who runs out of chances is the person who stops taking them,' she trilled, switching motorway lanes. Scout wondered if this was supposed to make her feel better. As far as she had known, she hadn't been taking any chances. The same for the crisis which could be wasted or not. Why wouldn't Joanie speak plainly? What had the letter said? No chance of knowing now. It was obvious Joanie wasn't going to tell. Perhaps she should have opened it herself. Then she'd have known what was what.

'Where *are* we going?' she asked. The seaside seemed too vague a destination. In a moment they would drive by the M&S they'd stopped at on their way up the motorway.

Circles, round in circles, Scout thought, suddenly fighting to keep her eyes open. It was almost 11.30.

'Bournemouth, Poole, Torquay, Torbay.' Joanie was chanting seaside town names, which suggested to Scout she wasn't entirely sure herself.

When Scout woke up, they were in a car park looking out over the sea. She could hear the waves lazily slapping against the sea wall. Joanie looked like she hadn't even been to sleep. She was sitting on the bonnet of the car with a pink Ikea blanket wrapped round her, smoking a cigarette and flicking the ash out beyond her. When she saw Scout was awake, she spoke through the windscreen.

'Bacon sandwiches and tea. That's absolutely what you have to have the first morning at the sea.' She craned her neck, and looked farther up the sea front. 'It looks like there's a van up there. I'll go and see what I can find. You stay here. I'll be back in a tick.'

Scout rubbed her eyes. She was covered by her duvet. Joanie must have put it over her in the night. Her seat was reclined. Scout pushed the button to restore it to upright and the sea came into larger view. The duvet smelt of the flat. She pushed it into the foot well. She stretched her arms and yawned. Her face felt grubby. She looked properly at the water. She saw a small ferry. To the left of it were some huge houses built on sandbanks out into the bay. In the distance on the right she could see a small island, with what looked like a castle. She looked to see if there were children on the beach. Stupid thought, they would be at school. She realised she wasn't sure what day it was. The sign beyond the car told her that Joanie had plumped for Poole.

Joanie came back to the car with two bacon and tomato rolls, and two teas in paper cups with lids. 'Come and sit on the sea wall,' she said, 'eat this and take a breath of fresh air. This will do us the world of good. Don't know why I didn't think of it earlier – it's almost June and we were stuck miles from the coast. Much better to be here. You can play on the beach when I'm working.'

Scout took the roll and started to peel back the wrapping. She felt as if the bacon would choke her unless she asked the question. She'd woken up with it still perched on the tip of her tongue. No point hesitating. Sometimes it was just better to blurt it right out.

'Did we do anything wrong?' She looked fixedly at the horizon. 'Did we do anything wrong to make them come looking?'

Joanie paused, and took the lid off her tea. She blew through the steam, and followed Scout's gaze out to sea.

'No, nothing wrong. Nothing known to be wrong. I just don't want their fingers in our pies. We can be free as birds. They're not telling me what to do, where to go.'

'But why would they want to, unless we had done something wrong?'

'Because they're nosy that way. Just nosy.'

'So, we did nothing wrong. We definitely did nothing wrong?'

'I'm telling you we did nothing wrong. Just let it go. I don't want to hear the word wrong again – okay? Wrong does not apply to us. It is not our word.'

'Definitely not our word?'

'Completely not our word.'

Scout bit into her sandwich.

Later, when Joanie went to buy cigarettes and a newspaper, she let Scout buy a quarter of sherbet lemons. Scout decided this was not the time to worry about when she had last cleaned her teeth. She sat next to Joanie on a bench, while Joanie looked at the job ads. She bit down on a sherbet lemon, filling her mouth with fizz.

Joanie had been quiet, but now she was chatty.

'Look at this,' said Joanie, 'there's a pottery factory here. It's recruiting. I could try my hand at decorating. You stay near the car, and I'll try my luck.' She came back an hour and a half later, having talked herself into a trial session.

'I said I'd had previous experience in Stoke-on-Trent. Everyone's worked in a pottery there.'

'What did they ask you to do?'

'Sponge paint a few dolphins around the edge of a plate. Believe me, it's harder than it looks.'

'What were yours like?'

'Mussels. Blurry-edged mussels. There's a lot more to dipping a sponge in paint than you'd think. Not exactly bottle-nosed, that's what the supervisor said. No way I could persuade him differently. I think I'll have to set my sights lower.'

In the Situations Vacant column she found an ad for a housekeeper/breakfast cook in a guest house one row back from the sea front.

Standing on the front step of *Calm Views*, Scout wondered if she and her mother looked like a pair of raggle-taggle gypsies. Joanie had brushed their hair, standing barefoot at the edge of the waves. She'd put Scout's up into a topknot and given her a big kiss on her forehead. They had cleaned their teeth by swigging from a bottle of water and spitting into the sea. Joanie had produced a clean T-shirt for Scout. Scout felt cleanish. Cleanish was probably the best to hope for.

She had never seen such fierce net curtains in her life. Every window of the house was impenetrable, guarded with stiff, white rigidity. There were window-boxes at each of the ground-floor windows. They contained alternating rows of marigolds and pansies. The glass in the windows was sectioned into small diamond shapes. The driveway was made of coloured cement, patterned in fake bricks. The whole front of the house looked like a geometry diagram. The sign that swung on a hinge by the gate said *No pets, sorry* and *No smokers, thank you.* It also said *FULL,* but Scout noticed a cobweb laced over that bit so wondered if it was reliably changed. When Joanie rang the doorbell, Scout straightened her back. First impressions, she thought, and did her best at posture. Joanie spotted it, and pretended to do an exaggerated army salute. She pulled back her shoulders and stuck out her chest. She was winking at Scout as the door opened. Scout was trying not to laugh when a sour-faced woman of medium height looked them up and down.

In the kitchen, Mrs Eastman ran through Joanie's duties. She was to set up the dining-room for breakfast, and cook Full English upon request. Also, freshly prepare toast and lay out a selection of preserves. Assortment of cereals and muesli to be decanted into glass bowls. Afterwards, restore the kitchen to order, and then make a start upon the beds. Sheets only to be changed for new guests, not daily or even alternate. 'For Mother Earth, for saving resources,' Mrs Eastman said, with a self-satisfied little incline of her head. Scout wondered if it was as Mrs Pearson-Smith said, and that the tide of the Amazon spilled into a guest house in Poole too. 'Nothing about saving Daz and her electricity bill,' Joanie said later.

'I'll make an exception for your daughter,' said Mrs Eastman. 'The job comes with a small bedroom at the top. There's room for a little fold-out bed; there's one in the store cupboard on the landing. She's to keep herself out of the way of the guests, and not make any undue noise. Will she be going to school?' Scout wondered if Mrs Eastman thought she was an idiot or if she could not answer for herself. She wanted to ask what undue noise was, but thought she'd probably find out.

'No,' said Joanie airily, 'not much point with just a few weeks of term left. She's home-schooled anyway. I find that more suited to her intellect.' Scout thought Joanie was putting on that voice when she talked more precisely than she usually did. She suspected Mrs Eastman was too. She hoped Mrs Eastman wouldn't come upon her mother saying *bollocks bollocks bollocks* when she caught her ankle with the Hoover or dropped something on to the floor.

Joanie and Scout put the fold-up bed in their room. Scout estimated that she could lie in it and hold Joanie's hand as she lay in hers. Joanie would be able to reach over and nudge her like she did when they laughed about things. The room didn't have a proper window of its own; what light came in, came through a Velux in the ceiling. It was mostly obscured by a large splodge of seagull mess.

'I'll get that,' Joanie said. She wet some toilet roll, balanced on the bed, and hooked her arm out of the window until she had wiped the mark away. 'All gone?' she asked. Her head was turned away with the effort of reaching through the window.

'Yes. All gone.'

'See,' Joanie said. She climbed back down and lay on the bed, and patted Scout's bed for her to do the same. 'See how cosy we are. We might not be able to see the sea, but we can see the sky. Bird's eye view you could say, which is better than the bird's poo view we had a moment ago.'

Scout looked up at the sky. It did seem freshly blue, more truly blue than the sky she had looked up at in Birmingham. Perhaps the wind off the water kept it blown clean. Joanie was making an effort. Scout felt she ought to too. She laughed at her mother's joke, but was just a beat too late.

'I bet she's got a zillion rules,' Joanie said. 'I'm guessing we only had the first instalment. No food in bedrooms, that'll be written somewhere. She's probably got a smoke alarm hidden away just to catch out the unsuspecting smoker. She had eyes like a lizard. Did you see that, the way she blinked? I'm guessing smuggling you a Full English will be out.'

Later, Scout was trying to fall asleep. Joanie was already snoring softly. Joanie had been given a lesson on the linen cupboard in the afternoon; which sheets went into which room, how Mrs Eastman liked them folded. Joanie was to be economical with cleaning products too; no lax swooshing of Cif all around the rim of the bath. Products were to be applied to a cloth, and then to the area to be cleaned. Far less waste. Scout had sat at the top of the stairs, her chin cupped in her hands, listening. She wondered how Mrs Eastman couldn't hear that quality in Joanie's voice, the merest hint of laughter, of finding the whole thing ridiculously funny. The cupboard that the sheets were in, Scout thought, just looked like any old normal cupboard. It wouldn't compare to the linen press at Houghton; certainly not after a few days of her mother's folding.

In the kitchen Joanie was shown where all the tableware was put. 'Dishes for if a whole table wants scrambled egg,' Mrs Eastman said. 'It looks so much smarter on the table. Handle with care, it's Royal Doulton. Any chipping from careless handling and I'll dock it from your wages.' Scout could have told her if it had been silver it would have been holloware. She could have told her the stainless steel flatware and cutlery was Thread and Fiddle too, but she sensed Mrs Eastman preferred to pretend she was not there. On the phone, by Reception, she'd leaned against the little glass-topped counter, talking to a friend. Yairs, yairs, Mrs Eastman said, she'd filled the position. Hopefully the woman would be up to scratch by the time high season started. A child in tow; a pale, thin, little thing. One step behind. She hoped she didn't get under her feet.

Scout turned over in bed. She could feel the two ridges which allowed the bed to fold into three. I am like the princess in *The Princess and the Pea*, she thought, only less delicate. Faced with only a pea, she thought, I'd have been asleep hours ago. It was obviously a sign she was not of noble birth, if another was needed. Maudie Broughton-Fowler would probably have got up from the bed in complete despair. Scout tried to wriggle her weight off the ridges. Joanie's foot was protruding from beyond the sheets. Her mother had square, strong, chunky feet. Scout considered them and thought they looked like feet capable of walking a long way. On her own, you could see the fan of bones that spread out to each toe. Scout curled and flexed them. She sighed, and wondered if she blew hard enough, she might mist the Velux.

Outside in the street, she could hear someone walking past, laughing softly, and then somebody's heels, and then a cough, and then a gate shutting precisely. She heard a car door closing and, beyond that, the gravel-sucking sound of the sea. Not much chance of hearing *wanker* here, she thought. Mr Groves would like it. She could see him taking his afternoon walk along the front. She thought of his old white gloves. He'd have had the dining-room of *Calm Views* shipshape and sorted.

After Joanie's induction had finished, they'd gone for a walk and some supper. Joanie had bought haddock and chips, and they'd eaten it sitting on a bench. Joanie had picked up some leaflets from a Tourist Information office near the front. 'You can read that tomorrow,' she said, 'that counts as Geography.'

Scout had put the leaflets carefully under her bed. She'd thought of putting them on the bedside table, but Joanie had placed her hand cream, eyelash curlers, nail varnish remover, and mascara there. Scout thought it probably wasn't a good bet, spill-wise, for any neat work. Mrs Pearson-Smith probably wouldn't even count the leaflets as Geography. Maybe she'd understand, though, that it was the best Scout could come up with thus far.

Outside, out to sea, she heard what sounded like a ship's foghorn blowing. She imagined a ferry full of people sailing off somewhere. She resolved tomorrow to walk around the block a few times. Perhaps all it took was some repetition, a few patterns, to make a place feel like home.

22

Scout sat on the wall outside *Calm Views* and sucked her Calippo. The melted juice had run between her fingers, and she licked away what she could. She seemed absorbed in her task, like a cat cleaning its paws, but in reality she was looking beyond her, to two girls who were a little farther up the pavement. They wore school uniform. Scout was trying to work out the motif on their polo shirts. It would be a school bell, or a squirrel, it was always something like that. The girls weren't playing anything in particular, they were mostly whispering to each other. Scout looked at them, and then turned her head away. She wondered if she had forgotten the rules in relation to girls her own age. She'd been watching them for over a week now, each day after school. They hovered just beyond her. 'They could be your friends,' Joanie said, when she glimpsed them from the window.

Yesterday, she'd asked them their names. 'Emily Matthews,' 'Cherry Mitchell,' they said. They'd looked her up and down, and then Emily Matthews had whispered something behind her hand. Scout wondered what she looked like to them; no school uniform, some egg on her T-shirt, and decided she didn't like thinking about that. Now, they were walking towards her.

'Your mum works for Mrs Eastman, doesn't she?' Emily said. 'She told my mum. We own *Palm Trees*.' She said 'own' with extra emphasis. With a nod, she indicated the small hotel a little farther along the road. 'My mum says it's hard finding any sort of decent summer labour. Does your mum always do this? Why don't you go to school?'

Scout was watching Emily's lips while she talked. They made a rectangle shape. Emily Matthews had already reached a view on her. She could tell that. Scout waved her hand airily.

'Just don't,' she said. That was what Joanie would say.

'Are you some kind of pikey?' Cherry asked. 'Emily says you're probably a pikey.'

'No. Of course I'm not.'

'Well, what are you then?' Emily said. 'Mrs Eastman told my mum she's only letting you stay out of the kindness of her heart, and that you're not to make any noise or disturb the guests. You're supposed to be super-quiet.'

Scout debated whether Mrs Eastman had any kindness in her heart. It certainly wasn't evident.

'She could put a cat flap in for you, then you could get in and out and not disturb anyone,' Emily added.

They laughed behind their hands. Scout could see their eyes moving quickly to check no grown-up was watching.

'If I were at your school, I'd beat you in a spelling test,' she said. 'No question.'

Emily's voice was quick to change tone, from wheedling, needling to a sharp edge of malice.

'Oh, we're so afraid of that, Miss Spelling Bee. Now you've really got us. Fact is you aren't, are you? We're at school and you're a pikey with egg on your T-shirt and time on your hands.'

They moved off up the pavement. Scout could hear them laughing. There was no point telling Joanie. She couldn't change anything. She'd probably just laugh about the land-ladies' stuck-up view of themselves. It would be hard to join in. Scout folded her Calippo wrapper into smaller and smaller rectangles. In the periphery of her vision, she saw a white net curtain flick.

The front, ground-floor room of *Calm Views* was beginning to perplex her. Yesterday morning, she'd been out on the street playing hopscotch and she'd seen the curtain flick twice. Her hopscotch would have made Mr Mohammed proud. She did not use chalk to write the numbers on the pavement – she gauged that would count as disturbing the outlook of *Calm Views*. Instead, she played from memory and multiplied each number in the sequence as she stepped on it. This, she decided, was admirably tricky, as she had to do the Maths at the same speed as she was hopping or scotching. While playing yesterday she'd turned twice and looked over her shoulder, feeling someone was watching. The curtain looked frozen. She saw Joanie pass before an upstairs window, plumping up a pillow. Her mother had waved to her and blown her a cheerful kiss.

Joanie seemed happy at *Calm Views*. Granted, she spent most of her time laughing at it – Mrs Eastman, the guests, the rules, the routine – but she seemed jolly and carefree. That morning, she'd dropped a fried egg on the floor. Scout had been sitting on the bin in the corner of the kitchen and saw her do it. 'Sod it. Floor's clean,' she'd said, 'can't believe it hasn't broken,' and she scooped it right back on the plate, and added a tomato garnish. Scout watched her put a tea towel over her wrist, just like Mrs Eastman specified, and carry the plate out and put it in front of the woman from Bedroom Six.

'Swear to God, half of them aren't on holiday, they've been secretly taxidermied,' Joanie said in bed at night. 'I'm going to spice up that dining-room, just watch me.'

She was cultivating some kind of sashaying walk. 'I am a Turkish belly dancer,' she said to Scout, swaying her tummy and holding up a plate of two sausages, a fried tomato and white bread toast. She was also adding her own little touches to the menu. When guests asked for eggs, she didn't just say poached, fried, scrambled or boiled. If they said fried, she'd ask, 'And how would you like it? Sunny side up? Over easy?' ('Like in an American diner,' she told Scout. 'In my head, I'm working in San Francisco, and my diner looks out over the bay.' Scout thought this demonstrated some imagination.) Scout also thought perhaps Joanie's Pink Flame lipsticked mouth at breakfast made some of the guests uncomfortable, especially when she pouted at the end of reading out the menu choices. The guests were very mild in comparison. They owned things like matching walking boots which they put neatly and helpfully on the rack labelled *Outdoor shoes* in the hallway, and they had rain jackets which folded into small Velcroed pouches which they put on the breakfast table, ready to take out with them for the day.

'Tomato saucy,' Joanie said, as she carried bottles out on a tray, pushing open the swing door from the kitchen with her bum. Scout looked beyond her and watched Mrs Eastman on guard at the reception desk in the hallway. Joanie's wiggling would get short shrift if it came to her attention.

Now, Scout picked up her hopscotch stone and sat down on the wall. She looked over her shoulder at the net curtains of the ground-floor room. Mrs Eastman went in there sometimes. It was just beyond her glass-topped reception desk, with its small silver bell and a vase with four pink carnations. The carnations practically stood to attention. Mrs Eastman would open the door just a sliver and slot herself in, like an envelope. Scout thought she had heard voices, possibly even music, but nothing of which she could be certain. Joanie had never mentioned going in there. Scout was wondering whether to ask her if she had. It was the only door not to have shiny gold numbers on it. Somebody must be in there, or how did the curtains move?

Scout looked back from the house and out towards the sea. Her reading of the tourist information leaflets had taught her two things. First, that the stretch of houses along the sandbanks was known as Millionaires' Row; footballers lived there, apparently, and all kinds of celebrities. Scout didn't think they would be what Mr Groves called Grand. Probably no herbaceous borders, no vegetables grown under glass cloches. No Breakfast Room with kedgeree or eggs benedict served from silver holloware. Not a roller in an outhouse kept exclusively for the croquet lawn. Not the village fête held in the garden. Not a large area of the churchyard with ancestors going back for ages, the same names given over and over to each generation; the saddest graves for the boys lost in the Great War. The women in the Millionaires' Row houses probably had nail extensions and big shiny handbags. She couldn't imagine they knew how to tie and pin a stock. They didn't count as properly rich, not respectably rich. Mr Groves would confirm that.

The second thing she'd learned was that the island was called Brownsea. It was one of the last places in the country where red squirrels had not died out because of grey ones invading their territory. Scout had a residual fondness for red squirrels. When they had moved to Alice's house, she'd found old copies of *Squirrel Nutkin* and *Jemima Puddleduck*, and she had read them repeatedly. She liked the thought that Brownsea Island was a haven for red squirrels. She hoped appropriate checks and restrictions were in place to stop a grey one getting a foothold. Would that be someone's job, she wondered, making sure a grey squirrel didn't suddenly make a dash for it? Scout had to acknowledge these two pieces of learning didn't add up to much. She'd also found out that what she thought, on the first morning, was a castle on the island, was an old house which now belonged to John Lewis and was used for staff training purposes. She wasn't sure why she found this faintly disappointing. She'd always liked going to John Lewis.

It had been hard for her to be productive since they'd arrived in Poole. A little mental Maths hopscotching didn't add up to much. It was partly the bedroom, which did not have a table to write at, and partly the feeling that what was most important was keeping out of everyone's way. Being what Emily called super-quiet required a deal of concentration. Perhaps all she'd achieved was a GCSE in eating Calippos. *Specialist subject?* the host on Junior Mastermind would ask her. *Eating Calippos.* This would not make Mr Mohammed or Mrs Pearson-Smith proud. This did not count as being excellent.

Scout wondered if, instead of excellence, she could achieve a feeling of being completely invisible. She was working on it, and felt she was making significant inroads. When she crossed from the dining-room to Reception, she held her breath so as to disturb the air less. When she walked up the four flights of stairs she pressed herself to the banisters and minimised the space she took up. Along the landings she walked close to the walls, following their lines and curves until she felt she was absorbed into them. Was it possible to lose bone density, mass? She practised a new way of walking where she rolled her foot down like a length of dough, starting at her toes and rolling through to her heel. She made almost no sound; she felt like a small, silent cat. Mrs Eastman had rounded on her at the corner by Bedroom Four and said, 'Good God, child, are you moving on wheels?' Sometimes, she imagined she was some kind of maid, just as Mr Groves had described at Houghton Hall. She plumped for scullery maid, thinking that was probably the lowest point of entry. She imagined herself with an ash bucket and a broom, scurrying between rooms and scooping up ash, minding not to smudge her pinny, while the rooms' inhabitants ate breakfast below. She blanked out the fact that each of the bedroom fireplaces in Mrs Eastman's had been filled in, and had an ornamental bird in each grate to tally with the room name and door key fob. Sometimes, she felt, you just had to give your imagination free wing.

Now, as she slipped back inside the house, she paused by the unmarked door. It was open the tiniest fraction. It was tempting to put her eye to the crack. There was no one at the desk. She took the smallest step sideways.

'Come in if you want to,' said a voice. 'I know that you're there.'

Scout pushed the door slightly ajar.

Such a cramming of that room, such a filling with things. Full of things to be straightened, twitched, adjusted. Scout looked at the walls. There were theatre posters, faded leaflets, old photos of a women's dancing troupe, dressed here in trousers, there in tap shoes, here in satin and looking like great white birds. There were also paintings of angels – angels bewinged, in flowing robes, or holding a huge set of scales. There were statues of angels, made from plaster, coloured glass, and china. Cherubs held fat chins in their upturned palms. Angel hands reached out, angel necks tipped sympathetically as if listening to what might be said. A small cluster looked wounded, with chipped or broken wings.

The room smelled of parma violet sweets. Had someone been eating them? In a bowl on the left were some greying Mint Imperials. In an armchair in the middle sat a woman, looking straight back at her.

She looked like Judy, Mr Punch's wife. Her skin hung in powdered folds about her face. What was left of her hair grew tuftily upwards, showing the pink of her scalp. Her lips were painted bright red; the lipstick seeped into the wrinkles around her mouth, looking like a river and its tributaries. Her hands were weighed down with rings which winked from her fingers. Scout swallowed, and thought of making a dash for it but felt she was too far in.

'So, finally you are here. Would you like a Mint Imperial?'

'No, thank you.'

'Always important to offer. To show hospitality. Always important to emphasise that whatever you have, you'd share it, just in case.'

'In case of what?'

The woman gestured around her. 'You know, when angels come calling. Unannounced. *We should not forget to entertain strangers lest we entertain angels unawares.* That's the Bible.'

'But I'm not an angel.'

'You could be. They never announce themselves, just stand there, wings invisible, adding you up.'

'I'm definitely not an angel. I'm the housekeeper's daughter. I'm not adding anything up.'

'You add up when you're playing hopscotch. I've watched you doing it. How am I to know whether it's good deeds and bad deeds that you're counting? I shall not be found idling. I'm waiting for the Archangel Michael to put me in his scale pan and weigh up my deeds. I'll not be off guard, even if you do look suspiciously like a housekeeper's daughter. Do you leave any footprints? Angels don't leave any footprints. You certainly walk quietly. That might be a halfway house. I'm on the alert. You stand well. Do you dance?'

'No. I've never danced in my life. Mr Groves taught me posture, Mr Groves of Houghton Hall.'

'Well, I can show you a thing or two about dancing, if you want to come in here of an afternoon when you've finished with your business of the hopscotch. I can also tell you a little of the angels. And that will give me the leisure to decide whether you're an angel or not.'

She pushed herself up from her chair.

'I'm Gabriella Douce,' she said, 'I am Mrs Eastman's mother.'

She said it in a way that might expect a drum roll to follow.

Scout thought of Mrs Eastman saying *yairs, yairs* down the phone to her friend. It was hard to imagine her as a child, holding on to Gabriella Douce's ring-heavy hand.

Gabriella Douce gesticulated around the room at all the posters and photographs. 'Take a look, take a look.'

Scout inched towards the ones nearest to her. *Gabriella Douce and the Sunshine Girls at the Palladium. Gabriella Douce at the Wychwood. For only three nights!* A young woman stared out from the pictures, her hair fashioned in waves down the sides of her head, her eyes rimmed with black. Scout stepped back to the centre of the room.

'I was always the lead. In this song', she gestured to the record player, 'some of the girls just stood there with huge tulip-shaped hats on their heads, swaying from side to side. Like giant bloody lampshades they looked. No skill in that. I was always the one called to go tiptoeing, always sashaying left and right, lifting my skirt above my knee, sometimes higher, depending on the audience.'

She reached down and put on a record; a man's voice creaked out into the room. 'Nick Lucas, nineteen forty-four,' she said, and lifted her arms to meet above her head, and pointed one foot in front of her like a ballet dancer. The voice sang . . .

Come tiptoe to the window, By the window that is where I'll be, Come tiptoe through the tulips with me. Oh tiptoe from your pillow to the shadow of a willow tree, And tiptoe through the tulips with me . . .

Like a mechanical figure plucked from a music box, Gabriella Douce began to dance, steadily lifting her feet which were shod in pink fur-trimmed tweed slippers, and holding her skirt in one hand, revealing her bony knees. She turned around and around, her mouth peeled wide and sustained in a smile. Scout reminded herself to breathe. Four times Gabriella danced round the room, with Scout standing by her chair. After the fourth time, she said, 'Now it's time for my rest. If you'd like to come back tomorrow, I'll tell you about Tobias and the Angel. And I'll dance for you again. You could learn something.'

She sat slowly back in her chair, and fell abruptly asleep. Her red mouth snagged to one side, beaded with a small glisten of spit.

Scout stood in the middle of the room, her fingertips pressed to her lips. She pricked up her ears to check if she could hear Mrs Eastman by the desk. From the centre of the room she could see above the net curtains to where she had been playing hopscotch. Gabriella Douce had a bird's eye view. Scout shifted from one foot to the other.

Entering this room had been difficult, but leaving it could present problems. She plumped for stepping sideways, crab-like, towards the door. She could not explain why this felt appropriate. Mrs Eastman's mother was snoring softly, holding a ridge of her cardigan in her balled-up hand.

Listening to confirm that it was silent beyond the room, Scout scooted into the hallway, and shot up the stairs, sucking in great lungfuls of air. She rubbed her palms against her cheeks. It felt like cobwebs were stuck to them. She sat on the edge of her camp bed, her knees tucked up to her chest. Gabriella Douce was quite unexpected. Scout couldn't decide whether she was frightening or intriguing. She was certainly unusual. Perhaps she'd be a good way to fill up some time.

Scout pictured her slumbering in her armchair three floors below. Perhaps she danced by herself, every afternoon, surrounded by her photos and all that host of angels, waiting for her own angel to come and count up her good deeds. She thought of Mr Groves, alone in his flat, polishing his cutlery, his shoes, his brasses. Perhaps a great deal was lost during a life. Old people tucked up in small rooms by themselves. There probably weren't enough ten-year-old, curious, own-learning girls to go round.

23

Joanie had sneaked out to an internet café while Scout was listening to the radio in their room. Location Order, Location Order was buzzing around her head. It ambushed her when she changed beds, poached eggs, cleaned a loo. She'd decided to Google it. Perhaps this was one of the rare occasions when knowledge would be power. Not exactly, she'd concluded, when she was walking back to Calm Views. Googling the definition of a Location Order hadn't been as productive as she had hoped. The first three definitions had been detailed, but were on Australian websites. The law probably wasn't the same. They certainly weren't to be banked on. All that she'd achieved was being distracted by the thought of Bondi Beach and the affirmation that, in comparison, Calm Views in Poole really sucked. Location Order had also taken her to the directgov site. Of this she had been hopeful. In the event, clicking on it pulled up ticket touting, speed limits, picketing and picket lines. There was evidently no connection. Joanie was beginning to hope a Location Order was such a dusty, insignificant piece of the law that, like a net little used, it was full of holes and no good at catching anything. She might just elude it. She was returning to the house no wiser than when she left. It probably wasn't a good move to think that just because she'd failed to find any information, a Location Order didn't have teeth.

What was starting to bother her each night before she fell asleep – admittedly not for long as Mrs Eastman's cleaning specifications were leaving her wiped out – was what she might call a different level of criminal behaviour. Joanie had totted up what she might call her dodgy behaviour thus far. A little shop-lifting as a teenager – a few mascaras, nothing significant. Some joints smoked, some ecstasy taken. A car not properly insured for a couple of months. A little bit of an understatement on the amount earned for a couple of years when she was filing her own income tax returns. Nothing that she thought counted as something majorly, criminally bad. Until this, which might be.

Part of her wished she hadn't put the letter in the toaster. She'd hoped to demonstrate to Scout that it was of no significance to them. Scout's little face had looked like wax when she handed it over. Joanie had hoped that the sight of it burning might take away her anxiety. Instead, the kitchen had been filled with smoke, and Scout had scrambled to open the window, and panicked about setting off the fire alarm. That hadn't gone according to plan. Joanie had tried to remember the wording of the letter so many times that she thought she'd probably created a version of her own, something that probably wasn't as exact, as clear as the original. *Criminal offence.* It definitely said it would be a criminal offence. But of what sort of magnitude?

Scout was her child, for God's sake. She tried to locate her inner sass. Since she'd been in Poole, she'd nearly killed herself trying to make Scout think everything was going swimmingly. She had been so unremittingly cheerful, she'd practically given herself toothache. Why should some stupid clinic, some Social Services team, some man she hadn't seen for years and didn't even know, presume to tell her what to do? She felt a stirring of resistance. *Sod it,* she thought, as she came into the guest house, *don't let them get to you.* Or at least not tonight. She was going out tonight. She'd order a lime margarita. She'd concentrate on some fabulous kissing. Perhaps she'd have another go at Googling tomorrow. Another route might turn something up. She'd prime Scout a little too, when the opportunity arose. Prep her to make sure she gave nothing away, nothing that could come back to bite them. Opaque; she'd teach her to be opaque. That way, if anybody asked her a question it would slide right off her. She looked at her watch and went quickly up the stairs. On the second landing, she passed Mrs Eastman, coming down.

'Back stairs, please, Mrs Simpson,' she said. 'And not three at a time.'

'Sorry, keep forgetting.'

'And now that you're settled in I do need to talk to you about financial details: National Insurance number, tax code, et cetera. I do pride myself on keeping a nice tidy accounts book. Also, some prior details: previous address, previous employers, et cetera. When you have a moment.'

Joanie nodded, and rolled her eyes when Mrs Eastman had gone past. She'd avoid all that business – if she did ask her in the next couple of days – by saying that she was self-employed. No need for any transfer of details – she'd tell her she took care of her own National Insurance and tax liabilities. Cash in hand; she'd get her to keep paying cash in hand. No paper trails. Invisibly one step ahead. God, it was exhausting. All this effort expended in seeking not to be found.

She started getting ready to go out. One of the benefits of this petty place was that she could go out at night with a carefree conscience. Not that she'd told Mrs Eastman she was going out, or asked her, casually, if she'd be prepared to keep an eye on Scout. Joanie felt confident she was leaving Scout in a safe environment. If the building burned down there would be a strategy to hand, one which probably involved Mrs Eastman in a bri-nylon nightie, blowing a whistle, and shouting at sleepy guests; Scout could be relied upon to tag along. Anyway, Scout didn't seem to mind her going out. That was always the best indicator. She would soon be asleep. Joanie dabbed her fingers along her jaw line, making sure her foundation had no visible rim.

Scout was lying on the bed reading aloud from the *Rough Guide to Paris*.

'You can take a trip to the sewers. You can actually walk along the sewage pipes. And by Notre Dame there's a church called Sainte-Chapelle. Apparently, the stained glass windows are made of such jewelled colours that when the sun shines through them it's like butterflies dancing on your skin.'

'Really? That sounds pretty. Not the sewers, obviously.'

Joanie had always privately wondered if guide books didn't over-egg the pudding a little. She'd lost count of the times she had traipsed up to some monument, lyrical descriptor in hand, sandal straps cutting into one or both of her feet, to find a shambling pile of stones, or something infinitely more faded and peeling than the image in the book. Once, on a tour in Pompeii when she was in her mid-twenties, the guide, Signor Carmine (why should she still remember his name?) had walked right over a mosaic. Just like that, with nonchalant shoe soles. *Should we also walk on it?* asked a well-meaning Texan woman. Signor Carmine had shrugged. *We have so many,* he said. Perhaps that was the better attitude.

Scout, anyway, seemed motivated at the prospect of butterflies on her skin. 'Apparently,' she continued, 'there is a plainer chapel downstairs which was used by the servants, and upstairs, with the glass, was for the aristocrats.' Upstairs, downstairs, Joanie thought. Always some nicely made distinctions. Scout had been using the word *apparently* since she was very small. Where had she got it from? Joanie herself never used it. Perhaps it revealed a tendency to doubt the reliability of what was said. Joanie hoped that wasn't learned behaviour.

Joanie pulled on a turquoise lycra dress. She tugged it over her tummy and smoothed the fabric over her hips. 'With belt or without?' she asked Scout, cinching a belt at her waist. Scout put down the book and paid her the courtesy of looking.

'Not quick enough,' Joanie said. 'Already decided. I look like the Pilsbury Dough Boy.'

She pulled off the dress, and put on some leggings and a long top. Much better, she thought; they also allowed her to sit casually cross-legged on the beach, channelling a little free spirit vibe, rather than having to sit with her legs out front, poker straight, drawing attention to her ankles which increasingly she felt did not stand up to close scrutiny.

She'd met Dave in a pub. Perhaps she might try and start calling him David. It had so much more presence, and also there was no way to say Dave without sounding a little gormless. He was a boat builder. She had been practising tripping that sentence off her tongue while cleaning the fat-spattered oven. *David's a boat builder. Yes, he's a boat builder.* Joanie liked summations that were instantly evocative. Even saying it – while scrubbing round the rings with a Brillo pad – conjured up someone solitary, soulful, and at one with his surroundings, planing beautiful, bleached-out, seasoned oak, perhaps on a beach somewhere, gulls wheeling overhead, the lines of the boat shaped by the sea's soothing sound. Quite lovely. The reality, she knew, from a quick, sneaky glimpse into his workplace was different. He worked for Sunseekers, making vast boats for rich men. Not much solitary oak-planing going on inside there – it looked more like the BMW plant where she'd worked for a short time in Oxford. Dave had initially entertained her with his accounts of luxurious specifications. Couches covered in cashmere, tables made of glossy walnut, speakers which piped out music underwater (*for when swimming off the boat,* he explained, *so that you can continue listening*). 'It started with Aristotle Onassis,' he told her, 'the bar stools on his yacht were made from the foreskins of whales.' Joanie wasn't sure if this was apocryphal. It sounded gross to her; to be perched on a white leather bar stool that was in fact a whale's foreskin. She couldn't see Jackie Onassis comfortable with that, with her pearls and her big sunglasses and her deck shoes and all those chic little jackets.

Joanie suspected she might tire of listening to the inventiveness which catered for rich men's tastes. Dave went on a bit. There seemed no end to his appetite for recounting bespoke options. On the plus side, he was an unbelievable kisser. Scout was still talking. 'Mmm, really?' Joanie answered, aware that she had been told something but having no idea what it was. On those occasions, you just had to cross your fingers it wasn't something significant.

Joanie kissed Scout goodnight before putting on her lipstick. Scout smelled of the peach soap-on-a-rope Joanie had found at the back of a cupboard. (It must have been there years; what was the harm in a little re-gifting?) Perhaps good mothering consisted of listening all the time. Were there women who actually listened to *everything* their children said, who weren't mentally elsewhere, musing, following their own line of thought? It was so easy to get distracted. The way children's minds worked, Joanie thought, in reality you could never be off your guard. Just when you thought they were rambling about flapjacks or red shoes, they could throw in something which needed action, like a bloke had flashed them on the way home from school. Scout had never had this happen. Joanie was confident she would know. She had hoped that Poole might be a little less solitary for Scout. She'd had high hopes of the two girls who hung about outside after school. Scout had seemed to swim at their edges, just into their view, and now nothing, no sign of any budding friendship at all. Joanie hoped her disinclination for friendships with her own sex could not be genetically transmitted. At a parents' evening two years ago, having listened, blah blah, to how clever and motivated Scout was, Joanie had leaned forward and asked the teacher, with what she hoped was uncommon spirited eloquence, 'But does she have a talent for friendship? This is what I am more interested in.' The teacher looked back at her calmly. 'No more or no less,' she had said, 'than any other child of eight.'

She certainly had a talent for not complaining. At this she was awesome. Joanie produced a packet of chocolate raisins as she left the room. 'Oh, thank you,' said Scout.

'Remember to clean your teeth,' said Joanie. As she said it, she could have bitten her tongue. Stupid to re-awaken any anxiety as to dental provision.

She got to the bench where she was meeting Dave. She sat down, lit a cigarette and looked out over the water. Was that a cruise ship she could see ploughing its way to Southampton? So many rows of windows and lights; it signalled so much internal activity. When Joanie thought of all the dross jobs she'd been doing, she reflected she could just as well be doing them on a cruise liner. Then at least she'd get to feel part of the outside world, rather than stashed away like some mad old gal in Mrs Eastman's attic. Joanie had never been on a boat as vast as a cruise ship. Lying in a bunk on what she was sure were probably the most lowly decks kept for the crew, it must be like being cocooned in the belly of a slowly swimming, purposeful whale. Much more to her taste, she thought, than sitting on its pale, soft foreskin.

24

Joanie was cleaning the kitchen floor. She had a Vileda mop and a red plastic bucket with a built-in wringer. It was apparent that each new swoosh of the mop was mostly redistributing the dirty water squeezed out the moment before. The floor didn't look any different.

Alice couldn't abide mops. She felt the only way to clean a floor was on your hands and knees with a scrubbing brush. She'd actually died doing it. Joanie thought there was perhaps something heroic and fitting about this: to die doing something for which you'd always made a case. The valour in a properly cleaned floor. Alice had two old towels she used to tie round her knees to reduce the impact of kneeling. She'd answer the door sometimes forgetting that she had them on. When her heart wheezed to a stop one morning, it was only a neighbour, coming round the back when she failed to answer the front door, who was sharp-eyed enough to spot Alice's outstretched arm, scrubbing brush still clasped, her body spread-eagled between the fridge and the cooker. The ambulance men had trodden across her spotless floor to get her on to a stretcher. That wouldn't have pleased her. Neither would turning up at the hospital with her knee towels still tied on, but Joanie rationalised that the point of death was a pretty reasonable moment to relinquish control. She arrived at Alice's house when it was all over and couldn't help but notice one of the ambulance men's boot prints next to the pedal bin. She'd wiped it away with a bit of kitchen roll. She'd hoped Alice would see it as a fitting tribute, despite it not requiring much elbow grease or endeavour. She liked to think that the fact that she knew it would matter should be credit enough. So, mopping the floor always put her in mind of her mother. Mostly, in imagining Alice rootling in the corner, teeth gritted, making sure the wainscot was perfectly clean, whereas Joanie just gave it a bit of a lethargic swoosh with her Vileda.

Mrs Eastman cleared her throat to signal she was behind her. 'Mrs Simpson?' Joanie turned. She was letting the Mrs remain uncorrected. She suspected Calm Views may have been less than comfortable with any alternative.

'Mrs Simpson, a moment?' Mrs Eastman had a notebook in her hand. 'As I said yesterday, I'm just keen to confirm a few details, so that all my records are straight. Do you have your National Insurance number and your tax code, and then I can put you on my P.A.Y.E. system?'

'Oh, you won't need any of that. I'm self-employed. If you have more than five employers in the course of a year, which I've had, obviously, then you take care of your tax affairs yourself. I have my own book-keeper, I tell her all the details, and she files my tax return each spring. You don't have to worry about me. Cash in hand is fine. I can write you a note to confirm I'm self-employed; that's all you need to show your tax office, should they ever enquire about who you are paying.'

'What about a previous employer, a previous address, something I can note down which isn't just the here and now?'

'No, not really, because we've lived in hostels, caravan sites, all kinds of places so it's not possible to chase those up. And, the last three months I worked as a live-in for a lovely old lady suffering from dementia. She had to be taken into a home when I left, could hardly remember her own name let alone mine. She would be of no use to you, and it would be unkind to trouble her in a nursing home.'

'So you're telling me there's nothing you can give me, nothing I can write down in a formal way?'

'Sorry. Nope. That's the way it is.'

'Well, I'm not so sure. It could be construed as a little fishy. Perhaps as having something to hide. It's very unusual that you have nothing to offer up at all.'

'Well, Mrs Eastman, you could either dwell on the unusualness of that, or the difficulty of finding someone to replace me at short notice just at the start of high season should you find my terms of engagement, at you say, fishy. I assure you I have nothing to hide. Just a clear boundary as to where your business stops and mine begins.'

Mrs Eastman tapped her pencil on the cover of her book. She pursed her lips and turned on her heel.

'Bedroom Four's bathroom needs a good going over this morning.'

Joanie tipped her bucket into the sink, went to the back door and lit a cigarette. She bent her knee so that the sole of her foot was pressed to the rendered wall behind her, and blew her cigarette smoke up towards the drainpipe. She'd read once about Catholic acts of devotion; God knows why she'd been reading that. It must have been in a waiting-room somewhere. Three sisters, to show their dedication to their particular saint, had gradually bricked themselves up in an ante-room of their church, until there was no opening available to pass them food or water. Years later, the parishioners had knocked down the wall and given the bones martyrs' burials. Joanie had been less interested in the women's religious fervour than in whether the sisters had squabbled, as it got hotter, more airless, as their thirst and hunger increased. Perhaps they'd turned into three spindly crabs, waving their arms like pincers at each other and gasping for air. The stench must have been appalling. The image had remained with her. She couldn't think of anything worse than bricking yourself in, reducing the space around you, until you obscured your ability to see anything at all. On reflection, maybe that's what she was doing this summer, not in a way that would starve her, or cause her to suffocate, but to feel surrounded anyway, by a neatly mortared wall of her own deceptions, each one smoothly bonded to the one that preceded it, until all that she could see, all that she could think of before she opened her mouth, was the amalgam of lies told, bricking her in.

A piece of tobacco seemed to have worked its way free of her cigarette. She spat with conviction into the drain cover. Other people's questions. Other people's agendas. Other people's dirty bloody bathrooms. She went back inside to the cleaning products cupboard, took out some Cif and some Domestos and went up to Bedroom Four.

25

Gabriella Douce would have triumphed if her Mastermind subject had been Angels. It turned out that Tobias was helped by the Archangel Raphael. Tobias's father was blind, and Tobias helped to heal him. Raphael told him to mix the heart, liver and gall from a fish into an ointment and dab it on his father's sightless eyes.

'Miraculous,' Gabriella Douce said, 'bloody miraculous. Twenty-twenty vision.' Also, she told Scout, there were two angels at opposite ends of the earth. They threw wicked souls back and forth, causing them to wander ceaselessly. This wasn't a happy thought. Scout looked for consolation at the glass angel beside her. He didn't look capable of making someone wander ceaselessly.

Gabriella was persistent in her determination to see Scout as an angel. 'No tread marks in the carpet,' she said triumphantly as Scout got up from the footstool and walked to the door. 'No footprints. See, perhaps you're starting to give yourself away.'

Scout pressed down with her heels. If the carpet hadn't been so bald there would be a chance of making an impression.

Later that night, when Joanie had gone out again, Scout lay in bed trying to sleep. Gabriella Douce's angels were beginning to trouble her. Not the angels themselves, but what they snowballed into. First of all, Tobias, off finding a fish to heal his blind father's eyes. That had made her think of illness and

Joanie. What if something happened to Joanie? What if she
was suddenly ill or struck down? The Archangel Raphael
wouldn't turn up with a solution, still less a magic recipe for
ointment. This realisation caused her to squirm a little into her
pillow. Who could she ask? Who would be of help? She
couldn't see Mrs Eastman storming to the rescue.

Secondly, she was anxious about Gabriella Douce's hope of
her being an angel. This was definitely ridiculous, and not a
concern in itself, but its ripples bothered her. Generally, when
adults wanted you to be something, hoped you were some
kind of solution, it was a ticket to nowhere. Expectations
dashed, even if you'd never raised them. Gabriella refused to
call her by her name; she hadn't even asked it. 'Angels have no
names,' she said, and seemed determined not to allow her one.
She called her Hopscotch Girl when she wanted to attract her
attention. Gabriella Douce's pinned hopes gave Scout a pain
in her chest.

Thirdly, the image of the Archangel Michael and his scale
pan was giving her additional discomfort. There was a large
painting of him over Gabriella's chair. Michael was vast and
golden. His wings were studded with all-seeing eyes. Next to
him stood a human being, forlorn and stooped, and in the two
pans of the scales were heaped their good and bad deeds.
Gabriella assured her that this was what would happen on
Judgement Day. Scout thought back to the letter in the toaster.
All her anxieties kept trickling back to that. It must be something bad that Joanie wasn't admitting to. Perhaps it was there,
ready to hop into the scale pan. Maybe it was sitting there
already, hunched and scabby like a cross, old, toad.

She shifted in her bed. She felt like a camel with a hump full
of worry. A hump full of worry that was compounded by
knowledge of the angels.

She couldn't get to sleep. No matter how she lay, her arms
felt like they were jabbing into her body. She lay on her

stomach and bent them at the elbow and folded them across her chest. She was reminded of stubby, sprouting wings. She quickly dangled her arms from the sides of the bed and flexed her fingers into fans. Nothing resembling a wing. Perhaps now she could sleep.

Later, she heard Joanie coming up the stairs. She must have finished her Chinese with the boat builder quickly.

'Are you still awake?' Joanie said. 'I thought you'd be asleep hours ago.'

'I'm just thinking, you know, just thinking about some things.'

Joanie sat down on the side of the bed and started brushing her hair. Her face had a purposeful, decided look. Scout waited for what would come. Maybe she would say 'What things?' and she'd have to spill. Instead, Joanie said, 'Just thinking is mostly better than saying. And often, the less you say the easier things are.'

That was a surprise.

'I don't understand.'

'You know, if someone asks you a question, the less information you give them the less they have.'

'Have to what?'

'Have to use, I guess, however they want to.'

'But nobody asks me questions. Why would they?'

'Good. But it's a useful habit to acquire anyway. You know, keeping your cards close to your chest, giving nothing away.'

'How do you mean?'

'Well, for example, if anyone asked where we lived before this summer, instead of saying Moreton, Oxfordshire, just say in the Midlands. If anyone asks where I worked before, just say a big hotel and instead of saying Birmingham, say something that takes the conversation sideways like the fact that nobody ever managed to eat their way through the "Eat as much as you like" Sunday brunch.'

'Did anyone ever manage to eat their way through the Sunday brunch?'

'I don't know, I just made it up, but that's not the point, Scout. It's more interesting and memorable than saying Birmingham, as you just proved.'

'So, if anyone asks me a question you want me just to say something interesting and memorable?'

'Yes. I'm just asking you to create a diversion. I'm not asking you to lie, just to give nothing away.'

'Why?'

'I like us to be private. I want you to bat stuff right back. I don't want anybody knowing our business. Okay?'

Scout nodded. Now there would be interesting and memorable diversions to worry about, as well as not having the Archangel Raphael standing by should anything happen to Joanie. This on top of not being the secret angel Gabriella Douce wanted her to be, or anything else any adult as yet unknown might expect of her. Furthermore, Gabriella wanted her to leave no footmarks, which could only be disproven by stamping on the floor. Mrs Eastman wanted her to make no noise, no disturbance, which meant walking quietly. Just moving around was problematic, let alone opening her mouth and deciding what she was supposed to say. Scout was tempted to take a bite out of her pillow.

Joanie undressed and got into bed. She fell asleep really quickly. Scout reached over and touched her arm in the dark. No response. Now there were even more reasons not to get to sleep. She rubbed at her elbows.

When she finally fell asleep, it was by staring fixedly at a seagull on the Velux window. He kept his white wings pressed firmly to his sides, and for this she was grateful.

26

Ned sat in his parked car outside a tower block in Birmingham. This was where Scout had been located. Accidentally, it seemed, fortuitously, after a neighbour had reported to Social Services that a child was not going to school. Should he regard the coincidence as showing that finding her was meant to be? The thought would be consoling. He found himself more preoccupied with the question of whether he had chased Scout to here, or from here, or both. He reassured himself that the initial letter which had sparked Joan Simpson's flight from Oxford had been the one from the clinic's legal department, on which he had been merely copied. The letter she received here, however, had warned her of the Location Order he had sought. Apparently they had left the night she had received it. He didn't like to think of the detail of that. He looked around. He hated to think he had been the catalyst for any of this.

He peered upwards. What a godforsaken place. Grey, grimy, graffitied and litter-strewn. How had Scout passed her time here, especially as she hadn't gone to school? How could anyone shape a life productively, with all this to contend with?

A gang of youths walked past, carrying vodka and Red Bull. One of them casually, nonchalantly, gave him a V sign. There was something perversely magnanimous in the gesture: at least it acknowledged him, included him. And, the boy hadn't scratched a key down the length of his car. Beyond him, by the lift, was a gaggle of gum-chewing girls. One or two had babies in push-chairs. Most of them looked as if they were not long out of them themselves.

Pulling away from the kerb was a mobile library van. It didn't look as if it had been stampeded by readers. Ned remembered how his father used to take him and his brothers to the local library each Friday. He could see his library card, right now, still crystal clear, as if held in his palm. He'd loved the smell of the library, the cardboard slot inside each book to contain the return date card, the reassuring *whump* of the librarian's stamp as she marked the cards. *Ned's my bookish one*, his mother always said. She was proud of his reading. In the scramble of boys that was their household, she'd liked it that he often sat quietly, his nose in a book. Might Scout be bookish? Might such things be manifest even if no one had ever taken your child to a library? Would Joan Simpson have done that? Ned couldn't even begin to guess.

He got out of the car and walked into the communal garden. Garden was an over-ambitious title. He sat down on a bench, which was sprayed brightly with *Twat!*, and watched an old man making a painstaking round of the pathway in the late afternoon sun. He was a surprise. It looked as if he had been beamed into a context with which he had no connection. He wore a tweed jacket, a waistcoat. His brogues gleamed with polish. Ned was surprised a gang hadn't taken a pop at him. There was no sanctity to old age, particularly in places like this. Round the man walked, gingerly, carefully. He was frail, but not stooped. His posture was impressively good. His eyes were rheumy, milk-ringed, but clear in their gaze. He looked at Ned as he passed him, said 'Good afternoon' politely. Ned greeted him likewise. It was borderline absurd, a lesson in the unexpected, this dignified, immaculate man inching his way slowly past barren flower-beds.

Ned felt hungry. He had left straight after school and driven up the M40. He had not told Elisabetta where he was going. She would have offered to come with him. It was hard to admit, but he hadn't wanted her to come. Scout was half his, not hers. Any decision they made was mutual, but the complexity of physical connection, that was his and his alone. Perhaps that was why he was here, sitting by himself on a bench that said *Twat!* Dissolving residual guilt was his problem alone. He needed to make his own connection to Scout; to feel himself moving, however haphazardly, towards her.

Last week, he'd gone for a drink with John, an old friend. He'd told him. 'Here's the thing,' he'd said, and rattled it all off. John, to his credit, had taken a minute to absorb the detail.

'And?' he'd asked which, on reflection, Ned concluded was an even-handed way of allowing him to say what he felt.

'And I don't know how I'm supposed to react. I had a child with a stranger because the baby was supposed to be immediately ours; all trace of the actual mother gone at birth. It didn't seem such a huge factor at the time. Now I've got an eleven-year-old daughter who's been raised by a woman I know nothing of.'

'Maybe in the same way as if you'd slept with someone at university and they'd had a child and never told you.'

'But at least in that scenario, I'd have known her. There would have been some connection. It wouldn't have happened unless I'd liked her.'

'We all remember ourselves as more discriminating than we were. Don't tell me everyone you ever slept with was meaningful.'

'You have a point. Maybe. But now I'm supposed to be clear about what I hope to gain from trying to find her and I can't get my head past the initial process, or move on from a feeling that I might be hounding her, hunting her down. I don't know whether I'm being honourable, selfish or irresponsible.'

'So who's judging? What does it matter? From where I'm sitting, you don't look like the child-catcher in *Chitty Chitty Bang Bang*. If you find her, have contact with her, and build a relationship with her, you'll be offering her something good. You and Elisabetta can have clean consciences on that. Look what you've given Maia. And how can you be expected to know at this stage if you're hounding her, or rescuing her from a life less well lived? She might need your input in ways you can't imagine. You can't punish yourself for your lack of knowledge. The mother could have chosen not to lie in the first place or not to bolt earlier this year and then most of what's troubling you wouldn't be an issue.'

Ned was glad they'd talked. He could, however, have done without the picture of the child-catcher who now sat, top-hat cocked, alongside his own image of a snuffling bloodhound, ready to keep him awake at night, and worry about what he was doing.

He looked down at his feet. He scuffed the toes of his shoes in the soil. She had been here. She had lived here. His daughter. Something inside his chest stirred. Too fanciful, he thought, to think of it as emotion; love shaking itself down, ready for the off. But a stirring all the same, some kind of reaching toward, some sort of connection. His daughter had been here. She assumed an aspect of feisty courage and resourcefulness in his mind.

He looked across the garden and saw a corner shop at the base of the flats. A small child was looking through the slats of the venetian blind that covered part of the window. She looked younger than Maia. Ned approached the shop; she waved to him, and then ducked back down inside. He went in and bought some chocolate, and a can of coke. The man who served him lifted the child on to a little stool and retied her shoelace. In his pocket, Ned had a photo of Scout. It had been given to him by Susan Philips at lunch-time, along with a statement from her previous school. Ned toyed with the idea of taking out the photo and showing it to the shop owner. Perhaps she would have come in here – didn't all children buy chocolate, sweets? He could ask him *Did you ever see her, did she come in here, what was she like?* He felt himself pathetically grasping at straws, standing in a queue, holding coke and chocolate. Who was he kidding? In this kind of place there was probably little sense of community. Probably all manner of disparate inhabitants, trying to make a life behind multi-locked doors. Why should he presume that this man would even know Scout's face? He went back to the bench. The old chap had hobbled away. The bench seemed more desolate now he was alone. What had Elisabetta said? That even if they didn't find her, one day she might find out that they had tried. He had tried to become her father. There was good intent in that. The alternative was probably unjustifiable.

He looked at the photo. There was something earnest in her expression. Her face had a thin, slightly old-fashioned quality. Her head was tipped to one side, like a little bird. Her hair was brown, perhaps auburn? Her eyes looked blue-green but perhaps this was the effect of the blue background. Why did schools always choose a fake sky as a backdrop for photos? She had the slightest suggestion of freckles. Her hair was worn in plaits. He wondered if she did this each day or just especially for the photo. One of the plaits was wonky, and lay crooked on her shoulder. Her school uniform looked clean. She was sitting self-consciously upright. Her two front teeth weren't quite through, almost but not quite. She seemed to hold her top lip in a way that was sensitive to the fact. He looked at her face. What was he looking for, what did he expect to see? His own genes writ large, some confirmation that she was his? From what he could remember, she didn't look like her mother and she didn't look like him. His lost child; that was what he found himself calling her. Lost mostly to him, even though she was lost in a way that differed from his first understanding, all those years ago.

In the statement, Scout's teacher had written *I was very sad about Scout's abrupt departure. She was a very valued member of our class.* Bright, she called her. Inquisitive. Motivated. Conscientious, she said, and always diplomatic.

Ned thought diplomatic was an unusual word to describe a child of almost eleven. Should he be worried about that? Was diplomacy, he wondered, a skill she had had to learn?

27

Scout felt, two weeks later, as if she had been tiptoeing through the tulips for miles. Gabriella Douce's lipstick was still compelling. She began each day with a mouth painted as neatly as a china doll's but, by bedtime, it had migrated in spidery lines to her nose and chin. Her hands seemed too trembly to paint it on herself. Did Mrs Eastman pop in and apply it first thing? Perhaps that was what being a good daughter eventually came down to. Scout could imagine Joanie still being keen on her make-up however old she got. She didn't expect she'd want to dance around a room repeatedly to the same song, but she was confident her mother would think of something to keep herself happy. Scout didn't think Joanie would run short of ideas.

At Calm Views, there was never any mention of a Mr Douce or a Mr Eastman; no photo of Mr Douce amongst all the angels and showgirls. No suggestion of fathers or husbands. Only mothers and daughters. The parallel to her own life made her feel a little uncomfortable. All the men were invisible, completely lopped off; no explanation given. Maybe, she thought encouragingly, in Mrs Eastman's rooms, there might be a memento of Mr Eastman. A photo from their wedding day or sitting on the beach? He'd be wearing one of those jumpers which did not have any sleeves. Perhaps, also, grease on his hair to make it slick backwards. Scout found herself quite partial to the image she'd created of him. She rustled him up a job. He could sail the ferry to Brownsea Island, and have a machine which printed and clipped tickets, like a conductor on an old bus.

Alternatively, in Mrs Eastman's rooms, perhaps there was no evidence of his existence at all. Maybe he was as lopped off as Mr Douce and her own dad. Totally invisible. When Scout had hypothesised about his whereabouts, Joanie said, 'Probably buggered off years ago. Wouldn't you, faced with waking up to her each day?' Scout wondered why the buggering-off option was Joanie's most easily reached for conclusion. She positively zoomed to it. Perhaps it was influenced by her own experiences. Perhaps that's what Scout's dad had done. That would explain why Joanie seemed to think most men were bolters.

Scout was working on building routine into her days. She would wake just before Joanie, in time to see her mother whack the alarm clock to stop its beeping. Downstairs, she would sit in a corner of the kitchen while Joanie made the breakfasts. She would eat peanut butter on toast, and then help stack plates in the dishwasher, or nip into the dining-room if Joanie had forgotten to put out ketchup or marmalade. 'Two for the price of one,' Joanie said. Scout wasn't sure Mrs Eastman saw it this way. She'd checked Joanie was buying bread herself for Scout's toast in the morning. 'I've got enough trouble making ends meet without extra mouths to feed.'

When Joanie started cleaning the bedrooms, Scout went back to their room and listened to the radio. Radio Four, she decided, was absolutely the station for own-learners. This week, she'd learned that bees in America were transported in great lorries from the east coast to the west, to pollinate the flowers of cranberries and blueberries, and then the flowers of oranges, lemons, and grapefruit. No wonder they were called worker bees. But, disastrously, they'd been fed corn syrup, not fructose, which was cheaper but not as nourishing. This was why they had become infected with a virus which was killing them.

Scout wondered if learning was always like this. The first
bite you took out of a subject was so uplifting, so surprising
– imagine, all those vast containers of bees on the highway –
but then the further along you got, there was always something
sad or disappointing. Each surface you scratched had something beneath you'd rather not know. Now, instead of seeing
the bees zipping between destinations, stuffed with cranberry
pollen and looking forward to orange blossom, she saw them
being force-fed cheap corn syrup and getting sick and dying.
It was another thing to fret about. Perhaps Mrs Pearson-
Smith had been intending to lay that one on them in the
summer term. The environmental collapse of the rainforest
would have been topped by the catastrophe of nothing being
pollinated. Surely Nicola Tate wouldn't be sitting through that
still saying *Boring, boring, I'm dying of boring?*

When she'd had enough of listening to the radio, she would
creep down the stairs and go outside. Her invisibility walk was
now what Mr Groves would have called top-notch, first-rate.
She had not compromised posture, she had just upped its
elasticity. She felt she descended the stairs with the fluidity of
a Slinky. She had also mastered opening and closing the front
door without it making a single creak. If there *had* been a cat
flap, she was confident she'd have worked out how to get
through that silently too. It was only the twitch of the net
curtain which told her Gabriella Douce could be relied upon
to be watching.

She'd walk along the front for a while, and sit and look at
the sea, challenging herself to find the right word to describe
its colour. Blue, green, slate-grey; they didn't even begin to
touch upon the possibilities. Without wishing to complain –
she was sure that geographically it must have taken millions of
years to produce – she wished that the outlook at Poole was a
little wilder, a little more rough-hewn. Given a chance, she'd
have thrown in some cliffs, some steep, narrow paths, some

nooks and crannies with hidden bays at their feet, some sheer, dizzying drops, some massive, craggy rock faces. And more kinds of birds, some really big, high-wheeling ones, not just the pesky seagulls who had grown fat on sandwiches and chips. It was too flat and smooth, she had decided. The benefit of this was that it looked like it couldn't possibly rear up and make a tsunami. One less thing to worry about, she consoled herself, warming to its basin-like appearance.

Sometimes, she watched the cars queuing to get on to the ferries. There had been families last week – half-term, she guessed – and there were cars crammed with duvets, and food, and shoes squashed against the back window. Some of the children stared back at her, looking up from their game boys and their portable DVD players. She liked thinking about where they all might be going. One day, she spooked herself thinking someone might open a car door, scoop her up and kidnap her to France. She did some practice escape running, abandoning all the invisible and silent constraints. She arrived back at the B&B, cheeks scarlet, heart pounding, but reassured she was speedy. If a car door opened and someone reached out for her, she'd be off like Usain Bolt.

Most days, when she'd eaten her packed lunch (this week she was favouring bread and butter and a hard-boiled egg with a sprinkling of salt – she didn't like to ask Joanie whether the egg was theirs or Mrs Eastman's) she'd go back to *Calm Views* and play a little mental Maths hopscotch on the pavement. The problem was she was beginning to know the answer to all the permutations of hops. To get round this, she'd started playing it backwards, but she felt this was fudging it as it was only the same sum in reverse. When the net curtains twitched twice, she knew it was time to see Gabriella.

Gabriella Douce wasn't building into quite what Scout hoped for. She wasn't an uplifting distraction; not cosy company like Mr Groves or teaching her something properly like Mr Mohammed. The angel stories were making her feel uneasy. Gabriella said that every blade of grass had an angel hovering over it saying 'Grow! Grow!' This initially sounded appealing; Scout liked the idea of nothing being too small to escape encouraging attention. Then, when she considered it further, she thought 'Grow! Grow!' could be said in a variety of tones. There was a possibility it could be barked as an order. Bossed about, terrified grass wasn't quite as appealing.

Gabriella also told her about Yode'a, the Angel of Losses. She said he watched lives unfold, recording each detail before it faded. She said he had servants, and his servants had servants, and each one of them carried a shovel, and they spent all their time digging, searching for losses. She showed Scout a picture of him, with a huge shovel, and enormous great hands like a gardener. When Scout went for a walk afterwards, she couldn't escape the feeling that someone was behind her, digging softly but diligently. She imagined she heard the sound of spade steel against soil, the clink as the blade hit a stone. She didn't like the idea of life being a series of losses. Or of losses being buried in soil, growing cold and damp, and being wriggled through by worms. She didn't want to think about what she might have lost, and what might be beneath her feet, being recorded by angels. She kept trying to focus on the fat cherubs who sat next to Gabriella's armchair. They looked as if they'd mostly concentrate on cake.

She was also unsettled by the table of broken angels. They had chipped wings, or whole ones broken off. Gabriella said if an angel committed a sin, it was banished from Heaven. It became a fallen angel, and demons in hell ripped out its wings. Fallen angels, she said, were ones who had lost their way. Scout ran her finger over the broken stubs. She imagined white feathers tumbling, quills scattered around angels' feet. So much losing, so many lost ways. She was beginning to think about not coming to Gabriella's room any more, but was spooked by the thought that Gabriella might dance slowly upstairs and find her.

She was relieved, therefore, each afternoon, when it was time for the tulips. At least she could stop listening and all she had to do was clap. Gabriella tiptoed through the tulips five or six times, one day accessorising what was left of her hair with a large diamanté pin, another day exchanging her slippers for a pair of grey satin high heels with bows.

The song was perplexing too. Was the singing man to be trusted? While silver stars were gleaming, he was *scheming, scheming to get you here my dear.* This didn't sound very honourable. Gabriella Douce didn't seem preoccupied by the moral difficulties of this. Mostly, she would sing along, or be mean about the other women in her dance troupe. 'Carmen Lafite,' she said, 'legs like tree-trunks, no turn on her ankle; Jolene Dubarry, the fluidity of a wooden spoon.'

'Were those their real names?'

'Of course not. Nancy Barber, Maud Coles, Eileen Scott. We all came down from Bolton together.'

Scout decided it would be better not to ask if she had begun life as something other than Gabriella.

Today, Gabriella wore a peacock-blue feather behind her ear. She'd also put on what seemed to be a garter, just above her knee. When she lifted her skirt (which was prompted by *Knee deep, in flowers we'll stray*) there was a flash of ruffled sugar-pink ribbon. As she did so, she managed her widest possible smile. Scout couldn't help feeling it looked as if her face had cracked open like an egg. At the end of the song, Scout clapped enthusiastically. Mrs Eastman's mother particularly relished the clapping part. She would perform a low, swooping curtsy, and extend her arm to Scout, and make gracious nodding gestures with her head tipped to the left. On the days she was wearing the diamanté hairpin, it caught light from the pendant fitting, and winked at Scout. Scout clapped until her hands were red. There was no end to Gabriella Douce's appetite for clapping.

Scout reflected afterwards that it was probably the vigour of her clapping which had masked the sound of Mrs Eastman entering the room. Now, as she turned to face her, Mrs Eastman was standing with her hands on her hips, her face in its beakiest severest form, shouting, '*WHO SAID YOU COULD COME IN HERE?*'

Behind her, Scout sensed Gabriella had flumped down into her armchair. The peacock-blue feather fluttered down to land by Scout's foot. Gabriella appeared to be scrabbling to remove the garter. Scout's lips reached for words, but her mouth remained stubbornly all air.

'Cat got your tongue?' accused Mrs Eastman. 'We will never speak of this again. Out of here, NOW!'

Scout flew up the stairs. She was glad she had practised being Usain Bolt. As she reached their room, she reflected on the expression *Has the cat got your tongue?* Wasn't that what Mrs Eastman had said? It seemed a peculiar thing for a cat ever to have tried to do.

Later, Joanie came into the bedroom, shaking her hair from her scrunchie and removing her apron.

'What's up?' she said, sitting down beside her.

Scout wondered where to begin. She described the room, Gabriella Douce, the angels, the dancing, the repeated tune, and Mrs Eastman's fury. Joanie's response was not what she expected.

'Show me the dance,' Joanie asked, 'show me what she does.'

Assuming the same split-faced smile, and with each gesture committed to memory, Scout danced in the small space between the beds, singing in a quavering voice.

Joanie paused for a second before starting to laugh. 'Encore! Encore!' she cheered, doubled over at the sight of Scout dancing and singing like a small, poised, arthritic crow. When

Joanie filled the room with her round, warm, full-bellied laugh, Scout felt so safe, so sure of where she stood. Nothing seemed strange or startling or worth getting into a tizz over. Scout laughed too. The memory of Mrs Eastman's face dissolved. Scout started singing again, and put some extra va-voom into her twirl.

28

A week later, Joanie was doing some tiptoeing of her own. 'Ssshh!' she whispered to Dave, as he followed her up the stairs, both of them clutching their shoes. Joanie suspected she was a little bit pissed. Mrs Eastman would kill her if she caught her. NO OVERNIGHT GUESTS. She'd printed that, in block capitals, very clearly at the top of her contract. Joanie stumbled and nearly dropped one of her shoes. Dave appeared to be holding one of his between his teeth. His free hand seemed to have found its way to her bum. 'Shhh!' she said again, although she had to admit his caressing hand was impressively silent. They were going past Bedroom Four. The trout-faced occupant from Maidenhead had sent back her breakfast this morning, claiming the bacon was burned and the egg over-cooked. Where did she think she was, the Ritz? Her husband didn't seem to mind whatever was put in front of him. He spent most of the time when she was taking the order looking at Joanie's breasts.

'Hold on a minute,' she said, 'just a sec,' at the top of the third flight of stairs. Christ Almighty, she'd forgotten Scout was asleep in the room. Not just in the room, but six inches from her bed. Where could she put her? The fact that she had an eleven-year-old daughter wasn't something she'd exactly dwelt on.

'Wait here,' she said, 'shut your eyes, wait on this landing and I'll call you up when I'm ready.' In the half-light she could have sworn he almost licked his lips. God, how men loved the promise of a little womanly mystique and preparation.

Scout was fast asleep, curled up like a kitten. Her hands were clasped and tucked to her chest, as if she had fallen asleep saying her prayers. Joanie kicked away her own clothes from the floor to make a gangway. She leaned down, scooped up Scout, and went down the back stairs to reach Bedroom Six. Scout murmured in her sleep. Joanie froze until she was silent. She leaned her bottom on the door handle to open it. She laid Scout on one half of the double bedspread while she peeled back the other, then she slid her in between the sheets, and tucked the covers around her. Genius, she said to herself. She kissed Scout on the forehead, and tried not to stumble out of the room.

Upstairs in their bedroom, she shoved all the clothes she had tried on earlier under Scout's bed. She rummaged through her drawer – did she have nothing that passed for exotic night-wear? That was the problem with promising a little forethought, a little eroticism – you had to deliver. Everything in the drawer looked like something Alice could have slept in. How did she not have to hand something made of a wisp of satin? With a sudden flash of inspiration she stripped off completely. She put a thick slick of transparent gloss on her lips. Men liked mouths that looked wet and slippery. She looked down at her vagina. Three days ago she'd been to a salon at lunch-time and had a little pubic art. No ruthless Brazilian. The shape of a butterfly hovered over her labia. She crept out on the landing and whispered 'You can come up now.' She assumed the pose of a Greek statue, bearing an amphora, arms raised above her head. She sucked in her stomach, crossed her feet at the ankles. She tilted her breasts up and out; they would look sumptuous. Nothing like half-light to show a mature body to its advantage. Dave came creeping up the stairs. She could already see the erection through his trousers. She laughed softly. This was the kind of Location Order she could handle.

29

When Scout began to stir, it was her feet that told her something was different. As she stretched out her legs, she did not hit the wall, but more mattress. She opened her eyelids a fraction. Her own duvet was cornflower blue, with large white stars. She was now smothered by something floral, with a stiff ruffled trim. She turned on to her right side and opened her eyes a little wider. On the bedside table was a box of tissues covered in scallop-edged white lace. Beyond the bedside table, she could see into the bathroom. A spare toilet roll was covered by a shepherdess in a raspberry knitted skirt. She swivelled her eyes across to where she suspected a fireplace might be. Perched daintily in the grate was a china replica of a great-crested grebe. If she was not mistaken, and by now Scout was sure she was not, she was in Bedroom Six, Great-crested Grebe. Currently unoccupied, new guests expected after 11am. Scout was flawless in her knowledge of which rooms were vacant, which due to be occupied. Joanie had a schedule pinned to a board by their basin in order to ensure that the sheets were changed on time. Scout always looked at it when she brushed her teeth. She had decided that memorising it daily probably took up the two minutes recommended for brushing.

Scout thought back to the night before. She had gone to sleep in her own bed. Joanie had gone out. She had spent ages deciding what to wear. When Scout went to sleep, it was like being in the middle of a changing-room floor. She'd listened to the radio for a little while, and watched a fat seagull perch on the edge of the Velux. She'd had beans on toast for her supper, and they lay heavily on her stomach. So how had she got here? The great-crested grebe looked equally mystified. She coughed lightly as she rolled over on to her back. 'Who's there?' called Mrs Eastman's passing voice. Scout prepared to be caught red-handed again which didn't seem entirely fair.

'You again!' said Mrs Eastman, swooping in, eyes blazing. 'What are you doing in here, messing up my rooms? You sneaky, deceitful girl.'

She whisked the bedspread off Scout. She grabbed her arm and pulled her out from between the sheets. Her hands, Scout thought afterwards, seemed to be fighting the temptation to hit her. They made swatting movements just above her head, wishful, it seemed, of landing square on her ears. Mrs Eastman took her by the shoulder and propelled her up the stairs.

'We'll see what your mother says about this. We'll see if she has an answer for this.'

Scout saw the door of Bedroom Five open just a fraction. It wasn't clear whether there were eyes pressed to the crack or whether it was just for easier listening. Scout thought it probably counted as early morning entertainment. She didn't have time for her rolling-dough walk. Her bare feet sounded like wet fish slapping on board, so quick was Mrs Eastman's stride. Her fingers were digging into Scout's right shoulder. How satisfying it would be to turn her head and sink her teeth right in.

Say what you want about Joanie, Scout thought, you couldn't fault her hearing. Scout and Mrs Eastman weren't even at the bottom of the flight of stairs that led to their room before you could hear the scuffling within. Joanie said afterwards that with the gift of a wardrobe she'd have probably got away with it. She would have claimed Scout had sleep-walked, she'd had that tendency since very small. Instead, a man, deprived of a wardrobe to hide in, came out on to the landing. He had trousers on (thank goodness, thought Scout), his other clothing held in his hands. He went quickly past Mrs Eastman and attempted a sheepish 'Good morning'.

Mrs Eastman's face and throat looked like a turkey's. Such an inflating, such a purpling. She stormed towards Joanie. All her manners, her careful way of saying words, slid off her like butter.

'How dare you turn my house into a knocking shop? How dare you put your daughter in one of my guest rooms at forty-two pounds fifty a night and then have a man back here? You know that's against the rules. Bet you wouldn't have changed the sheets in Room Six either, just smoothed them over, spared yourself the job, you lazy slut.'

Scout thought afterwards that her mother seemed to have taken it well. She'd managed to get her dressing-gown half on, and she didn't look at all embarrassed. If she'd lit up a cigarette and started eating something, she'd have managed to blow all the rules at once. The bedroom looked like a bomb had hit it. The pillows seemed to have been flung everywhere. There was a bra hanging from the headboard of her bed. There was a half bottle of vodka on her own bed, and one of the man's socks. There was a packet of condoms by Joanie's nail varnish remover. Scout didn't want to look any more closely.

'You're more trouble than you're worth. Your cleaning's slapdash, your cooking is woeful. I let your daughter stay here as well and this is how you thank me. You can take yourself and your silent ghost of a child and be out of here by eleven.'

Mrs Eastman slammed out of the room.

Scout was perplexed. Besides the embarrassment of all this, wasn't silent meant to be how she was behaving?

Joanie rolled her eyes at Scout, and shrugged. 'Sorry about the rude awakening.'

'Can't be helped,' Scout said, but she thought it probably could. There was no point, however, splitting hairs.

As she packed up, Joanie was singing and humming. She didn't seem the least bit bothered. Scout retrieved her pencil case and put it into her rucksack. She was sad to leave the radio and patted it twice.

As they walked downstairs Scout could have sworn every door was ajar. Mrs Eastman had put a sign on Reception which said that, due to circumstances beyond her control, a cooked breakfast would not be offered today. She was standing by the desk, her arms folded like a shelf for her bosom.

'Good riddance,' she snapped to Joanie. 'You're over-easy, like your bloody eggs.'

Scout stood in the driveway, waiting with their bags while Joanie walked to the car park and brought round the car. Joanie was not walking with any degree of shame. She seemed to be doing what she called her red carpet walk, head up, shoulders back, and toes pointed. She wore a low-cut T-shirt and swivelled her hips as she walked. Scout could sense eyes behind the net curtains. Surely Joanie wouldn't rotate through 360 degrees and stick two fingers ceremoniously at each one of the watchful windows. Was she whistling, too?

The ground floor nets twitched. The curtains parted and she saw Gabriella Douce's doll-like face. It was without lipstick or powder. She looked as pale as milk. She raised one hand, and gave Scout a melancholy wave, and blew her a mournful kiss. In her other hand she was holding up one of her small, broken-winged, fallen angels. Straining her ears, Scout thought *Tiptoe through the tulips* was playing. It was surprisingly bolstering. She put her hands together and gave Mrs Eastman's mother a small clap. Gabriella responded by dipping her head to the left, and dropping a curtsy. The fallen angel dipped too. When Joanie arrived with the car, Scout was singing. She helped her mother cram in the bags, all the while straining her ears. *Knee deep, in flowers we'll stray; We'll keep those showers away.* She wondered if this episode counted as a shower. They'd made a dash for it twice now. She tried not to think of the two angels who threw wicked souls from one end of the world to another. Scout felt a wash of longing for her old bedroom in Alice's house. This episode must surely have convinced Gabriella Douce that she wasn't anything special. Nothing angelic at all.

30

'Why did you move me *to* Room Six when I was asleep? Why didn't you move me *out* of Room Six when Mrs Eastman was still asleep?'

Joanie laughed. Scout hadn't intended to be funny. They were sitting in an internet café.

'Couldn't you have stayed at his house, or somewhere else? Couldn't you have thought of something?'

'No, Scout, evidently I couldn't. Evidently I didn't. I didn't exactly plan for it to turn out that way.'

'I could have seen it coming. I knew it was against the rules.'

'Well, clever you. Perhaps I should consult you at two in the morning. Come on, Scout, give me a break. I'm sorry she hauled you up three flights of stairs. I'm sorry we've had another sharp exit but what do you want me to say? It wasn't our only option. It's not like it was the answer to our dreams.'

'But at least it was somewhere.'

'Tsk. Somewhere anywhere nowhere. Live a little, Scout. We'll find somewhere else. Admittedly without your very own lipsticked dancing geriatric.'

'That's not fair.'

'What's fair got to do with it? What's fair got to do with anything? Come on, eat your breakfast. There's no point us arguing. I need to find another job.'

Joanie turned back to the screen. She was looking at the Gumtree website. Scout resisted saying that there was no point reading the details of an ad for a gardener on the

Blenheim Estate, because Joanie had no experience whatsoever of growing peaches and other hothouse fruits. She looked out of the window, eating a packet of Rolos. That probably shouldn't count as breakfast either.

Eventually, Joanie finished her timed session and Scout followed her outside. Joanie sat down on a wall and lit a cigarette, and blew out long, contemplative streams of smoke. She tugged with her teeth at the cuticle of her ring finger. Across the road, an elderly woman walked by with a chocolate-brown poodle. The dog lifted its feet daintily like a circus pony. Scout watched them disappear around the corner. Two boys came past, bouncing a ball on the pavement between them. The Chinese takeaway next door started cooking for lunch, and Scout could smell chicken, garlic, noodles. Still Joanie smoked and chewed at her finger. The car, Scout thought, would be getting hot, packed as it was with all their belongings. The plastic of the bin bags would be starting to smell. Scout wondered if she'd feel sick if they drove any distance. She stopped eating the Rolos. She could regret them later.

She looked up and watched two birds wheeling in the sky. Yesterday, on Radio Four, listening to a programme about a fictitious garden through the seasons, she'd learned that a flock of starlings, when just beginning to group together and swirl, was called a flag. A flag of starlings. She liked this; it captured their density and their movement. Scout liked expressions which made perfect sense. She'd also learned that long-tailed tits had four different names depending where you lived in England. This was proof, if more proof were needed, that moving around a lot meant you couldn't even name some things properly. Wouldn't have a clue.

Joanie finally spoke. 'Come on,' she said. 'It's not as if we need to be in a hurry. No one's expecting us. Let's get some noodles from the takeaway and go and spend the afternoon sitting on the beach. It looks as if it's turning into a nice day.'

She slid off the wall and fished for some money in her pocket. Scout followed her into the Chinese. It would have been nice to know what they were going to do, where they were going to go. She wondered if asking counted as pestering.

Joanie looked at the menu board. She tossed back her hair, feeling she was shaking *Calm Views* right out of it. She felt pleased to be leaving, give or take the less than ideal exit. Poor Scout, being dragged up three flights of stairs by the old witch. Noodles probably didn't go very far in making it better. Still, it was good to keep moving, good to stay on their toes. What did she sing as a child playing catch? *You can't catch me for a toffee-tee.* And the gingerbread man; *Run run as fast as you can; you can't catch me I'm the gingerbread man.* She thought of the letter, the Beechams' hopeful faces, the social worker's interfering, unwanted intrusion. Stuff them all. She'd stay one step ahead. Run to earth. Box clever.

31

Elisabetta had stuck Scout's photo to the fridge. Each time she walked past it, or it caught her eye, she would allow herself to ask it a question. What is your favourite colour? What do you like best to eat? Can you skip? Can you draw? What is your favourite film? She didn't try to guess the answers, but wondered if accumulated knowledge counted as knowing a child; knowledge being separate and distinct from love, but relevant all the same, and the ability to predict behaviour or choices being only one step removed from intuitive understanding.

Elisabetta spoke to Scout in Italian. This had come as a surprise; she even dreamed in English now. Elisabetta taught Italian three days of the week, and spoke Italian to her family on the phone, and yet, as she made dinner, cleared the table, moved about her kitchen, she also spoke Italian to Scout, stuck on the fridge with her sky-blue background. Mother tongue. Elisabetta acknowledged that she spoke to her in her mother tongue. That was the only flimsy maternal dimension that remained to her in relation to this child. It would have been different had she been handed to her as a tiny newborn, but this was probably better not dwelled on. She might well feel motherly towards her, might love her one day, but she would never be her mother. Joan was that. Joan had kept that for herself. There was some kind of resolution in articulating this. Odd that in the process of seeking, there was a letting go.

Ned had told her he had gone to the flats in Birmingham where Scout had been located. He had not asked her to go with him. He'd evidently decided he preferred to go alone. She'd had to let that go too – any feeling of being marginalised or sidelined. He had not wanted her there. He had not needed her there. Whatever had prompted him to go to Birmingham, and whatever he felt when he was there, he had preferred to feel first, alone, for himself. Elisabetta decided that some processes were solitary, however hard you tried to disguise it. They involved winching yourself along a series of emotional adjustments until you arrived somewhere different and ready to talk about it. He had given her the photo. The way he had handed it to her seemed like a tacit apology.

When she walked past the photo with Maia in her arms, she would point to it and say *Scout!* Maia would say it back, as cheerily as she might repeat banana, or cherry, or helicopter, or postman. For Maia, Scout was just another thing to be named, labelled, recognised. Elisabetta envied her simplicity. She had never spoken any Italian to Maia. The first fourteen months of her life Maia had heard only Mandarin, and the adoption authorities had advised that it would help her development if she and Ned spoke consistently in English. So, Elisabetta felt that speaking Italian with Maia lay in the future, stacked and preserved as if in ice. *Ti amo*, she would allow herself to say when Maia was fast asleep. *Ti amo. Ti amo.*

She did not say that to Scout's picture. It would be inappropriate, presumptuous. Probably absurd. But she would like to tell her, one day, that she had loved the idea of her, had loved the thought of her, the prospect of her, the budding reality of her.

Heart wounds, Elisabetta felt, did not heal with silvery scars like skin; did not become smooth to the touch, to be explored without pain. Instead, they became dusted with new reflection, until they assumed a shape of their own, layered and layered with private thought and grief. Loss was a determined companion. It hunkered down for the long haul. Sometimes, when she was out running, it was there, placid and determined, tucked neatly in her heart, shaped like a foetus and washed over with blood.

However much she accepted it, Elisabetta didn't like to think of Ned sitting alone at the foot of a tower block. If she felt Scout's absence, how must it be for him? Perhaps as if part of him had been extracted, transplanted. What would he say to her in the precise Latin that he dealt with daily? *Te amavi. Amo. Semper amabo?*[1]

She was making risotto. She pounded some saffron in a pestle and mortar and mixed it with a little wine. Maia was asleep upstairs. Thank God for Maia. Accepting the fact that she had been denied being Scout's mother, could never be Scout's mother, had been eased by the fact that she was Maia's. Of this she was in no doubt. She felt heart-spillingly grateful to her small, sleeping child upstairs, who had healed more wounds than she could ever imagine. Everyone assumed a child adopted from an orphanage was being given the gift of a wholesome life. The gift was reciprocated; of this Elisabetta was sure. She could absorb the complexity of Scout because of the security of Maia. For this she gave thanks, and because of it, felt able to give space to Ned.

She ladled stock on to the arborio rice, and stirred it in figures of eight. Usually, she found this soothing and therapeutic in its easy repetition. It had started raining. Ned was playing tennis with some colleagues from school. They had told no one at work about Scout. They had decided they couldn't bear the constant requests for updates. *Any news? Have they found her? What does your solicitor say?* Someone would suggest hiring a private detective. She knew it would be

[1] I have loved you. I love you. I will always love you.

well intentioned. And Scout would begin to sound like one of the lost girls in the newspapers, snatched in sleep, or from their bike, never to come home. Elisabetta didn't want those words to settle on Scout.

If they had not already finished playing tennis, the rain would chase them off the court. It was heavy, for June. It began to drum on the kitchen window. The dust by the bird bath bounced into the air. It was worth it, she thought, for the way the grass, the trees, would smell afterwards.

As she stirred the rice, she looked over her shoulder at Scout. The thing that hurt most, the thing that seemed so monstrously unfair, was that Joan had so effortlessly, nonchalantly, successfully given birth to Ned's child, which had been so beyond Elisabetta herself. Looked at that way, she thought, looked unabashedly straight in the eye, it was easy to feel that love had little to do with achieving anything at all.

32

Where to go, where to go, where to go.

Joanie plinked pebbles into a small tower by her left-hand side, and smoothed a small furrow of sand around the base. Beyond her, at the water's edge, Scout was standing in the frills of the waves. The evening was drawing in. Earlier in the afternoon, she'd been jumping over them. Now she looked a little aimless. Her feet kicked at strands of seaweed. She'd been standing there some time. She kept looking over her shoulder at where Joanie sat on her jacket. The beach had emptied. The afternoon hadn't materialised into quite the sun-streaming one Joanie had forecast.

Scout looked back at her again. Joanie made a small *tsk* of frustration. What was she hoping for – a small plume of smoke like at the Vatican when they'd elected a new Pope? Did Scout expect her to stand up and yell down to the shoreline 'I've cracked it! Now we'll do *this*.' If only it were that simple.

Of all the things single parents didn't get recognition for – and from Joanie's perspective what they mostly seemed to get was a steady stream of disappointed blame – was the relent-lessness required in being the only person capable of making or taking a decision. No credit given for always being the one who conjured something out of nothing. She knocked down her pebble tower.

On the horizon, she noticed clouds rolling in. It was going to start spitting with rain. That would top the afternoon off perfectly. It would be spiteful English rain, feeling like drawing pins on her skin. She shifted on the sand. It was scratching her legs. She blew heavily through her lips. Perhaps one of her mood indigos was about to come rolling through too.

She took out her phone. No messages, no unread texts. She wondered about texting Dave, but couldn't summon the enthusiasm. In the slate light of the evening, he didn't seem worth the effort. Funny how it could evaporate – boom! – in one little gesture. Last night in bed he'd started asking her questions about where she'd lived before. She'd been evasive and he'd said 'Why are you so mysterious? My mystery lady.' If that hadn't been corny enough, he'd nuzzled his face down to her breast in a movement that was weirdly infant-like. Even through the haze of too much vodka, it was oddly repellent. She would have called time on him soon anyway.

Scout was still at the shoreline. Her feet looked blue from here. Bless her for not whining. It would be completely reasonable for her to be whining her head off. Joanie lay back on the sand and looked up at the clouds. They were busy scudding off somewhere, blown by the wind with no independent decision-making required. A wasp settled on the lip of the noodle carton by her side. She wafted it away with her hand. The best thing was probably just to get in the car and drive. Somewhere. Anywhere. Just away. Mrs Eastman with a grudge could be a fly in the ointment if she stayed here. Perhaps Bournemouth? Torquay? Brighton? Joanie felt sick to her back teeth of the English seaside. She sat up and brushed the sand from her arms. She waved to Scout, who turned and walked slowly towards her.

33

Susan Philips was working late. She sat at her computer going through extant cases. There were always more cases than time, she thought, and always the underlying anxiety that the one you took your eye off would turn out to be the miscarriage of justice that marked your career.

Scout Simpson. She'd slipped through the net. The Location Order had, inadvertently, located her, only to lose her again. Another fabulous example of joined-up thinking between Social Services and the police. Sometimes she couldn't script it; the seemingly limitless capacity for authorities to fuck things up. It was 17 July; there had been no new knowledge of Scout since mid-May. Susan wondered if the child's mother was feckless, or reckless, or both. Joan Simpson now knew Scout was the subject of a Location Order; to have absconded with her, knowing that, was a criminal offence. The letter would have made that clear. Joan Simpson had ratcheted up the seriousness of what she was doing. If they were found, Susan could press for the child to be the subject of an Emergency Protection Order. Scout could be deemed at risk. At risk of what, the law did not require her to specify in advance. The fact that Joan Simpson had committed a criminal offence, plus one debatable criminal offence at the time of the child's birth, meant that she wasn't scoring too highly in the fit mother stakes. If made the subject of an Emergency Protection Order, Scout could be taken into foster care, whether she wanted to be or not. That is, unless Susan and her chosen barrister were able to persuade a judge that it was a better option to place her with a father she didn't know, who, she would remind the court, could not be a more upstanding citizen. It never failed to achieve support in a courtroom, the appeal of a middle-class life solidly and decently lived. Even when it shouldn't have – when a child was adopted in a frankly disastrous mismatch of expectations – it punched above its weight. Susan had seen that so often.

Sometimes, when she thought about surrogacy, she wondered if it was a twenty-first century version of hiring a wet nurse. Certainly, when Hollywood film stars did it to preserve their figures, or when women worked for too long and then expected to have it all at forty-five. Out-sourcing; perhaps it was the highest order of out-sourcing. It was obviously not so after years of anguished trying, but it held a taint of that; the procuring of a robust womb, rented out for the physical stint. It must be difficult to hand over a surrogate baby; like the trauma of giving up a child for adoption without all the attendant counselling. How had it been, she wondered, the initial dialogue between the Beechams and Joan Simpson? The aspect that eluded her so far was what had prompted Joan Simpson to offer herself up at all.

Susan wasn't initially sure what she thought of Ned and Elisabetta. They seemed likeable enough – not that it was her business to judge. He was more hesitant. She detected sometimes an unwillingness to extrapolate upon exactly what he felt. Elisabetta had all the verve. It positively thrummed from her. She was beautiful too, as if perhaps to prove nobody got everything. After all these years had lapsed, perhaps their commitment to this process was like waking the dead. Except that she wasn't dead. Scout Simpson wasn't dead at all, but rapidly moving between Oxfordshire, Birmingham and God knows where.

To whom did she belong? That was the question. If they managed to find her, they could get to grips with that. Or at least the law would; the law, with all its multiple fingers, its precise, suckered tentacles. Perhaps Joan Simpson was only a sloppy parent. Now she was embroiled in this process she would be required to up her game. Joan Simpson engaging with figures in authority. From what had happened thus far, Susan thought it might not be the smoothest of rides.

What sort of love was best for a child? The family courts loved to ponder that. Mostly, they plumped for the middle-class sort, with five servings of vegetables, an emphasis on manners, good dental work, swimming classes, a belief in sustained endeavour, and optimally, a quiet, designated space for homework. Susan wondered if she was too young to be so cynical.

Maybe she should add a Penal Notice to the Location Order. That would mean, if found, Joan Simpson could be arrested in the street. Perhaps that would be a little heavy-handed. But it was a good option. She could apply to the Applications Judge in the High Court and have it up her sleeve.

If asked what made a good lawyer, Susan thought she might have the answer. Mostly, a combination of the lowest possible common denominator of expectation with regard to human behaviour, and a sleeve stuffed full of ammunition your opposition hadn't even dreamed you might acquire. Some bite, a sharp tongue, and a certain talent for peacockery. Received wisdom was that bravura was best left to the barristers. Susan disagreed. Bravura was mostly present in small measure. Instead, she thought, the barristers sweated the most; up on their hind legs, arguing the toss.

34

Joanie was driving fast. Scout had no idea where they were going, but Joanie was definitely driving fast. She'd headed in from the coast, but hadn't revealed her plan. Scout didn't want to ask. That would be a guaranteed mistake. Her feet felt grimy and sandy. She didn't want to put her shoes back on because she had seaweed trailed around one toe. She didn't want to pull it off because it would make her fingers feel even dirtier. She'd tried to dislodge it with her other foot, but it had simply migrated to the opposite toe. Her mouth felt sticky-sweet from the noodles, ice cream and crisps. Her hands smelt of rock pools. Her hair was all tangled too, from the wind off the water. A bath would have been nice. A bath and her own cosy bed.

It was getting darker, and the raindrops were getting bigger and splashier. The windscreen wipers hardly made it across to her side of the car before the screen was completely water-blurred again. The puddles at the side of the road splashed up over the bonnet each time they cornered. Joanie was sitting forward, hunched over the wheel. Scout wondered whether to ask her if she was tired. She was tired herself. It was getting harder to keep her eyes open. Joanie had stopped to get petrol and bought her a packet of prawn cocktail crisps. They'd filled her up; she didn't want dinner any more. She let her eyes close. Perhaps she'd wake up somewhere nice like when they first arrived in Poole.

Joanie looked across at Scout. She looked as if she had finally nodded off. She toyed with putting on the radio quietly.

Perhaps that would inspire her with a plan. She rubbed her eyes. The rain was getting heavier and heavier. Lorries overtook her and threw up great swathes of water. Her windscreen wipers were crap; the rubber had almost worn out. They made a scrawping noise each time they crossed the screen, which set her teeth on edge and left the glass smeary, worse than it was before. She felt tired, so tired; so suddenly worn out with what to do next.

There was a lay-by ahead. Perhaps the most sensible thing would be to pull in and get some sleep. Everything was always better either with a clean pair of knickers or a good night's rest. She pulled over, turned off the engine and reached into the back seat to get Scout's duvet. She settled it over them both. Scout's face still felt sticky from her lunch. The rain hammered on the roof of the car. It felt as if it was driving into her skull. She was parked beneath a huge tree. Extra raindrops plinked down from its sodden leaves, and were unexpectedly irritating. She reclined her seat and lay looking at the roof. As each car passed on the road, it threw a beam of light down the seam. Her blood felt as if it were fizzing and jangling in her veins. She felt blurry at the edges, less distinct, less herself. She made her toenails scritch scratch against the accelerator pedal. Anything to stop this emerging feeling of anxiety. Where the hell should they go? What would happen if they were found? She shifted uncomfortably in her seat. Sleep seemed unlikely.

35

James Baxter liked the days when he sat as Applications Judge. In the High Court, he would see people he liked to catch up with. Most of what he dealt with required only quick resolution.

Before him, on his desk, lay a written application to attach a Penal Notice to consolidate a Location Order. He recognised this one. It was the surrogate mother who'd had a change of heart; now, it would appear, located briefly in Birmingham and all trace of whom since vanished. How untruths snowball, he thought, and yet the instinct to scram, to flee in the face of them, remains shimmeringly appealing. No absconder conceives of the venus fly trap of the law. Both orders were ex-parte; it was highly unlikely Joan Simpson would appear to account for herself. The solicitor – who was she? – Susan Philips – had been quick off the mark. In truth though, probably naive. He attached so many Penal Notices, clamoured for by solicitors, and the police were hardly queuing up with suspects successfully identified and arrested in the street.

He wondered if the case would ever wash up in front of him. What would the mother be like? Susan Philips was suggesting the child may be at risk. Often hard to tell. Especially by the age of eleven when there was a high degree of loyalty, whatever the circumstances. It was an age when a child unhesitatingly plumped for the familiar, unless it was truly appalling. What would she want, if asked, this little Scout Simpson? He looked over his glasses at the case notes, at a small photocopy of her face. She was all neat and clean in a school uniform. That marked her out as different from most upon whom he was required to call judgment.

James signed the Penal Notice and looked at his next application. His mobile phone rang. The children had bought him an iPhone for his birthday. On it, applications were called apps. Apps sounded neat, vibrant. The term couldn't be applied to the papers in front of him. Its brevity didn't sit well with the debris of lives that these applications concerned.

James Baxter wondered, not for the first time, if language itself – even the archaic, precise, exact language of the law that he loved – was capable of rendering anything how it actually, really, was. And if you accepted that to be true, how could one ever pronounce accurate, reliable judgment at all?

36

Matilda had made an appearance. This was a first. As if it wasn't bad enough having Alice interjecting, the appearance in a dream of Matilda, who had never previously ventured from her water-butt, spooked Joanie in the night. She woke up – perhaps it was when the rain stopped drumming – and the image of Matilda remained, silent and sodden.

Matilda was Alice's mother. Joanie sometimes saw them as a kind of relay team; Matilda transferring a baton to Alice, Alice to Joanie, Joanie to Scout. She wasn't yet quite sure what the baton was, but increasingly wondered if it wasn't the ability to endure. That, or the possibility of passing on intact your own limitations or hang-ups to the next generation. Matilda's appearance didn't bode well.

Joanie had always been told Matilda died of a heart attack. Then, when Alice's own heart began failing, and Joanie went with her to a hospital appointment, the doctor asked if heart disease ran in the family. Alice shook her head.

'Don't be ridiculous,' Joanie interrupted, 'your own mother died of a heart attack.'

'No, she didn't,' Alice said, looking the doctor straight in the eye. 'She committed suicide when I was twenty-two and she was forty-six. She walked out into the garden in her Monday wash dress and climbed head first into our water-butt. I found her with her legs sticking out. She'd put on her good shoes.'

Joanie had had trouble assimilating this new picture of Matilda, not slumped in her armchair still holding her crochet hook, but upside down in the water-butt, her face distended and bloated from drowning, the hem of her petticoats frilling at the edge of the butt.

It was the thought of her best shoes, dutifully polished, that upset Joanie, and the notion of the horrible, confined, desperate contortions of someone upside down in a water-butt, fingers clawing at the sides. She had not thought about it for years and now, in her dream, preceded by shadowy legions of Location Orders which marched up and over the horizon at her, Matilda surfaced in front of the bonnet of the car, her water-butt now made of Perspex, her upside-down froggy face bulging obscenely, her tongue blue, fat and distended and lolling from her head.

'Law-breaker, promise-breaker, lousy selfish mother,' said Matilda, burping a little algaed water down her chin.

Joanie woke gagging for breath. If that were the truth, she wished her subconscious had picked a less disturbing vehicle to express it. She envisaged Alice and told her in no uncertain terms, *Matilda is your trauma to own, kindly take her back. She's got no place in my nightmares.* Alice didn't respond. She evidently preferred no comment. Joanie felt if she reached forward and touched the steering wheel it would spark shocks of blue.

'Fuck off, Matilda,' she said as the sun rose behind her. 'And keep your opinions to yourself.'

She shivered, and put her face in her hands. It occurred to her that she was what Alice would have described as *up to her neck in it*. That was presumably why Matilda had weighed in, clad in Perspex, just to add a little additional baton-transferring vibrato. Her sins, surely, were still in the realm of venial. How predictable, she thought, Alice's old Catholic words coming back to weigh her.

Joanie opened the car door. The sound made Scout stir. Joanie took six deep breaths. Some open sky, some fresh air, that was definitely what she needed. *Come on, giddy up*, she said to herself. *Hold it together*. She looked up through the wet leaves. Trees were over-rated. It was a middle-class conspiracy. If you swept up your own leaves they were less bloody appealing. Their ability to make you feel hemmed in and suppressed, to drive you freaking crackers, was rarely articulated.

Scout woke up and saw Joanie standing on the verge beside the car. She was holding her head in her hands. Had she been thinking all night? Scout stretched out her legs. The seaweed had fallen off her toes. It looked like a string of scabs in the foot-well. She felt even more grubby than when she had fallen asleep. She looked along the dashboard for a bobble to tie back her hair. Her T-shirt was dirty. The distance between her own clothing and a garment in a wardrobe at Houghton Hall must now be at its maximum measurement. There probably existed some kind of mathematical equation which expressed that if Miss Maudie's clothes were at x, Scout's shorts and T-shirt were currently at the furthest point from x, measurable in terms like those used to describe the distance to the sun. She opened the car door. Joanie looked up.

'Mum,' she said 'before we go to wherever we're going to, can we go somewhere for a wash?'

All things considered, Joanie thought, it wasn't an unreasonable request.

37

Joanie and Scout sat in a leisure centre café in Andover, looking over a plastic, chrome-rimmed screen at the swimmers beneath. A lifeguard had noisily blown his whistle, and was telling off some boys for diving. Scout had a hot chocolate, topped with whipped cream, with a Flake sticking out of it. She'd chosen it because she thought it might resemble what the Houghton children drank after swimming in the lake. She hadn't actually been swimming, but she'd felt cold after her night in the car so she thought that counted. She and Joanie had not swum at the pool. Joanie's idea had been far better than that. They had paid the £2.80 admission and gone straight to the showers. Joanie had bought a bottle of shampoo and some soap. They had stood under the hot water and washed themselves until they were pink from scrubbing. Joanie had bought Scout a T-shirt, some knickers, a skirt and some baseball boots. She'd forgotten socks, but they decided this didn't matter as they wouldn't be walking any distance anyway. Scout felt clean; so beautifully, perfectly clean.

Scout looked at Joanie. She'd bought herself a bright pink hair clip, and a cotton vest which had appliquéd butterflies clustered over one shoulder. She scooped her hair up and fastened the clip, gave herself a big kiss in the mirror and said to Scout, 'Now for our next adventure.'

Scout couldn't fail to detect the relish in her voice. She plucked up her courage. 'Can't we go home?'

'You asked me that before. I've told you we can't.'

'But why? Are you sure?'

'I am sure. Certain. Positive. Absoluto. Absoluto.'

Only Joanie could finish her sentence with such relish. Absoluto. It might not even be a word. It started off like absolve. That had been one of her dictionary words with Mr Mohammed. It meant to grant remission of a sin, or to pronounce clear of guilt or blame. That might be a harder question to answer. Definitely best not asked. She looked at her new baseball boots. They were a form of consolation.

Joanie now had her AA road atlas out on the table. She was flipping the pages and talking.

'I want a wide open landscape and the possibility of a suntan. Look at the colour of me – I'm grey. That's what you get for changing Eastman's beds all day. I'm going to get a job outside and see blue sky and sunshine – it's almost August for God's sake. Where do strawberries grow? And peas? Can you pick grapes in England like you do in France?'

'I think peas are harvested by machine. I've seen that on the Birds Eye advert on the television. I don't know about grapes.'

Scout sucked on her straw. The hot chocolate wasn't delicious. It left a grainy feel in her mouth, and when she dipped the Flake in the cream and ate it, it felt greasy on top of the graininess. She wanted to poke her tongue out to escape the feel of her gums. Had it been like this for the Houghton children? She expected not. Cook most likely made their hot chocolate from real chocolate, melted. Her own was made from powder. Maybe it wasn't even mixed with real milk; perhaps that was powdered too. The cream had been squirted from a tall, thin can with a nozzle. Maybe it was chemical cream, not truly from cows. No question, this was much worse hot chocolate than the Houghton children had ever drunk; perhaps than they had ever thought could even exist. She tried to imagine Miss Maudie sitting at a swimming pool in Andover and managing to drink it. Maudie wasn't pulling it off either. The other interpretation, slightly more depressing, was that things always looked or sounded nicer than they actually were, and therefore bound to disappoint, even when you did get them. Scout decided not to think about that any further. It wasn't just the hot chocolate that was different anyway. The Houghton children drank theirs on the terrace overlooking the herbaceous borders. That was different from the steamed-up, chlorine-smelling balcony she was currently sitting on. Joanie was still talking.

'Okay, strawberries, if we can find some strawberry fields. Or maybe hops? Is it time for hops? Don't they sell dried hop garlands for kitchens? Alice wouldn't have stood for that; dust gathering for no particular purpose, imagine – and dropping leaves.'

Scout wasn't really sure what hops were. She thought Joanie, if pressed, may not be too sure either, so she decided not to ask. She hoped picking hops wasn't too complicated, or didn't involve obeying hop growers' rules about what you did outside hop-picking time. That might end in tears. Strawberries sounded simpler. That wouldn't require any specialist knowledge. Wimbledon was over, she'd listened to it on the radio. Did that mean most of the English strawberries had already been eaten? Perhaps there were other varieties that ripened after June. Maybe there was a sequence to strawberry growing. That would be a comforting thought.

'Norfolk!' Joanie said triumphantly. 'We'll go to Norfolk. Come on, finish up your drink.'

Scout decided that to leave it would seem ungrateful. She curled her toes in her baseball boots and downed it in one.

Joanie got into the driving seat, singing and humming. 'M4, M25, M11, Norfolk here we come.'

She was tapping the steering wheel in time with her song. Scout watched the cars in the other lanes. Everybody was evidently going somewhere, with purpose and intent. She reached beneath the seat and felt for her folder of work from Birmingham. Still there, undisturbed. She adjusted her fingers so that she could pinch the width between her fingers. She'd learn some more in Norfolk. She'd make the stack grow bigger. There wouldn't be so many distractions if Joanie were out at work.

She sat in the car seeing their journey like the beads on Alice's old rosary. Moreton, Birmingham, Poole, Andover, Norfolk; would it carry on like this? Would her mother add on places until Scout couldn't remember the list any more? Would they continue to keep going until her AA atlas had no uncrumpled pages? Scout rested her head against the window and felt the small vibrations inch into her temple. Norfolk. Strawberries. *Accentuate the positive;* that was what Joanie always said.

38

Scout thought it was the fifteenth time of asking that Joanie came out of the pub clutching a hastily drawn map to a farm called Dent's which was recruiting fruit pickers. Joanie had started her search at an internet café in Norwich, but the websites she looked at said that most fruit pickers were recruited by word of mouth, and to ask in village newsagents and pubs. Scout had stayed in the car while Joanie nipped in and out. Her mother, she concluded, was quite speedy over a short distance. She didn't give up easily either. Taking no for an answer obviously wasn't her thing. She had a spring in her step, as if each footstep she put between herself and Poole gave her extra bounce.

The villages they went through seemed mostly quiet and deserted. Scout could see church spires for miles before they reached anywhere. She became bored at the vastness of the fields. Initially, she asked Joanie what was growing in each one, but then Joanie kept saying *sugar beet* without actually looking, so Scout gave up. It wouldn't count as reliable Geography anyway. Sitting alone in the car, she wondered if everyone who lived in the houses was out picking fruit in the fields. She suggested it to Joanie when she came back, but she said probably not. Apparently, most fruit pickers came from abroad and just worked for the summer.

It was hot in the car. Scout put her feet up on the dashboard. Something had bitten her ankle and she kept pushing her fingers into her baseball boots and scratching away at the bite. Joanie was reading from a leaflet she had been given in the pub.

'Strawberries now. Plums and apples in very late August. Apples and pears in September. Hops sometime afterwards. See, I knew there'd be hops! Hourly rate five pounds seventy-four and then piece rate after a week. Workers to take responsibility for their own tax.'

'What's piece rate?' Scout asked, wondering if they'd still be here in September. September was for going back to school, for daddy-long-legs on the door frame in the morning, for new shoes, for new exercise books. Joanie was obviously ready to give it all up for hops.

'It means you get paid for the amount you pick. It makes you work faster because you earn more money, and the farmer gets his crop picked faster before it rains or gets over-ripe. Ten kilos an hour for strawberries – that's a top picker's target. Ten kilos an hour – how hard can that be?'

Scout suspected it might be harder than Joanie anticipated. Her mother was now driving through a farm gate, past a sign which said *Register for work here. Accommodation available. Cash in hand daily.*

Another sign listed the paperwork needed in order to gain work. *British passport; EEA passport; Working Holiday Maker Visa; Bunac Blue Card.* Joanie rifled though her bag for her passport. 'Whoo hoo,' she said, 'I'm about to become a farm girl.'

In History at school, Scout had learned about the Land Army girls in the war. She tried to imagine her mother with her hair in a headscarf, wearing overalls and driving a tractor, keeping calm and carrying on. While she was trying to assemble this image, Joanie started singing *Country road, take me home* in an American accent. Scout wondered if sometimes, even if you had all the right papers, you might not be taken on.

The next blackboard listed the available accommodation in the nearby field. *Tent pitch £5 per week. Tent £20 per week. One-berth caravan £42. Two-berth caravan £70. Four-berth caravan £105.*

Joanie said that she couldn't face a tent. She managed to persuade the farmer that a one-berth caravan, with its additional child-sized flip-down bed, would be plenty.

'Add it up for me, Scout,' she said. 'We'll call it a Maths test. Let's say seventy kilos a day, six days a week at a pound a kilo, minus forty-two pounds for the caravan.'

'Three hundred and seventy-eight pounds.'

'We'll be in the money. Cash is king!'

It would sound grumpy to point out her mother hadn't actually picked any strawberries yet. Her ankle was really itching. She spat on her thumb and pressed it to the bite. So far, she hadn't even caught sight of a strawberry.

Joanie parked the car in the yard and they walked down a track. The ground was rutted and baked dry. They passed a shower block which Scout thought didn't look like somewhere you'd go to try and get clean. It smelled like a blocked toilet. People were queuing by the external tap, washing their faces, cooling their feet.

Scout realised, just before they turned a corner, that she could hear the site before she actually saw it. Such a babbling of voices, of languages. Dogs barking. Music playing. Laughing. Shouting. Each way she turned her head, it seemed that the language she heard was different. On the left-hand side were the tent pitches and tents. People spilled out of them, played guitars, drank beer, prepared food, laid fires, kissed. Quite a lot of kissing. About twenty caravans were placed in a group to the right of the track. Men sat on the external steps, smoked, called across to one another. Strung between the caravans were washing lines, with pegged-out clothes. Some Chinese men sat eating noodles from cups. A woman called out to someone in a language Scout couldn't even begin to guess. People sat rubbing their feet, their backs, their shoulders. A couple were quarrelling. The woman threw a can in the direction of the man's head. There was a smell of food cooking, wood smoke, sweat, and also, beyond all of it, a sweetness which Scout thought must be the strawberries. Joanie was looking happy. 'I am born to be a fruit picker,' she said, with a gesture that took in all of the site.

Joanie stood outside a small caravan with 17 painted on the door in big red numbers. It correlated to the number on the rectangular wooden key-ring in her hand. She opened the door and Scout followed her up the steps. A sign on the table said *If not left in the condition found, your deposit will be kept.*

The caravan was mostly orange. The walls were orange, the work surfaces and the table-top were orange. Not fresh orange – like the fruit – but pale. Orange, Scout felt, that was forgetting what colour it had started out being. The two bench seats either side of the table were covered in a bobbly fabric that was orange, yellow and brown. When the table was slotted to the side, the benches could be pulled out to make a bed. There was a small two-ring stove and oven, a toaster, and a little sink. The tap, Scout saw when she opened the cupboard, was attached to a drum of water like she'd seen people carrying.

'Perfect,' Joanie said, 'this will be just perfect. You look in all the cupboards and think where you want to put everything. I'll go back to the car and nip to the Spar shop to get us some food, and I'll bring down our stuff and we can get unpacked before eating.'

When she'd gone, Scout closed the door, in case anyone tried to come in, although it seemed pointless as it was thin as a tray. If she'd been one of the little pigs, the wolf could have huffed it down easily. Each of the cupboards was opened by sticking your finger into a little hole. Scout methodically opened each one. It felt like her doll's house but bigger. When

Joanie came back, Scout was sitting on the bench seat, her knees tucked to her chest.

'Look what I've got,' Joanie said, holding up a small portable TV. 'I just bought it from someone who was leaving. I checked it worked before giving him the fifteen quid.'

She put down two bags of food, which Scout started to put in one of the cupboards. Joanie turned on the oven. 'Pizza!' she said.

Later, Scout sat on the caravan steps with her mother and ate pizza as darkness fell. Joanie had bought some wine and was drinking it from a paper cup.

'It's peaceful and noisy at the same time,' Scout was saying of the music, the chatter, the voices from around the small fires.

'This will suit us just fine,' Joanie said. 'Tomorrow I will begin my campaign to become queen of the strawberries. Ten kilos or bust.'

Another bed, Scout thought later, although at least this one didn't have ridges like the one at Calm Views. It wasn't full-size, but she decided this made it feel snug and cosy. She lay in it, listening. Another set of noises to get used to. She thought back to the flats, to the sound of the 280 bus driving by, the footsteps in the corridor, the shouts from down by the communal garden. She thought of Gabriella Douce and the sound of her record player; *And if I kissed you, would you pardon me?* She recalled the ferries' foghorns out in the Channel; the sound of the rain on the car roof last night. And here, there was chattering, singing, a guitar strumming, someone shouting to someone else to be quiet. By the light of a small lamp, the caravan interior looked even more faded. It was, she decided, as she fell asleep, like lying at the centre of a vast fondant cream.

39

The morning routine, Joanie said, was like an army on the move. She'd bought a pair of wellies from someone the night before, and had them rolled down to the ankle like everyone seemed to be wearing them. She pretended to stand to attention. Scout saluted her and pushed out her chest. A tractor pulling a trailer came to the edge of the site. People were clambering up, carrying lunch-boxes, water, sun hats. There wasn't much chatter – it was still only 7.30 am, but they looked to Scout like a wave of people, washing up and over the vehicle, and settling on to its benches.

Joanie seemed to be swept up by the momentum. She kissed Scout and said 'Be good. Don't go wandering off. Don't put yourself in a position where anything bad could happen.' Scout wondered what she should do if anything inadvertently did. Joanie didn't seem to have considered that part of the equation. 'Get yourself some breakfast,' she said, 'I'll be back at five thirty.'

Scout thought the exit from the camp was like something from the Bible. In R.E., they had learned about Moses and the exodus. Mrs Pearson-Smith had held up a picture. It showed a great swarm of people with sheep, goats and donkeys, leaving to cross the desert. Moses stood in the middle with a big, thick staff. A glossy fat snake lay curled on a rock at his feet. Apart from the livestock, and Moses, and obviously the snake, Scout decided this had the same feel. The Red Sea had apparently parted. That must have been a sight; water rearing up like a wall. No danger of that here – it looked like there couldn't possibly be water for miles. Joanie seemed glad of the fact. She'd said *Good riddance, Matilda,* when she surveyed the vast, dry field. Scout thought better not to enquire.

She picked her way between the tents. All the stuff of lives was here: bowls with the remains of cereal and milk; cigarette packets; the odd boot or shoe; a twisted cellophane wrapper containing a few slices of bread; a jacket; a hat; a guitar; an empty beer can; a bottle; yesterday's newspaper. In one tent, someone had obviously not woken for work. She could hear thunderous snoring. She tiptoed past carefully. The sun was already warm. In the shadow of the tents, a couple of dogs were tied, and sleeping. She decided not to pat them. A dog bite would count as something bad happening. She didn't even have a plaster. Other than theirs, the caravans were all closed up. Their door hung open, slightly wonkily, on its hinges. Apart from the snoring man, she wondered if she was the only person here. Such a contrast to last night; all those bodies, all that chatter. At school, she'd read about a boat called the *Marie Celeste.* It was found floating at sea, everything within it as if the crew had just stood up to bring something extra to the table, or just stepped below having finished their jobs on deck. This was like that too; as if someone had clicked their fingers and magicked all the people away. The tap by the shower block dripped water into a small, solitary puddle.

Scout mooched back towards the caravan. If she'd been at school, she'd be on holiday now. From the middle of July, all those free weeks would have rolled out before her. Last year, she and Joanie had gone on a package trip to Greece. Joanie had drunk too much retsina each night, and woken daily with a headache, but Scout had swum all day in the sea, until her skin felt as smooth and gleaming as a mussel. The sea was the bluest she had ever seen. Joanie had booked the tickets on lastminute.com after they'd watched *Mamma Mia* at the cinema. Scout wondered at the time if Joanie thought being in Greece might mean you got to be in the same position as Meryl Streep, with three men who might want to marry you, one of whom was happily the long-lost father of your child. Possibly even look like her too. It hadn't worked out like that, although their hair was the same.

She returned to thinking about school. She would have started the long school holiday having done weeks of school-work. She couldn't pretend to have achieved that. At Mrs Eastman's she hadn't written a word. That wasn't to say she hadn't learned things but she hadn't written things down. That was the only indication of real, proper learning.

Scout folded away Joanie's bed, and restored the table to its place. She retrieved her work folder from the cupboard where she had put it the previous night. Joanie was attempting to be the queen of strawberry picking. Here, in the caravan, Scout would become the queen of own-learning. By September, when Joanie might be making an attempt at achieving the crown for queen of hops, Scout guessed she would not be starting at senior school with a new uniform and a rucksack for carrying her books. She'd have to step up the pace. She sucked on a Jammie Dodger contemplatively. Senior school-level own-learning probably had all manner of unknown complexities. She must get down to some proper work. The campsite in working hours was quiet and peaceful. With a small nudge to the imagination, she might consider it one vast, untidy library.

40

Jesus Christ Almighty, Joanie thought, was it possible to be in any more physical pain? Her back felt as if someone had stuffed a poker up it. Her spine was rigid. Even the muscles in her fingers ached. Her calves felt like they been podged full of walnuts like a Christmas stocking. A Chinese woman had mimed to her all the places where she might expect to hurt. She was bang on. A Polish student with perfect English told her it would pass after a couple of days. Ten kilos an hour looked like scaling bloody Everest. It wasn't even lunch-time. She swigged at her water-bottle. Why did all the best ideas end up having grit in them? There had to be easier ways to invisibly earn money. *Persistence*, she said out loud to herself. *Persistence, persistence.* Perhaps if she dug deep, she might discover a little bit of Alice. Her mother would have probably picked the entire crop of strawberries by now and tidied up the field afterwards. *All those clumps of straw*, she'd have said, *the smallest breeze and it gets everywhere.*

It never ceased to surprise her, the moments her mother chose to ambush her. Perhaps that was how it was with the dead. One minute, you're making an observation, or just getting along, minding your own business, and then they're there, by your side, telling you how it is through their eyes. Or standing alongside, in effective, wordless reproach. The dead, Joanie decided, must be committed to not allowing themselves to be forgotten. Alice's presence seemed to be getting stronger the longer she lay dead. Was it possible to mourn someone more intently, in more detail, three years after their passing? In the caravan last night, as she fell asleep, Alice was standing by the oven. She wiped her index finger along the rim of grease on the hotplate and shook her head with something akin to disappointment. She looked across at Scout, her arms folded across her scraggy bosom. *Don't give me any grief*, Joanie had warned her. Alice resumed her inspection of the oven. At least Matilda hadn't resurfaced in her dreams.

There was something oddly peaceful about fruit-picking; up and down rows methodically, left to the thoughts in your own head. If she could just acclimatise to the physical demands, she could see it would suit her. There was an amicable cama- raderie between the pickers which was warm in tone but without real interaction. People smiled as they deposited full boxes to be weighed, but passed each other on rows without raising their heads. Language was an issue – she'd lost count of the different ones she'd heard on the wagon. There was a woman who counted the boxes and who seemed to be able to say *No white patches, no stalks*, in just about every language. It was a relief to escape all that English. It gave your tongue a rest. No Mrs Eastman catching her skiving against the banister on the landing, and saying 'I presume you've already prepared Kittiwake?' No one capable of asking prying questions – there was a soothing peacefulness in that. Different tongues, different skin colours, different eyes, different noses, different jaw lines. Everyone's hands blushed and sweetened by the strawberries. You could always see things in common, and not get caught up with the detail. A lithe Chinese man had offered to refill her water-bottle. She'd nodded her head in thanks. How had he ended up in a field in Norfolk? Perhaps he'd made one of those journeys in a false-bottomed boat, or packed in a crate in a lorry. How much more peaceful it was just to nod thanks for the water and not to have to deal with any of that undertow; to be without the inclination, or the language, to ask.

At lunch-time Joanie sat under a tree and ate her tomato sandwich. She hadn't thought about Scout's lunch. She was sure she would find something in the cupboard. Maybe after a couple of days she would be allowed to bring Scout along on the wagon. She'd keep out of the way. She could sit by the weighing station, read a book, occupy herself. Perhaps she could pick a few herself. Her fingers were quick and nimble. Team effort, she thought, perhaps that's how they'd get to ten kilos an hour. She hadn't really thought about the safety of the campsite by day. It had felt so jovial last night. Perhaps she should have given Scout a little more instruction. She could lock the caravan door. Nobody would even know she was there.

Joanie sluiced her face with water. The sun was hot now. The fastest pickers had bagged the shade of the only tree to sit under. One thing never changed; there was always a pecking order.

Alice materialised by the weighing station.

'What's Scout had for lunch? I have to say you're excelling yourself in the maternal diligence department.'

Joanie turned her head to look in the other direction. Alice reappeared by the plastic crate stack.

'Sooner or later, you will run out of road.'

Joanie took a swig of water from her bottle and spat it out into the dust. She wasn't going to let that go without a response.

'Unlike you who never had any notion of a road beyond your own front door. Suffocating me with your bloody routine and order.'

A man passing turned his head, thinking she had spoken to him.

'I did my best,' Alice said, stooping to pick up a discarded apple core. 'Can you claim that?'

'Best for whom?'

'Same might be asked of you. Although even you'd have to admit' – and now with tartness in her voice – 'there's never been any question about whose interests you hold closest to your heart.'

Joanie turned her head again. Alice was increasingly beyond the pale.

When 5.30 came, Joanie was questioning whether she would ever again be able to stand up or sit down in one easy motion. She limped towards the wagon.

'You'll have Sunday to recover,' said the old toothless guy who drove the tractor.

Joanie thought this probably passed muster for sympathy here.

41

Joanie woke up. Was it possible to be woken by your own heart singing? She looked up at the caravan ceiling and beamed. One week in and her muscles no longer hurt. She was on the up, absolutely on the up. Alice seemed to have ducked out for a few days too. Mrs Eastman's kitchen, her sugar-pink bedspreads, her china birds in fireplaces, had receded into the distance. Hoorah! She pressed her fingers to her face. She smelled of strawberries, even though she had washed before bed. She smelled constantly of strawberries. She'd smelled like strawberries for over a week. This morning, she even felt warm and plump like a strawberry. In fact, she felt like Tess of the d'Urbervilles when the rich man had tried to put a strawberry in her mouth. Just like Tess of the d'Urbervilles, (she'd watched it on the BBC) but without any of the bad stuff.

She looked across at Scout in the flip-down bed. She was still sleeping. It was a pity there were no children for her to play with, but she seemed to be occupying herself. God knows how. What a gift that she was so easy.

Joanie peeked out of the window. Blue sky, and the promise of heat. What glorious, perfect timing – to cut out to Norfolk and coincide with what would probably be the only heatwave of the year. She'd get a tan quickly. Yesterday she'd worked wearing the smallest top she owned. Perhaps she could go into Norwich at the weekend and get some teeny shorts. Who cared if her arse looked a mile wide bending over a strawberry plant? Some blokes liked that anyway; something broad and slappable. Preferred it in fact to some bony little rump which was always accompanied by a thin, pinched face. What did the French say? That women got to keep either their face or their bum? Joanie pinched at the peach of collagen on her cheek. So far, she thought, she was hanging on to both. Double hoorah. And with tanned, toned thighs – surely to God they would be benefitting from all the stooping and bending she was doing, she no longer felt as if someone had set fire to her hamstrings – who was to know whom she might attract?

A tumble in the strawberry beds. That would be a nice keynote as July slipped into August. She imagined her body blotted with strawberry pulp, with smudges of fruit pressed into the creases of her skin. How lickable she would be. How gloriously summery and juicy; like one big strawberry. She smacked her lips together at the thought. She scooched her breasts together and sat up in bed. She'd be strawberry-nippled, breastilicious. She reached over to put on her new balconette bra. Tits up. Tits out. She shimmied her shoulders and got out of bed. She pulled on her shorts. Today was definitely a day for going commando. Just the thought of it, just the knowledge of it, as she queued for the wagon which would take them to the field, would give her a twinkle in her eye. It would be detectable to any man who knew what to look for, and how to convert it.

She put a slice of bread into the ancient toaster that came with the caravan. She stuck her finger into the jar of Nutella and sucked it while the toast cooked. She toyed with the idea of tracing it down the length of her cleavage. Strawberries and chocolate. My, would she be delicious.

She scooped up her hair, and tied it into a scrunchie. She could already feel a warm fine sweat gathering in the nape of her neck. Today would be hot. Hot hot hot. She opened the door of the caravan and sat on the step to eat her toast.

In the caravan opposite, the eastern Europeans were awake. One of the women was cooking some sausages over a fire, slicing them and stuffing them into huge hefts of bread. That probably counted as good housewifery; doing the menfolk's lunch. Bollocks to all that. Not that Mrs Sausage Cooker wouldn't be queuing for the wagon too, and the one who looked like her sister. The two men wore vests and jeans. Joanie eyed the muscles of their torsos. Ripped. Definitely ripped, if not great dentally. She allowed herself the luxury of imagining the strange words of their language pouring urgently, at the point of ejaculation, into her ear, grubby vest rough to her breasts. She licked the Nutella from her fingertips. She sucked each finger clean with a swift *moue* of her lips. The woman by the fire caught her eye. *Good morning!* said Joanie and waved with her free hand, as if butter wouldn't melt.

When she went back into the caravan, Scout was beginning to stir.

'Morning, sleepyhead! Rise and shine!' Joanie said. 'Do you want me to put some toast in for you?'

Scout sat up in bed. Joanie edged through the gap between the beds and planted a kiss on Scout's head. God, this was so much better than Calm Views! Joanie felt liberated. Her anxiety in the lay-by had completely receded. It seemed ridiculous now. Some of the Romanian women had rigged up a washing line, and already their clothes were flapping in the breeze. Spirits could be like that, Joanie decided; strung-out, visible, animated. Bright, external splashes of colour.

Scout still looked a little bird-like, a little watchful. Joanie thought she perhaps hadn't managed to shake the thought that they were somehow in the wrong. If Scout didn't ask her again, she wouldn't bring it up. Better to let sleeping dogs lie. Here, under this blue sky, with the prospect of a strawberry-filled day, the possibility of being in the wrong seemed ridiculous anyway. Location Order, splocation order. Who cares? What had Alice said? Sooner or later you will run out of road. Nonsense. A road was as long as you chose to make it. She'd get Scout's hair cut at the weekend. Maybe that was what was making her face look a little over-shadowed. Alternatively, she could cut it herself. The woman opposite looked as if she would have scissors that were up to the job.

She turned back to Scout.

'It's another beautiful day. Why don't you come over to the field with a picnic at lunch-time? Get your school-work done first. We're in the second field on the left from the top of the track.'

Joanie blew Scout a kiss, took her sun hat and went down the caravan steps. If her voice weren't so rubbish, she'd be tempted to belt something out.

42

Scout locked the door after her mother left. It got hot and stuffy by mid-morning but it made her feel safer. She got herself a Weetabix and some milk and sat cross-legged on the bench and ate it. Today she would study Venice. She'd marked the pages in the *Rough Guide* already. It would count as History and Geography combined. She put her cereal bowl on the draining board and quickly got dressed. She'd start with her sense of direction.

She studied the map intently, and tried to learn the way from the Rialto to St Mark's Square. Then, she re-drew it in bold pencil strokes, and got all the left- and right-hand turns correct. If this were senior school sense of direction, she'd be an A★ candidate. With her red pen, she marked with a dot a restaurant in San Polo which offered eighty different types of pizza. That was where she would stop for lunch. How long, she wondered, would it take to read the menu? The fire station in Venice was in the Dorsodoro. Instead of red fire engines, it had red launches moored under a bridge. She was satisfied this still communicated urgent.

She read about the church of Santa Maria della Salute, where pilgrims processed to give thanks for their health. It had a roof in the shape of something called the Marian star. Scout made an attempt at drawing it but thought it looked more like a Christmas decoration. She decided to have a go at recreating one of the church's artworks, and plumped for St Mark Enthroned with Saints. She debated how much artistic freedom to give herself with regard to the plague saints, Cosmas, Damian, Sebastian and Roch. Would they sport a whole host of boils, or just one or two weeping sores? She wondered whether Titian had included a plague-spreading rat. She decided to add one to the bottom corner of hers. St Roch looked particularly appalled.

Her crayons were blunt. This was getting in the way of her drawing's effect. St Mark was currently not what Joanie would have called a show-stopper. His face, Scout decided, looked a little long-suffering, rather than saintly. It was hard to capture the distinction between goodness, smugness and resignation. She fingered the blunt tips of her crayons. She could try sharpening them by pointing them upwards and slicing at them with the bread knife. Joanie had done that once, but she had expressly told Scout never to try it for herself. Joanie's attempt had met with only limited success. The crayons were cut in a crinkle shape. Joanie had also nearly taken off the top of her thumb. Scout thought that instead she could walk to the Spar shop, and buy lunch for the picnic, and a pencil sharpener for herself. She imagined a crisp £20 note and pencil sharpeners priced at 55p. How many would she be able to buy? She suspected this was babyish Maths, not even complex multiplication and division. If she'd still been seeing Mr Mohammed daily she'd have left that behind long ago. She'd probably be on logarithms, or trigonometry, things she only knew as headings in his book. Mr Mohammed had said she had the potential to become *an excellent mathematician, a mathematician of the highest order.* This was increasingly hard to believe. The division of £20 by the price of a pencil sharpener, and mathematical hopscotch, probably weren't steps on the road to achieving this.

Scout twizzled the knob on the TV. The only channel that came through clearly was showing the Jeremy Kyle Show. A girl with seven earrings in one ear was complaining *He cheated on me while I was having his baby*. Her friend chimed in and said she *saw his car parked outside his previous girlfriend's house*. Scout switched it off. That definitely wasn't own-learning. She packed her papers and books away in a neat, size-graduated pile. She pushed and prodded with her finger until it was perfectly, precisely stacked. She liked them that way. David Beckham had an obsessive compulsive disorder. She'd read it in a newspaper she'd eaten chips from in Poole. He vacuumed in absolutely straight lines and all the ornaments had to be in exactly the right place. She nudged the *Rough Guide to Venice* with the pad of her thumb. If it was good enough for David Beckham, it was good enough for her.

She pulled on her baseball boots and picked up the caravan key. The wooden tablet with 17 painted on it was too large to push into her pocket. She locked the door behind her and stepped lightly down the stairs. Then, she retraced her steps and checked she'd locked the door properly. Initially, she'd been worried that it was too insubstantial to prevent all their stuff being stolen. However, when she'd looked with a careful eye over what they actually owned, a door that could be pushed open with a nudge seemed barrier enough.

It was hot already. Joanie wouldn't be wearing sun screen. Scout could take a bet on that. Last night, she'd come home with red marks along the length of her bra straps, and asked Scout to rub in some Johnson's baby lotion. She said 'Oh God that's agony' every time Scout touched the red bits. The doctor's surgery opposite the Spar shop had two signs about sun screen. One said *Sun screen makes sound sense*. The other said *Sun burn fades; sun damage doesn't*. Scout had told Joanie this while applying the baby lotion. Joanie said some people had to go red before they went brown. Scout didn't think this was a scientific principle, although she wasn't sure she could count on herself to recognise one.

Science. She wasn't doing anything that could even be remotely described as science. She crossed the road and walked over to a ditch. She looked to see if any wildflowers were growing. Mrs Crawshaw had recommended a picture book on the seven life processes. If Scout could spot a flower, perhaps she could see if it was doing any of them. Transpiration. That would be tricky to detect. She saw only a patch of nettles. The same book had said that the presence of nettles showed there was too much nitrogen in the soil, and was often evident at the edge of intensively cultivated fields. The soil in the field wasn't visible beneath the ripening wheat. Apparently, when wheat was ready to harvest, it made popping noises. She crouched next to it, her ear pressed up close. As Joanie would say *Nothing. Nada. Zip*. No combine harvesters required along here. Scout moved off down the road.

Outside the Spar shop was a metal loop where you could tie up a dog. A Jack Russell lay there in the shade, his pink tongue out on the pavement. She decided not to pat him. He looked as if he would like to lick an ice cream. She went into the shop and wondered what was the best thing to buy for a picnic. What would Mr Groves have suggested, she wondered, what would he recommend? She squidged with her fingers a waxed packet of Soreen malt loaf. Mr Groves would probably say that was better for tea-time, spread thickly with butter and served with tea, properly, in a pot. Not that they'd be having Soreen malt loaf for tea at Houghton Hall. He'd told her Cook used to make tea bread with alcohol-soaked raisins and sultanas. Scout had concluded that Cook was very good. She wished Mr Groves hadn't told her what the Mistress had said about sun hats and Cook's skin. It was unspecific enough to be misleading; Scout hadn't been able to get a clear image of exactly the nature of the problem. Whenever she pictured Cook, now stirring tea loaf dextrously, or carefully melting chocolate, her face was emblazoned with a mixture of port wine stains, sun burn and freckles which Scout felt probably wasn't entirely fair or accurate.

Luncheon meat. The words leapt out at her. If she disregarded the word *Spam*, she could think of luncheon, the perfect luncheon, and buy it for the picnic. She thought Mr Groves would approve.

As she walked back to the caravan, the plastic bag knocked against her legs. She craned her neck backwards to look at a bird above her in the sky. It was singing and singing, a song which seemed to thread along the road with her. Perhaps it was a skylark? She'd read that skylarks could sing for eight minutes without stopping. Perhaps it was a swallow. She squinted skywards and tried to see the shape of its tail. Through the mesh of her eyelashes, the sky and the bird looked as if they had been trapped in a very fine net.

43

In the caravan, Scout made sandwiches with luncheon meat, mayonnaise and some red grapes cut in half. The addition of the grapes had come to her in a flash of inspiration. She thought the colours might go well – the pink of the meat and the purple of the grapes. As she squidged the slices of bread together with the heel of her hand, she briefly questioned her judgement. With the sheen of the mayonnaise, the contents were starting to look a little too flesh-like and bruised. She mentally made a note to avoid banging the bag against her legs as she walked.

Other homes – Emily Matthews' in Poole, for one – probably had Tupperware to contain sandwiches for picnics. Or a zipped-up chiller bag with a padded bottom which supermarkets sold with their names printed across. Or, even, whole hampers designed just for the purpose of picnics. In John Lewis once (Joanie had been buying a snow-white towel because she felt every woman should have one – *Not a towel, Scout, a bath sheet. Like Marilyn Monroe would have had*) Scout had seen a picnic hamper, packed beautifully and ergonomically. The spoons, knives and forks were slotted symmetrically together; the plates held in place with elastic webbing; the cups arranged in a row on the inside lid of the basket. She had gazed at it, closing and opening the sturdy clasp, until a shop assistant had said sharply 'Can you not touch that unless you intend to buy it.' Scout tried to envision a life which included a picnic basket tucked neatly under the stairs, ready for the off. It was hard to imagine.

Scout locked the caravan again, and walked back up the track towards the fruit field. The sky was definitely bigger in Norfolk. It was easy to believe, under this sky, on a day like this, that Heaven might be up there, with God on a vast throne and all the dead people – Alice included – living and worshipping, as she remembered being told by the rector, on a different shore. This phrase had stuck in her mind because she thought it particularly confusing. Why, when everything else about Heaven positioned it in the sky, did this description of the afterlife make it sound like it was on a beach?

The world looked flat when you were in Norfolk. Of this Scout was also increasingly convinced. She understood how people had believed for centuries that it was so. She felt as if she were walking along a huge, smooth plank, which at any moment might up-end and send her spinning and tumbling towards the horizon. A television programme she'd watched said there was a formula for calculating your distance to the horizon. It was something to do with knowing your height and multiplying it by a certain number. She couldn't remember the detail. Would Mr Mohammed have known? She hadn't thought to ask. Maybe it would have followed on from negative numbers.

If Joanie were ever to ask about the pros and cons of own-learning, Scout would have told her there was a definite disadvantage. If you didn't know your height, and you didn't know the formula, the distance to the horizon would remain a mystery for ever. All the own-learning in the world, however diligently pursued, wouldn't change that.

The sun was really hot now. Scout rubbed her palm against the back of her neck. It was sweaty and sticky all at once. Her feet must have swollen a little too, as she was aware of the back of her baseball boot rubbing at the bone of her heel. Today would have been a good day for wearing socks. The plastic handle of the carrier bag was digging a groove into her fingers. In an effort to stop it banging against her legs she was holding it out wide, which was making it twist and tighten its take on her hand. She hoped Joanie was hungry. She hoped she would like the sandwiches. It was always a possibility that her mother might lie back on the grass and say 'Not for me, darling, I'm happy with my smoke.'

Scout spotted her mother before her mother saw her. Joanie was leaning up against the weighing station. Her elbow was against the stack of empty crates and the side of her head was cradled in her palm. She was looking up and smiling at a man who was wearing a plaid shirt. At least, he'd worn a plaid shirt earlier in the day and it was now knotted around his waist. His chest was bare. He was somebody who didn't go red before he went brown. Joanie had her left foot tucked behind her right ankle, and her hips were jutting slightly forward. Her mother was doing that thing she did when she talked to men. She lifted up her chin as she laughed, and touched her two front teeth with the tip of her tongue. Even though she couldn't hear her voice, Scout knew it would be higher than normal, and peppered with laughter. She stopped for a moment, and stood, the bag spinning in her fingers, and waited for her mother to look in her direction.

When she spotted her, Joanie waved to Scout with a long, lean wave, her arm extended and her flat palm making confident, sweeping arcs. Scout scanned her mother's face as she approached her. The tricky part was guessing what she was supposed to say. Should she mention the picnic? Had Joanie forgotten they were having a picnic? Was the man joining them for the picnic? She hadn't made him a sandwich. Joanie would *have* to just have a cigarette. The man was staring at her now too. She was conscious her T-shirt had a jam smear. She tried not to limp. Her heel was beginning to sprout a blister. *Try not to look like a jam-stained limper*, she said to herself, all the while mesmerised by her mother's wave. *Jaunty, if possible,* she told herself, and mimicked the wave back.

'Is there a problem, Scout?' Joanie asked brightly. 'Anything wrong, darling? I was just chatting to my new friend Gus – we were thinking of driving into the village in his truck and having a cold cider at the pub.'

Scout switched the bag to behind her leg. 'No, just passing,' she said. 'I got fed up of my lessons and thought I'd come out for a walk. I wondered how the strawberries were coming along.'

Joanie leaned forward and gave her a kiss. She smelled of strawberries – right there in the smooth curve of her neck. Scout noticed her mother's shoulders were really sunburned. She seemed to have wiggled her straps right down to the tops of her arms. No amount of Johnson's baby lotion was going to soothe that.

'Strawberries, strawberries,' said her mother. 'I'll be picking strawberries in my sleep. Lucky old Gus just has to drive them to Tesco's. Do you need anything?' she asked, smoothing the hair back from Scout's forehead with a hand which was similarly fragrant.

'No,' Scout mumbled. 'I was just walking. Just walking before I did some more school-work.'

'Such a little scholar, my girl,' Joanie said to Gus. 'She won't be picking strawberries for a living.' She nudged him with her elbow as she said it. Gus seemed to be looking mostly at her mother's breasts.

Scout watched as Gus gave her mother a leg-up into the cabin of his lorry. He webbed his fingers together, and Joanie put the sole of her foot into his hand, like a fine lady getting on to a horse. Scout turned and started to walk back to the caravan. Both her feet were bothering her now. How had straw got into her baseball boots? She stopped and picked it carefully from between her toes. Her eyes were prickling too. That

was probably dust from the fields, or something else agri-
cultural. Perhaps it was pesticides. She'd read a lot about
pesticides. That was another thing to worry about. Instead of
breathing in great chestfuls of healthy fresh air, she was probably inhaling toxic chemicals; they would be elbowing and
jostling their way into the tiny pathways of her lungs, the soft
pinkness of her eyelids. She decided to breathe more shal-
lowly. The bag was tapping against her leg as she walked. She
talked out loud to herself to the rhythm of its sound. *Easy
thing to forget*, she said, *easy thing to forget. She was probably not
properly awake when she suggested the picnic.*

Back in the van, she flipped down the table and laid out the
picnic. The sandwiches were looking doubly oily now. Would
that be oily^2? It wouldn't be the square root of oil. She didn't
know what a square root was – only the name – but it wouldn't
be that, of this she felt confident. She bit into the sandwich.
The luncheon meat tasted like cling film. It wasn't the kind of
meat Mr Groves meant as luncheon meat. This would *not* be
his definition of luncheon meat. Mind you, as she looked at
her neatly washed plate from breakfast, she knew jam on toast
wouldn't count on his terms as breakfast either. Kippers fried
in butter, he'd told her. Eggs benedict. Kedgeree. Kedgeree
was made from fish, eggs, rice and cream, with spices and
parsley. Mr Mohammed, meanwhile, had told her that the
English borrowed many words from India ('while they were
busy belonging our land'). 'Gymkhana,' he'd said. 'And jodh-
purs. Pyjamas. Veranda. Kedgeree.'

Scout felt that if you looked hard enough and long enough
you could always find the place where two people overlapped;
the bits of their lives that gave them something that was the
same rather than something that was different. And there it
was, stumbled upon while eating a frankly sickly sandwich.
Kedgeree. Kedgeree. The point in the Venn diagram where Mr
Mohammed and Mr Groves overlapped. A place swimming in

rice, fish, parsley and spices, edged on one side by what she envisioned to be a silver serving platter, like the ones on the home shopping channel, and on the other by a map showing somewhere like Mumbai or Delhi.

If she'd been in Mrs Pearson-Smith's class long enough – if the alphabetical order had reached her name so that it would have been her turn to give an assembly to the class – she'd have done her assembly on her Venn diagram theory. She would have called it *Working out the Overlap.* The boys mostly did theirs on things like *Why I will Love Liverpool Football Club until I Die*, with the exception of James Burrows who'd drawn a schematic diagram of the Battle of Thermopylae – even a Spartan combing his hair leaning against a rock. Until then, she had thought she had nothing in common with him. Now she knew they overlapped on the Battle of Thermopylae. It had been harder to find common ground with Lisa Merrow's assembly on *Why my Terrapins are FUNNY!*, but Scout had been willing, also, to give her the benefit of the doubt. What did she, herself, know about terrapins? She was in no position to contradict.

Scout finished her lunch and went back to her drawing of St Mark Enthroned. Try as she might, she couldn't get his face right, and the plague rat at the bottom left looked like a hamster. She wondered how she should wrap up her school day.

Perhaps a little foreign languages learning. Today would be a good day to make inroads into Italian. She flipped to the back of the *Rough Guide*. She scanned the section that focused on food and drink. *Aglio et olio* – tossed in garlic and olive oil. Perhaps she could think of her greasy sandwich like that. She moved on to Basic Phrases. *Wait a minute! Aspetta!; I'm here on holiday; Sono qui in vacanza.* She rolled the words around her mouth as she imagined them to sound. This would be so much easier with some kind of recording to follow. *Quickly, Slowly,*

Quickly, Slowly, she said to herself. *Velocemente, Lentamente.*
She swung her legs down from the bench where she had been
sitting. That probably counted as enough foreign language for
a day. She went outside and kicked at a few tufts of grass. She
was hungry again. No sign of Joanie. Perhaps she would fry
an egg. An egg, eaten with a spoon, sitting with her back to the
caravan, looking out over a huge empty field, before all the
noise started. That, Scout thought, should be an uplifting kind
of supper.

Later, she undressed by the sink, and filled a bowl with
water. She'd read that Romany gypsies were fastidious about
using separate bowls – one for food and utensils, and another
for washing themselves or their clothes. Mr Mohammed had
told her that Indian women with tiny babies cooked their food
in separate pans to ensure that they ate no spices. Scout liked
this fastidiousness, this clarity of conduct. She rubbed her
flannel on the soap and washed her neck and ears thoroughly.
Emily Matthews had said she was a pikey. Not with these
clean ears she wasn't.

Much later, as she lay in her bed, listening to the caravan
creak and release as it cooled from the day, she heard Joanie
come back. She could tell she wasn't alone. She heard two
voices, two bodies, laughing softly as they came across from
the track. 'SSSHHH!' said her mother. Scout could imagine
Joanie putting her fingers to her mouth like a picture in a
cartoon. She heard her mother stumble on the uneven ground.
'I've gone right over on my ankle,' she said. 'Bloody hell!' It
was said without pain. 'Take your boot off, take your boot off,'
Gus was saying, 'in case it swells up. Here, give it to me, I'll
pull it off for you.'

'Ooh, that's lovely,' Joanie was saying. 'Clever you to be so
good at foot massage.' Gus said something that Scout couldn't
quite catch. Her mother laughed again. 'I'm practically under
the caravan already!' Scout pulled the pillow over her head.

Aspetta! Aspetta! Sono qui in vacanza, she repeated to herself. Joanie's voice came again, more muffled this time. 'You're a one! You're a one!'

A one what? Scout wondered. Not the One Day My Prince Will Come. Not that one. Not *the* one. That didn't look as if it would happen any time soon.

44

Joanie still felt happy. This was awesome and unusual in equal measure. Maybe she was born to be a fruit picker. She was picking up to eight and a half kilograms an hour so she was also collecting a satisfying wedge of money at the end of the day. Quite how much of it she would cough to the tax office she had yet to decide. Or the route by which to do it, if at all. Where to stash it was becoming an issue. Some of the groups had theirs collected by some sort of gang leader (she didn't want to think about that too closely; what tangles of human misery lay there); others trekked into town to put it in the bank or post office. That would be too risky. If she opened a new account they'd ask for identification; maybe it would go on to a computer database – that might trigger something. She'd ruled that out. It wouldn't be safe to hide it in the car. She had close on £1,000. It was getting too much to keep stashing about her person. There were only so many nooks and crannies to be used. Perhaps she should hide it in the caravan, although Scout was all over the van like a squirrel so would find it in hours. If Scout knew where it was, that could potentially compromise her safety. She didn't want her sitting swotting in there most of the day, alone with a biscuit tin crammed full of money. Joanie rolled it up and stuffed it down her bra.

There were only a few days of August left. They'd be switching to plums soon. Then, she would smell like Christmas cake. Her strawberry moment would be over. She'd liked her night with Gus. She would always think of it, she'd decided, as her summer strawberry tumble. Gus was all right. He had a wife and two kids in Newmarket – didn't they all? – but it was a nice distraction. Just what she'd needed. This job had been just what she needed. She hadn't made friends with anyone, but she felt she did a lot of enthusiastic nodding. This was all she required. She loved the noise of the site – 'What a hulla-baloo,' she said to Scout. She loved the pattern of the day, the mass exodus when the tractor came at 7.30, the scramble for the wagon, her bum perched on its broad smooth planks. She liked working her way up the rows, the sight of her plastic crate filling. The strawberries felt warm to the touch. Would it be the same for the plums? She'd always loved the feel of a September morning, the dew a little heavier, the air a little cooler, the afternoon sunshine all the lovelier for the waiting and wanting of it.

Not long before she and Scout had left Oxfordshire, she'd been working in Sainsbury's. Strip lighting, a polyester uniform, ripping open cardboard boxes to stack shelves, destroying her hands. Here, dressed in a T-shirt and shorts and rolled-down wellies, she felt she could break into a dance. She had taken to whistling as she went along the rows. One of the Polish students had told her that when the English season finished, some of them went across to Spain. Or Israel, he told her. Joanie's heart leapt at the thought.

Alice was frowning. At her shoulder on the rows, Alice was often frowning. *You're a thirty-nine-year old mother,* she told her, or asked *What was so wrong with living in my house?* On one occasion, Joanie swore she heard her say *Liar, liar, pants on fire.* Alice dead was obviously more confrontational than alive.

The problem was, and Joanie could see it, acknowledge it, as she sat eating her lunch leaning against some packing crates, the problem was that she liked this way of living. There was something about respectable, monotonous stability which made her want to heave. Scout could cope with it too, Scout seemed to be coping brilliantly. Only last night she'd told her some frankly tedious details about the building of the Coliseum. She would have read all the *Rough Guides* cover to cover soon. Joanie could buy her some new books; with all this money Scout could go into a bookshop and choose some new ones for herself.

They'd be like rolling stones, they'd gather no moss. They'd free-wheel. Free-fall. Do whatever they chose. The Location Order would soon be at the bottom of the pile on somebody's desk. You could always rely on people to fill up a vacuum with a new store of misery or someone else's appalling behaviour. All you actually needed was a big fat slice of time. That, pushed between yourself and anything unpleasant, usually made things come right. She liked the calm logic of this thought.

In the toilet block that evening, Joanie hummed as she queued for the shower. Scout chose not to use the shower in here. Joanie suspected she felt uncomfortable with the jostling assortment of semi-naked bodies. Scout said she preferred to use a flannel and a bowl in the van. She'd elaborated by adding something about washing like a Romany gypsy. Joanie decided not to pursue that one. Sometimes, the things that stuck in Scout's mind were best not given over to scrutiny. In the shower, Joanie sang gustily as she washed the dust of the day from her body. She tilted her foot to make sure she got it properly rinsed. The swallow tattoo on her ankle seemed to soar higher on its wing.

As she approached the caravan, she swore under her breath. Before she'd gone to the shower block, she'd taken out the tank from the chemical loo, and had meant to empty it before showering herself. Now she'd have to do it when she felt all fresh and clean. What a kicker. It couldn't wait until the morning. Scout was bound to need the loo before bed.

When she looked up from where she had left the tank on the grass, she saw Scout sitting on the caravan steps, and a woman was standing beside her. Her heart skipped a beat. Was she someone from the authorities? Looking at the way she was dressed – she was wearing Crocs on her feet – no, she couldn't be anyone important. She looked pretty annoyed, though – she was scowling as Joanie approached. Probably some petty request, some infringement of some kind of rule. For once, Joanie was at a loss to think of even a minor transgression she'd committed.

'Hey Scout,' she said warmly as she came towards the steps. She tilted her head to draw in the woman's physical presence. The woman wasted no time.

'Bitch,' she said, 'd'you think I couldn't smell you on him? D'you think he came home at five in the morning with anything like a convincing story? His kids waited up for him. Waited for him to come back at bed-time to read them a story. Not that a slapper like you cares. Your own child obviously knows nothing like. Let me tell you this: you heave your fat arse anywhere near my husband again and I'll let you know about it. Just you even try.'

Joanie rolled her eyes. Jesus, just what she needed. Gus hadn't been that great; certainly not worth all this performance. Scout seemed to be trying to melt into the spaces between the steps. The eastern Europeans were agog. She wasn't sure exactly what they understood, but the drift was obviously accessible. She took a deep breath.

'Firstly, with regard to my fat ass, let me say from this perspective it's looking half the width of yours, and certainly not as slack. Secondly, any woman who blames another woman for her husband cheating is looking at the wrong person. Look in a mirror, or at the father of your children. Thirdly, I'd be grateful if you'd take your even larger, slacker arse off my caravan steps, and go home and yell at Gus. I didn't have to persuade him into anything. Perhaps you should dwell on that. It might be more helpful.'

'You cow. You brazen fucking cow.' Gus's wife stepped forward and Joanie thought for a minute that she was going to lunge at her. Oh God, how tacky, now she'd have to do some slapping and hair pulling. Instead the woman went for the toilet tank, and rapidly unscrewed the top. Surely she wouldn't . . . The woman turned on her heel and threw the contents all down the side of the caravan. A splatter hit the sleeve of Scout's T-shirt.

'You might not be sorry,' the woman screamed, 'but enjoy cleaning your own shit up. That's what you're worth. Scrabble in your own piss and shit. Be my guest.'

She stormed off, her face scarlet, through a path that automatically cleared through the small crowd. The footbed of one of her Crocs had caught a small puddle of pee. Later, Joanie thought wearily, that might be a satisfying thought. She refocused her attention.

'Thank you,' Joanie said turning to the crowd, with a shooing gesture of her arms. 'Show's over. Tonight's show's over. No more entertainment at Caravan Seventeen. Thank you for your attention. Now please return to your own lives. Glad mine has been of interest.' She clapped her hands together. The onlookers didn't even look sheepish.

Scout had run into the caravan. She had taken off her T-shirt, and was putting it into the bowl which she said was only to be used for washing clothes. Joanie reached out to touch her arm but Scout pulled away.

'Why, Mum, why d'you have to do it? All those people. All that staring. All the mess on the caravan wall.'

She had started to cry. Not small suppressed sobs, but huge great tears. Her nose was running too. She wiped it with her elbow while scrubbing furiously at her T-shirt.

'You might have known she would come.'

'I didn't. Truly I didn't. I'm sorry; I'm really sorry. I had no idea she would pull a stunt like that.'

'But why, why did you have no idea? You always do these things and never guess what comes afterwards. Mrs Eastman's and then this. How many times will it happen?'

'Look, I had no idea he'd be such a hopeless liar. We didn't even discuss what he would say. How could I guess that? It's not my fault.'

'You *always* say sorry, and you *always* say that it's never your fault. Whose fault is it then? It can't be my fault. I'm tired of it. I'm tired of all this.'

'I think you're just tired anyway because it's late, it's bed-time and it's been a long hot day and we both could have done without this. And I *am* sorry, properly sorry, but it *wasn't* my fault. I'm not married. I'm not cheating on anyone. Other grown-ups have their own decisions to make. I'm not forcing anyone to do anything. You have to try and see that, even though I know it's a big ask. It really *wasn't* my fault. I accept that's hard to believe. One day we might laugh about this. I promise you we might. Our summer of crazy women; dancing crazy women, septic tank throwing crazy women. We'll have our own private collection. We could make a pack of cards. Faces we met on our summer of fun.'

'It doesn't feel like a summer of fun. I'm just here on my own all day. I'm fed up. I'm fed up of this. I'm fed up of trying. I'm fed up of accentuating the positive. I just want *normal*. I just want *normal*.'

Scout sank to a crouch on the floor, her head resting on her crossed arms. Joanie knelt down beside her.

'Look, you're tired, you're upset. I promise you it won't seem so terrible in the morning. It's just a stupid bust-up. Just a stupid angry woman. Let me put you to bed. Your

T-shirt's fine. Never been cleaner. Let's fill your other bowl and give you a wash. I'll make you a drink, and tuck you up in bed. When you wake up in the morning, I'll have everything spick and span. You won't spot a trace. Everyone who was watching will soon forget; they'll move on to someone else's dirty laundry. It wasn't so unusual. Scout, trust me, she was just some sad old cow with a husband who doesn't want to sleep with her. The world is full of them except they don't usually make a habit of throwing septic tanks down caravan walls.'

Joanie lifted Scout on to the bed, and peeled off her jeans and her pants. She rinsed a flannel in some warm water and washed and dried her. Scout lifted her arms to ease Joanie putting on her pyjama top. God, Joanie thought, she hadn't put her to bed for years, hadn't helped her into her pyjamas for years. When had she ducked out of that? When had Scout started taking responsibility for all that? She looked so much smaller, so much younger, naked. Joanie reached over to the sink and squeezed some toothpaste on to Scout's brush.

'Open wide. I'll brush your teeth for you. I'll be like your own private dental hygienist. I promise I'll keep going for two minutes . . . You don't have to check your watch . . .'

Scout had settled to sleep, but not as quickly as Joanie had hoped. She wouldn't meet her eyes, and had turned to face the caravan wall. *Go on, forgive me,* Joanie had cajoled, rubbing her back. *Maybe,* Scout said. She'd cried for a little longer, the sobs subsiding into small liftings of her ribcage. Later, as Joanie sluiced disinfectant and fresh water over the side of the caravan, she didn't really want to think about it. Scout hadn't sounded angry, she seemed more desperate than that. Her voice sounded broken, as if whatever sustained her had temporarily sputtered out. This perception was probably best not pursued. Not when Joanie had only just recently got her mojo back.

Through the window she could see Scout's neatly piled stack of books. God in heaven, her fastidious, order-seeking, intense little daughter. Would she be storing up all this disorder like coins, ready for a jackpot of recrimination? Years of all the embarrassment and pain she had caused, all the times when she'd been a crap, negligent mother?

Joanie glanced around the vicinity of the caravan. She'd expected Alice to make an appearance. How wily of her to remain absent. Just when it would have been helpful to have the distraction of a little sparring. She hadn't even material-ised to tut-tut about the thoroughness with which she was cleaning up all the mess. Alice was becoming more strategic. Surely this wasn't allowed?

Joanie sat on the caravan steps and lit a cigarette. Hard to believe she had been singing happily in the shower. You could always count on other people to fuck things up. Always count on them to batter you with their own agenda. Maybe Scout wouldn't mention it in the morning. Maybe it would be stashed away with the collection of things they didn't go back and dwell on. Maybe she'd be receptive to the idea of dismissing it all as part of a collection of female crazies. This one more of a harpy. Completely mad eyes. Even though it had been embarrassing, Joanie had to commend Gus's wife's conviction.

Children mostly woke up in the morning ready to put their best foot forward. Scout would do that. Joanie felt she could count on her to do that. She put aside the small, surfacing anxiety that if the Location Order worked, and anyone ever asked her about all this, it wouldn't stand up well with Social Services. They'd be on to this kind of an incident with barely disguised glee. Once they started assessing you, you were mostly shafted.

Hell, who says they'd find them? Joanie tried to revert to the calm logic of the power of a big fat wedge of time. Location Order, splocation order, she tried to say to herself with her previous chutzpah. Problem was, the words seemed to die before they even reached the end of her cigarette.

45

When Scout reflected on it – which she did, at length – she had to hand it to the police. They came at a very clever time. If they'd come later in the morning, they'd have found her alone in the caravan, measuring out triangles with a ruler, preparing to calculate their area; and a couple of fruit pickers who'd overslept and were still in their tents. This would not have counted as what she learned later they called a good bust. If they'd come in the evening, at nightfall, there would have been a lot of scurrying away, a lot of melting into the shadows. Pickers could have crept out of the back of their tents, and legged it across the fields. The police were obviously wise to all this. So, instead, they came at 7.30 am, 7.30 am exactly, because Scout had been sitting on the van steps, having waved to Joanie with almost restored enthusiasm (it was a few days after the incident with Gus's wife), looking at her watch and eating her toast. First, they surrounded the wagon. About ten of them stood around it, the people heaped on it as usual, looking like a bonfire with too many guys, and the tractor driver looked at one of the policemen and turned off the ignition and shrugged. Other policemen had dogs. They skirted the edge of the camp, and positioned themselves at equal spaces. Two policewomen started poking their heads into tents. If anyone was still sleeping, they told them to wake up, get their papers, and go over to the wagon. The policewoman who found Scout seemed a little surprised.

'Do you speak English? English?' She asked her. She mouthed 'English' the second time.

Scout nodded.

'Who are you with?'

Scout pointed in the direction of the wagon. Had the cat got her tongue?

'Go over to them, then. Go over to the adult who is in charge of you.' The policewoman opened the door of the caravan and checked there was no one else inside.

The policemen were making the workers climb down from the wagon and get into lines. Joanie was standing with her back to them, looking across at Scout. She held out her arms to her, and gestured, and Scout ran to her and took her mother's hand.

'EEA passports in this line; Bunacs here; WHMCs here,' shouted a policeman. 'Anyone who hasn't got their papers on them queue in this line for an escort to your tent.' Another of the policemen was rigging up a desk and taking out a laptop.

The first thing that surprised Scout was how many people had their papers on them. What a flurry of hands, retrieving papers tucked away in clothing, boots, hats. They all seemed to wear so little, and yet it was enough for safekeeping. The second thing Scout was surprised by was the sheen of sweat on Joanie's upper lip. It wasn't at all hot yet. Her mother's hand was sweaty, too. Joanie walked to the line where you were to go if you needed an escort.

'Lovely morning for it,' Joanie said to the policeman as he walked them to the caravan. Scout thought that he didn't look in the mood for jokes. Maybe, also, if you were a policeman, there was no such thing as a lovely morning to do all the things you were required to do.

'Must be so complicated, this kind of operation. Illegal workers. Illegal immigrants. The languages for a start. I don't envy you having to make yourself understood, or understanding them all. Swear to God, in the fields all day I never hear a word of English spoken.'

Scout thought this wasn't entirely true. Some of the Poles, particularly, spoke English really well. Joanie must be trying a different tack. She was laughing nervously in between her sentences.

'What you'll get from me is a British passport. A lovely uncomplicated British passport. Bet you don't get to see those very often in this kind of thing. Just doing a little holiday work. Lovely part of the world. Lovely environment for my daughter. Lovely thing to be doing in the school holidays.'

'Your daughter's school must be back late. My kids have already started,' he said.

Scout thought now probably wasn't the time to jump in with the own-learning explanation. Joanie obviously wasn't keen to offer it as an option.

They reached the van. Joanie went inside and returned quickly with their passports and handed them over. Scout noted that she kept her hand out, palm raised, in the space between them, as if to encourage him to hand them back quickly. She was also doing the back arch which pushed her breasts out. Scout couldn't help but feel that the policeman wouldn't be very impressed, although perhaps her mother could be relied on to be the better judge of that.

'See, couldn't be simpler. Straightforward British citizens. No additional permission required. Hoorah!'

The policeman hadn't looked at the passports. They were still closed, in his hand. Joanie reached forward, rotated her hand and put it confidingly on his arm. She took a moment to look at his badge.

'Officer Colston, once you've checked them, do you mind if we just wait in our caravan until the check's all done? I expect you will find a few illegals, or whatever it is you're looking for. I just don't want my little daughter witnessing anything distressing, you know, people can get so outraged. Between you and me, I think there's some fairly dodgy gang leaders collecting up money at the end of the day. Shocking really. When you think how this sort of work used to be the backbone of the community. That part of England's fabric's gone really, hasn't it? Maypoles and all that.'

Joanie seemed to be looking at him, Scout thought, through her eyelashes. She was also a little perplexed as to why Joanie seemed to be yearning for an old-fashioned England. It seemed a little random. Mostly, she'd always laughed at school's attempts to teach them maypole dancing (*Outdated nonsense*, she said) and last night, when they were eating, she'd gestured across the site and said to Scout, 'Isn't this great, this is how the world should be, one lovely big mix-up.'

The policeman still hadn't looked at the passports.

'Sorry, madam,' he said, 'I'm afraid you'll have to go through the same procedure as everyone else. We'll do our best not to make it upsetting for your daughter.'

Joanie bit her lip.

In the queue for British nationals, there were surprisingly many.

'My favver, he born here,' a man two in front of them said.

'Bequeath you a fake passport did he, mate?' said the officer, and gestured him to move to the left, to a steadily growing huddle.

'What will they do with them?' Scout whispered to Joanie. Her mother didn't answer. Scout asked again, and nudged Joanie. Joanie evidently wasn't listening. Beyond them, one of the groups of workers was being herded into a van. Scout wondered if this was a good thing or bad. She'd thought before that some of them looked as if this might not be work they were choosing. One of the women was always crying.

When it came to their turn, Joanie handed over the passports with less of a flourish than to Officer Colston. Scout had

thought she might say *Ta-daah!* when she gave them to him
and go on again about being British. Joanie didn't say anything.
The man typed their names into a computer. Scout noticed
Joanie was biting her nails while he made the mouse rove over
the screen. She couldn't see what he was clicking on. His brow
was furrowed with the attempt to discern the details on screen
with the sun rising behind him.

'Joan Simpson? Scout Simpson?' he asked. Scout wondered
afterwards why he put the question into his voice. It was
evidently them; they'd just given him their passports to prove it.

'Can you step to one side? My colleague will assist you.
Looks like Scout Simpson is subject to a Location Order filed
by Social Services and a private individual. A Penal Notice
too. I assume you're aware of it. I'm afraid you're under arrest.'

Scout turned to look at her mother. Her own mouth was so
wide open with shock she thought her tongue might just fall
out on to the ground by itself. A cat could get it just strolling
by. Joanie bit the cuticle on her fingernail so savagely it started
to bleed.

'Fuck,' said her mother, 'fuck fuck fuck fuck fuck!' Scout
thought this perhaps wasn't what a fan of the fabric of old
England and maypole dancing might be expected to say.
Officer Colston was looking uncomfortable, anyway.

Later, Scout dwelled, amongst other things, on this. First, if
her mother had anticipated other workers getting cross, her
own response to being bundled off was surprisingly muted.
Secondly, Scout could have sworn, as they were taken to a
police car separate from all the other pickers, that her mother
had unwittingly raised her hands above her head, just like in a
cowboy movie. If Scout had drawn it later, she'd have put a
speech bubble coming out of Joanie's mouth and in it she
would have written *Hands up, I surrender.* The thing that
bothered Scout, as she shifted uncomfortably in the police
car, was *what* exactly was she surrendering *for*?

46

Other than when she swore, Joanie hadn't said anything. Scout thought she looked as if she was thinking, though – thinking like mad.

It occurred to her – as she looked out of the car window at the fields receding into the distance – that sometimes just shifting one word in a sentence made things sound completely different. She could say to Joanie *We* did *do something wrong,* and that would sound final, complete, most definitely guilty of something. It might even sound as if she was accusing her mother. Or, she could just switch round the first two words and say Did *we do something wrong?* This would become a question, would have no blame about it, would leave the door ajar for the possibility that there had been a terrible mistake which might be resolved shortly and leave them in the clear, ready to go back to the caravan. Alternatively, she could say nothing at all. That was probably the best bet. *Least said soonest mended,* Alice used to say, although she probably didn't imagine it applied to being escorted into a police car and driven to the nearest station. Alice definitely wouldn't have imagined it in relation to that.

Scout bit her bottom lip to stop it wobbling. She reached across to take Joanie's hand. Her mother looked at her. 'Sorry, Scout,' she said, 'I'm really truly sorry, Scout.' She looked like she might cry. Scout wanted to say *What for?* but she thought the two policemen in the front would be listening to every word. Them, and possibly St Michael. Hopefully, whatever

Joanie was sorry for would be none of their business. Hopefully, it was something very truly small. After Gus's wife, Scout didn't feel up to a showdown.

At the police station, she and Joanie waited in a reception area, where a policeman was sitting behind a vinyl desk. It could have been a hotel reception desk, except there were no carnations like on Mrs Eastman's, and rather than notices telling you about tide times, or boat trips, or gardens that were open, there were stern warnings about assaulting officers, drunkenness, and access to solicitors, and details about how bail could be paid. The floor wasn't very clean. In the right-hand corner there was a dried puddle of sick. Scout decided to sit on her hands rather than have her thighs pressed to the chair. It would be easier to wash her hands properly afterwards.

Joanie was asking for a solicitor. She produced a roll of money from her bra. This was a surprise to Scout. Was it something they taught pickers, when they first arrived at the fields, this ability to squirrel all manner of things about themselves and not have them drop out along the rows? 'I can pay,' Joanie was saying. 'I can pay. I don't need legal aid.' The policeman rolled his eyes at her wearily.

'Do you have any idea how much it costs?'

A policewoman with a round face, and earrings in the shape of four-leafed clovers, approached Scout. She crouched down on one knee so that her face was at the same level as Scout's. Scout wondered if she'd checked the floor for sick first. The crouching was always a bad sign. Grown-ups did this when they were going to speak very slowly and very clearly, whilst maintaining eye contact. Scout made the space between them greater by sucking in her ribs and her stomach. She wondered whether she should try looking dim. Was this an appropriate time to create an interesting and memorable diversion?

'Scout,' the policewoman said, 'we need to talk to your mum. We need to take her into a room by herself. I'd like you to come with me and sit in a different room until they've finished having their conversation. Don't worry, you haven't done anything wrong, I'll just be keeping you company. My name's Sergeant Lindsay, but you can call me Dawn.'

Scout wasn't sure if she wanted to call her anything. Joanie turned round from the desk and said, 'It'll be all right, Scout. You go with her. I won't be long.' Joanie looked as if she was trying to give her a usual smile. It wasn't a usual smile though. It didn't push beyond the corners of her mouth. Joanie's cheeks stayed right where they sat when she wasn't smiling.

Scout followed Dawn into a small side room. There was a camera in the corner but it didn't have a light on and it wasn't making a noise. She wondered if they interviewed criminals in here. Did all the rooms have cameras? She sat down on a red fabric chair.

'Are you going to ask me questions?' Scout said.

'No, but you can ask me some if you'd like.'

'What sort of questions?'

'Any sort you'd like. You can ask about police work, the police station. Anything to help the time pass more quickly for you. Or, if you want, I can ask you some. Not about anything serious, just what you like doing, your favourite things, you know. I'll start by asking if you want anything to drink. We've got a dispenser down the corridor. You can have hot chocolate, chicken soup, tea, coffee, warm blackcurrant.'

'Hot chocolate, please.' She watched Dawn get up and leave the room. Could it get any worse? Maudie Broughton-Fowler drank Cook's hot chocolate on a terrace overlooking the garden. Scout had drunk it at a leisure centre in Andover and now in a police station in Norwich. The distance between herself and Maudie, she thought, was an unbridgeable abyss.

What would Mr Groves think? Dawn returned with the hot chocolate. A glob of undissolved powder floated on its top. Scout poked her tongue around the edges of it like a hesitant cat.

'So,' Dawn rallied, 'what do you like to do in your spare time?'

Spare time from what, Scout thought. It seemed that most of her time was spare.

'I like to learn things, you know, stuff.'

'Give me an example,' said Dawn brightly.

'Mostly, the mathematical area of shapes, the types of patterns of silver cutlery and flatware, good posture, the meaning of uxorial, how to walk from the Rialto to St Mark's in Venice.'

'That's nice. That sounds interesting.'

Dawn didn't look as if she meant it. Although, when Scout ran through the list again in her head, she thought it didn't really show all its possibilities.

She looked up at the camera. It still didn't look like it was whirring. If it had been, it would have recorded what she'd said. On television programmes they said everything you said could be taken down as evidence. If they showed that to a school inspector, an own-learning inspector, it might pass as an acceptable account of herself. Scout arched her spine and tried to look out of the window. It was too high to do so. She guessed that most people, sitting in here, wouldn't want to be seen from the street.

'Venice,' Dawn said. 'I've never been to Venice but I went to Rome on a school trip once.'

Scout wondered whether to tell her about the construction of the Coliseum. Dawn didn't exactly look as if she had always been dying to know. She had retied one of her shoelaces and was now smoothing her eyebrows into an arch using the tips of her ring fingers which she'd lightly licked.

256   *Kay Langdale*

'Would you like something to eat?' Dawn asked. 'I can fetch you something from the canteen.'

Scout shook her head.

When the door opened, a little later, and Joanie came in, she was accompanied by a different police officer, and a woman who told Scout she was called Jackie Broom from Social Services. Scout wondered if she knew the social worker who'd knocked on the door in Birmingham, but decided it was better not to ask. Presuming people might know each other or were friends was probably a mistake. There could be thousands of social workers. Joanie sat down on the chair beside her and scooped her hair back from her neck.

'I've got something I need to talk to you about, Scout. Unfortunately, these people have got to listen to me telling you too.'

She took Scout's hand in hers, and kissed her fingers.

Jackie interrupted. 'Your mother has not been entirely truthful with you, or with others. She has to tell you something she could have told you a long time ago.'

'Thank you, Jackie. I don't need you introducing anything I have to say to my daughter.'

'There's no need to be hostile.'

'There's no need for you to interrupt.'

Scout shifted in her chair. Once Joanie got off on the wrong foot with someone it didn't usually go well. She turned to look at Joanie, who had started to speak.

'It's about your dad,' she said, as simply and straightforwardly as she might say, 'It's quarter to four.'

After she finished speaking, Scout thought of what Jackie had said, just before Joanie spilled the beans. *Your mother has not been entirely truthful with you, or with others.* When she said this, Scout toyed with the idea of how big a lie could actually be. If it were made into something physical, something able to be held, how big might it actually be? A grit-sized fib? A pebble-sized mistruth? A whopper the size of a boulder? An absolute cliff of a lie? However she'd guesstimated, it would not have been as big as this one turned out to be. That was what a small voice inside her head said. Not a voice that was angry, she felt clear about that. But a voice which pointed out that she had lived all of her life not knowing she had a dad who had wanted her too.

Jackie was now looking calmly at Joanie. Scout thought her face wore a practised, kind-looking expression, but each of her features, when examined separately, lacked any kindness at all. Her lips were thin and mean. Her badge said she was a Family Court Advisor, and also part of the Looked After Team. She would take a bet that Jackie's definition of being Looked After might not be the same as her own.

All those years of worrying she had no dad when he was out there all along. She could have sent him one of Mr Mohammed's Father's Day cards. She could have sent him a miracle of paper engineering. At school before Christmas, they'd watched a film called *The Railway Children*. At the end, the mist cleared and the girl said *Daddy! My daddy!* Scout had managed not to cry; it seemed a little unnecessary now.

When she was very young, Alice had bought her *A Child's Treasury of Fairy Stories and Legends*. It was the biggest book she had owned. To hold it required the whole length of her arms. At the time, she thought all the babies got stolen in that book; swaddled in cobweb-thin mohair and taken away by the fairies, by old women who came to the door, or by servants, hidden and smuggled away in caskets. Had she been stolen too? Stolen from her father by her mother, but in a way that was more scientific, more medical, than any of those stories could have anticipated. Carried away not in a blanket or a casket, but a test-tube. When she visualised the test-tube, it acquired a soft blue glow.

Jackie was talking to her. Her tone of voice, and the way she was looking deeply into her eyes, irritated Scout. She wondered how much of this summer had been spent either pretending to be, or being thought to be, dim. It could get to be a habit.

'Secure accommodation,' Jackie was saying, 'we'll be moving you both to secure accommodation in the short term. Just while there's a preliminary hearing in Norwich. There's an application for an interim hearing in the Royal Courts of Justice in London in a fortnight, just so everything can be talked through properly. In the meantime, I'll spend some time with you and you can say what you are thinking and feeling so that everyone knows your views. Your mum under-stands that and is happy with it. I'm here to make sure your views and thoughts are listened to. You can trust me for that.'

Jackie told her they could have waited some more weeks while a psychiatrist assessed Scout's ability to handle the news, but Joanie had felt Scout was perfectly able to absorb it. Scout thought it felt like trying to swallow a house brick. It would require some extra effortful swallows, but she would work on it.

Jackie finished speaking. Scout looked across at her mother. Joanie was staring out of the window. Scout followed her gaze. A dog on a lead was peeing up against a tree. She didn't think Joanie was looking at that. Perhaps she was staring right through it all. She looked as if she would welcome a cigarette and her pink Ikea blanket. Was that back in the caravan? Was it in the Corsa? Perhaps you lost track of things, living like this. Maybe most things got lost, and all you were left with was the memory of them.

'What's my dad's name?' she asked Jackie suddenly. Jackie looked a little surprised, and flicked through her papers.

'Ned Beecham,' she said, 'he's called Ned Beecham.'

And so there it was, after all that wondering, all that pondering about what the other part of her name might be.

Scout Simpson Beecham. Scout Beecham Simpson. *Simpson Beecham*. Saying it together made it sound as if you had hiccups, or it was the name of a station where a country train might stop.

Joanie was rubbing at her face with the heels of her hands.

'When can we go to our secure accommodation?' Scout asked.

'Now if you want,' Jackie said, 'I'll just ring and sort out a car.'

47

Secure accommodation sounded as if it might have an extra large door. Perhaps one that had an eye-hole for peeping at whomever was knocking on it, or a series of bolts on the inside to be drawn across with a reassuring *whump* at night. In fact, the door didn't look like that at all. It was a normal size, the paint was peeling a little, there was no eye-hole, and there was only a piddly chain on the inside to be added if required. Scout looked extra hard for some kind of security pad which would require a pass or key to be slotted into it. No sign of any such thing. Nothing. Perhaps secure accommodation meant something you could count on.

There were mothers and young babies in the unit. There were onlookers who seemed to watch everything the young mothers did, which from what Scout could immediately gather was mostly smoke and listen to their iPods. There were women with older children. One had a face covered in bruises and cuts, and what looked like a broken arm. There was someone called the warden who sat at yet another desk in the entrance hall. Perhaps he was the one who stopped anyone suddenly making a bolt for it – she imagined one of the young mothers making a dash with a push-chair. He didn't look up to much speedy chasing, or to preventing the person who had bashed the woman's face coming back to give her another licking.

Joanie and Scout were shown to their room. There was a small electric hob, and a sink, and a little en-suite shower and loo. There were two single beds with turquoise covers. Joanie was still wearing the clothes she had put on to work in the field. Social Services were going back to the caravan to fetch them some more. Joanie pulled off her boots. She lay down on the bed and crossed her arms over her eyes. Scout asked her if she was hungry. 'Not really,' Joanie said, 'are you?'

Scout wondered if it was inappropriate to be ravenous on a day like this. It was four in the afternoon and she'd had nothing since the powdery hot chocolate. She confessed that she was, and Joanie went out barefoot to the warden, and then a woman came in with a can of beans and some bread. Joanie lay back on the bed and put her crossed arms back over her eyes. Scout opened the ring-pull of the bean can and tipped the contents into a little saucepan. Joanie was silent and still. Perhaps she was busy swallowing a house brick of her own.

When it was dark, and they were in bed, Scout felt more able to speak. Her mother was obviously awake, even though she had hardly spoken.

'Why did you do it? What made you do it?' Scout asked. She had been searching for the best way to ask since she had been stirring the beans. *Why didn't you tell me I had a dad, and that you'd promised me to someone else?* seemed too risky an opening.

'Why did I do it? It probably sounds odd but it seemed fair at the time. You felt like only mine. At the beginning, when you were made, I hadn't even considered wanting to be a mother. I was just doing it because of something I saw on TV. And then suddenly, I did want to be a mother. I really wanted to keep you. I didn't know how to explain that, and I didn't really want to have to either. So I lied, and I ran. I'd done that in other situations. It usually worked. It seemed simple and obvious and so straightforward then.'

'Did Alice know?'

'No, she hadn't a clue. No one had. She put you down to some passing bloke. Telling no one made it seem smaller, less true. After a while, with the passing of time, even I forgot. I just thought what you'd never had you'd never miss. Your dad or you. My dad died when I was so young. I didn't really see how it could be any different.'

Scout considered saying it *was* different. It was completely different. Alice hadn't told any lies; her husband had died in an accident, no one could prevent that. Joanie had promised something and then broken her promise. Scout couldn't inch round that not being fair, not fair to her or to the couple. Joanie only saw things from her point of view, from how it affected her alone. Scout felt her eyes prickle with tears. She reached over to take her mother's hand. The problem was, knowing this didn't make Scout love her any less.

'I'd like to meet him if that's okay. I always wanted a dad. I always wondered what he was like. I minded that you'd never talk about him.'

'I didn't know him to tell you anything, apart from all these circumstances which I didn't want you to know. It felt like a slippery slope, so I thought best avoided.'

Scout reflected. Her parents hadn't known each other at all. Not at all. There was no escaping its strangeness. Her father had an Italian wife, and another child who was adopted. He was a teacher. He taught Latin at a boys' school. That was all Jackie would say. Scout felt there was a lot extra that might be said. The Italian woman was meant to be her mother. Joanie had planned on giving her away. She didn't know how to even begin thinking about that. She thought of Alice. *Least said, soonest mended.* Perhaps least thought, soonest mended too.

She switched her mind back to her dad. If he was a Latin teacher, he'd understand all the mottos and inscriptions on buildings. He'd know what all those ornate, elaborate words meant. She racked her brains to see if she knew one word of

Latin. She couldn't come up with anything. Not a single word. If she were able to meet him, would he think she was dim too, even if she wasn't pretending to be?

When she met him, she'd pretend she was Maudie Broughton-Fowler. She'd walk in like Maudie Broughton-Fowler, and offer her hand, back straight, first-rate posture, like Mr Groves had taught her. That might be a good start.

48

It was September the second. Ned was in the garage of their London home, hosing down wet suits and deck shoes to rid them of salt and sand. He'd hung the wet suits in descending sizes on hangers, and stuffed the deck shoes with balled-up newspaper to keep their shape through the winter months. He'd rinsed through the outboard motor of their little dinghy, and strung its paddles to the wall with a bungee cord. Elisabetta teased him; such order, she said, such obsession with order. They'd returned from Cornwall late last night. She'd gone through the house this morning opening windows, sweeping up dead flies from sills. She shook blankets and rugs, and opened the french doors into the garden. Anyone would have thought that they had been gone for years. Maia's beach clothes were pegged out along the washing line. Maia was following Elisabetta around the house, rediscovering her toys.

They hadn't found Scout. All those weeks in Cornwall he had found himself waking up, crossing from the bed to the window, opening the blind and looking out at the vast expanse of water, and making some kind of wordless prayer to a God he wasn't even sure he believed in; *Please, might today be the day?* And none of them had been. After a while, everybody had stopped asking. His father, the last to quit, over breakfast, from behind his paper; a short peremptory *Any news?*, the tone disguising empathy. *A Scout-shaped space*, that was what his mother had called it, and so it was. At the dinner table, on walks, on the terrace in the evening before dinner, a

Scout-shaped space which silently, persistently, nestled among them, finding its way to the crook of his arm, to the inglenook by the fireplace, to the turning corner of the stairs where there was a small wicker chair. Perhaps it was ridiculous to expect they would ever find her. Maybe they would spend years looking for Scout in this curiously passive way.

When his mobile rang, he couldn't fish it out of his jeans pocket. His hands were wet and slippery from the hosepipe, and when he tried to slide the phone open, his thumb shot off the screen and ended the call. He turned off the hosepipe, wiped his hands down his jeans and waited for it to ring again.

'They've found her,' Susan Philips said, 'she's in Norwich. Joan Simpson was working on a fruit farm. I've filed for an interim hearing in the Courts of Justice in two weeks. She's asked to see you. Social Services have agreed to the request.'

Afterwards, Ned couldn't really recollect how he had crossed the driveway from the garage to the house, how he had found Elisabetta doing whatever she was doing. Was he shouting, was he calling, where did he put the phone? When he told Elisabetta, she dropped an armful of laundry and ran into his arms. Perhaps it was inappropriate that they both cried. Perhaps it was making assumptions, that would be horribly premature.

49

Jackie Broom had it all lined up; she held her three folders and tapped them officiously on her desk. She pushed back on her chair and reached for her coffee mug. She'd talk to Joan Simpson first, then Scout, then the Beechams. Information gathering. She always liked that part of her job. Then the mulling, the consideration, and the coming to a conclusion. It would be wrong to deny she liked the process. The unveiling and dissection of people and their lives, what might be called their suitability. So many of the people she encountered – haphazardly floundering towards Social Services after a call from a well-meaning doctor or a referral from the police – had no idea of the power, the sanctions, that she was in a position to wield. Regularly she took children from mothers she deemed unworthy. Regularly she decided that couples were not suitable candidates as adoptive parents. Regularly she restricted, or withdrew, mothers' contact hours with their children. *It's not personal; it's professional,* she would tell them, *you have to respect the process.* The power of process. If ever asked to consider, she might truthfully acknowledge that once, in the middle of the night, she'd seen the procedures she implemented as a combine harvester; threshing and hacking everything that stood in its way. Once, a woman from whom she had taken a child, stood, tears streaming down her face, screaming, *Is this what you call doing good? Tell me how this is in the best interests of my child?*

You got immune after a while; immune from the abuse, from the accusation you were playing God. You got bolstered too; by the knowledge that due diligence to process mostly meant keeping your own back covered and that, at least in the magistrates' court, most magistrates would agree mildly to any measure you suggested. They were the last ones to want anything bouncing back in their faces. What had made her job easier, Jackie decided, what had made it so much easier, was a reduction in the confidence of most magistrates to challenge or think independently, and a climate of caution which meant acquiescing to whatever Social Services recommended. A judge at the Royal Courts of Justice, though, may be a different matter.

It still meant she could be chummy; she was good at being chummy. She called her clients *darling* and *sweetheart*, and complimented them on their boots, their new haircut. She always said she was so sorry, how sorry she felt for them, whenever she told them of a new decision which was basically shafting them. She had perfected an expression, her head tipped sympathetically to one side, her palms facing the ceiling, a wobble in her voice as she said it was the process, not her. She reminded herself of a painting she'd once seen in a gallery; someone pious, holy. Often she blamed decisions on her manager, or the team lawyer, safely tucked behind the frosted glass of the inner office. In reality, the power was mostly hers to wield. She liked that; some days she saw it as a gleaming Arthurian sword.

Joan Simpson. She didn't look the type to roll over and cooperate. She'd been sharp once or twice already. She'd learn that wasn't the way to get on. Jackie picked up her pen and drummed it on the edge of the table. Which opening gambit would she choose? How could she get her to give the information she wanted? She skimmed through her options and alighted on *How would you describe yourself as a mother?* That was the one that usually put them at their ease and made them open up more than they intended.

'That's a ridiculous question. I wouldn't choose to describe myself in that way.'

Joanie could have kicked herself. That wasn't the best opening response. Why answer honestly? That was almost never the best policy. All the way in the taxi she'd repeated to herself *Smile. Be nice. Don't give them anything to hang you by.* If she could just strike the right note, surely they'd be on her side? And now she'd blurted that out. Calling Jackie Broom's first question ridiculous probably didn't count as the most sensible start.

'It may be ridiculous, but could you have a go at answering it for me, anyway?'

This was said in a tone so patronising, Joanie would have liked to lunge at her with the scissors on the desk that Jackie had used to cut a sample of Scout's hair. She took a deep breath.

'Isn't that something celebrities do in magazines when they want to portray themselves as the all-loving, all-attentive, perfect woman? It's not really an appropriate question, is it? How would *you* answer it? Come on, how would *you* describe yourself as a mother?' (Always, she thought, as the words tumbled out of her mouth, always this inability to rein herself in.)

'Whether I have any children or not is irrelevant to this conversation. I'm trying to ascertain what kind of mother you think you are.'

'But it's not irrelevant to me. If you are considering and judging what kind of a mother *I* am, at least I deserve some insight into what you think is best practice. Look at it from my perspective. Scout is eleven, has never been in hospital for any kind of injury or broken bone, has never been reported at school for any sign of neglect, is healthy, and well-adjusted and, until this summer, highly focused at school. If you're looking for poor or neglectful mothering I suggest you look elsewhere.'

'Neglect isn't just physical. Perhaps we could discuss that a little more.'

'I see. So you'll try and get me on emotional neglect. I see you. I see what you are doing.'

Jackie looked down at her notes. Joan Simpson was not demonstrating an appropriate level of subservience and respect. Some of them came out boxing like this; still thinking they were slugging it out, as individuals, one to one, or thinking she was just some kind of gatekeeper and that the real authority figures would come later. They didn't know she had the combine harvester behind her, ready to tear up the ground they thought they were standing on.

'I think perhaps you need to think a little about your attitude. Aggression or argumentativeness towards us is something we take very seriously. If I can give you any tip, I'd suggest you make a better attempt at co-operation. Put at its simplest, you've put yourself in this position, now we get to decide.'

'Decide what? What have you taken it upon yourself to decide?'

'At its most extreme level, to decide whether we put your daughter in foster care because you have shown yourself to put your needs before hers.'

'That's ridiculous. Why would you even say that?'

'I think the facts of this summer speak for themselves. You defied a Location Order. That's grounds enough. We have testimonies from all of your employers, some neighbours. Please don't doubt our ability to gather information.'

'I wouldn't begin to doubt your ability to gather information. I'm doubting your ability to see what's right in front of your face. Scout doesn't need you taking her into foster care. It's the last thing she'd need.'

'So give me an example from this summer where you put her needs first.'

'Scrabble.'

'I beg your pardon?'

'Scrabble. Scout loves playing Scrabble. She'd play it for hours every night if she could. I can't bear the game. I hate each and every plastic tile. Yet I play Scrabble – at least two or three nights a week. I don't pretend to lose; Scout wins every time. But it takes hours, hours and hours. There's a nice piece of selfless mothering for you. Put that down in your notes.'

'You honestly expect me to take this as an example of putting Scout's needs first?'

'No, because in your view of the world you're not interested in simple things which make a child happy. Scout likes Scrabble, and doughnuts in bed, and reading all manner of books, and learning things off by heart, and putting things in very tidy piles, and adopting some ridiculous Romany system of washing herself and her clothes. And so whatever you think of my mothering, I'll tell you this, Ms Broom. I know her; I know what makes her tick, and I've got an eleven-year head start on anyone else you might want to consider to care for her.'

'So you see yourself as beyond reproach, beyond criticism?'

'I didn't say that.'

'No, you didn't say that. So perhaps instead of asking you to describe yourself as a mother, perhaps I should have cut straight to the chase, and asked you what you could have done better or differently. Would that style of questioning suit you better? Would you be a little more forthcoming?'

'I'm not sure it's worth talking to you at all. You look to me like someone who's reached a decision before I even open my mouth. What do you want me to do? Plead with you to let me keep my child? I expect that would make you feel good, sitting there tapping your pen on your desk. You make me sick.'

'Being rude to me doesn't help you in any conceivable way. I'm going to draw this meeting to a close. Perhaps you need some time to think of the seriousness of the situation you're in, and work out a way of handling yourself so that my report doesn't just say that you were hostile and unable to communicate in any meaningful way.'

Job done. Jackie flicked the file closed. Sometimes, everything was so much easier when you actively, instinctively, disliked the person you were assessing.

Joanie continued to sit at the desk after Jackie left the room. *Damn it.* So often her good intentions were left trailing behind her. She'd intended to co-operate – why hadn't she left it at a little bridling, rather than becoming all-out hostile? Damn her mouth. What did Alice say? *You might as well be hung for a shilling as a sixpence?* She'd probably achieved that. No point chasing after Jackie down the corridor. No point trying to be all warm at the next encounter. Perhaps she should send her an e-mail, putting her attitude down to nerves or stress. Jackie Broom didn't look like she'd be particularly sympathetic to that. Joanie got up and decided to go outside and have a cigarette. Jackie would be talking to Scout next. She wondered if Scout would unwittingly shop her. There ought to be rules to make sure it was fair.

Scout sat waiting in a small room in the Social Services offices. They'd cut off a little piece of her hair for a DNA test. Joanie was annoyed and said there was no question that Ned Beecham was her father, but they did it anyway. She said Scout was born thirty-nine weeks and six days after implantation and how much more precise did they want her to be? Joanie's tone was quite stroppy. Scout sat quietly while Jackie Broom sawed away at her hair with a very small pair of quite blunt scissors. This seemed another magical piece of science; that her hair could prove beyond doubt that Ned Beecham was truly her dad.

Jackie was having a meeting with Joanie now, and then coming to talk to her. Scout hoped it was going well, although despite everyone painstakingly telling her each stage of the process, she wasn't sure what counted as going well. She hoped Joanie wasn't getting cross. She obviously didn't like Jackie. Cross was a definite possibility.

Family Room didn't seem the right word for this place. There was a total absence of any people looking like a family. Also, there were a lot of printed notices warning you not to hit or abuse anyone who worked here. That didn't sound very family-like. The walls were plastered with the same poster titled *Adoption and Fostering: Working together to change lives for the better! Give us a call!* Underneath the title was a photograph of a girl in a bubblegum-pink puffa jacket, laughing by a swing in a park, her mouth so open you could see all her teeth. Scout wondered if you got asked before your life got changed for the better. Jackie looked bossy. That was the only thing she was sure of.

Another social worker would sit in on the meeting to support her and to see that the questions were clear. 'What will they ask me?' she'd asked Joanie in the taxi.

'I don't know for sure. I expect what we've done this summer, who you've met, what you've felt like, what you would like to do next. That sort of thing.'

When Jackie came in, she was carrying a folder which had Scout's name across the front.

'Hello my darling,' she said. Scout didn't think she was her darling at all.

'I've just had a lovely chat with your mum about how this summer has been, and thought it would be nice to go through it with you, you know, just to understand things from your point of view.'

Afterwards, Scout wasn't sure what to think. She'd tried to be as factual as possible; to say where they had gone, where they had stayed, who they had seen. Jackie didn't seem that keen to note down what Mr Mohammed and Mr Groves had taught her. Or to learn about the mobile library, or Gabriella Douce and the angels. She mainly seemed to want to know things that might get Joanie into trouble. Things about men; about Dave at Calm Views, and Gus at Dent's Farm. Scout just said she was embarrassed; that seemed a non-blaming sort of word. Jackie looked like someone who could take your words and twist them into something to whack Joanie with. She asked Scout how she felt about not having been told about her dad. She'd replied she was glad she knew now. It was a bit like walking a tightrope. She thought the best thing was not to use too many adjectives. Adjectives were describing words; sometimes they gave away more than you intended. Scout tried to speak in small sentences. Jackie would think she was stupid, but it was better than saying more than she meant. She said *hmm* a lot, to try and avoid some of the questions and give herself time to think, not like mad, but carefully. Eventually Jackie seemed to get frustrated and asked her to write a list.

'A list?' Scout asked.

'Yes, a list of what you like and what you'd like to do in the future.'

Scout took a pen from Jackie. The future seemed safer territory. She hoped her handwriting wouldn't be too rubbish; it was ages since she'd sat at a desk, and it was hard to do so now, with two faces watching her every move.

Afterwards, when she left the room, Jackie had to credit the child. Beneath her apparently hesitant cooperativeness, she could see she was thinking hard. She did better than her mother; she had been careful throughout; had demonstrated thought before everything she said. She hadn't sung like a canary; Jackie wished she had. She preferred it when that happened; you could scoop up armfuls of evidence and swagger out like a pirate.

The Beechams were good. Whether it was practice – Jackie assumed the process of adopting a Chinese child meant you sang brilliantly from the same song sheet – or whether they were the genuine article, a happily married, stable, couple, it was hard to deduce. They didn't exhibit any overly hostile resentment towards Joan Simpson; Elisabetta said she felt very let down, but that it was a long time ago and there were more important things to think of now. They were interested in putting the child's interests first, however that played out. They seemed open to as little or as much contact as Social Services were prepared to recommend. They seemed familiar, she guessed through their experience with their adopted daughter, with grafting someone new on to a family environment. Their expectations seemed appropriate, measured. They ticked all the commendable boxes. Ned looked keen; she always liked it when fathers looked motivated. She thought he'd get on with his daughter. Jackie didn't usually allow herself such sentimental, irrational conjectures.

After the meeting with them, she went back up to her office. Time to mull, time to ponder. Time to decide who got what. In one case, a client had said plaintively *I thought the court got to decide.* Not really, Jackie wanted to say, but thought the woman was better left with her illusion.

50

Waiting for Scout, Ned had butterflies in his stomach, and his palms were sweating. The meeting with the social worker had been curiously bland and factual. Now, Elisabetta hadn't spoken for the last quarter of an hour. They were waiting for Scout to walk through the door. Had it been as it was planned, they would have greeted her swaddled, freshly born, perhaps even been present at her birth. Instead, they had mourned the possibility of her, and now, on this day, she was going to walk into the room, his daughter, aged eleven. He tried to push the image from the school photo out of his mind. Children never looked like they did in school photos.

He looked towards the door; he could hear voices behind it. Elisabetta reached over and took his hand. Another social worker came in first – God, there were legions of them – 'Here's Scout,' she said simply, holding the door open for his daughter to enter.

A child, under-sized for her age but standing tall and with eyes that looked at him intently, put out her hand to shake his.

'Hello, I'm Scout,' she said.

'Like in the book *To Kill A Mockingbird*,' Ned said. (What a ridiculously formal thing to say, what a dyed-in-the-wool schoolteacher thing to say, he thought, but how was he supposed to begin?)

A shadow of indecision flickered over her face. 'No, not that,' she said, 'people often think that. My mum named me after Demi Moore's and Bruce Willis's daughter. That's where my name is from.'

'That's good too, I think that's good too.'

Scout smiled hesitantly. 'I'd like to read the book though, if I'm old enough.'

'I could read it to you, if you want.' God, how eager he sounded, he thought. Was that a ridiculous thing to say to an eleven year old? Did you still read to children at that age? Anything to build a bridge to this child.

Scout turned to Elisabetta. Elisabetta reached towards her and put both her hands around Scout's. She surprised herself by speaking Italian. It was her mother tongue that sprang from her lips in a dialogue that had begun with Scout's photo on the fridge. It was not something she had planned.

'*Ciao; come sta? Molto lieto.*'

Scout looked puzzled, and then she said, '*Aspetta! Sono qui in vacanza. Velocemente. Lentamente.* That's all I've got. I'm only just beginning. I'm probably not saying it right because I didn't have a tape.'

Elisabetta reached forward and hugged her. (Much easier to be Italian, Ned thought, all that spontaneous physicality.)

'You are saying it beautifully.'

Scout sat down on a chair and looked across at Ned. 'Always I imagined how you would be. You're not burly.'

Ned laughed a little awkwardly. 'Yes, sorry, I'm not burly.'

'That's not a problem. That's actually good. Can you understand all the mottos on buildings and crests?'

'Yes I can actually. Do you look at them and want to know what they mean?'

Scout nodded. 'Sometimes, and I will do more now, because now I can ask you.'

'You can ask me anything. You can ask me anything at all.'

51

Like a dancing monkey, Joanie thought, like a bloody dancing monkey. If you listened to a solicitor long enough, if you listened to what Social Services wanted for long enough, that was what you would become. Jackie said a Care Plan would be required. A Care Plan which detailed where they would live, how they would live, how she would work. Accountable, monitored, measured up to the hilt. Skewed on benchmarks of other people's making. It made her want to spit. The last week had been bad enough. She was not allowed to leave the building with Scout unaccompanied. She'd had to hand in her car keys and passport. Even alone, she'd had to account for where she was going, what she was doing and the anticipated time of her return. It was torture.

What she had forsaken, she realised, in the gamble that began with her bolt in the spring, was the right to a private life, to a life lived invisibly with Scout. *That'll teach you*, Alice said, from her position, arms folded, in the corner of the room. Maybe Alice might rustle up some sympathy soon. What she actually said was *I told you it would rebound; all these years of upping and offing when the wind changed or it suited you.*

Joanie knew how it would be in court. A long litany of her misdeeds, all her shortcomings, and she would have to stand looking suitably contrite. 'Wear something sombre,' her solicitor had said, 'that always shows you are engaging with the process, that you are taking it seriously.' Should she go shopping, and buy a cheap little suit and a sensible white blouse?

Alternatively, she could go in with a red lipsticked mouth, and a T-shirt emblazoned with *All you need is love!* or *Who's the daddy!* and confirm all their preconceptions. This was evidently not one of her better ideas.

And in all of this, there was Scout. Coming back to their room at the centre, dropped off by Jackie, having spent time with the Beechams, evidently a little aglow but not wanting to appear disloyal. She wondered what they talked about. How could they possibly begin? *So, the last ten years, how was it for you?* Scout had taken all her pristine school-work to show them. At least they might be relied upon to engage with appropriate enthusiasm.

Could she cobble together a statement for a care plan; commit to something that was sensible and steady? *Why break the habit of a lifetime?* chipped in Alice. Really, she was getting beyond the pale. Joanie thought back to the strawberry fields, to the arching blue sky. There, she had felt free.

Joanie gave herself a little shake. Alice disappeared. Her solicitor came through the door, ready to discuss the process of the interim hearing.

The vision of a stable and child-centric life squatted down before Joanie. Why did it cast such a depressing shadow? She blinked to try and put it into context. Would it be a stable and child-centric life back at Alice's or somewhere different? Somewhere close to the Beechams in Putney? How weary it made her feel. She was suddenly so tired. So impossibly tired. All these demanding people hanging off her like puppies from multiple teats. She wished for the fruit fields, for Scout waiting for her on the caravan steps, for couscous eaten from cups with a spoon, for the smell of plums on her skin. No chance. She could see that wouldn't be an option. Once the authorities were on to you, it was like ticks burrowing into your flesh.

'Joanie, are you listening?' her solicitor said. Joanie heaved her concentration back to the business in hand. *Yes,* she said, but she wondered if she actually was. *Blah blah blah,* continued the lawyer. Joanie tried to rally her attention. It wasn't that she didn't care, it wasn't that she didn't love Scout: of this she was sure. It was just that the prospect of the hoops she would be required to jump through made her want to lie down on her belly on the floor, and hold her breath until the room spun black.

52

James Baxter sat in his study going through the papers he would adjudicate upon tomorrow.

Molly was cutting dahlias in the garden in the late evening light. He watched her through the window. She turned to face him, standing in the middle of the border, her arms full of jewel-coloured blooms, and he was struck by how the young woman he had fallen in love with was still there, still there in the way she turned and faced him, chin tilted upwards, eyes clear. Hadn't he read her *The Waste Land* nearly forty years ago in a punt in Oxford? How seriously they had taken themselves. *They called me the hyacinth girl.* And there she was with dahlias, still his, with her arms full of dahlias. He watched her come into the house. 'Supper in ten minutes,' she called.

Her father was ailing. She'd spent most of the day at the care home. Some days he barely registered her presence, yet still she went. Minty had telephoned while she was out. *Can I speak to Mum?* she'd asked. He'd explained that she was with Grandpa. 'Will I do?' he'd said.

'Sorry, Daddy, no, but thanks. I'll call back later.'

She wanted her mother. She wanted only her mummy. Intractable, complex bond.

Would Scout Simpson want only her mummy? Would that be what Joan Simpson wanted too? And what account would she give of herself?

He went into the kitchen. Molly was slicing pears into a watercress salad.

'You look preoccupied,' she said.

'I am. Tomorrow. A tricky decision tomorrow.'

She asked him to elaborate, and James did so, standing in the kitchen with his wife while she lifted fish fillets from a pan, combined lemon juice with coriander and red chilli and melted butter.

'Rather you than me,' she said when they sat down, and reached over to squeeze his hand in a gesture of solidarity.

James was confident her insight would more than equal his.

53

Scout thought Joanie didn't look anything like her usual self. She was buttoning up a white, sensible blouse, and had bought a neat, blue skirt and a pair of shoes that Scout would never have previously imagined to have come within a mile of her mother's feet. Joanie stood in front of the small mirror in the room.

'Too much make-up, too little make-up?' she said to Scout, dabbing at herself with a powder brush. Scout shrugged. Even though she felt everything had been explained to her at length, nothing had touched upon what you were supposed to look like in court. Joanie seemed to be taking it as an opportunity to experiment with a very different version of herself.

'I don't think they'll be looking at your lipstick.'

'Everything communicates.'

'But it's not a competition, is it? Jackie says it's more like a discussion about how things might be worked out.'

Joanie didn't answer. She put on some earrings, and then squeezed hand cream from a tube held high above her palm.

Scout got out of bed. Joanie was catching an early train to London, and a social worker was going to collect Scout and take her to the Family Centre for the day. She folded her pyjamas and got dressed. Joanie had put the kettle on to boil, and a teabag into a mug. She sat on the edge of the bed. Normally, she would have been cross-legged, and have been twisting her hair into some sort of bun. Now, she sat with her feet planted docilely on the floor, her knees together and her fingers plaited around the white, chipped mug. Scout thought the clothes probably made you sit like that. This morning, her mother looked like someone who worked in a bank, or perhaps a receptionist at a desk.

'Heigh ho,' Joanie said, and reached over and kissed Scout on the cheek.

Scout felt as if there was something very heavy sitting in the middle of her chest. Everyone's words about what would be good for her would be flying about the court today. They'd be like a flag of starlings, swooping and swirling beyond her. She wished she could be with Mr Groves, where everything was polished and clean and neat and orderly, and he would tell her stories about Houghton Hall which made the world sound as if it slotted perfectly and solidly into shape, rather than dissolved and re-formed so that everything you thought you knew was recast differently, uncertainly.

Her dad had shelves of books. She had specifically asked him. He had also taught her a sentence in Latin. *Quintus in hortus est.* Now, if ever it was required, she could say Quintus was in the garden. He said he would teach her some more the next time he saw her. She would like to eat Latin sentences for breakfast, or Maths formulae, or History dates. Given a chance, she might actually take a bite out of a page.

Scout brushed her teeth. Joanie was putting on her coat. Scout wondered whether she was supposed to say Good Luck. Instead, she wiped the toothpaste from around her mouth and gave her mother a minty kiss.

'I love you,' she told her.

'Me too,' Joanie replied.

After she had gone out of the room, Scout put aside the thought that her mother's response might technically mean Joanie loved herself too. That would be unfortunate. She had obviously been distracted. What Joanie had meant to communicate was that she loved Scout. Scout felt sure of this. If asked by anyone, she would have said with all confidence that she knew her mum loved her. What might be harder to explain was that Joanie had her own particular way of loving which, to an outsider's eye, might be difficult to read. She had wondered about trying to explain this to Jackie, but had decided that it was better not broached.

She sat down on the bed and waited for the social worker to arrive. At school on Sports Day, before it was banned on health and safety grounds, they used to have a tug of war. At each end of the rope, two classes would pull and heave. Perhaps it would be like that in court today, but over her instead of a rope. Perhaps all the fine legal words in the world couldn't disguise that was actually what it was.

54

Mrs Eastman was there. Joanie walked into the courtroom and saw that Mrs Eastman was there. Good God, if she hadn't felt so tense, she would have burst out laughing. Her own hastily appointed barrister (who didn't look old enough to have a baby-sitting certificate) told her that Social Services had called Mrs Eastman as a possible witness, and that she'd written a very fulsome statement about her impression of Scout and Joanie, and Joanie's state of mind. 'They've also got a statement from the neighbour who originally contacted the Birmingham department,' the barrister said helpfully.

Joanie looked across at Mrs Eastman, who was wearing a hideous hat. How she must be relishing this. She'd have had to get an early train. Safe to say cooked breakfasts and dining-room supervisory strolls had not been an option this morning. Mrs Eastman looked as if she would be hopping on one foot, hand up in the air, wishing to be chosen to give evidence. She looked as if she could hardly restrain herself from licking her lips. Joanie tried not to be distracted by her. She looked across at the Beechams. They were soberly dressed. Ned didn't meet her eye, but the wife did. Her intent was difficult to gauge. The Beechams' solicitor looked alert, on edge. She was briefing their barrister who seemed focused on looking at his papers. Fingers crossed he didn't have a full grasp of the detail. Jackie Broom was sitting there, upright like a meerkat. She'd greeted her enthusiastically in the foyer. The measure of her insincerity would be gauged by how much she criticised her in the report which would be read out. *You are not my friend*, she wanted to say, when Jackie stepped forward to greet her. *You are the person who has the presumption to think you can recommend what is best for my child.*

Joanie pinched her thigh. She should stop looking at all the faces and start to listen up. It was hard to feel that she was not weirdly sleepwalking; on the train down to London, on the tube to the Royal Courts of Justice, and now here, to Courtroom 41 where they were putting her and Scout under a microscope. The Location Order which she had dreamed of in the lay-by had located them all right. Located them and plonked her squarely on this uncomfortable bench, while Ned Beecham's barrister stood up and identified who everyone was. He then said:

'May it please my Lord before we embark upon the evidence, I would like to clarify some points of principle. Were this a final hearing, rather than an interim hearing, we would no doubt consider the initial deception which is the catalyst to today's situation: namely, sustained deception after a surrogacy agreement. It is, you might say, a crime for modern times, and the statute book has yet to catch up. We are not here to judge the rights, wrongs and implications of Miss Simpson's falsehood in nineteen ninety-seven. That may be for another day. This case is not about an evolving point of law about to whom this surrogate child belongs. It is Mr Beecham's and Social Services' hope that just such a process can be avoided if a mutually supported plan can be decided upon today for the care of Scout Simpson Beecham. Since discovering Scout's existence, my clients have approached this matter with immense sensitivity and a child-centric view, with Scout Simpson Beecham's interests uppermost. All my clients wish for is an opportunity to have contact with Scout, to develop a relationship with her, and to give her the opportunity of getting to know them, and of offering her a more stable, ordered life should she eventually so choose. With that in mind, I would like to ask Miss Simpson a number of questions in due course.'

Joanie's own barrister stood up and asked her to go to the witness box. She asked her to confirm her name, that she was Scout's mother, and to agree that she had written the statement she was now showing to her. As she held out the statement, Joanie could have sworn that the young woman's hand was shaking. Great, when the Beechams' barrister looked utterly poised at the prospect of biting it off. Her own barrister didn't ask her anything further. She scuttled back to her bench and looked relieved to be sitting down.

The Beechams' barrister stood up, and looked at her in the witness box. She pinched herself again. No possibility of bolting. She was struck by his resemblance to a fox. A small tweak of his nose and jaw and it would elongate into a snout. There was something predatory about his lips, his teeth. Snap snap he would go; scattering the hen-house chickens. Joanie braced her foot against the witness box. His appetite for humiliation, she gauged, probably knew no bounds. He was tall and rangy; his face was clean shaven but there was a gingery tinge which seemed reflected in his cheek. Fantastic Mr Fox. Joanie bit the inside of her lip.

'Miss Simpson. Can you confirm you have had sole charge this last eleven years of the daughter you claimed to have miscarried?'

'Yes.'

'And that you have, up until recent events, never given her any indication of the circumstances of her conception.'

'Yes.'

'That you have lived your life mostly in an itinerant fashion, with a failure to hold on to any job for more than three months, and with your daughter attending a rapid sequence of schools until you inherited your mother's house?'

'Shall I just say yes to everything? You seem to be basing your questions on that assumption and I expect it's far more effective to get me to condemn myself out of my own mouth.'

'You may answer, Miss Simpson, whatever you like, but may I remind you that you are under oath. To continue. When you received the first letter notifying you that the Tavistock Clinic wished to discuss with you the veracity of your claimed miscarriage, you left your home that afternoon, shortly after your daughter returned from school?'

'Yes.'

'And when you received a letter from Birmingham Social Services giving you notice of a Location Order, you absconded similarly quickly, that same night?'

'Yes.'

'And on both occasions, your daughter was bundled along in your slipstream with no explanation as to why you were going?'

'Yes.'

'Would it be fair, Miss Simpson, to call you impulsive and self-centred?'

'I'm guessing you're going to anyway.'

'Were you ever concerned during the last six months for your daughter's safety while you were out at work?'

'No, not really. Scout's sensible.'

'Not in Birmingham, when you left her for long hours in a small flat, or in Norfolk, where she stayed mostly in a caravan while you worked nine-hour days?'

'I had no specific cause for concern.'

'Even when she was out roaming the shops or pursuing friendships without any supervision?'

'By my assessment, the mobile library was hardly a risk.'

'It wasn't just the mobile library, was it? Did you actually have knowledge of where she was at any point in the day?'

'No, not exactly.'

'I see, not exactly. And let's just confirm, Scout was eleven on July the fourth?'

'Yes. I expect you're happier when I just say yes.'

'This isn't about my happiness, Miss Simpson. Would you agree childcare could be defined as having a child within eyeshot and earshot?'

'I suppose so.'

'During the summer, what proportion of an average day was Scout in eyeshot or earshot or both?'

'Very little, I suppose.'

'And let me just restate, she was eleven on July the fourth?'

'Yes, but you have to see that it wasn't always like that. When we lived at my mother's house, Scout went to school daily. I met her from school probably twice a week. If we hadn't been forced to leave, she wouldn't have been in Birmingham, or Poole or Norfolk.'

'But you weren't forced to leave, Miss Simpson, were you?'

'I was asked to come to a meeting.'

'That's rather different. You chose to leave, to avoid a meeting with the Tavistock Clinic and Oxfordshire Social Services. Had you chosen to sit down and discuss your decision of nineteen ninety-seven, Scout would have been at school, as usual, the day after you received the letter. That's right, isn't it?'

'Possibly.'

'I suggest definitely. Have you made self-centred decisions this summer, causing your daughter disruption and unnecessary harm?'

'She has not been harmed.'

'On two occasions this summer has Scout been aware of the nature of your relationships with men?'

'Yes, but you make it sound worse than it was.'

'But on both occasions did you cause embarrassment to your daughter.'

'Yes. But she got over it quickly.'

'But she was embarrassed, wasn't she?'

'Yes.'

'Looking forward, should the court decide that your daughter's emotional needs and interests are best served by remaining with you, can you commit to stop embarrassing Scout and to providing her with a stable life, supporting her in her endeavours and choices? . . . Miss Simpson, you have paused now for several moments.'

'I need to think. I don't know.'

'Let me turn to the report submitted by Jackie Broom of the Social Services' Children's Team. In the course of a meeting with her, you were asked to provide details of something you did which proved you put Scout's needs and interests above your own. Unless I'm mistaken . . .'

'Which I expect you very rarely are.'

'Unless I'm mistaken, the example which most readily sprang to your mind was the playing of Scrabble, which you say is Scout's favourite board game. Now you've had more time to consider, are there any other examples you'd like to share with the court?'

'No. Not off the cuff. You make everything sound small, anyway. I love my daughter. I'm not perfect but I love her, and I haven't got everything wrong. It was probably a mistake to lie to the clinic, but you're not here to judge me on that. You're here to decide what's best for Scout now. I love her. You can't tell me I don't.'

'And I have no intention of so doing. That you love her is not an issue. It is the kind of loving which you offer that this court needs to assess. I have no more questions.'

Joanie watched him sit down. Snap snap; jaws crunching. Chicken heads everywhere. A few white feathers floating down around the witness box, necks and legs splayed at odd angles around her feet. She had to credit him; it was an impressive performance. A complete and utter shafting. He could not have been more effective if he'd tattooed *unfit mother* across her forehead. She took a deep breath. She wasn't sure how much more of this she could stand.

Ned Beecham looked across at Joan Simpson and felt an unexpected pulse of compassion. Susan Philips had told him the barrister she'd chosen was highly effective. Outside the court earlier, he had been urbane, charming. No hint of tooth or claw. The cross-examination was like something from the Coliseum; Joan Simpson harried and hamstrung, positively thrown to a lion. Some of her answers had an unexpected dignity. Odd that he should almost like her more, now, when they were facing each other in court. She was right too, about not having got everything wrong. Scout was testament to that.

The lawyer for the local authority stood up.

'Miss Simpson, I'd like to draw your attention to the report submitted by Jackie Broom on behalf of the children's services team. Its focus is very much on the interests of the child, and the primacy of Scout's needs. Have you had a number of conversations with Jackie Broom?'

'Yes.'

'And do you feel you have a clear understanding of some of the options available to Scout?'

'Yes.'

'And Jackie Broom made it clear to you that absconding when learning of a Location Order may result in the subject child being taken into foster care?'

'Yes. She made that clear.'

'Whatever reservations the Children's Team has about some aspects of your parenting, you have had sole charge of Scout for her entire life. She is undoubtedly attached to you. To place her in foster care would be traumatic. To order residence to her father, whom she has currently met on only three occasions, would not be an option without your complete and sustained support, which we presume we cannot count on. What I am interested in gauging is how much you are prepared to work on aspects of your own parenting. For example, if Scout were made the subject of a Supervision Order for the next two years, whether you would be prepared to work co-operatively with us in the imposition of a more supportive, ordered life?'

Joanie looked down at her nails. What poking words. Poking noses. Poking fingers.

'I can't say yes until I know exactly what your expectations would be.'

'I see. You don't feel able to offer a complete commitment to putting your daughter's needs first?'

'Can I have a break? I just need some time to think.' She looked across at the judge. 'Can I just have half an hour – I'd like to go and sit somewhere by myself.'

Mr Justice Baxter looked at her. 'It is almost one o'clock, Miss Simpson, when the court would adjourn at any event. Let us reconvene at two pm.'

55

Joanie came out of the courtroom and slipped into an adjacent conference room. The waistband of her skirt was killing her, and her prim little shoes seemed to have squeezed most of the blood from her toes. Her head was spinning. She was desperate for a cigarette. She was also in danger, she could see, of being completely trounced. Damn them all. And their bone-crunching, ruthless, remorseless, meticulous process. She remembered telling Jackie Broom it was all none of her business. She had replied tartly, 'You made it our business, through absconding and ignoring court orders. If you want to apportion blame, start with yourself.'

Joanie followed the exit signs and made her way out of the building. She walked down to Lincoln's Inn Fields, and sat on a bench in the soft September sunshine. She lit a cigarette. She thought of Scout's fastidious Maths folder on top of the greasy cupboard in Birmingham. She thought of her playing hopscotch outside Calm Views on her invisible pitch, her lips working furiously, counting to herself. She thought of her spilling over with *Rough Guide* facts, and washing her clothes and herself in her double Romany bowls. Scout was different from her, separate from her; someone who would not live the same life, or make the choices she had made. Nor could she be expected to continue her life as an adjunct, a tag-along, to Joanie's own. But she loved her. In her own unreliable fashion, she loved her. What had Scout said when

Gus's wife had come to the caravan? *I just want normal.* It was an understandable request. Why should the verbal commitment to it seem such a momentous life sentence? She thought of the prospect of Scout's next few years at school. *You are invited to a parents' evening to discuss GCSE choices.* She was unsuited to all that. She saw she was unsuited to all that.

The Beechams were just as she remembered them. The wife had hardly aged at all. Ned looked only a little different. He had been holding his wife's hand. Perhaps they'd spent the last twelve years doing that. Scout had something of his colouring; she could see that now, and his way of tilting her head to the right when she listened. When Joanie looked at Elisabetta, Elisabetta looked straight back at her, without aggression but certainly eye to eye. What did she expect her to do? Apologise? Say she regretted it? What was done was done. She'd hardly snatched a baby from her arms, but perhaps that was how Elisabetta would see it. She'd have liked to say to her *Whatever you may become to her, Scout will be my blood child always.*

Joanie looked across Lincoln's Inn Fields. There was no hint of autumn in the air. Beyond her, a woman was walking, holding a very small child by the hand. She was patiently explaining something to him. Perhaps though, she was thinking about something completely different. What was good mothering? What did it mean to actually *be* a good mother? Was it sometimes, on the rarest of occasions, a shard of insight that helped you to recognise that what you had to offer wasn't what your child needed at all? It seemed an unspeakable, impossible line to cross. The memory of Fantastic Mr Fox's questions pinpricked her skin.

Joanie took a pen and notepad from her handbag and started to write. *To Mr Justice Baxter.* Her solicitor and barrister wouldn't expect this. They wouldn't have seen this coming. But maybe in their position they didn't expect very much from anyone at all. Least of all a pre-emptive strike, to avoid being flayed alive.

56

James Baxter sat in his chambers, taking advantage of the longer adjournment to think. It wasn't looking good for Joan Simpson. He could see that she sensed that too, but she didn't seem to be taking the life-rafts offered to her. Perhaps he was being presented with the rarity of a witness who was actually telling the truth, who actually wasn't sure if she could cut the mustard. He turned his mind to the child. What had she written in her interview list? *I do not want to be deracinated.* Where had she fished up a word like that? And did she mean deracinated from the itinerant life she had been living with her mother, or from the stable, more conventional life that she had briefly led before? It would have been helpful if Jackie Broom could have clarified this. Social Services were so wary of leading, of influencing, particularly children of this age group, and all manner of ambiguity slipped through the net.

Joan Simpson seemed unwilling to give a commitment to a more stable, monitored life. For some people, just the notion of being accountable was guaranteed to make them want to run headlong the other way. Other than the three years she had lived at her mother's house, Joan Simpson had shown little taste for a consistent environment. *I want to go to school,* the child had written. How did that square with her mother's plans, or in fact, the absence of anything that resembled a plan?

Social Services had ventured that they thought the child could possibly be at risk. This was increasingly their stance.

Too many cases in the media which had come back to bite them, where children had been allowed to stay with parents and sustained all manner of grievous harm. Scout was not at risk of physical harm, they had clarified this. But Joan, they said, seemed unable to put the child's needs before her own. This had been demonstrated a number of times, not least in the circumstances surrounding the child's conception when she had decided to deprive Scout of the possibility of a relationship with her father.

Was putting the needs of a child first a requisite of mother-hood, James wondered. Was it, in fact, a form of self-sacrifice? He thought of all the years that Molly had run around for their own children's needs. He'd never asked her *Is this what you thought it would be? Would you have liked a life lived, less sacrificed?* Was it something she privately dwelt on, now they were all grown up?

Joan Simpson, Social Services said, showed a predisposition to form potentially inappropriate relationships with men with little regard for Scout. Furthermore, when asked for character references, she had not been able to supply the name of one single adult who could testify to having been part of her life for more than a few months. This, they concluded, could lead to the risk of emotional isolation, a failure to nurture relationships, and chaotic, disrupted emotional attachments for Scout. It didn't add up to a great picture. And yet, and yet. There was something likeable about the mother. She seemed perversely honest about her shortcomings. That wasn't something he encountered frequently. Might she be coaxed into assuming a life more stable?

He considered his current options. It was serious to abscond in the face of a Location Order. It was also extremely inappropriate if Scout had been aware of sexual interaction between her mother and men. Foster care would be an option if that was to be a pattern, despite the fact that the child had not said anything which indicated inappropriate knowledge. Happily, none of the parties was suggesting foster care. Scout evidently loved her mother. (What had she written? *I really love my mum, even if she makes mistakes.*) She had been positive about discovering her father's existence. It would be an unfeeling decision to place the child with strangers elsewhere; for her to have discovered that she had two parents and then to be living with neither.

James considered Ned Beecham's perspective. Elisabetta Beecham added a dimension. The child had been promised to them both, conceived for them both. Did this give Elisabetta Beecham some sort of claim to Scout, too? There was an adopted younger daughter. This suggested the Beechams had jumped through all manner of hoops to prove their suitability as parents. The Beechams were both school-teachers. This seemed a good fit with Scout's stated desires and preferences. They would support her in her schooling, in her homework, in establishing an ordered daily routine. Did good parenting actually come down to this? Structure, order, routine? Even if it didn't, Ned Beecham deserved the chance to see if he could build a loving relationship with his daughter.

Perhaps the Beechams and Joan Simpson might share care between them? Might this be something they could negotiate without rancour? It would be understandable if Ned Beecham felt residual hostility. Perhaps, also, a feeling of being somehow violated. The Beechams might justifiably detest Joan Simpson. Could this be managed, or would it be damaging to Scout?

Where to go next? James anticipated that the local authority lawyer would complete her questioning of Joan Simpson after lunch. Perhaps during the break she would have taken instructions in respect of inviting him to make a Supervision Order. Perhaps it would be necessary to call other witnesses. In the front row sat a woman who used to be Joan Simpson's employer. She looked desperate to be called. She was clutching the straps of her handbag, all ready, guns blazing, relishing the possibility of pronouncing her own judgement upon Joan Simpson with the luxury of a captive audience.

James looked up from his papers. He thought again of Solomon and the two women who came to him, both claiming the child as their own. The real mother abandoned her claim when Solomon suggested cutting the baby in half. No such easy discriminator here.

He looked across at an oil painting on the wall. How easily dilemmas were resolved in art. A perspective chosen, a side taken, a brush dipped in paint. Here, Samson having his hair shorn by Delilah. Delilah always got the short end of the stick.

His thoughts were interrupted by a knock at the door. 'A note, m'lord,' said the clerk, handing him a folded piece of paper. It was addressed to him. It was admirably succinct, if a little enigmatic.

Love isn't always enough. Scout deserves different, better. I do see myself clearly, if only occasionally. If you grant what my solicitor explained as incremental custody to the Beechams, I will help smooth it with Scout. She would thrive in their care. It pains me to admit it, but it's true.

Joan Simpson had signed it with an autographical flourish.

A few moments later, James Baxter stood up and prepared to re-enter the court, note in hand. 'Court rise,' said the clerk. As everyone rose to their feet, he was struck by one thought: sometimes grace came from the most unexpected quarters.

57

Joanie sat in the train with her head leaning against the window. Her breath was misting up a small part of the glass. She gnawed at the side of her thumbnail. Her brain was clattering in her skull. It felt as if it might skitter to the distant horizon and back. She tried to steady her breathing. Perhaps then the feeling of being winded would recede. *It would have been nice to tip me off*, her barrister had said shirtily when the judge read out the letter. *It would have saved me some time to know you were heading in that direction.*

The assumption of pre-thought was something Joanie decided to take as a compliment. Rather that, than explain she'd made her decision on a park bench at lunch-time, watching a woman lead a child by the hand. Perhaps she should have said it was like most of her decisions – made in a finger-snap, and implemented upon impulse. That didn't seem like something that was going to change anytime soon. Evidently, she wasn't going to be a surprise late developer when it came to making considered decisions. She thought back to her decision to become a surrogate, to her fleeting wish to be powerful in a unique way, to her notion of motherhood as something which would make her feel complete. Now, faced with a fox-like barrister and a couple who seemed committed to going through life holding hands, she had thrown in her maternal cards, or at least put them up for grabs.

Had she set something in motion which she would come to

regret? It wouldn't be the first time. It was tempting to cock her ears, to sniff the air in the carriage, to see if she'd get a snatch of what might be to come. Not that she didn't know already. No point pussyfooting around that. In the courtroom as the judge read out his decision, she sensed the direction the wind would have blown. What was it that he said? *The decision must come down to where the child's best interests lie.* She should congratulate herself on spotting that compliance was a smart, pre-emptive strike. It wasn't that difficult to gauge where Scout's best interests would lie. Scout was more suited to life with the Beechams. It was patently clear. The trick now would be to make the transition as smooth as possible.

Putting Scout first; that would be a novelty. Maybe that was what would keep a soft footfall of guilt from creeping into her bones. *A mother who didn't fight to keep her child*; that was hard to swallow. *A mother who held her child's best interests at heart*; that was more like it. Let Jackie Broom stick that on her.

She felt overwhelmed by an urge to sigh. Perhaps she should think of the plan as shared child care. God knows in the past she would have valued that on occasions. If Scout were unhappy, she was sure they could revert to how it was now. It was better not to think of it as a door clanging shut.

How much would she miss her? Her heart did a small, involuntary flip. Eleven years together; Scout's small sweet face. Yet, if she tried to summon her up, aged five, aged six, aged eight, it was all something of a blur. Was that normal? Most of her memory seemed shaped by photographs and there were precious few of those. She bit her lip. She loved her daughter. Was letting her go loving her too little, or loving her best? She swallowed down a sob. The old guy opposite, if he noticed, would bury his head deeper in his newspaper. What would the English do on trains without papers to preserve their apartness?

She would not cry in front of Scout. She would make the

changes sound exciting. She would fish up images of her doing new things she would like. And, she would stay close by until she could see that she was settled and happy. She would do the right thing by her child. Scout deserved more than to sit in a caravan waiting for her to return, reeking of soft fruit. Oh, but she loved her. In her muddled, inconsiderate, selfish way she loved her. *Don't think about that*, she repeated to herself. The old guy looked up, surprised. Had she said it out loud? She lifted her head from the window. She stiffened her spine and took a deep breath. She rummaged for consolations. Perhaps she would work on a cruise liner one day; she would pick fruit in Israel, work in a taverna in Greece. She could do things on a whim, on an impulse. That had always been her way. The thought of the Beechams' daily life made her want to hurl herself from the carriage window. Scout would still love her, even if her daily importance faded. Her daughter would always love her. Love, she was confident, could be tough as old boots.

The old guy opposite reached over from behind his paper and worldlessly passed her his handkerchief. Joanie put her hands to her face to find it wet with tears.

58

The room was dark when Joanie came back. Scout had told the duty officer she was tired and wanted to go to sleep. She lay like a tin soldier in her bed, her palms pressed to the side of her legs. She tried to trace the outline of the light in the moulded ceiling.

When she heard Joanie's key in the door, Scout flicked on the lamp. Joanie looked smudged when she came in; as if someone had lightly pressed down on her with a large, smooth thumb. She took off her shoes, and tugged down her hair. She wiped a flannel over her face and then started unzipping her skirt.

'How was it? What happened? What did the judge think?' Scout leaned up on her elbow. Joanie looked at her fixedly as if her eyes were taking a photograph.

'Wouldn't you prefer to talk about it in the morning? You must be tired now.'

'No, I'm wide awake. I've been thinking about it all day. I've been sitting in the Family Centre with a social worker called Beth who kept trying to get me to draw pictures of autumn trees.'

'And did you?'

'That's not important. I asked first.'

'Well, the judge was very nice. I think he was wise. He wasn't scowly and short-tempered like the ones you see on the television. There was a barrister like a fox, but that's a different story. They talked about everything for ages. Everybody was very focused on making the right decision for you. In the end it all seemed straightforward and calm.'

'How?'

Joanie sat down on the side of the bed and took Scout's hand in her own.

'Well, everybody thought that you should have a turn at doing the things *you* like doing best, the things that make you happiest, and that this might best be met if you have a little go at being with your dad and his family. Not all the time straightaway, we'll share until you know what you think. Social Services are going to get me a flat near where he lives and I can meet you from school and have dinner with you or go to the cinema. See you as much as you want, and lots at weekends, and if you're not happy, you can come back to just me, but first you'll get a chance at a life that isn't always changing, isn't always to do with me and my ways. You know, have a chance at the normal you said you'd like when we were in the caravan.'

'But I don't mind your ways. I only know your ways. It's only ever been your ways.' There was a rising note of panic in her voice. Joanie's voice sounded older and wearier and flatter than Scout had ever heard it.

'I know, but my ways aren't necessarily best. In truth, we both know they're a little bit rubbish sometimes. You don't have to live like me. It's okay to choose something else.'

'But I'm not choosing anything. I wouldn't know what to choose.'

'I know, and that's why I'm helping choose for you, so that you can be clever and accomplished and have choices and live exactly as you want to when you are grown up.'

Joanie got into bed beside her.

'I'll always love you, and I'll always be your mum. Nobody and nothing can change that. I'm thinking about what's best for you. I'm trying really hard to do that. We both know it's probably a bit of a novelty. I really want you to understand that's what I'm trying to do.'

Scout's head was spinning. She laid her cheek on her mother's shoulder, and inhaled her warm, familiar scent.

'Your dad's going to arrange for you to go to a really smart school. You'll learn Latin, and wear a blazer and tie. We both know you'll love that, so let's not even pretend that you won't. And you know what, you'll play lacrosse. I've always wondered if you might have a talent for lacrosse.'

'Lacrosse? You've never even mentioned lacrosse.'

'I know, but I've thought about it. I was storing up my hunch. I've always thought you might be a superstar at lacrosse.'

Later, when Scout was sleeping, Joanie was ambushed again by tears. She pressed the pillow to her face so as not to wake Scout.

So, she thought, a little delayed, but she'd functioned as some kind of half-assed surrogate anyway. She'd given Scout up to the Beechams; eleven years after promising, but given her up all the same. Just after a few hapless years trying to be a good-enough mother.

The judge had commended her on her note to him, and for putting Scout's needs first. It was ironic when to outsiders she must appear at her crappiest, her most selfish. She reflected that today she had discovered the element of self-sacrifice she'd always resisted in motherhood. Perhaps she'd call it her Giant Octopus moment.

Alice appeared at the end of the bed. The edges of her mother's body were less distinct; she looked blurred, fuzzier. Her mouth seemed partly erased; she looked less capable of chipping in. Alice looked tired. Joanie wondered if she had worn her out living and now she was wearing her out dead. She waited for her to say something but instead Alice just reached over and took Joanie's hand in hers. She looked as if she might speak, but had decided better of it.

59

March 15th, 2010.

Dear Mr Mohammed and Mr Groves

I am writing this letter to you both in the hope that Mr Mohammed will visit you, Mr Groves, and read it to you. I think you will get on together anyway, but if you are unsure, you overlap on kedgeree. You might discuss this for starters.

I am writing to tell you about where I am now. We left in such a rush because my mum did something wrong before I was born, but it has all been sorted out and everybody is looking forward; not looking forward to something in particular, just not looking backwards.

Now I live, most of the time, with my dad, who's a teacher, and his wife who is also a teacher. They are lovely and help me every way I can think of. In the summer I will go with them to Lucca, in Italy. They are going to take me to Venice. I am excited already, and know the restaurant where I want to eat lunch. It has a choice of 80 pizzas. At half-term, I went down to Cornwall to meet my new grandparents. They are very impressive. I liked them a lot.

I have a new sister who comes from China, called Maia, and she is just a little older than Nona. She's very funny and sweet. I am teaching her to count. She is almost as quick a learner as Nona. She hides under my bed when I get home from school.

I go to a new school where I wear a blazer and a TIE. You will be pleased to know, Mr Groves, that I learned to tie it very quickly, and I am keeping up my practice of good posture at the bus stop. I've not yet had any difficulty with soup.

At first I had extra catch-up lessons in school because of missing so much last year, but my form teacher says I am a VERITABLE HOOVER. My Maths teacher says she thinks I will be in Division One after Easter. This is thanks to you, Mr Mohammed; I will always try to be excellent at Maths. I have started learning Latin too. I do not ask my dad for help with my homework. I get very high marks. My teacher says it must be in my genes.

My mum has a flat nearby and I see her lots, except now she is leaving for six weeks to go and work on a cruise ship. She says she will send me e-mails daily which will always start with 'Ahoy there!'. She is supposed to be working as a cleaner on board, but she says she intends to learn ballroom dancing. She says she will come back and teach me the cha-cha-cha, and will be laden with gifts like a Christmas fairy. I am hoping the Captain isn't particularly burly. I spend Sundays with her, but we don't eat Kentucky Fried Chicken any more. We've moved on to Mexican Burritos which has made a nice change. Wherever and whenever she goes, I know she will always come back.

I think of you often, and am still grateful for all the kindness you showed me when I lived at the flats. When you see Mrs Crawshaw, Mr Groves, could you please tell her I say hello. My school has an enormous library with computers and everything. She would like it very much. She would have much more room to move.

After leaving the flats, we lived by the sea for a while and then on a farm in Norfolk, where my mum picked fruit. Although I learned a lot of things, I am much happier staying

in one place. My mum says in this I am like Alice, my grandmother, which she says is probably not a bad thing. She says
Alice probably has a view.

One day soon I would like to visit you both. My dad came
there once, after we left, but I don't expect that you saw him.

I hope you are both well. I am very happy. See you both
soon, I hope,

Lots of love

Scout xx

ACKNOWLEDGEMENTS

Many thanks to:

Sue Fletcher, my wonderful, wise editor; Swati Gamble, super-efficient and kind assistant editor; Sheila Thompson, David Mitchell and the first-rate team at Hodder & Stoughton who guided this book to press.

Helenka Fuglewicz, at Edwards Fuglewicz, my staunch ally and agent, who remained resolute and clear-sighted at each and every stage; Julia Forrest who, as ever, gave perceptive editorial advice, and Ros Edwards who deftly and cleverly carried it over the line.

Barbara Bradshaw, Claire Batten, and Linda Longshaw, who read drafts and were, as always, generous in insight, encouragement, and time given.

David Freeman, and in celebratory memory of Joanna Isles Freeman, for 'Tiptoe Through the Tulips'.

Rachel Langdale for counsel on the intricacies of Family Law. All mistakes, inaccuracies and embellishments are absolutely my own.

Georgia Stevenson, who read the manuscript first, and who, in asking when the next chapters would be ready to read, helped me to believe that Scout and Joanie were potentially on a roll.

Hamish, Finn, Hal, Noah, and Georgia again, for matters of the heart and home.